"Mama, there's a boy waving."

Jo Beth waved back excitedly, and Marlee noticed a man standing at the end of the runway.

She throttled back, unable to take her eyes off him. It flashed through Marlee's mind that from a distance the raven-haired, broad-shouldered man reminded her of Cole, her husband, before he'd taken ill and his fine body had wasted away. Suddenly her hands shook and the plane dipped.

She quickly regained control, but landed with an irritating hop—a beginner's mistake that unnerved her as she powered down. Ripping off her headset, Marlee leaped from the cockpit and shook out her hair, only to discover as she watched the taciturn Wylie Ames that he watched her, too.

Marlee hurried around the plane's nose to assist Jo Beth. For some reason, Marlee disliked the fact that Ames was too far away for her to tell the color of his eyes. Ace-of-spades black would be her guess—to go with the scowl he wore.

Dear Reader,

I read an article in a rural newspaper about the area's inclusion in a much-needed and longed-for volunteer life-flight organization. The article discussed the vital role these groups play in helping with critical-care patients living in remote regions of the United States.

Intrigued, I began to look up and gather information on the many groups of volunteer pilots that exist across this vast country.

If my fictional flight group, Angel Fleet, bears any resemblance to a real mercy flight corps, it's purely accidental. The services they provide, of course, are similar, but my characters are totally of my own making.

Since my books are first and foremost love stories, I wanted to integrate my characters' work with a story about how they meet and fall in love.

The first of these two linked books is *Angels of the Big Sky*, Marlee Stein's story. It's about renewal and finding love a second time around. Book two, *On Angel Wings*, will be about her twin, Mick Callen. They're both accomplished pilots who, for different reasons, return home to remote Montana. It's where they were born and raised, and where they come full circle to find true happiness.

I enjoyed writing about their reunion and showing what creates the fabric of their new *and* their old lives. I hope you hate to leave them at the end of their respective books as much as I did.

Best always,

Roz Denny Fox

I love to hear from readers.
Roz Denny Fox
e-mail rdfox@worldnet.att.net
P.O. Box 17480-101
Tucson, AZ 85731

ANGELS OF THE BIG SKY

Roz Denny Fox

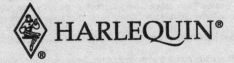

TORONTO • NEW YORK • LONDON
AMSTERDAM • PARIS • SYDNEY • HAMBURG
STOCKHOLM • ATHENS • TOKYO • MILAN • MADRID
PRAGUE • WARSAW • BUDAPEST • AUCKLAND

ISBN-13: 978-0-373-71368-4
ISBN-10:   0-373-71368-1

ANGELS OF THE BIG SKY

www.eHarlequin.com

Printed in U.S.A.

ABOUT THE AUTHOR

Roz Denny Fox made her first sale to Harlequin Romance in 1989. She moved to the Harlequin Superromance line a few years later and has published over twenty-five novels to date. Roz has been a finalist for the prestigious RITA® Award and also for the Holt Medallion and the Golden Quill award, among others. She lives in Tucson, Arizona, with her husband, Denny. They have two daughters.

Books by Roz Denny Fox

HARLEQUIN SUPERROMANCE

1046–WIDE OPEN SPACES
1069–THE SEVEN YEAR SECRET
1108–SOMEONE TO WATCH OVER ME
1128–THE SECRET DAUGHTER
1148–MARRIED IN HASTE
1184–A COWBOY AT HEART
1220–DADDY'S LITTLE MATCHMAKER
1254–SHE WALKS THE LINE
1290–A MOM FOR MATTHEW
1320–MORE TO TEXAS THAN COWBOYS

HARLEQUIN AMERICAN ROMANCE

1036–TOO MANY BROTHERS
1087–THE SECRET WEDDING DRESS

HARLEQUIN SIGNATURE

HOT CHOCOLATE ON A COLD DAY

CHAPTER ONE

MARLEE STEIN TOPPED a ridge, leaving behind Whitepine, Montana, the town closest to where she'd been born and raised. She rolled down the driver's window, breathing in the autumn scent of the piney wilderness, and felt herself relax. Until then, she hadn't been aware of how tense she'd gotten on the long drive from San Diego.

Who was she kidding? She'd been riddled with tension for the past five years.

But now, on this lonely stretch of highway with nothing but fall sunlight sprinkling pine-needle patterns across her windshield, she began to shed the stress that had become so crushing.

She'd realized that the sense of heaviness and regret might always be with her. It was barely a year since she'd lost Cole to the ravages of lymphatic cancer. Too young. His life snuffed out at thirty-six. There was so much they hadn't done. One of the many things they'd talked about but never got around to was visiting this beautiful country Marlee loved.

They'd been introduced by mutual friends. Had dated for a whirlwind thirty days, married on base in a fever pitch driven by the demands of their jobs—she, a navy helicopter pilot on the verge of shipping out; he an officer with an eye to one day commanding his own ship. It seemed a lifetime ago, those scant six years they'd shared. Or not shared, since much of it had been spent apart. But...so many dreams, all left in tatters. Widowed at thirty-four, Marlee was running home to hide.

No, to rebuild a shattered life—according to her twin brother, anyway.

Mick Callen, her twin, knew about rebuilding a life. A pilot, too, he'd been shot down over Afghanistan—what was it—four years ago? Mick had come home to Whitepine and forged a new life. On almost a weekly basis during the past awful year, he'd insisted that Marlee could do the same. She wanted to believe him.

Averting her eyes from the ribbon of highway, she glanced in the rearview mirror of her packed-to-the-ceiling Ford Excursion. Jo Beth slept on. Without doubt, her daughter was the most precious part of her too-brief marriage.

Maybe their lives could get back on track. Mick thought so, or he wouldn't have badgered his twin to join the family airfreight business, Cloud Chasers, originally started by their grandfather, Jack Callen. Everybody called him Pappy. He'd taught her and Mick to fly anything with wings, and they'd developed a love affair with flying.

It seemed unreal that they'd both come full circle. Fate, maybe? In the days immediately following Cole's death, Marlee had thought about the circle of life, but Whitepine was the last place she'd envisioned herself ending up. Big plans, she'd discovered, were best left to starry-eyed innocents. Reality made its own claims. And to think she and Cole had worried that her naval career presented a greater risk of death. She, who'd done two tours in the Gulf.

Releasing a sigh, she wiped a sweaty palm on her jeans. Really baggy jeans, she noticed, and grimaced. She'd lost weight—was down to a hundred and five pounds. Skeletal, her lieutenant commander had growled when he'd signed her discharge papers.

Mick would probably be shocked. Or maybe not. He'd suffered through his own months of hell in military hospitals after he took a legful of shrapnel and debris from his F/A-18, when a handheld surface-to-air missile blasted him out of the sky.

The Callen twins, who'd left Whitepine for the naval academy with grandiose ideas, had come full circle, all right.

A mile to go. Nervous, Marlee wasn't altogether sure what to expect. Three years ago Mick had said he'd found Cloud Chasers in sad shape. Pappy Jack apparently suffered from arteriosclerotic heart disease, which caused bouts of dementia. It must be true; otherwise he'd never have let the business decline.

Through hard work, Mick said he'd enticed old customers back and added new accounts. He regularly groused about needing an extra pair of hands. Marlee hoped he truly did. Because it was crucial to end her former mother-in-law's influence on Jo Beth. Rose Stein spoiled her and undermined Marlee's control. It had taken an unpleasant court skirmish to defeat her attempt at custody.

Dipping into the last valley, Marlee was finally home. The family holdings, house business—the whole panorama—was a welcome sight. The main log house and the three smaller cabins that were added over the fifty years Pappy built Cloud Chasers.

Marlee battled tears as she saw the runway, still with that tacky wind sock at the end. Home looked refreshingly the same. As did the metal hangar with its add-on maintenance bay and cubbyhole office—so small an area their mom used to complain about it daily when she answered phones and kept the books. Before Shane and Eve Callen were killed coming home one foggy night. At an unmarked train crossing out of Whitepine. Two more senseless deaths.

Marlee blinked rapidly and swung onto the gravel drive. Memories of the parents they'd lost when she and Mick were starting junior high threatened to overwhelm her; instead, she busied herself counting planes. A single-engine Piper Arrow and a newer turboprop Piper Seneca, a silver gleam in the last bay. The battered, refurbished Huey army helicopter she loved sat in the clearing between the smaller two cabins.

Marlee could handle every machine there. But she'd told Mick she wouldn't fly. As Jo Beth's sole guardian, she owed it to her daughter not to take any more risks. Her brother had expressed disappointment, but in the end he'd agreed that if she reduced his overflowing paperwork and helped ride herd on Pappy, who sometimes tended to wander, it'd be enough. A godsend, in fact. So here she was.

Her thoughts of Mick and Pappy Jack must have made them materialize—there they were, looking solid and welcoming and, well—beautiful.

She jammed on the brakes and the Ford's tires skidded. Uncaring, Marlee jumped out, flinging her arms wide. Hugging Mick, she felt her tears on his blue cotton shirt. Still tall and blond and muscular, her twin squeezed her hard. And when he let go, Pappy Jack hugged her, too. At eighty-five, he was thinner than she remembered. His full head of hair was nearly white where it'd been nut-brown. Still the same, though, were his aquamarine eyes, a trait borne by all Callens. And his shimmered with unshed tears.

All three began talking at once. They were stopped abruptly by a wail from inside the Excursion. Spinning, Marlee dashed to the open door. She tried unsuccessfully to quiet the sobs and coax five-year-old Jo Beth Stein out to meet her uncle and great-grandpa. "Hey, tiddledywink, I'm right here. It's okay, I haven't left you. Jo Beth, this is our new home. Come say hi to Uncle Mick, and to Pappy Jack. Remember I showed you pictures of them before we packed my albums?"

A little girl with a mop of brown curls and weepy hazel eyes held a soft-bodied doll in one arm as if her life depended on it. She scrubbed her cheeks with her free hand but didn't venture out of the SUV.

Marlee turned to the men. In an undertone she said, "Maybe if you went back inside to wait... I explained about her crying jags and temper tantrums, didn't I? They started after Cole died

and escalated through my tug-of-war with Rose. I'm hoping…"
Marlee raked a hand through her tawny gold hair as her eyes
begged her brother's understanding.

"No problem, sis. We'll take your luggage. Mrs. Gibson
swabbed out the largest of the cabins for you. Or if you'd rather
sleep in the main house until your furniture arrives, your old
room's made up. It has twin beds if you want Jo Beth to share."

Marlee waved a hand toward the Ford. "What you see is our
life in a nutshell."

Pappy peered in the windows of the SUV. "That old broad
stole your house, furniture and everything?"

She corrected his misimpression. "Cole and I rented a fur-
nished condo because we were rarely home. As soon as I got
pregnant, we decided to buy a house." Marlee looked pained.
"Pappy, it was during house hunting that I noticed Cole seemed
tired. Finally, after weeks of tests, he was diagnosed."

She would have let it go, but her grandfather said, "So, where
did Cole's mother get off trying to take your kid away from you?"

"Didn't Mick tell you?" Her glance darted to her brother,
then back to Pappy Jack. "Right after Jo Beth was born and I went
off desk duty, I got orders to ship out. That's when we let the
apartment go and moved in with Rose. At the time we didn't
know how else to manage, what with a new baby and Cole un-
dergoing treatments. We…just, uh, counted on the treatments
working." She sighed and fiddled with Jo Beth's cap of curls.

"Don't sweat it," Mick said, ruffling his shorter, sun-lightened
hair. "The cabin has the basics. We can add stuff as you figure
out what's missing. If you open up the back, Pappy and I can haul
in your suitcases."

Nodding, Marlee retrieved her keys. "Maybe we'll sleep in
the house until Jo Beth gets more comfortable. Set the two small
bags in my old room, okay? Everything else can go to the cabin."
She couldn't help but notice Mick's prominent limp even before

he picked up the suitcases. That gave Marlee pause. He'd told her he was fine now.

It took the better part of forty minutes to convince Jo Beth that she needed to go inside.

"Sis, I have freight to pick up in Kalispell for an early-morning delivery," Mick announced. "And I've got an appointment, so I'll be gone a couple of hours. Settle in, and if you feel up to it after dinner, I'll show you around the office. You can take over where I left off billing. I'm warning you, I haven't done any paperwork in months."

"Filing's time-consuming nonsense," Pappy snorted. "All you need to keep the IRS guys happy is a record of income versus outgo. Most years, the latter tops the former," he said, sounding more savvy than her brother let Marlee believe.

"Frankly, Mick, I'm anxious to start. I want to earn my keep. I hope you don't object to Jo Beth playing with her toys in the office while I work."

"Why would I? Mom raised us out there until we were old enough to tag after Dad and Pappy."

A smile blossomed, the first genuine smile she'd felt in weeks. But then she watched Mick walk toward the Piper Arrow. She wasn't mistaken; he favored his left leg. Maybe his old injury was affected by weather. The ground here looked as if it'd rained not long ago.

She took Jo Beth by the hand. "Pappy, while Mick's gone, I'll unpack a few boxes and suitcases and find storage space in the cabin. I want to dig out Jo Beth's toys so she'll feel at home. Care to tag along?"

"Nope. I let myself get involved in one of those silly afternoon soaps. You and the little squeak just come on back to the house whenever the spirit moves you."

Marlee laughed. Pappy used to call her *little squeak,* too. Being home felt good. Natural, as though she hadn't grown up and been left to deal with grown-up matters. If anybody deserved to kick back in the afternoon with TV it was Pappy. He'd worked from dawn to dusk for most of his life.

Already in a better frame of mind, Marlee struck out for the cabin. She'd forgotten the rustic charm of the knotty pine walls and cedar plank floors. Mick hadn't been kidding. The cabin was basic, all right, boasting only the bare essentials. But Marlee didn't want a lot of memories hanging around. It was better to leave them with Rose, who'd made one room of her home into a shrine for her husband, and a second for Cole.

Time passed as she unpacked. Before she knew it, two hours had disappeared. Now the cabin had a few personal touches, making it hers and Jo Beth's. Collecting toys for her daughter, Marlee put them in a tote. Together she and Jo Beth wandered back to the main house.

Pappy appeared to be engrossed in another program, so Marlee set Jo Beth up near the couch, and emptied the tote onto a worn braided rug.

"Do they have a dining room, Mama? I'm hungry," Jo Beth said suddenly.

"Me, too," growled Pappy Jack. "I hope you can cook, girl." Shutting off the TV, he leveled a hopeful glance at Marlee.

Since they'd come in, he'd been rocking contentedly in a scarred rocker Marlee knew had belonged to his dad. She remembered every square inch of this house, while Jo Beth had only ever lived in Rose Stein's decorator-designed show home. What a contrast.

"Pappy, I wish I could say I was a great cook. I picked up some tips from my mother-in-law, but whenever I was at the house, it…just seemed easier to let her cook. It was, after all, her home."

"Maybe you shoulda brought her. Mick says I put stuff on to cook, then go off and let it burn. Hell, he's a fine one to talk. Half the time he gets to tinkering with engines and can't remember it's time to eat."

Jo Beth looked up from arranging her Polly Pocket hairdresser and fashion model sets. "Mama, that man said a bad word."

Marlee had Rose Stein to thank for Jo Beth's prissy attitude, too. The woman had been married to an admiral, but even before his passing she'd insisted the profanity prevalent among military personnel not invade her home. Cole rarely slipped. Marlee often did and got taken to task by Rose. Jo Beth mimicked her grandmother.

Rather than take issue now, Marlee redirected the conversation to what she should fix for supper. Another difference for her daughter—in Rose's home they *dined*.

But she needed to shut off her mind. Preparing a meal seemed a good outlet. She found steak thawing in the fridge, and fresh corn in the vegetable keeper. There were baking potatoes in a bin that had always been in the pantry. Just as she patted herself on the back for remembering, the wall phone rang.

"That's the business line," Pappy said, glancing up. "Mick says taking orders is gonna be your job. You might as well answer it and get your feet wet, twin."

Marlee reached for the receiver and smiled. Another thing Pappy used to do—call one of them by their given name and the other *twin*. Sometimes he used *boy* or *girl*. "Hello," she said, her voice reflecting the remnant of her smile. The caller mumbled that he must have dialed incorrectly.

"Wait—you've…reached Cloud Chasers." She grabbed a pen and hunted for paper. "You're Wylie Ames?" Marlee's eyes sought Pappy's, but he was watching TV again. "I'm sorry to have to ask if you're an old account of Mick's or a new customer. Mick? Oh, he's gone to Kalispell. I expect him back anytime. Who am I? His sister." She stopped short of adding isn't any of your concern. Not a good idea to annoy a customer her first day on the job, the man was curt to the point of rudeness.

Her smile turned into a frown when it became apparent the guy didn't trust her to deliver a message. Tersely, he said, "I have a generator on the fritz. The parts house in Kalispell promised to have my order ready for Mick by the middle of next week." He sounded even more ill-tempered when Marlee asked if Mick knew where to deliver the goods, and snapped "Yes." He clicked off without saying goodbye. Glaring at the receiver, Marlee banged it back into its cradle.

"Disagreeable jerk," she muttered as her brother walked into the house, his limp more pronounced. There were fatigue lines around his mouth Marlee didn't recall seeing earlier.

"Who's disagreeable?" Mick shrugged out of a battered brown flyer's jacket. Marlee remembered fondly when he'd saved up to buy it, or one just like it.

"A customer by the name of Wylie Ames." She rattled off the reason for his call.

Mick took the message she'd scribbled on a corner of a brown grocery bag. "Wylie's a good guy. He's a forest ranger who lives year-round on a remote station on the Glacier Park perimeter. He's the only official presence in thirty square miles."

Marlene wrinkled her nose. "He could do with some manners." Turning, she slid the potatoes in the oven and began to shuck corn.

Pappy had stirred when Mick entered. Stifling a yawn, he said, "You probably wanna steer clear of Ames, girl. Old-timers up-region say his wife disappeared in the dead of night. Just like that." Pappy tried to snap his gnarled fingers.

Looking up from peeling corn silk, Marlee's mouth sagged. "You mean people think he—" She broke off and cast a worried frown toward Jo Beth.

Mick hobbled to the couch, sat and picked up one of the child's plastic dolls, turning it in his big hands. "Don't pay Pappy any mind," he said. "Those are crazy rumors, sis. You know how folks in the backcountry love to gossip. With each repeat, their bear stories get fiercer and fish tales bigger. Wylie's a good man raising his son alone. Dean is a few years older than Jo Beth. So, you said Wylie expects his stuff when?"

Her mind shifted from Pappy's warning. "Next Wednesday, he thinks, or Thursday. He said you could call Morrison's parts house if you don't hear by Thursday morning." She found the griddle for cooking steaks and plugged it in.

Pappy Jack faced Mick. "What did the doc have to say about your hip?"

Marlee's ears perked up.

"Same old, same old, Pappy. Hey, isn't it good to see Marlee fixing us some decent food for a change?"

Pappy spiked a bushy brow. "Same old, how? You mean the bone doc still wants you in ASAP to replace that socket."

"Mick? You need more surgery?" Alarmed, Marlee straightened and anxiously twisted the top button on her blouse.

Her brother pursed his lips. He took his time arranging Jo Beth's doll in a tiny chair. He even clamped a bonnet hair dryer from the toy set over the doll's head.

"You mean the boy didn't tell you he's put off havin' that joint replaced nigh on four months now?" He turned to his grandson. "When Rusty Meyer called to say he couldn't fill in to fly our freight runs, I thought you told him that it was okay 'cause Marlee was due in and she'd handle the route?"

Mick sent his grandfather a killer scowl. "Pappy, why do you forget what the hell day it is, and whether or not you took your blood-pressure medicine, yet you remember every frigging detail of my private business?"

Even as Jo Beth pointed out her uncle's bad word, Marlee presented him with her back while she slapped steaks on a grill beginning to heat up. "Mick...I—"

He broke in. "I know, you made it clear you didn't come here to fly. Josh Manley at the flying school in Kalispell has a student close to qualifying for solo. Unless the weather turns bad, he thinks the kid could manage our day runs. If he graduates in time. Of course, I'd have to notify Angel Fleet to take my name off their roster for mercy missions."

"They still operate here? Why don't people just use 911?"

"Oh, you city girl. Out here volunteers for Angel Fleet *are* 911."

"I didn't know you flew sick, injured or dying people around, Mick." Marlee spun toward him, hands on her hips. "What else have you neglected to tell me?"

"Cloud Chasers is the charter service best situated to airlift needy folks out of the remote wilderness. Besides, most flights are tax-deductible. It helps offset the red."

"Doesn't Glacier Park have a search-and-rescue team?"

"Summers. They have a couple of small choppers. Since I've come home, I've seen an increase in accidents. They mostly occur in new, fairly inaccessible bed-and-breakfast sites or at fishing and hunting lodges. Tourists have discovered our area, Marlee."

"I know you said one outfit cleared trees and put in a vineyard. And another planted a huge apple orchard. I suppose their workers might get hurt," she said unhappily. "I'm just not sure about this growth…."

"Growth is good for Cloud Chasers. More lodges laying in food, liquor and such. I fly customers in and out. I didn't think it'd be right to make money off tourists and not fly them to hospitals if they get hurt out here."

"I suppose not. Besides, you know firsthand how a quick rescue can spell the difference between life and death. Which brings us back to the surgery Pappy said you need." Marlee flipped the steaks. When Mick remained silent, she asked him again.

"Things aren't that desperate yet," he said, heaving a sigh.

When Marlee glared at him, she noticed him rubbing his face wearily with both hands. "Dammit, Mick, let's have the truth," she demanded, totally ignoring her daughter's hissy fit over Mom's swearing.

"The local sawbones says if I don't get the socket in my left hip replaced soon, it's gonna wear away the ball joint. Today I got a second opinion. Same report."

"Pain?" She didn't let up.

"Yeah. More all the time. I can't take anything except industrial strength, over-the-counter, anti-inflammatory meds and still fly. But it's my problem, Twin, not yours. I've got my fingers crossed that Manley will pass that student. My routes are straight-up flying. As a rule," he added.

"I've seen some of those rinky-dink landing strips," she said drily, dumping corn into boiling water. "Do you feel like setting the table?" she asked, changing the subject.

He climbed slowly to his feet. Marlee saw what it cost him to try to do that with panache. She said nothing else until they were all seated at the table, and Jo Beth had offered a simple prayer. Pappy alone dug into his meal.

"Out of curiosity, Mick, what timetable does the doctor give you for getting back in the saddle after surgery?"

"Eight to ten weeks. But I heal fast. I figure I can take the controls again later in the winter. Between more lodges, and more outpost rangers stocking up before snow socks 'em in, I get busy. After November, calls are sporadic until spring thaw, except for an occasional emergency. And your military training qualifies you to handle those."

Marlee nibbled a thin slice of steak. Jo Beth loved baked potatoes. She was making a healthy dent in the one Marlee had cut and buttered for her.

Pappy devoured his food, tuning them out. Marlee heard him humming. It wasn't until he wolfed down everything on his plate, shoved it back and went outside without a word, that she revisited a previous topic. "Mick, I want to help. With a little refresher on fixed-wing aircraft, I can fly your route. Even into the winter, if need be. For God's sake, I landed choppers on carriers in all kinds of weather. But...two things. It's imperative that you agree to let me name you as guardian for Jo Beth should anything happen to me. It'll probably take a codicil on my current will. And...after surgery, how do you propose to manage here if I'm on a flight? You'll be on painkillers at first. Jo Beth can't be given the freedom you apparently allow Pappy."

"What would you say to taking her along? I mean, we flew with Pappy and Dad from the time we could crawl into the cockpit. Mrs. Gibson—Stella, a widow from down the road—does light housekeeping here now. She can look in on me'n Pappy. She often prepare meals for us to pop in the oven."

"Taking Jo Beth wasn't something I'd considered. I'll have to think about that." Standing, she started stacking plates. Jo Beth had excused herself to play with her dolls. Marlee wondered if her daughter would like flying. Until Cole got really ill, on weekends Marlee sometimes rented a plane and flew him out over the ocean he loved.

They'd told Jo Beth what her mother did for the navy—fly. Marlee had planned to request a discharge at the end of her first Gulf tour. But while she was on active duty, Cole had better medical coverage as a spouse than he did once he took a medical discharge. Marlee had let Rose talk her into signing on for another two years. She'd never once dreamed the Navy would promptly deploy her again. She'd already missed too many of Jo Beth's formative years. Missed being on hand when Cole's conditioned worsened. Hey, maybe a flight now and then would be good for her daughter. Except for her new tantrums, Jo Beth seemed far too serious.

Shaking off her sudden blues, Marlee carried her load to the sink. "I see you had a dishwasher installed. That's a four-star improvement."

"Yeah, but not in the cabins." With a hint of the old Mick, he teased, "Guess that means you'll have to fix all your meals at the main house. You don't want to end up with dishpan hands."

"I can afford a dishwasher, brother dear. Fighting Rose in court didn't go through my entire savings, even if my lawyer did his best to see I didn't end up too well off."

"Ouch…life's a real bitch, sometimes," he said, lowering his voice.

"All God's chilluns got trouble," Marlee quipped back. "Let me put these dishes in to wash, then why don't we go take a gander at your office?"

"I guarantee my plane engines are in better shape. While you finish up here, I'll see where Pappy got off to."

"You said he runs off?"

"Wanders. He's usually messing around in the workshop. It's important to lock the doors on the planes. Can't trust him not to get it into his head to fly. That's why I let him ride along, especially if I'm going to the fishing lodges. He loves gossiping with his old cronies."

"I hate to see him going downhill, Mick. Is his health okay other than the arteriosclerosis? Is that what they used to call hardening of the arteries?"

"Uh-huh. He's got the usual health issues of a man his age. His cholesterol's sky-high. The doc said to limit red meat and dairy. Bad though I am in the kitchen, I did try. First time I told him no more steak he walked all the way into Whitepine and ordered rib eye at Sue Jensen's restaurant. I went nuts when I couldn't find him anywhere on the property. I called the sheriff, and Pappy gave us both what-for. So, call me negligent, but I let him eat steak or roast a couple of times a week."

"I'd never call you negligent, Mick. Cole bucked his doctor's orders, too. He loved the beach. One time, Rose summoned me home from the Gulf when things looked grim. Cole rallied and begged me to drive him and Jo Beth to the beach. He wanted to build sand castles with her. But he was too weak, so he persuaded me to build them for him. We dug in the damp sand while he watched. He kept urging us to build more." She bit her lip. "Jo Beth was having fun, and I didn't realize the sun had dropped. It's always windy at the beach…but Cole got really chilled. He had no defenses to fight off infection. Rose accused me of hastening his death. I don't know," Marlee said slowly, almost absently. "He laughed that day, Mick. We saw his old sparkle." Her throat worked and her voice had grown raspy.

"Leave the dishes. When we come back, I'll help. Pappy heard us talking about the office, and I'll bet he decided to straighten up."

Grabbing the chance to shake off her thoughts of Cole's last days, Marlee rounded up Jo Beth and found them both sweaters. They kicked through fall leaves, saying little until Marlee noticed Mick rubbing his hip and leaning into his left leg.

"When did your doctor think he could schedule surgery?"

"Next week if I give the word. If I called tomorrow, he'd probably have me under the knife on Tuesday."

"That doesn't give us much time to draw up an addendum to my will, or for me to check out the fixed-wing planes. But…do it, Mick. I can't bear to watch you suffer like this."

"Are you sure? I've got a run tomorrow. Nothing again till Thursday. Supplies going to Finn Glenroe's lodge. You remember him and Mary?" As Mick opened the office door, Pappy turned, feather duster in hand. Mick hadn't exaggerated; the place needed cleaning. The place looked junky. The desk held an ancient, dusty computer, nearly hidden by stacks of invoices.

"What about Finn?" Pappy flipped his duster, and they all choked. "Oops," he said, "should've stepped outside."

"I was telling Marlee which jobs are firm. Oh, I almost forgot Wylie's generator parts. They go out whenever Don Morrison calls."

"You tell Marlee that Wylie Ames is part Blackfoot?"

Mick shook his head. "He's Chinook Native. But what's that got to do with anything?"

"He's tight-lipped. I hear the boy's got no native blood. Like maybe the woman he married cuckolded Wylie. Could be why he did her in—if'n he did."

"Pappy, honestly! Shirl left him. Uh, that cop show you like is on in ten minutes."

The old man surprised them by locating a pad and pencil. He handed both to Jo Beth. "Draw me a picture to hang on the fridge," he said before he left.

Mick demonstrated his computer program for Marlee. They discussed flight plans and talked for an hour while shuffling papers.

"I'll dig into this filing mess first thing tomorrow," she promised. "It's pretty straightforward. Same system Mom set up, except for the computer. Maybe you could build a better tracking system while you recover."

"I swore you wouldn't have to fly. You *sure* you want me to call the doc about the surgery?"

"Do it before I have second thoughts. Besides, seeing the planes and all...well, what flyer ever voluntarily grounds him or herself?"

Mick grinned cheekily and dusted his knuckles over her softer chin.

THE NEXT DAY he did phone Dr. Chapman. "It's all set," he told Marlee. "I'll watch you fly touch-and-goes in the Arrow this weekend. Monday you take me to Kalispell for pre-op tests. By Wednesday I'll be the proud owner of a space-age hip."

"I'll write up a note to attach to my will. I'm sure the hospital has a notary."

"Sounds good. By the way, I'm taking Pappy with me today."

That gave Marlee a chance to begin establishing a routine for

Jo Beth. All in all, the girl threw only one small tantrum, insisting she wanted Grandmother Rose.

Marlee didn't hate Cole's mom. But with her own worry over him and the fact that Marlee was gone often, Rose had usurped her role as Jo Beth's mother. The first time she'd come home on rotation, and Jo Beth refused to have anything to do with her, hurt more than Marlee had ever let on. Each trip, the gap widened. Still, after Cole died it'd been a shock when Rose sued for legal custody of her granddaughter.

The remainder of the week passed in a blur. Marlee spent four hours a day bringing order to the office. The rest of her time she divided between getting reacquainted with Jo Beth, flying, and leafing through her Mom's old cookbooks.

She'd totally forgotten about Wylie Ames until she picked up the phone in the office on Saturday and heard him say, "You're still visiting, huh? It's Ranger Ames. Tell Mick that Don Morrison will have my stuff by noon on Wednesday. I'd like them delivered Thursday."

"Okay." Marlee jotted herself a note, but when she began to say she'd be the one flying in with his order, she discovered Ames had hung up. Muttering about his rude phone manners she slammed down her receiver.

She and Mick spent Sunday afternoon discussing his regular customers and their expectations. He talked about their landing strips. "Most are primitive, sis. Only a couple of them have lights, so I try to arrange morning deliveries. The smoke jumpers' camp has an asphalt strip. Wylie wired lights on either side of his. If he knows I'm coming in late, he'll fire 'em up with his generator."

"I'll make sure I only fly in daylight, Mick. I'm glad Ranger Ames's parts don't have to go out until Thursday. That way I can visit you in the hospital after your surgery, and collect his order in Kalispell."

"Call him Wylie. Don't want him to think you're uppity."

"Mick—all that stuff Pappy said about him… I, uh, plan on taking Jo Beth along. Is he…is it safe?"

Mick laughed. "As a rule, I time his deliveries so I can eat lunch with Wylie. His son, Dean, is a great kid. He's home-schooled and I take him books on wild animals. He's always healing a bird, a raccoon, deer or squirrels. I have a couple of books waiting to give him."

"I don't plan to socialize, Mick, only off-load the order."

Over the next few days, what with Mick being in the hospital, Marlee had so much on her mind that Wylie Ames took a back seat until it came time to pick up his order in Kalispell. Even then, her mood was much improved because the surgery had gone well. She left Mick flirting outrageously with an attractive nurse, and went to refuel the Piper Arrow. She was glad the plane handled like a dream.

Thursday was a beauty for flying, with a clear blue sky and thready white clouds. Below stretched the orchards Mick had told her about, and the vineyards, laid out like quilt blocks. Jo Beth was excited about getting to fly, and Marlee, who'd worried how her daughter would do, finally relaxed.

Having decided to make the ranger station her first drop, Marlee spotted the landmarks Mick had mentioned. It wasn't long before a runway came into view. She circled once to get the layout and to test the wind. As she started down, Jo Beth pointed. "Mama, there's a boy waving." Jo Beth waved back, and Marlee noticed a man standing at the end of the runway.

She throttled back, frankly unable to take her eyes off him. His dark presence embodied every last one of Pappy's innuen-dos and warnings. It flashed through Marlee's mind that from a distance, the dark-haired, broad-shouldered, narrow-hipped man reminded her of Cole before he'd taken ill and his body had wasted away. Suddenly her hands shook and the plane dipped.

She quickly regained control, but landed with an irritating little hop. A beginner's mistake that unnerved her as she powered down. Ripping off her headset, Marlee leaped from the cockpit and shook out her hair, only to discover, as she watched the taciturn Wylie Ames, that he watched her, too.

Marlee hurried around the Piper's nose to assist Jo Beth. For some reason, Marlee disliked the fact that Ames was too far away for her to see the color of his eyes. Ace-of-spades black would be her guess—to go with the scowl he wore.

A shiver of apprehension wound up her backbone seconds before she decided not to let Pappy's rumors affect her. She purposely stiffened her spine.

CHAPTER TWO

WYLIE AMES MOTIONED to his excited eight-year-old son, Dean, to stay back until Mick Callen's charter plane came to a full stop. Then the ranger saw a woman at the controls. Where was Mick? Damn. Wylie always looked forward to the bush pilot's visits. So did Dean. Their outpost did get lonely. Not that Wylie minded solitude so much, but it was hard on his son, who was by nature more sociable.

Whoa! Not one but two females had invaded his bastion, Wylie saw, as the woman hurried around the plane to assist a child from the passenger side. A curly-haired girl.

The pilot studied him warily. Wylie figured she must be the woman he'd talked to on the phone—Mick's sister. He couldn't help but wonder what she might've heard about him. Right now, while Wylie stared into the sun, she had the advantage of checking him out. Even shading his eyes with a hand allowed him only sketchy impressions. So, he moved into the trees.

She was tall for a woman, and thin as a conifer sapling. Her hair was something, though. Like honey fresh from the comb. The thick mass fell to well below her shoulders. *Nice. Very nice.*

As she stepped out of the sun and he was afforded a better view, Wylie felt a kick to his sternum that left him gasping for air. He told himself to get a grip. He'd banned reactions of that kind long ago.

He clamped his back teeth tight as Dean bolted past on his

way to greet the new arrivals. Feet welded in place, Wylie had some furious thoughts for Mick Callen. What the hell was his friend thinking? Of course, it was his right to put his own plane at risk. But there was the matter of Wylie's shipment…. Parts for his ancient generator came at a premium and were getting harder to locate. Out here in the wilderness, a generator was vital, especially during tough winters.

His son's chatter, followed by a higher-pitched response, shook Wylie from his thoughts in time to see the pilot lift a wood crate from the cargo hold. It was evident from her stiff steps that the crate weighed probably as much as she did.

"What do you think you're doing?" he demanded, striding over to relieve her of her load. Up close, it looked to him as if she'd break more easily than a sapling. Irritation made him muscle her aside none too gently, and he carried the crate the rest of the way. "I don't know why Mick sent you, but he should have his head examined. This stuff's too heavy for a woman."

Marlee, already simmering at being assessed by this backwoods oaf, glared up—and at just over five foot nine herself, there weren't a lot of men she had to tip her head back to meet eye to eye. Confronted instead by Ames's broad back, she wheeled and stalked to the plane to haul out another crate.

His expression was dour as he hustled toward her and reached for her load. Marlee offered a slight curl of her upper lip that some might mistake for a smile…seconds before she let go of the box. She knew her aim had been true when she heard him swear. Marlee glanced over her shoulder and saw Ranger Ames hopping about on one square-toed boot.

Satisfied, she returned to the plane for a third box.

The kids, still yakking up a storm, had progressed from the passenger side of the Arrow to its nose. A gangly boy with sandy red hair, freckles galore and lake-blue eyes said, "I'm Dean. Is it all right if Jo Beth goes with me to the tire swing my dad hung in our apple tree?"

Marlee paused to take in the pair of eager faces. This was the most animated she'd seen Jo Beth since before Cole's death. "Is it far?"

"Nope. You can see our house from here." The boy waved a hand toward a cabin visible beyond a forest of trees more diverse than the ones that grew in Whitepine. At a glance Marlee identified spruce, fir, larch, cedar and hemlock. Each emitted its unique scent—aromas Marlee had grown up with, but had forgotten. For too many years, she'd spent her days and nights at sea on the deck of a carrier where she smelled mostly jet fuel mixed with sweat.

All the same, the old familiar sights and scents settled her jumpy stomach. Jumpy because she'd more than half believed Pappy Jack's gossip surrounding the supposed disappearance of Wylie Ames's wife, this outgoing little boy's mother. But Dean Ames certainly seemed happy and well cared for.

Marlee shot a surreptitious glance to where she'd left the grumpy father, only to discover he'd collected himself and hovered like a dark gloom over her shoulder.

"Dean, these folks won't be here that long. I just need to transfer these last two crates and check the paperwork, and they'll be off."

"But, Dad, you made gumbo and baked bread. And you said we were having company for lunch."

Wylie cleared his throat. "I, ah, expected Mick."

"I'm sorry to disappoint you," Marlee said drily. "I suppose I ought to introduce myself. I'm Mick's sister, Marlee Stein. We spoke on the phone. Twice. I'm making deliveries because Mick had hip surgery on Tuesday. I'll fly the route until he recovers."

Ames pushed mirrored sunglasses into his hair and frowned. "Is Mick okay? I'm sorry as heck. He's had…what? Four or five operations?" A cloud of sympathy filled eyes Marlee expected to be almost black, but which were a dark gray that didn't conceal emotions well. His concern for her brother spurred Marlee to loosen up a little.

"We hope Mick's new hip will mean his last hospital stay. I saw him yesterday before I picked up your parts. He came through the operation well enough be flirting with a pretty nurse."

Unexpectedly, Wylie's eyes crinkled at the corners as Marlee's words elicited a knowing masculine grin.

"Before I forget," she said, oddly feeling easier in his presence, "Don Morrison at the parts house mentioned that he wasn't able to scare up everything you need. He said there's no single supplier who stocks everything for your generator. He suggests you consider purchasing a newer model."

The big man slid the heaviest crate from the plane. "I'll have to remind Don that the powers that be in D.C. seem to think forest rangers should be able to live totally off the land." His grin flickered. "Third time they've cut Parks Department funds so they can give more to the military."

"You're speaking to a very recently discharged navy flyer who cursed those same powers in Washington every time we had to scrounge for parts to keep our choppers aloft."

"If you bounced the navy's aircraft around the way you did the Piper when you landed, I understand why they broke."

Gone was the fleeting goodwill she'd felt over his sympathy for Mick. "Look, buster, I assure you the navy regarded my flying skills very highly. I can fly anything with wings, I'll have you know."

Wylie merely grunted, presumably under the weight of the box.

Dean Ames, who'd stood patiently by while the adults traded insults, pulled on his dad's sleeve. "Da...ad! Jo Beth and me could've gone to the swing and been back."

Wylie raised a black eyebrow as if deferring the decision to Marlee before he continued over to the other crates.

"Oh, go on," she said, removing the last item from the hold.

"Jo Beth, I'll call you when I'm ready to fire up the plane. It won't be long," she warned.

Even before her last word was out, the kids had darted up the trail into a thick stand of timber. Straining, Marlee could see the ranger's cabin…and a window box overflowing with colorful marigolds? A trailing vine awash in red blooms? She gawked, which slowed her progress and allowed Ames to catch her off guard when he pulled at the crate in her hands.

"Hey, watch it," she grumbled, trying to yank the box back. "Mick said part of our service is loading and unloading a customer's freight. Which leaves said customer free to check the contents of a delivery," she added pointedly.

"Well and good, but you aren't Mick."

"Ranger, I'm not a weakling," she called after him. "A few months ago I was swooping into enemy territory and carrying shot-up soldiers to my chopper."

Wylie offered no response. After dropping his load at the end of the runway, he returned for the bill of lading she'd retrieved from the cockpit, then silently strode to the crates and sliced open the first one with a wicked-looking knife Marlee hadn't seen; it had been strapped to his boot.

She shuddered at the sight, but her attention quickly moved to the rippling of muscles beneath the ranger's khaki shirt. Something about him reminded her of Navy SEALs she'd run into. A go-to-hell cockiness. Her gaze moved from his broad back to the tanned hands pawing through shredded paper. If indeed the man had Chinook blood as Mick claimed, Ames's skin was probably the same smooth bronze all over. Marlee ran her tongue over dry lips as the simple image slammed desire into her stomach.

She caught herself up short, feeling heat flood her cheeks. What in heaven's name had gotten into her? For years she'd worked mostly with men, and she'd never fantasized about what they looked like under their shirts.

Pushing aside her inappropriate thoughts, she joined Ames. "Does it all look okay? According to Morrison, a turbine you want should be in next week. The pump he wasn't sure about. He said he'd call you, or us, when he tracks one down."

A short nod was the only response Marlee got. "Uh, since you don't need me until you're ready to sign the invoice, I'll just walk up the trail and get my daughter." She jerked a thumb in that direction, but then realized he wasn't listening.

Wylie felt her leave his space. He didn't want to, but he stopped checking his order and watched her go. The scent of whatever fragrance she wore lingered. He sniffed, trying to identify it. He couldn't. But it was something feminine. Nice. Compelling.

He didn't consider himself the total recluse he was rumored to be. After all, he got together three or four times a year with his fellow rangers and their families. Mainly to catch up on everything that happened in other sectors of the sprawling national park—but also to give Dean an opportunity to play with other kids.

Wylie rarely looked twice at the women at those gatherings. Not even when one or another friend introduced him to a new, single female ranger. And there had been several who'd joined up since Shirl hightailed it. For the life of him, he couldn't recall if any of them had worn such a tantalizing perfume. On second thought, he decided, he'd remember if they had.

In the distance, he heard the woman, Marlee, call for her daughter. Muttering under his breath, Wylie dived into his task. He didn't glance up again until the sound of feet shuffling through pine and fir needles on the trail interrupted him. Marlee Stein's worried expression yanked Wylie right out of admiring the picture she made. "Something wrong?"

"I found the tire swing. The kids aren't there. I called for Jo Beth, but got no response. My daughter's not used to being in the woods. She could easily get turned around."

"Dean probably took her out to the animal pens." Wylie, who'd been down on one knee checking the largest of the crates, stood and brushed off the needles stuck to his khaki pants.

"Animal pens?" Marlee's face paled. "Oh, I suppose you keep hunting dogs?"

"Our pens house wild creatures that Dean and I have rescued."

Marlee raked a hand through her hair. "Wild—oh, Mick said something about that. Isn't that dangerous? Jo Beth's a city girl. Where are the pens?"

"It's a fair walk. I'll take you."

"How far?"

"We keep the environment as close to normal for the animals as we can," he said in explanation. "So when they heal, it's easier to release them back into their natural habitat." He led the way to a junction in the trail Marlee hadn't seen on her trek to the swing.

She had a hard time keeping pace with the ranger's long stride. Suddenly he stopped. Slightly winded, Marlee caught up.

He parted the dense foliage. "That's where they got off to, all right. I can hear Dean explaining how he stumbled across Boxer after a rancher shot its mother."

"Boxer?"

"A griz cub. Yea big." Wylie shaped his hands to the approximate size of one of the smaller crates.

"Griz, as in grizzly bear?" Her pitch rose, along with her anxiety level.

He nodded and Marlee found herself noticing how deep they were in the forest, enough so that every ray of sunlight was blocked. She prided herself on having a good sense of direction, but now realized she hadn't paid attention to their route. She was at this man's mercy and it unnerved her. That and the nonchalant way Wylie Ames discussed grizzlies and gun-toting ranchers.

Marlee bit her lip. "I don't hear voices." Closer to the runway, birds chirped and squirrels chattered, but here, surrounded by undergrowth, it seemed uncannily silent.

The ranger placed both little fingers to his lips and rent the air with a shrill whistle. Moments later he repeated the call.

As if Ames had flushed out small varmints, Marlee heard scuttling in the brush. Then an answering whistle sounded, quite some distance off. Very soon, though, childish giggles followed. And in no time, two bright heads burst out of a thicket. One sandy red, the other toffee-brown. Relief unfurled in Marlee's stomach.

Dean Ames stared curiously at his dad. When the girl traipsing at his heels stumbled on a knobby tree root, the boy instinctively reached back and kept Jo Beth from falling. "Did you want us, Dad?"

Marlee rushed over and pulled Jo Beth tight against her legs as if to shield her from any threat. The woman's frightened expression gave Wylie an idea of what he was dealing with.

"Son, you told us you were going to the swing. You shouldn't have gone to the animal pens without telling anyone."

Dean screwed up his nose as he squinted at his dad. "Where else would I be?"

"Mrs. Stein had no idea. You worried her."

The freckle-faced boy gaped at Marlee. "Sorry," he mumbled. "I told Jo Beth about my pets and she asked to see them."

"Mama," the girl broke in. "Dean's got his very own bear. The kind we saw at the zoo at home, only littler. Boxer got hurt, but Dean and his daddy are making him better."

"That's...commendable," Marlee said with a quaver in her voice. "Tell Dean goodbye, Jo Beth. We have an order to deliver to Glenroe's Lodge."

"You're going into the backcountry? Dean, run to the house and get Mary's pie tins." He turned to face Marlee. "Last time

Mick came out, Mary Glenroe sent along a couple of fresh apple pies. Can you tell her thank you?"

"And tell her she can send us more pies," the boy said.

"Dean, that would be ill-mannered."

"Doesn't that tell Mrs. Glenroe we liked her cooking?"

"Well, yes, but…" Flustered, Wylie clammed up. He was more dismayed when Marlee laughed. The soft trill seemed to coil around places inside him long untouched. It was a nice sound, even if her laughter was at his expense.

"I'll tell Mary you loved her pies, Dean. I recall enjoying a slice or two of her peach pies when I wasn't much older than you."

Marlee hadn't realized that the roundabout path Wylie led them down now would end up not at the runway but at the back door of his cabin. Not until Dean darted ahead and she heard the screen door slam. The boy reappeared with pie tins before the others emerged from the woods into a clearing that held a vegetable garden fenced with chicken wire. She'd been so worried about not finding Jo Beth at the swing earlier, she'd completely missed seeing the garden. The neat rows of vegetables surprised her nearly as much as the flower box had. Ranger Ames was domestic, which one wouldn't imagine looking at his very masculine body.

"Dad, the soup smells yummy. I'm hungry. Can't Jo Beth and her mom stay and eat with us?"

Wylie and Marlee whipped out a simultaneous denial.

Jo Beth pouted and stamped a foot. "I'm hungry, too, Mama. Why *can't* we eat with Dean?"

For the life of her, Marlee couldn't find a way to tell the two children, who'd obviously hit it off, that neither she nor the boy's father wanted to remain in each other's company.

Ames reacted to his son's disappointment by ruffling the boy's red hair. Then he sighed, giving in to the pleas of the children. "Won't take long," he said to her, sounding gruff even though he smiled at the kids. "A matter of filling bowls and slicing bread."

Marlee, who'd never felt more like turning tail, wasn't about to be the bad guy in this setup. "Sure, okay. I'd hate to have Mary think she had to fix us something." She gave a quick shrug. "They must be getting on in years, Mary and Finn. I haven't seen them in...fourteen years."

Wylie opened the back door and stood aside to let his guests enter. "Been three for me. Dean and I had to take a run to the lodge on the big snow cat that winter. Finn had complaints about a couple of guests. Whit Chadwick claimed they chased his sheep, and he'd recognized Finn's snowmobile. The kids turned out to be Mary's great-nephews, come from Dallas to celebrate her sixty-fifth birthday. And Finn's even older."

"Definitely not spring chickens." Marlee followed Dean and Jo Beth through a laundry room into a country-style kitchen. She didn't know what she'd expected—surely a cluttered mess much like she'd found at Mick and Pappy's. Not so. The Ames' kitchen was spotless. Cheery curtains hung at the windows and bright place mats graced the table. A Crock-Pot on the counter emitted puffs of steam. Good-smelling steam. "Dean's right," Marlee said, stopping to close her eyes and sniff. "The soup smells delicious."

The big man seemed to have retreated within himself once they'd left the great outdoors. He stepped to the sink to wash up, and quickly began to fill the bowls sitting out on the counter. Because he had to open a cupboard to retrieve a fourth bowl, Marlee was reminded that Ames had planned for Mick, and that she and Jo Beth were interlopers.

"Jo Beth, you and I need to wash, too."

"Dean, show them to the main bath."

The boy grabbed Jo Beth's hand. Marlee trailed the chatty pair. As she passed Wylie on her way into the hall, she sensed that he relaxed as his kitchen emptied. His son was his exact opposite. Dean and Jo Beth couldn't seem to shut up, odd since her daughter was usually one to sit quietly, taking in everything around her.

That behavior had worried Marlee on her rare visits home. She'd worried that spending so much time with Cole during the worst of his illness might affect Jo Beth's ability to relate normally. Her concern eased as the kids discussed what to feed a growing bear cub.

"Dean, that reminds me," Marlee broke in. "Mick sent a couple of books. They're still on the plane. Would you like me to go get them now or give them to you when we're ready to leave?"

"When you leave's okay. Wow, I wonder if he found the book I read about on the Internet! *Bears as Good Neighbors.*"

"I don't know. Before he went for surgery, he gave me the sack and told me to be sure to bring it when we flew your father's generator parts in."

"I'm glad you came 'stead of Mick." He stuttered suddenly. "I—I didn't mean—gosh, I like him, but you brought Jo Beth. I know she's littler than me, but it's neat having another kid to play with."

"I understand." Marlee inspected Jo Beth's hands. "And this one is mature for her age. She spent a lot of time with her dad and grandmother."

"Does Jo Beth read and write? If she does, we can e-mail. That is—if it's okay with you. A ranger friend of my dad's won't let his kids use a computer. They're both older'n me, too."

"Jo Beth doesn't read well enough to handle e-mail. She's just five."

"Can we talk on the phone? I know it costs more, but we can take turns." His eyes shone with hope as he shoved back a shock of hair with a still-wet hand.

"Yeah, Mama. I want Dean to call and tell me if Boxer's

well enough to go and act like a real bear. He said maybe we can come watch when they let him out of his cage to go live in the forest."

Dean lowered his voice. "That won't be for a while yet, Mrs. Stein. Dad and me hafta teach Boxer to forage for berries and roots, and how to fish in the river."

"If it's okay with your father, Dean, you can call me Marlee. Jo Beth's grandmother is 'Mrs. Stein.'" She laughed. "I used to be Lieutenant Stein, but I'm out of the navy now, so that no longer applies."

"I think it's cool that you and Mick both fly planes. I can't wait to get old enough to learn. I wanna be a veterinarian who flies to ranches and takes care of animals. Oh, maybe Mick sent a book on planes. We were talking last time he was here about all the different kinds."

"Dean," a deep male voice said outside the bathroom door. "Quit talking their ears off. The gumbo's getting cold. I expected you to wash and come straight back."

Without looking guilty, the boy scooted from the room. "Dad, can I call Jo Beth one night a week so I can update her on Boxer? Marlee said it's okay with her if it's okay with you. Oh, and she said Jo Beth's grandmother's Mrs. Stein and she's Marlee. Well, she used to be lieutenant, like Mick. Now she's not."

"Can you tell Dean's glad to have someone to talk to?" Wylie said with a wry grin. "Let him know when your ears are blistered."

Marlee just smiled. But as they ate, had it not been for Dean's endless chatter, it would've been a quiet meal indeed. Marlee barely managed to extract one-word responses from her host.

"Ah, this is whitefish gumbo? I've only ever had it with shrimp or okra."

Wylie passed around thick-cut slices of bread. "Uh-huh."

Dean nattered on about the animals they currently had in their makeshift hospital. "Jo Beth, you didn't see my gray squirrel, or the porcupine with the broken leg. I think they were asleep in their cages. Next time you come, maybe they'll be out."

"I really like this bread. Whole wheat with Parmesan cheese?" Marlee asked.

"Oat." Wylie scooted the butter dish closer, again lowering his gaze to his bowl.

Marlee couldn't fault the man's manners. And he controlled his son's swinging legs with a touch, accompanied by a look Marlee called, "parents' evil eye." Smiling, she spread a thin layer of butter on her bread. "There are so many personal touches in this cabin, it makes me think you've been a ranger for quite a while."

"Sixteen years."

"That long? I guess that answers the question as to whether you like your job."

"Yep."

In the background Marlee heard Jo Beth ramble on to Dean about her two favorite spots in their old hometown. SeaWorld and the San Diego Zoo. "Honey, quit talking and eat. We have to stop at Glenroe's, and I'd like to make it home before dark." Also, Marlee didn't want her daughter telling strangers why they'd left a city the child chose to rhapsodize about.

Wylie pushed back his chair, went to the counter and returned with the remaining soup. "Seconds anyone?" He lifted the ladle.

Dean held out his bowl, but Marlee declined any for herself and Jo Beth. Although, if they'd found any common ground, she might have stayed. The gumbo was superb.

When Jo Beth slurped up her last spoonful, Marlee quickly snatched the girl's bowl and stacked it with hers. Repeating the process with their bread plates, she then started to carry the lot to the sink.

"Leave the dishes," Wylie ordered.

Startled by his tone, Marlee let the stack of dishes clatter back to the mat. "Well, then. I hate to eat and run, but…" She pointedly turned her watch around and studied it.

"Wait a minute," Dean implored. "You said you'd give me the books Mick sent."

"So I did. Tell you what, Dean. I have to run through a pre-flight check of the Arrow. If I'm ready to take off before you finish, I'll send Jo Beth to the house with the books." Marlee swung her daughter into her arms. "Much obliged for the lunch," she said, tossing her casual thank-you at the back of Wylie Ames's head of shiny black hair. Without further ado, she left the cabin as they'd entered, via the back door.

As Marlee started her check, she couldn't recall ever enduring such an uncomfortable forty-five minutes. Not even in the most stressful days she'd spent with Rose Stein. Which said a lot.

"Wow, Jo Beth and her mom are really, really nice, don't you think, Dad?" Dean gushed as he shoveled in the last of his second helping of gumbo, plainly anxious to run after the departing duo.

Wylie paused, a soup spoon halfway to his unsmiling lips. Truthfully, he didn't know what he thought about this woman and her child.

Hell, who was he kidding? He found too much to like about Mick Callen's twin sister. She had grit, and he admired that in a woman. She seemed to like Dean, which was more than could be said for the boy's mother. Shirl had left him a mere babe in arms. He scowled. Marlee smelled—well, feminine. Sweet and sexy, the way a woman should smell.

"They're okay," he drawled reluctantly, letting as much time lapse as he dared. "Thing is, son, we don't get deliveries often. Mrs. Stein didn't say how long it'd take for Mick to recover. Soon as he's well, he'll fly our orders in again."

"Dad! She said to call her Marlee. Mrs. Stein is Jo Beth's grandmother."

The mention of the girl's grandparent suggested another question. *Where was Mr. Stein? Junior, not the girl's grandfather*.

Divorced? Probably. Hadn't Jo Beth rattled on and on about their life in San Diego? City folk. Even if Marlee Stein had once lived here, he knew how it was when women had a hankering for city living. Of course, he'd had other issues with Shirl than just her dislike of the backwoods. Like the fact that she'd lied to him.

"Dad…you aren't paying attention. I finished my soup. Can I go and get the books Mick sent? One's about bears, I bet."

"Yeah."

"Aren't you coming to say goodbye?" Dean had jumped up from the table, but he hovered half in, half out of the doorway, clearly expecting his father to follow.

Wylie's first tendency was to tell Dean to run along. The more often he let the image of Marlee Stein burn into his brain, the more discontent would invade his jaded soul.

But he knew how excited Dean got watching planes land or take off. He couldn't trust the kid to keep well away from the propeller. "I'm coming," he said.

After Dean got his books and the pilot was strapped in for takeoff, Wylie hauled the boy far enough back to avoid the wind from the prop. Dean and Jo Beth began waving madly at each other. Wylie extracted his sunglasses from his shirt pocket and covered his eyes. He curbed the temptation to wave to Marlee. They hadn't become fast friends as the kids had. Still, he stood at the end of the runway and watched her lift off much more smoothly than she'd landed.

He looked up and kept track of her slow circle. As her flight pattern brought her back over his head, Wylie noticed she dipped her wing the way Mick always did. His way of saying *so long*.

IN THE AIR, MARLEE COULDN'T resist making one last flyover of moody Wylie Ames. The guy didn't even bend enough to acknowledge her leaving. He'd just covered his eyes with those damned mirrored shades and lazily hooked his thumbs in his trouser pockets as he stood immobile. The arrogant wide-legged stance served to warn any newcomer off this corner of the world. *His corner of the world.*

"Mama, I like Dean," Jo Beth said into the mouthpiece, as Marlee had shown her to do before the trip. "Can I call him when we get home?"

Marlee's lips twitched. She thrust the elder Ames out of her mind. "Listen, kid, you're a little young to be running up a phone bill talking to a boyfriend."

"Ma…ma! Dean's my *friend*—friend is all."

"I'm teasing. How about if I let you call him next week if his dad's auxiliary motor doesn't come in? If it does, I guess we'll fly it up here." She wouldn't have expected the possibility of a return trip to the ranger's cabin to bring a sense of excitement. But for whatever reason, it did.

"Oh, I hope the motor comes, Mama. We can stay for lunch again. And I'll get to see Boxer Bear." Jo Beth bounced excitedly.

Marlee dropped her sunglasses over her eyes to cloak her reaction to the memory of their recent lunch. "Don't count on it, tiddledywink." In spite of a definite sexual awareness the man had stoked in her, Marlee wouldn't put it past Wylie Ames to garnish his gumbo with fish bones next time—if he knew that she and not Mick was slated to make his delivery.

CHAPTER THREE

GLENROE LODGE SAT in a pocket carved out of conifer trees. A single fire road led in and out of the site. Someone had constructed a runway that was little better than two grass tracks long enough to clear the trees on takeoff. Bush pilots loved the adventure and the challenge of taking off and landing in tricky conditions. Marlee wasn't so far removed from hitting the deck of a carrier in a pitching sea that she enjoyed the thrill provided by Glenroe's runway. But she was nevertheless pleased when she set the Piper Arrow down sweetly. If Ranger Wylie Ames had seen this, he wouldn't have accused her of bouncing a plane around.

In the backcountry, a plane's arrival was cause for excitement. Marlee barely had her door ajar when she saw the lodge owners on the porch. Guests rushed out of rustic cabins tucked almost out of sight deep in virgin timber.

Once she left her plane, Marlee lifted Jo Beth down, then pulled out the first box of Glenroe supplies. They'd ordered mostly dry groceries, such as bagged rice, beans and pasta, canned vegetables by the case and fifty-pound sacks of sugar and flour.

Unlike Wylie, Finn and Mary Glenroe let her carry the delivery to the lodge.

"Land sakes alive." Mary elbowed her husband's ribs. "It's not Mick Callen bringing our order. If my old eyes don't deceive me, it's his twin come home. Marlee, what a pleasant surprise. When we saw the little girl run out from the plane, Finn and I were racking our brains trying to recall if we forgot to write down a family due to check in today." Mary wrapped Marlee in a warm hug.

Marlee introduced Jo Beth, then hastily repeated the information she'd given Wylie about Mick's latest bout of surgery.

It wasn't until Finn Glenroe limped over to open the lodge door and pointed to where Marlee should stack the supplies that she remembered a tractor had overturned on Finn years ago and caused him to lose one leg.

Three dogs, ranging in size from large to miniature, rushed the opening and got tangled in Marlee's feet.

"Mama, dogs!" Jo Beth squealed. "May I pet them?"

"Lord love you for asking so politely," Mary chimed in. "Tinker Bell, the Chihuahua is skittish. Lola, our spaniel is the offspring of our old dog, Daisy. Your mama may remember Daisy. Lucifer is Finn's bluetick hound. 'Bout all he's good for is eating, sleeping and hunting." The plump woman smiled at Jo Beth. "You sit yourself down yonder in one of the wicker chairs, those animals will gather round begging for attention."

Jo Beth's eyes grew big. "My grandmother said we couldn't have pets while my daddy was sick. But Pappy Jack said he and Uncle Mick might get a dog. I hope they do." The girl sat and, sure enough, the dogs bounded up to lick her.

Two of the guests—city-folk-turned-fishermen-for-a-week by the looks of them—offered to help Marlee carry supplies from the plane. She revised her thinking that Wylie had muscled her aside because he thought her puny. She'd forgotten in the real world, men assisted women. In the military, everyone pulled his or her own weight, and that's what was expected. She let the men take some boxes, and thanked them.

"Marlee, have you two eaten lunch? I can easily scare up sandwiches."

Marlee started to say they had to head home straight away,

but Jo Beth piped up, "Me and Mama ate lunch with Dean Ames and his daddy. Dean's got his very own bear."

"A bear, you say? That doesn't surprise me much."

Marlee halted beside Mary. "I almost forgot. Ranger Ames sent back two pie tins. I put them in one of your supply boxes."

The last of Glenroe's guests, who'd plunked down a sack of flour, paused halfway down the steps. "Little lady, you'll wanta take care flying into Ames' station. Heard tales floating around a year or so ago up along Kootenai River. Mary can fill you in. Fact is, a lone woman and a girl…you can't be too careful."

Marlee frowned as he whirled and trotted off in response to a call from his buddies who were gathered at the lake. Colorful fishing flies fluttered around the brim of the man's floppy hat.

"Dave Modine, don't be an old gossip." Mary shook a finger at his scrawny back. "Sit a spell, Marlee. I have fresh cake and coffee. Catch me up on what all you've been up to since last you flew in here with Pappy. How is he? Mick said he has good days and so-so ones. Finn looks at Pap's iffy health and says we've maybe got a couple good years left. Then we've gotta think about selling out and moving to town."

"Gosh, Mary, you've had this place since before I was born." Marlee stripped off the gloves she'd donned to better grip the bulky crates, and pulled out a wicker chair. "I take it neither of your boys plans to keep the lodge?"

"Nope, we sent them off to college where they met city girls. Matt's an insurance broker in Spokane, Washington. Lewis teaches history in Bozeman. So does his wife." As the woman spoke, she dashed in and out of the lodge, setting plates and cups on the glass-topped table sheltered from the afternoon wind by an ivy-draped trellis. "I'm surprised to see you back in White-pine. Mick, now I understand."

Marlee knew, of course, that she'd have to explain about Cole. She hadn't expected that merely mentioning his death would be so difficult. After all, it'd been a year. And in her heart she'd guessed some six months before that, they were losing him. She lowered her voice and stumbled through minimal facts.

Mary listened, sad eyes cutting to where Jo Beth sat petting an oversize cat that had curled up on her lap. "I'm right sorry, Marlee. A woman your age shouldn't have to lose her man when she's still raising young'uns. How do you cope?"

"The navy chaplains do a fair job preparing personnel to accept loss." Marlee patted the chair beside her, encouraging the older woman to sit. "Mary, when you scolded that fisherman, Dave, for gossiping, did you mean there's no truth to the rumors concerning Wylie Ames?"

"Jo Beth, honey," Mary called out. "Inside and down the hall is a place where you can wash up if you'd like a slice of chocolate cake. Would you like milk or juice?"

"Mama, may I have cake and milk?"

"Yes, sweetheart. Ms. Mary asked *you,* though. You can answer her directly."

"Grandmother said I should always ask before I take anything to eat from a stranger."

Marlee felt a twitch. Her mother-in-law had rules on top of rules. But this one made sense, and was one Marlee would have instituted if she had raised her daughter. "Thank you for checking with me first, Jo Beth. You don't know Mary and Finn, but I've known them since I was little."

"Then, yes, please." The child carefully set the big gold cat onto the porch and slid out of her chair. Mary waited until the screen door closed to address Marlee's question. "I'll go on record straight away. I think Wylie's gotten a bad rap. No one knows for sure what happened to his wife. He's not much of a talker. But the kind of man who'd trek in here on snowshoes in the dead of winter, him carrying an infant son in a front pack, just to see how a couple of old folks are getting along, isn't a man who'd mistreat a woman. I know him to be generous, honest and polite. Wylie's raised his boy to be the same. And something else…those two rescue and treat injured animals. That doesn't mesh with the rumors of foul play."

"Was his wife's disappearance investigated?"

"By whom? Rangers are more or less police themselves. Did something happen over at Wylie's?" she asked.

Marlee spent a moment in thought. "Actually, no. It's just that Pappy Jack mentioned the rumors, too. I have to say, though, I didn't find Ranger Ames sociable."

"Jo Beth said he served you two lunch."

A ghost of a smile flickered at one corner of Marlee's lips. "Dean invited us to stay. His dad tried every way possible to wiggle out. Lunch was delicious but far from the most comfortable time I've ever spent. Saying he's not much of a talker may be too big of a stretch."

As Jo Beth skipped out of the house, her mother's smile broadened. "I was about ready to send out a search party. What took you so long to wash?"

"I saw another fluffy kitty and stopped to pet her. Gosh, that cake looks yummy."

Mary patted a chair. "Climb up, and dig in. See if it tastes as good as it looks."

Rising, their hostess excused herself to fetch Jo Beth's milk. When Mary returned, the three ate slices of cake while the adults discussed how much Northwest Montana had grown in the years Marlee had been away.

"Growth's another reason Finn's talking of selling out. Used to be word of mouth brought in enough guests for us to make a decent living. Now there's a resort, a lodge, or bed and breakfast in every scenic byway." Mary stacked her plate and Marlee's as she talked. "Owners have to advertise with the tourist bureau, the Ranch Vacation Association and the Board of Outfitters.

We're told we need a Web site that's accessible through the chambers of commerce of nearby towns. People used to just call and book a cabin, and ask if Finn had time to show them the best fishing holes. Now they ask if we have certified river guides, liability insurance and oh, a lot of silly stuff. It's like they want to claim they're roughing it, but their kids demand cable TV, DVD rentals, a hot tub and swimming pool."

Marlee shook her head in commiseration. "And in the few days I worked on Mick's books, I saw how property taxes have tripled."

Inside the house a phone rang. Mary excused herself and went to answer it.

"Are you almost finished with your cake, Jo Beth? Nice as this visit's been, I want to head home before much more of the day slips away."

The girl's lower lip protruded. "I want to stay and play with the dogs. They like me, Mama. See, they're all waiting for me to be done eating."

Marlee glanced down at the ring of eager pet faces. She thought it more likely the animals were hoping for a crumb.

Mary burst out of the house clutching a cordless phone. "Marlee, it's Pappy for you. Gordy Maclean has been gored by a rogue bull at his ranch near Whitefish Lake. Angel Fleet called to see if Mick would fly him to the Kalispell hospital."

Marlee's stomach dropped. She accepted the phone with a shaky hand. "Pappy, Marlee here. Mick said he'd ask Angel Fleet to remove Cloud Chasers from their roster until he's able to fly again."

The old man either wasn't hearing the fear in Marlee's voice or else he didn't understand. *She didn't want to handle mercy flights.* Her grandfather kept repeating Angel Fleet's request. Finally, he took a breath and said, "Twin, here's the deal. There's no other plane available. Gordy's wife told Angel Fleet he's gonna bleed to death if somebody doesn't transport him to a hospital fast."

Marlee was rattled further by that news. The last thing she

needed was for Jo Beth to see anyone else on the verge of dying. "Pappy," she began, but he had hung up.

The cake and coffee Marlee had just consumed balled in the pit of her stomach along with the gumbo she'd eaten at Wylie's.

"Are you all right, Marlee?" Mary collected the phone, which was sliding from the younger woman's grasp. "Are you worried about landing without an airstrip? Gordy will have harvested his wheat. I think you can land in his field. If you look at Finn's wall map, you'll see exactly how to reach Gordon's ranch. Will that help?"

"Probably." Marlee stood on legs that felt pulpy. She concentrated on the issue front and foremost. No other plane was available. She tried not to think about what Pappy had said about a man maybe bleeding to death.

"Jo Beth, we need to make another stop. Please go to the bathroom if you can, and hurry."

The girl scuttled off while Marlee checked the map showing an excellent overview of the northwest woods. She mentally logged coordinates. "Mary, thanks for the refreshments. If you'll send Jo Beth out, I'll go warm up the plane."

Her daughter appeared before Marlee had climbed aboard. She boosted her in and helped settle her earphones.

Before Marlee taxied to the end of the runway for takeoff, she radioed Pappy. "This is Arrow one-three-six-niner. Come in home base." Her radio crackled. "Pappy, I'm in transit to Maclean's. Do you have any other word on the patient? Out."

Pappy didn't answer until after Marlee was fully airborne. "Affirmative on first directive. Negative on second."

Marlee would've asked if he'd spoken with Mick today, but Pappy cut off their transmission. She'd heard a woman's voice in the background. Probably Mrs. Gibson, the occasional housekeeper Mick had arranged to keep tabs on Pappy.

If she had to fly the injured man to Kalispell, she'd stop by and see Mick. It'd be good for Jo Beth to visit her uncle, and see him improving. Each hospital stay of Cole's he'd gone progressively downhill.

The Maclean ranch had been hollowed out of an aspen grove. White-barked trees were resplendently decked in yellow and gold. Grassy fields were thick with cattle. Marlee banked and came around for a sweep at a lower altitude.

Mary Glenroe had suggested she land on wheat stubble, but Marlee spotted a gravel road running from the house to the barn and beyond to lodgepole pine corrals. There was room to set down there as long as the people who'd run out of the house didn't get in the way. A huge yard flanked all four sides of a two-story farmhouse. If the grass wasn't too soft it'd give her room to turn around and be headed outbound again.

She executed another perfect landing, and once again said to herself, *Wylie Ames take that!* Not that she gave a damn what Ranger Ames thought about her piloting acumen.

"Jo Beth, don't unbuckle. Here comes our patient." Two men were carrying him out of the house. "Honey, I just need a minute to assess his condition, then we'll leave."

A dark-haired woman and a girl of about fourteen ran up to Marlee as she exited the plane. Worry had settled in the woman's eyes. "Angel Fleet said we should expect Mick Callen. I pray to heaven you've come to move Gordon."

"I'm Mick's sister. Did Angel Fleet happen to say if they've arranged for an ambulance to meet us at Kalispell airpark?"

"The dispatcher said they'd handle everything. My son and our hired hand tore up a sheet and wrapped Gordy's chest real tight. But the blood has soaked through. I'm so worried. Is it okay if Josh goes with his dad? He's old enough—sixteen."

"The problem is, Mrs. Maclean, I have my daughter with me, and this is the smallest of Mick's planes. Can you tell me approximately what each of them weigh?"

"I'm guessing Gordon's one-eighty. Josh is maybe one-fifty."

Marlee did some rapid calculations. "The only space I have available is the cargo area behind the seats. From the look of it, your husband needs to lie flat. I'll depend on your son to anchor his dad in place on bare floor. Do you have a sleeping bag we can use to cushion him?"

The woman directed the teenage girl to run to the house and check in the hall closet with the camping gear. No one said much thereafter.

The hired hand and Maclean's son worked to stabilize Gordon in the spot where the freight had been. When the man cried out, Marlee took a deep breath and stepped back. Irritated by her uneasiness, she told herself this mercy mission work wasn't so very different from rescues she'd flown for the navy. Once she made that connection, her jitters dissipated.

"He's not far from help now," she said to Mrs. Maclean in much the same way she'd reassured field medics who'd entrusted her to save lives.

However, her discomfort with the situation returned when she had to gather speed across the lumpy gravel road. As stoic as Maclean had tried to be when the younger men had manipulated him into the awkward space, his face now turned pasty white and sweat drenched his forehead. Even with earphones on, Marlee heard him scream seconds before she soared aloft. Jo Beth, however, calmly turned sideways in her seat and reached back to pat the injured man's shoulder.

Marlee dredged up a warm smile for the child. She'd thought Jo Beth needed a break from all reminders of her dad's long illness. Then Mick had announced he needed surgery, and now this unexpected mission for Angel Fleet. Neither fazed her daughter.

Some fifteen minutes out of the airpark, Marlee sensed more than saw that Gordy Maclean's breathing had become shallower. What if she lost the first patient placed in her care? She unhooked a fleece-lined jacket Mick had draped over the back of the passenger seat. "Cover your dad with this," she told Josh, as she coaxed more speed out of the Arrow. She recognized shock. God knew she'd seen enough men and women suffer from it during her two deployments. The big difference now was she wasn't facing flying bullets.

So why was she a nervous wreck by the time she called the tower at the Kalispell airpark? She consciously restrained any shaking in her voice as she spoke to the controller. "I've got a man on board who needs immediate medical attention."

"We've been expecting you, Arrow one-three-six-niner. Ambulance and medic are parked at runway four. You're cleared to land. Do you have any special requests?"

"Blankets, blood, Ringer's," Marlee responded automatically. She knew this emergency routine well. More's the pity, she thought.

The red lights of the ambulance cut through the thickening dusk, moving toward them slowly as Marlee set the Arrow down in the smoothest landing she'd made all day. This time she didn't let visions of the smug Wylie Ames intrude—much. She braked, removed her headphones and was out the door, racing around the tail section to throw open the cargo doors well before the propeller stopped spinning.

A paramedic team hustled to load the patient onto a rolling stretcher. One medic strapped on a blood pressure cuff while another attended oozing wounds, then swabbed Gordon's arm before inserting needles for blood and Ringer's solution, which would keep him hydrated and hopefully from going deeper into shock.

Marlee lent a much-needed third pair of hands. It wasn't until she heard Jo Beth's shoes hit the tarmac behind her that she realized she'd reacted as she would have at her old job. In so doing, she'd left her daughter to fend for herself. Awash in guilt—of the type Rose Stein had heaped on her at their recent custody hearing—Marlee removed herself from the scene at hand.

She gathered Jo Beth against her. Mom and daughter stood with arms wrapped around each other, watching medics load the gurney and boost Josh into the ambulance. The doors slammed and the vehicle roared off into the night with sirens blaring.

Her part in the rescue was over and she didn't personally know Maclean. But she recalled the fear etched on his son's face. Marlee had spent more time in Josh's shoes than she cared to think about. The kid was sixteen. What if his father's injuries were too massive, and Gordon died in spite of their efforts?

"Mama, you're squeezing me too tight."

"Sorry, Jo Beth." Marlee loosened the arm anchoring her daughter to her. Stifling a sigh, she raised an unsteady hand and rearranged her hair, which had come out of its clip during the afternoon.

"Why don't we go inside to see if we can rent a car to drive to the hospital?"

The child looked up and nodded solemnly. "That would be good, Mama. Josh might need us. He'll have to sit in the hospital waiting room all by himself."

The understanding filling the eyes of her five-year-old surprised and concerned Marlee. "Honey, Grandmother Rose never left you alone in the waiting room. Didn't you stay next door when Daddy went for his treatments?"

"Sometimes he had 'mergencies at night. Grandmother didn't have time to wake up Mrs. Griffith."

Marlee battled more nagging guilt. Of course, over time she'd come to realize Cole had kept the truth about how sick he was from her. He'd outright lied during her last ten-month deployment. But Jo Beth's admission meant Rose hadn't been honest, either. She had denied the extent of Cole's illness. It stood to reason his mom would do that, she thought, as she opened the door to the so-called terminal office.

A single clerk stood at the counter working a crossword puzzle. "May I help you?" he asked, glancing up.

"I just landed the Piper Arrow. Do you have a car available to rent or if not, the number for a cab?"

"That Mick Callen's plane?"

"Yes, he's laid up at the moment. I'm his sister."

"And you don't trust that eyesore he parks here? Can't say I blame you. Mick claims he leaves it in my lot so his grandpa can't hop in and take off."

Marlee found a smile. "Is it a '62 Caddy, robin's egg blue and cream?" At the man's nod, she said, "Mick and I learned to drive in that old tank." She studied a cork board filled with tagged keys behind the clerk. "I don't suppose Mick keeps a key to it here."

The young man turned and lifted one from a pushpin and handed it to her. "Now I *know* all pilots thrive on danger."

"How late is someone here?"

"I'm here till midnight. If you come back later, park the car in the same spot and shove the key through the mail slot in the door."

"Is midnight when the tower shuts down?"

"Yep. And that's when we turn off all runway lights except for number one. That stays lit for emergency landings."

"We'll be back long before then."

Marlee helped Jo Beth into the back of the Caddy, and dug for a seat belt wedged under the seat.

"Mama, this backseat is the biggest I've ever seen. I bet it's as big as my bed."

"This was your grandpa's car. They made them bigger in the old days." If Jo Beth had been older—a lot older—Marlee might have joked about modern cars not being nearly as good as this one for making out.

Behind the wheel, she cursed the engine that wouldn't turn over. It took five minutes but finally it caught. As she left the lot and merged with highway traffic, she decided she'd been wrong to tell Mick that she absolutely wouldn't fly for Angel Fleet. If Gordon Maclean pulled through, it'd be due in large part to the fact that she'd had a plane in the area and been willing to help.

A sign on the highway told her where to turn for the hospital.

Marlee debated whether to go to Mick's room first or try to locate young Josh Maclean. Stopping to see Mick won out, because she knew where his ward was. Maybe a nurse there could help her track down Gordon.

Two women in print smocks and white slacks were helping Mick out of bed when Marlee and Jo Beth walked into his room. The anguish on his face made it clear that standing was very painful. Marlee hovered in the doorway, not sure she should've brought Jo Beth, after all.

Mick hailed them. "There you are. What the hell, sis? Pappy's called here three times in the last half hour. Didn't you take your cell phone today?"

She quickly dug the phone out of her back pocket. "Oh. I thought I'd put it on vibrate, but it's shut off. Is something wrong?"

"How's Gordy?" Mick had been bent over with his weight distributed between the two nurses. He straightened marginally.

"So you know about my side trip? I don't know yet how Mr. Maclean is. He looked pretty rough when we landed. Maybe a little better when they loaded him into the ambulance." Marlee stepped into the room. "Why has Pappy been calling you? He reached me at Glenroe's. I told him I'd take the Angel Fleet job."

Mick mustered a brief smile. "According to Pappy you didn't agree without dumping some harsh words on me. Not that I don't deserve every one. I totally forgot to ask Angel Fleet dispatch to delete us from their roster. I feel doubly bad that you had to make a run without us ever discussing the process."

"Yeah, that would've been helpful," Marlee agreed, with a smile to soften her words.

"How it works is a coordinator phones the volunteer nearest to a victim. If the volunteer's plane is free, we go. At the scene we touch base with Angel Fleet to let them know we're underway. And volunteers sign in again after transfer is complete."

"Ah, so I didn't phone them nor did I contact Pappy from the airpark. It's my turn to apologize, Mick. I'm not a novice at rescue. I guess since most missions I flew in Iraq were under strict radio silence, I didn't even think to call in."

"Pappy wasn't the only one worried about your whereabouts. Wylie called Cloud Chasers twice. He apparently decided you'd fallen out of the sky."

"Wylie, as in Ranger Ames?" Marlee's chin shot up several inches. "Why, in heaven's name? I left his place ages ago."

Mick shuffled a few feet, but had the nurses take him back to bed. Once they'd settled him, he unclenched his jaw. "Pappy said it started out with Dean Ames phoning to speak with Jo Beth." He found a real smile for the little girl who still hovered in the doorway, staring at him with huge eyes.

She waltzed up to his bed, finally. "Mama said Dean and me could call each other." She slid her small hand into Mick's larger one. "Do you hurt a lot, Uncle Mick? Can the nurse give you a pill to make the pain go away? That's what they did for my daddy."

One of the nurses involved in exercising Mick flipped through his chart. "The doctor ordered Vicodin as needed. I see you've refused any pain meds up to now."

"I'd rather not use painkillers. The months I spent in military rehab, I saw far too many guys hooked on prescription drugs."

Marlee broke in. "On the other hand, Mick, won't you heal faster if you take the edge off your pain?"

His features relaxed into a grin. "I wouldn't be in pain if the nurses were nicer. If they didn't barge in here and force me to get up and walk. Four times today," he drawled, clearly angling for sympathy.

The petite brunette holding his chart rolled her eyes. "You're so full of bull." She glanced at Marlee and backpedaled, "Uh… we're just following doctor's orders. By the way, I'm Tammy, his evening nurse."

"Don't pay any attention to Mick. He's squeaked by on charm since he was born. You have my permission to whip him into shape before you send him home. 'Cause we sure won't be pampering him."

"I'll pamper him," Jo Beth declared loyally.

"How sweet." The nurse glanced at her patient. "Funny, I don't believe you mentioned having a daughter, Mick."

"I don't," he said. "This is my very best niece." He tugged at one of Jo Beth's curls. "Tell Nurse Tammy what a fantastic uncle I am, kid."

"You're my *only* uncle," she scoffed. "Dean thinks you're okay. He said you care a whole lot about kids and animals."

"Hear that?" Mick winked at the young woman, but she was talking to Marlee, who had asked how to find Gordon Maclean.

Jo Beth leaned on Mick's bed. "Dean said to say thanks for the books. And he asked if you got the dog you told him about on your last visit. I said no, but I wish you'd get one, Uncle Mick."

"You do? We'll have to see what your mom thinks of that idea. I'll have time to train a dog while I'm recovering at home, I guess."

"Train him to do what?"

Mick stopped rubbing his leg below his sore hip, and tweaked the girl's nose. "To help keep track of you and Pappy Jack, since I'm not going to be fleet of foot for a while. Hey, it sounds as if you and Dean got along famously."

"Uh-huh. He's nice. And he's smart," she said, clearly enamored of her newfound friend.

"I agree. So, does your mom feel the same about Dean's dad?"

Jo Beth wrinkled her nose and twisted her mouth from side to side before she shrugged both shoulders.

Mick turned to his sister, who'd just parted from Nurse Tammy, and was now using his bedside phone. "Marlee, did you have a problem with Wylie Ames?"

"Problem?" She smoothed a strand of hair behind her ear. "An earthworm is probably a better communicator. What? No, not you, Pappy. It's Marlee. Sorry I'm late phoning. Jo Beth and I are with Mick. No, I don't know his status. Hold on a sec." Marlee put a hand over the receiver as the nurse breezed back in.

"Mr. Maclean is still in surgery," Tammy said. "From what I gather, it's going well. His son is one floor above us in the B Surgery Suite waiting room."

"Thank you so much. We'll run up shortly to see how Josh is doing." She returned to her call and relayed an identical message. "Are you anxious for us to get home, Pappy? Are you on your own?"

She listened intently. "Why should I phone Ranger Ames?" After an irritated toss of her head, Marlee tried to temper her sharp response. "I'm sure everyone who lives in the backcountry is a friend of the Macleans, but I can't call them all. Okay, Pappy. *Someone* will notify you and the ranger as soon as any report comes out of surgery. Mr. Maclean's son is here. Maybe he'll call everyone after he updates his mom. Pappy, I've gotta go. According to Mick, I need to call Angel Fleet."

"Don't!" Marlee put down the phone and held up a hand as her brother opened his mouth. "I know the ranger's your friend. But he rubbed me the wrong way, okay? If you asked him, he'd say the feeling is mutual."

"I was just going to give you Angel Fleet's number."

"Oh. I thought you were going to…never mind then. What's the number?"

He gave it. "When you reach Arlene Thomas, their night co-ordinator, explain that I'm laid up. Have her take Cloud Chasers off the volunteer list until further notice."

"Uh…Mick. I've had a change of heart. I forgot how isolated people are up here. Leave us on the volunteer flight schedule."

"Are you sure? Gordy's accident is a one-time flight. Sometimes our requests are the beginning of a series of treatments or doctor visits for a patient. Angel Fleet operates differently than some mercy groups. They feel it's difficult enough when a very ill person has to be in and out of the hospital. If the patient gains confidence in a pilot flying them back and forth, it's one less stress."

Marlee knew what Mick was saying. "Surely no one expects weeks, months or years of continuous service. Rose drove Cole to treatments for four years."

"Six flights is the most I've made for any single patient. If care is ongoing, most people arrange to stay temporarily near the hospital."

"Then I can do this, Mick. What we went through with Cole was different. I'll have no close ties, no relationship with anyone who may need us." She broke away from Mick's unwavering gaze to check her watch. Then she stretched out a hand toward her daughter. "Jo Beth, tell Uncle Mick goodbye."

"Bye-bye. When I call Dean, is it all right to say you're still getting a dog?"

Mick's hearty laughter drowned out his twin's reprimand. "Yes," he said. "And *when* you call him, make sure you tell him how Mr. Maclean does in surgery. That'll save your mother from having to communicate with an earthworm." Mick pushed a button and lowered his bed. At once he groaned and grabbed for his bad hip, but he recovered enough to lean up on an elbow. "You two run along. Marlee, I'll call Angel Fleet for you tonight. I'll tell them to be kind to you."

She gave him a tight smile over her daughter's head. Mick's bringing up Wylie Ames again produced a well-formed image of his brooding, handsome face, which Marlee did her best to push out of her mind.

CHAPTER FOUR

MARLEE LOCATED JOSH sitting in the B Surgery Suite waiting room, as she'd expected. The boy had his head in his hands. He looked up when they came in, and stood when he recognized Marlee.

"My dad's been in surgery a really long time."

"Josh," Marlee said carefully, "it takes a while to prep a patient and get underway. I waited four hours for word the day of Mick's operation."

"Four hours?" The boy glanced at his watch. "I haven't been here for two yet."

"Did you let your mom know we landed?"

"It's a pay phone. She said to call collect."

Marlee dug in her purse. "Here's money for the phone. I know the wait's hard for you, but she's sitting at home with no idea of what's going on."

"Thanks. I'll pay you back."

"Don't worry about it. Would you like a soda? We passed vending machines in the hall. I'll go get us something while you make your call."

He accepted her offer, and Marlee and Jo Beth left the room.

By the time they returned, he was off the phone and looked markedly better. Marlee passed him the cold can and a ham sandwich.

"My Uncle Rod and Aunt Sammy are coming to help finish baling our hay."

"That's good. Will it take them long to get to the ranch?"

"They live in Spokane. It's a hundred and fifty miles. Mom asked them to swing by here to see Dad and bring me home. Uncle Rod's my dad's brother."

"I wasn't sure if I needed to fly you back to the ranch. Forgive me if I'm out of line, but it looks like you came straight from work. Do you have money for food?"

He glanced at his dirt-and-blood-smeared shirt and jeans. "Mark Hart, our hired hand and me…we were repairing a fence knocked down by Chili Dog. That's our bull. Dad went to track him. When we heard him holler, me 'n Mark dropped everything and ran to help, but the bull threw Dad against a fence post. Hooked 'im three or four times before we drove Chili Dog off." Hunching, the boy rolled the cold can across his brow. "Don't know what got into that ol' bull."

While Marlee tried to imagine the scene, Jo Beth went over and hugged Josh. "It's okay if you wanna cry. Sometimes I did when my daddy had to stay at the hospital. And if your tummy aches, crying helps."

The teen looked surprised, then looked guiltily at Marlee. "Did your husband get in a bad accident, too?"

Marlee shook her head, and took a long pull from her soda. "He had cancer. Of the lymph glands. Jo Beth and I are no strangers to hospital waiting rooms."

Like everyone she told, Josh didn't seem to know what to say. They were saved an awkward moment when the desk clerk told Marlee she had a call. She walked over, expecting it to be Mick. "Hi, there."

"How's Gordy Maclean?" The voice was familiar, but she didn't immediately recognize it.

"Mr. Maclean is still in surgery. Who's this?"

"Wylie. Ranger Ames. Mick transferred me. He said you're upstairs with Josh. Oh, and he asked me to relay a message. Pappy's about to go to bed, but he's leaving a light on in the hangar."

"Oh, well…thanks. Why don't I let you speak with Josh?"

His answer was a low, rolling laugh. "Sure, but I was trying my level best to communicate better than a worm."

Marlee choked on her soda, feeling the heat sting her face. She was going downstairs and she was going to murder Mick. "I…I…I…" She gave up trying to come up with something witty, and beckoned Josh over. "It's Ranger Ames," she muttered. "Asking about your dad."

Josh had barely said hello when a doctor in blue scrubs came into the room and headed straight for Marlee. "Mrs. Maclean, I'm Doctor Black. I was the surgeon on call when they brought your husband in."

Josh dropped the phone, forcing Marlee to scoop it up. "I'm the Angel Fleet pilot," she informed the physician. "This is Josh Maclean, Gordon's son." Into the phone, she hissed, "We should hang up. Mr. Maclean's doctor is here to talk to Josh."

"Wait. Take my number. Gordy and I are friends. I'd like to know his condition. If he's likely to be laid up for months, I'll organize help for his family."

Marlee didn't know Ames at all. She certainly had no reason to have formed a judgment against him. But she'd pegged him as a lone wolf. In a few minutes he'd blown that image to hell. "I don't have anything to write on," she murmured. "Can you call back on my cell in say, fifteen minutes?"

He hung up without answering or even muttering a goodbye. Definitely not verbose, she thought, turning to the surgeon, who was saying Gordon Maclean was in recovery. And after two pints of blood, his vitals had stabilized.

WYLIE WISHED he'd had longer to talk with Marlee Stein. He'd laughed when Mick told him what his sister had said about his lack of communication skills. Wylie knew he had the reputation of being a loner. It suited him to foster that with other rangers, especially after Shirl took off and left him to raise Dean. Friends were always trying to set him up. The rangers' wives thought his son needed a mother. So, to get everyone off his back, he'd dated a couple of the women. But maybe he should heed what they said about how he needed to learn to trust again.

Oddly, after one meeting, Mick Callen's feisty sister piqued his interest. She both disturbed him and revitalized a part of himself he'd kept locked up since Shirl. He'd met his ex after a long, lonesome winter. It was spring, and she'd been a pretty, flirty waitress in town. Wylie had found excuses to visit her. But she'd played him for a sucker.

So maybe Marlee Stein made an impression only because she didn't seem to give a damn if she interested him or not.

"Dad, didn't Marlee get Mr. Maclean to the hospital in time?" There was concern in the boy's voice.

Rousing, Wylie placed a hand on his son's shoulder. "She got there. I spoke to Josh. The doctor had just arrived to talk about Mr. Maclean's condition. I'll phone Jo Beth's mom back later for a better report. Meanwhile, you go throw a change of clothes in a backpack. Josh said they have a rampaging bull loose at their ranch. We should leave at first light so I can help the Macleans' hired hand corral it."

"But I want to talk to Jo Beth. When you call her mom, can I tell Jo Beth I found my whole set of medieval knights?"

"We'll see. It'll all depend on how late it gets to be."

IN THE WAITING ROOM, the surgeon laid out his plan for Gordon Maclean. "I'm sending him to ICU tonight. If he's not too groggy, I'll have the nurse give you a couple of minutes with him, Josh. Otherwise, you may as well go home. I make rounds at seven in the morning. If he looks good, he can go to the ward."

Josh seemed panicky. Jo Beth latched on to one of his limp hands and Marlee the other. "The Maclean ranch is too far away for Josh to drive back and forth. He has relatives coming from Spokane. My daughter and I will stay with him until they arrive."

"That's good of you." The doctor stripped off a mask that hung loose around his neck, rolled it and stuck it in a pocket sagging under the weight of a stethoscope. "You Angel Fleet people always go the extra mile. I don't recall them having a female pilot before, though. Not that it matters. I grew up north of here, and I've seen some of the so-called landing strips." He made a face.

"Yeah," Josh said. "My mom worried that a plane couldn't land at our ranch. Marlee did. But she scared the shit out of me taking off. Uh, sorry." He turned red when Jo Beth let go of his hand and tsked.

"Mama, Josh said a bad word!"

"It's okay, Josh. I'll admit I had a few tense moments clearing those trees."

The doctor was shaking his head. "Everyone believes *my* job takes nerves of steel. But I wouldn't trade places with you."

An older nurse approached. "Doctor, your patent's alert. Should we move him now?"

Dr. Black turned to Josh. "Ready to see your dad? Come with me."

The two started down the hall. "Marlee," Josh called back. "I see my aunt and uncle coming. Will you tell them what's going on and have them call Mom? And if Wylie phones again, will you bring him up to speed?"

Marlee didn't want to be a go-between for Wylie Ames, darn it. But Josh had already slipped through the door. She turned her attention to the approaching couple and met them with an extended a hand. "Hi. Marlee Callen. Josh has been allowed a minute with his dad. Mr. Maclean's gone from recovery to ICU."

A tall, lean rancher-type stripped off a straw cowboy hat. "We're Rod and Samantha Maclean. ICU? That's not sounding good for Gordy."

"A precaution, according to his surgeon. Your brother lost a fair amount of blood before we got him here. They've given him transfusions and stitched him up."

"Ah, you'd be the volunteer pilot who flew Gordy out?" said Samantha Maclean. "My sister-in-law says you're awesome. She'd read articles about Angel Fleet, and knew a family whose child the Angels flew to Seattle for a liver transplant. But she never dreamed they'd ever need Angel Fleet themselves. I guess no one ever does, huh?"

"I'm sure that's true. I didn't expect it, either. I was on a routine supply flight to a guest lodge when the call came in. My daughter was with me." Marlee indicated Jo Beth, who'd retreated to a waiting room chair.

"She looks ready to drop," Samantha Maclean whispered.

"We still have to drive back to the airpark, and then fly home to Whitepine. Josh said he'll meet you here and asked if you could call his mom. I wanted to keep him company until Mr. Maclean came out of surgery, but I think we'll be on our way now. If you're going to help out around their ranch, I hope you steer clear of that bull."

"Rod spoke with Gordy's hired man when we hit town," Samantha said. "A park ranger friend of theirs has arranged a kind of bull posse to chase down Chili Dog tomorrow."

Wylie. Marlee pictured him astride a horse. She shook off the image, but couldn't help wondering if catching crazed bulls was part of a ranger's duties. She imagined he'd be capable of that or any outdoor activity. *A few indoor activities, too.*

"Jo Beth, honey, we're going home." Marlee lifted her daughter. Before she left, Marlee rang Mick's room to say good-night.

He sounded tired, or else he'd taken pain medication. She didn't keep him on the phone, but promised she'd be in touch the next day.

Jo Beth fell asleep before Marlee exited the hospital parking lot.

Thirty minutes later, they were at the airfield. When her phone played its tune and she answered, she wasn't really surprised to hear Wylie's voice. Marlee figured he must've gotten an update from Mrs. Maclean.

"Time got away from me," Wylie said. "I've been organizing a few friends to help Gordy's family. How is he?"

"Out of surgery. Out of recovery and into ICU for the night. I heard you were rounding up a bull posse."

As Marlee unbuckled Jo Beth and locked the Caddy, she listened to his deep, thoroughly masculine laugh and couldn't resist smiling.

"For being in the backwoods, news does travel fast. Bull posse, huh? Did Josh come up with that, or did his little sister, Carrie?"

This didn't sound like the taciturn man Marlee had met. "Neither," she said. "Josh's aunt. I've left the hospital. In fact, I'm about to board my plane to fly home." Unable to help herself, Marlee yawned. "Sorry. It's not that late. Barely ten."

"Late enough when you've had a long day. Mick said this was your first flight in a while. I could tell he felt bad that you had to deal with an accident on your first day."

"If anyone could predict accidents they'd avoid them."

"Right." He was silent for a moment. "I figured you'd spend the night in Kalispell."

"Mick's planes are equipped for night flying."

"The plane, yes, but it's the pilot who takes off and lands."

"About that…not to brag, but I can probably count on one hand the number of times my landings haven't been glass-smooth."

There was a smile in Wylie's response. "No need to be defensive. We all make mistakes."

"I'm not defensive." She slapped the Caddy key down on the counter so hard the young clerk, deep in his novel, nearly fell off his stool.

Wylie stifled his muffled laughter when Marlee growled, "I'm hanging up. Do me a favor—wear a red shirt tomorrow when you chase that bull. On second thought, don't. With my luck, Cloud Chasers would get another call from Angel Fleet." She hung up and shut off the ringer, then shoved the phone in her back pocket while she strapped Jo Beth in the plane.

"Who were you yelling at, Mama?"

"I wasn't yelling."

"Grandmother Rose would call it yelling."

Marlee clipped her own harness and put on her earphones. And felt an insistent throb against her butt. Thinking Mick or Pappy might be trying to reach her, she dug out the cell. "'Lo."

"Call me after you land at home."

"You know, Ranger, it's been years since anyone's asked me to check in."

"Huh. That attitude could be why your husband took a powder. He did, I presume."

"My husband died, you insensitive jerk." She jammed her phone into her pocket, unaware of how every nerve in her body trembled until it took her three tries to contact the tower for permission to take off. All the while, she felt every quiver of her cell phone's insistent bleat, which she flatly ignored.

Her wings wobbled on takeoff. *Damn the man to hell and back.* Whoever was handling the tower would think she was a novice flyer, for heaven's sake.

The phone stopped pulsing. Marlee rolled her tight shoulders, and trimmed the wings. She probably shouldn't have snapped his head off.

Casting a glance in Jo Beth's direction, Marlee wondered what her daughter would say about that last outburst. The girl's soot-dark lashes had drifted down. Moonlight glittering through the side window splashed shadows across her baby's cheek.

The phone danced yet again. Marlee touched the metal case through the material of her jacket, then just as quickly withdrew her fingers, too tempted to take the call.

She massaged a pain lodged beneath her breastbone. *Heartburn.* Marlee was no stranger to it. In five years she'd been treated twice for peptic ulcers. The flight surgeon said she needed yoga or some other relaxation technique to combat what he diagnosed as increasing anxiety, resulting from Cole's worsening condition.

The phone finally fell silent. She expected the vibrations to start again. They didn't. *Well, he gave up easily.* She ought to ask herself why she cared that Wylie Ames thought her enough of a bitch for a man to divorce her.

Up here, alone with nothing but the night sky, a person tended to see too clearly. It hit Marlee like a wrecking ball. She'd lied to Mick earlier when she insisted his friend rubbed her the wrong way. She'd lied to herself. The real truth—Wylie rubbed her the *right* way. So right, she felt disloyal to Cole. "There you have it, Mr. Moon," she whispered. Of all the men she'd met in the year since Cole's death, it made no sense that the first one to waken her dormant emotions had to be the most unsuitable.

The reflectors of Mick's runway twinkled below. Bringing a bird safely home always sparked a joy that would be impossible to describe to anyone who wasn't a pilot. Home could be anywhere—the deck of a carrier, a military runway in a foreign land, or this slab of asphalt with its moth-eaten wind sock blowing in the wind. The sense of a mission accomplished was always the same the instant the plane's wheels down.

The fact that Jo Beth slept on as Marlee taxied the Arrow into the empty hangar Pappy had left lit made her homecoming sweeter.

Her first day on a new job was now officially behind her. Marlee tucked the clipboard with the daily log under her arm. When the propeller stopped spinning, she opened her door and dropped to the ground. Before she rounded the tail to wake Jo Beth, the cell phone in her pocket began to convulse against Marlee's waist. She smiled for no reason as she eased it out of her pocket. "Yes, I'm home," she said softly instead of berating her caller.

"About damned time," the gravelly voice said. "Now maybe Dean'll quit fretting and go to sleep."

"Dean's still up? Jo Beth dozed off ages ago."

She heard the man's tight breath. "Actually, Dean's fast asleep, too. Listen, about my earlier comment. I shouldn't have assumed…" His words trailed off.

Marlee knew he wanted her to relieve his guilty conscience. She didn't.

He cleared his throat. "I shouldn't have jumped to conclusions. I didn't want to leave what I said hanging between us, Marlee. I'm sorry, now I've apologized. There's no reason to mention it again. Uh…so long."

Like that, he ended the call. Marlee stared at the phone in exasperation. On a scale of one to ten, as apologies went, she'd rate his a two. Maybe a three. Hell, she'd be generous and give him five, she thought, juggling her clipboard while trying to remove Jo Beth's deadweight from the seat.

She whacked an elbow on the door casing as she stumbled into the dark house. That time the sound leaving her lips roused her daughter.

"Grandmother Rose? Why is it so dark? Is Daddy sick again?" The sob in the child's half-asleep voice ripped at Marlee's heart.

"Mama has you, hon. Everything's fine. We've been flying.

Remember? Now we're at Uncle Mick's." Marlee rubbed her cheek over Jo Beth's hair. "Pappy Jack didn't leave a light on inside. Shh, we don't want to wake him."

She made it down the hall and into her old room. After growing up in this house, she could navigate it blindfolded. Marlee located the twin bed with its mountain of stuffed animals.

"I don't wanna be at Uncle Mick's," Jo Beth sobbed. "I wanna go home. I wa...ant Grandmother Rose!" The child flailed her arms and legs.

Few things hurt Marlee as much as that did. With shaking hands she found the lamp with its night-light base. She hoped the soft, rosy glow would comfort Jo Beth and help her fall back asleep. According to the pediatric psychologist Marlee had consulted, time and distance were all that would get rid of these bouts she said were caused by worry and Marlee's absence.

Bouts her best friend in San Diego, Dana, insisted were old-fashioned temper tantrums. Dana had grown up with Cole. They were both navy brats. Dana's husband was a navy doctor, they had two model kids, and thought that made them experts in child-rearing. In fact, Dana had always been a full-time mom. Her husband had only ever been out of town on a few mandatory training exercises. Other than that, he worked regular hours at the Naval Hospital.

Their comments stung, and yet Marlee owed them. They were the first to point out that Rose was replacing Marlee with Jo Beth. And it'd been Dana who convinced Marlee that she should accept Mick's plea to return to Big Sky Country.

Filled with guilt or not, Marlee hardened her heart against Jo Beth's tears. She sat on a corner of the bed and calmly removed the girl's shoes and socks, then shook out a clean pair of Jo Beth's favorite pj's. It was a good thing the house was well insulated. Especially when her efforts resulted in Jo Beth screaming and ultimately sweeping her stuffed toys off the bed.

Although Marlee's instinct was to cradle her child, experience had taught her it only prolonged the bouts. The shrink said kids who'd lost a parent after a prolonged illness often grieved this way. Once she said that, Marlee found it easier to cope with the tantrums and with her own guilt for being an absentee parent. "Jo Beth, do you remember at lunch today Dean Ames said a person had to be very quiet and patient to heal wild animals like Boxer Bear? I'm afraid if Dean saw how you've treated your stuffed toys, he might have second thoughts about letting us watch them release Boxer."

Contrary to Rose's insistence that Jo Beth had no will of her own during one of these episodes, the girl stopped kicking at once. She rubbed her eyes with the tail of her pajama top, eyed her mom warily, then slid off the bed and hastily gathered the dogs, cats and teddy bears that littered the floor between the twin beds. Her arms full, her chin quivering, she gazed out of glistening eyes so like her father's that Marlee hurt. "I didn't mean to throw my toys."

"I know, sweetie." Though hesitant, Marlee lovingly straightened tear-dampened curls tangled around her daughter's pixie face.

"I miss Daddy."

"That's okay, baby. I miss him, too."

"But you don't miss Grandmother Rose," Jo Beth accused as she pulled herself free and dived back onto her bed. "You don't like her." The thin chest heaved from the aftermath of the tantrum.

Not for the first time since she'd arrived home, Marlee wondered if she'd been right to leave San Diego. There'd been a time when she did enjoy her mother-in-law's company.

At this moment, she chose to go with another piece of advice given by the child psychologist. "Jo Beth, would you like to telephone Grandmother Rose tomorrow?"

The little girl nodded, her hazel eyes clearing. Cole's eyes, but his mother's, too. Even if Marlee was so inclined, she couldn't deny Jo Beth's relationship to Rose Stein.

"If I call her, can I still call Dean? Mama, please don't tell him I was mean to my stuffed animals." She hugged each of her many pets and grouped them on her pillow. "I'd never throw a *real* dog."

The child's actions showed more remorse for the recent behavior than Marlee had seen thus far. "I won't tell Dean…this time, Jo Beth." Marlee thought it wouldn't hurt to leave the implication hanging.

"Okay." She lay back and her eyelashes fluttered down. "Let's go to sleep now, Mama."

If the incident hadn't left Marlee feeling drained as these fits always did, she might've smiled on her way to the shower.

Jo Beth was asleep when Marlee came out.

She sat on her bed to towel her hair dry, and spent a moment marveling at how perfectly angelic this child of such extreme emotions now appeared.

Dropping the towel, she picked up a comb to smooth out the inevitable tangles in her own hair. Marlee stopped a moment, thinking she heard something fall in another part of the house. She threw on her robe, tied it, and cracked open the door to listen. *Definitely noises*. She hesitated. This home was truly a sprawling rambler. A huge living room separated what had been Marlee's and Mick's bedrooms from two main suites. One had been used by their parents, and the other by Pappy Jack, whose wife had died shortly after she and Mick were born.

She hurried down the hall thinking Jo Beth's yelling might have awakened her grandfather. Indeed, she found him fully dressed, rummaging in a kitchen cupboard. The only light in the room came from the moon shining through the window above the sink.

"Pappy? I'm sorry if Jo Beth disturbed you. We should probably move out to the cottage. I can never predict what might set her off."

The man jerked his head around the cupboard door. "Who the hell are you?" He cringed. "What do you want? How did you get in my house?"

Marlee's fingers tightened on her comb. "Pappy, it's me. Marlee. Your granddaughter."

They stared at each other for several moments. Enough light filtered through the window that Marlee could see his confusion. This must be what Mick had meant when he claimed Pappy Jack suffered from dementia. He'd been so normal this past week, Marlee actually thought Mick had exaggerated.

"Granddaughter? Mick's married?" The gnarled hand let go of the cupboard. "When did that boy go and get hitched?"

"Mick's not married, Pappy. He's in the hospital having surgery on his hip," she reminded him quietly, hoping he'd snap out of whatever state he was in.

"Right. A guy from the military phoned today. He said Mick got shot down." Tears began trickling down the wrinkled cheeks. Ignoring them, he segued straight to his own time in the service.

"Yep, we lost some good men on that last mission. I counted five fighters going down in flames. Don't know why I was lucky. All I took was a little flak from those damned antiaircraft guns on the ground." He blinked owl eyed, and peered at Marlee. "Hey, are you one of them USO gals? Got some coffee? My last flight was plenty bumpy."

He jumped from one era into another so quickly Marlee had difficulty keeping up. She wished to heaven she'd asked Mick about how to deal with situations of this nature. But she hadn't imagined there being anything like this.

Reaching around the corner, she turned on the living room lamp. "I'll make a pot of coffee. Why don't you go see if there's anything interesting on TV?"

"Douse that light. We're under blackout orders, don't you know?" He moved past Marlee and plunged them into darkness again.

"Sorry." She didn't know what else to say. Nor did she know if she'd be able to find the coffee and measure out the correct amount with only the intermittent moonlight to guide her.

Sliding her comb into her pocket, Marlee resigned herself to the fact that half of her hair would resemble a rat's nest by morning.

"Have a seat at the table. Tell me about your mission."

He sat heavily in the chair she'd pulled out, planted his elbows on the tabletop and buried his face in his hands. "Our P-51 Mustangs got the shit pounded out of 'em. We might've got away if we'd been on our own, but our job was to protect Mama Bird and her bomb payload."

"Mama Bird?" Marlee found the coffee canister and counted the number of scoops she dished into the filter.

"The B-17. What a snail. But, thanks to us, she unloaded six ton of bombs on the enemy," he said, deep satisfaction tingeing his response. As quickly, his mood changed. "Yep, but not without a price. Our XO says we're winning this war. Sometimes I wonder. Four of those five guys who went down have wives and kids. Stinks, ya know?"

"It does." Marlee leaned on the counter, and sniffed as the rich smell of coffee began to permeate the air. The silence lengthened. She removed two mugs from a rack sitting next to the sink and carried them to the table. She decided she might as well indulge in a cup, too, especially since Pappy seemed stuck in the past. No matter how beat she was, Marlee wouldn't go to bed and leave him like this. *How often did these bouts occur?* Mentally she made a list of questions to ask Mick first thing tomorrow. How had he managed so long without any more assistance than the occasional watchful eye of Stella Gibson?

The coffee stopped gurgling. Marlee carried the pot to the table. She waited until the moon shone full again before filling the mugs. As she poured, Pappy glanced up in surprise. "Marlee, when did you get home, girl?" He squinted through the curling steam. "Long enough ago to get into pj's I see." He picked up the mug and blew across the hot liquid. "Is that hairdo some new-fangled city style? If so, I don't blame you one bit for mucking about the kitchen in the dark."

For a moment Marlee's temples throbbed. It was as if someone had flipped a switch.

"Mick said you planned to go up to surgery and see how Gordy Maclean fared." Pappy set down his cup and unfolded his body from the chair. "Dang, girl. Maybe you got night-vision eyesight. I don't." He marched across the room and snapped on the switch for the light that hung above the breakfast nook.

Blinking, she muttered into her cup. "Mr. Maclean's son was able to see him before I left, Pappy. Gordon lost considerable blood, but the doctor said the surgery went well. Gordon's brother, Rod, came from Spokane."

"Good. Good." Pappy opened the fridge. "Stella made apple cobbler today. I wanted to dig into it earlier. She slapped my hands. What's a woman thinking when she cooks something that smells so good but won't let you eat it? Want some?"

"No, but you go ahead."

He loaded a small bowl and topped it with enough whipped cream to make Marlee wonder about the condition of his arteries.

"Where's the little squirt? I'll bet she'd like some of this."

"Asleep, Pappy. She had a big day. Her first small plane ride. Then she chased through the woods with Dean Ames. You probably know he doctors wild animals. Jo Beth was very taken with his bear cub."

"The Ames boy and his pop phoned here a couple times tonight. You hadn't oughta get too chummy with that man, Marlee." Pappy filled his mouth with cobbler. Whipped cream stuck to his upper lip. Blue eyes no longer cloudy bore into Marlee's.

She sipped the strong coffee and felt her stomach object.

Whether to the brew or Pappy's vague alert she wasn't sure. "Mary Glenroe says there's nothing to the rumors about Ranger Ames."

"So, Mary knows what happened to Wylie's wife?"

"No." Marlee shifted on the hard bench seat.

"That's what I'm trying to tell you, girl. No one does 'cept maybe Ames."

Marlee found herself leaning forward. "Why doesn't anyone ask him? There's probably a simple explanation." The ranger's assumption that her husband had dumped her popped into Marlee's head. "They probably got a divorce. Maybe she filed. I doubt that would sit well with a macho guy like Ames."

"Joe Duff, he retired as county sheriff near when Mrs. Ames vanished. Joe said straight out there's no record in the county of them splitting the sheets."

"Oh. A divorce would be on file."

"Yep." Pappy Jack emptied his bowl, rose and set it in the sink, where he filled it with water. He brought the coffeepot back to the table and topped up their mugs. "As long as you don't marry the guy."

She found a grin. "No, Pappy, I'm not planning to marry again. I said Dean and Jo Beth could phone each other occasionally, though. She doesn't have many kid friends. I'm not going to keep her from talking to Wylie's son, Pappy."

"I suppose phone calls won't hurt. It's not as if you'll be flying up there again. For all Mick claims they're friends, Wylie orders supplies three, maybe four times a year. Mick'll be on his feet before another order has to go to Ames." Pappy strode to the sink and dumped the mug he'd just refilled. "One thing the navy didn't teach you, girl, is how to make a decent cup of coffee. If I drink more of this sludge tonight I'll never sleep. If your cooking's the same, woe is us." He stifled a yawn with a hand and promptly announced he was going to bed.

Left alone at the table, Marlee now had little desire to sleep. She nursed a mug of too-strong coffee while mulling over what had been said. She was aware, if Pappy wasn't, that she'd be making another trip or possibly more to Wylie's in the near future.

Just how concerned should she be for her safety and Jo Beth's? Who was right about Wylie? Mary Glenroe, who considered him a prince, or Pappy, who suspected he might be a murderer?

Was her own radar so far off the mark?

CHAPTER FIVE

MARLEE HAD HER DAY planned out when, not long after she'd checked on Gordon Maclean, an emergency call came in from the smoke jumpers' camp scrambling her schedule. A Captain Leonard Martin introduced himself, then said, "Have I reached Cloud Chasers? Is Mick around?"

"Yes. But Mick's laid up. I'm his sister. What can I do for you, Captain?"

"Sorry Mick's under the weather. Why I called him…well, I hoped we'd seen the last of fire season when I ripped September off our calendar. But a campfire got away from some hikers deep inside Flathead Forest. I sent a team in there an hour ago with a day's ration of bottled water. I'm expecting supplies from our regular source in Missoula late this week. But I can't wait. Generally I count on Mick to fly us in emergency supplies. Can you refer me to another air freight service?"

"I'm taking Mick's place until he's back on his feet. Where's the freight you need picked up, Captain Martin?"

"You'll bring my order? Fantastic! I can have a crew in Kalispell truck our delivery to the airpark by seven. I need water especially, ASAP."

Marlee, suffering from insomnia, had been sorting invoices since 3:00 a.m. She frowned at the stack of filing she'd intended to tackle after she cooked breakfast for Pappy and Jo Beth. Not two minutes before Martin phoned, Pappy had buzzed through on the intercom to say he and Jo Beth were up. Her grandfather had sounded groggy and grumpy. Months ago, when she'd insisted to Mick that a man in Pappy Jack's condition needed nutritious meals at regular intervals, Mick had said flatly it was impossible. Marlee now understood why.

"You estimate the weight of your order at twenty-two hundred pounds?" Marlee listened to her caller while she worried about her family obligations. She decided the best aircraft for this job was the Huey. She hadn't test-flown it. On the heels of that thought, she wondered how Jo Beth would handle the noise and a ride bound to be much bumpier than the Arrow would be. Would Pappy agree to go? Or would she have to phone Stella Gibson to see if she could spare a few hours today to ride herd on him?

Her mind jumped from one point to the next. At least the dawn was lovely. Birds twittered in the trees. A late-fall sun was beginning to streak the sky with lavender and orange. She'd gotten used to urban noise, so this was a treat.

"Roger that, Captain. You'll have your supplies by nine, or shortly thereafter."

Of course she'd never turn away a customer. Cloud Chasers needed every single one. Computer records showed Mick had occasionally hired young pilots straight out of training school to give him a break and help them out until they found permanent jobs. She also saw the strain the part-time labor put on their budget. That, no doubt, was why Mick tried so hard to do it all himself.

But why hadn't he told her he needed an infusion of capital? Surely he knew she had Cole's insurance to tap if necessary. She'd placed the money in a college fund for Jo Beth, but she could draw off the interest to hire some part-time help.

Maybe Mick could do everything. Marlee wasn't so sure she could.

Turning away from the invoices, she hurried to the house. There she found Jo Beth, face buried in the couch, sobbing. An unshaven, disheveled Pappy sat at the breakfast nook drinking coffee. Marlee had no more than walked in through the side door when the crying child flew at her and grabbed her legs.

"That man yelled at me, Mama."

Marlee looked aghast at her grandfather as she placed a protective arm around Jo Beth.

"I didn't yell." Pappy's scowl deepened.

"He did so. He said to hush up my crying. Bu...ut, Mama, you weren't in bed or in the living room or anywhere. I...th...ought you were go...gone," Jo Beth whimpered through great gulps of air.

Pappy huddled over his steaming mug. He occupied the same chair he'd claimed last night. But this morning he looked completely unkempt. "I don't know what's wrong with the girl, Eve. I told her you'd gone to the office."

Uh-oh! Pappy had called her by her mother's name. Marlee hitched Jo Beth up on her hip and swayed from side to side. "It's okay, tiddledywink. Remember this—I'll never leave the property without first telling you. Someone will know where I am."

"But the prop'ty is too big," the girl insisted, wiping her eyes on her mom's shirt.

"I know, and we haven't had a chance for you to explore it all. Pappy, have you taken your blood pressure medicine this morning?" Marlee crossed to the cupboard where Mick kept Pappy's pills. Most of the bottles on the bottom shelf contained vitamin supplements. She spotted his prescription bottle tipped on its side.

"I take 'em with food. Where's breakfast?"

"I'm afraid we're going to have to take breakfast potluck today. I just got a call to pick up a rush order for the smoke jumpers' camp. ASAP." She parked Jo Beth across from Pappy and shook out a tablet from each bottle. "Here. Swallow these with your coffee. Mick said he stocks fruit and breakfast bars for days like this. I thought we'd all make the run. It's a beautiful morning. I'll be flying the Huey."

"You two go on. I'm gonna tinker in the shop. Shane said yesterday the engine on that biplane runs rough. He's flying this weekend in the air show down in Polson, you know, Eve. It's probably just a piston misfiring."

Marlee's heart sank. "Pappy," she said gently. "You sold that old biplane years ago. Shane is dead and so is Eve. Mick owns the business now. I'm Marlee. I've come home to help Mick, remember?"

Jo Beth clutched the glass of milk her mother had poured for her. Her gaze skipped from one adult to the other over its rim.

One by one the old man picked up the pills Marlee had set out. When they were all in his mouth, he swallowed them with a swig of coffee. "A man shouldn't outlive his s-s...on." He rubbed a shaking hand over a rough-stubbled chin.

Marlee noticed tears collecting in the red-rimmed eyes. She clamped down hard on her lip and turned away. Pappy Jack's grief-filled words bore a marked similarity to what Mary Glenroe had said yesterday—that a woman shouldn't outlive her husband and be left alone to raise their kids. But somebody had to raise them. And somebody had to care for the aging, as well. It struck her that she and Pappy had much in common.

Marlee stopped fussing with the food for their unplanned trip. Summoning a smile, she went to her grandfather, looped her arms around his shoulders and rubbed her soft cheek against his bristly one. "Where would Mick and I be if you'd gone before our folks, Pappy? Please come fly with me today. It'll be like old times."

He reached awkwardly back and patted her arm. "I flew with my dad."

"I know. And Mick and I flew with you. Now it's Jo Beth's turn."

The old man's eyes tracked his granddaughter's movements as she straightened and scooped items off the counter. "Mick locks the plane doors and hides the keys. The boy thinks I don't know it's because he believes I've lost the stamina to fly."

What to say? "To pilot, maybe, Pappy. We'll all lose that one day. You'll always have the stamina to fly as a passenger. The physical sensation's the same."

"In the Huey? I'm not so old I don't know when you're pulling my leg, girl." His chuckle resonated pleasantly.

Marlee gave a relieved sigh. Once again his odd regression to bygone years seemed to have passed. Terrible as the thought was, maybe she and Mick would have to discuss finding some type of a residential care facility for Pappy. The very prospect of shuttling aside a man who had been her and Mick's rock when they most needed one weighed too heavily on Marlee's heart; she couldn't deal with it today. The clock was ticking down. Captain Martin counted on her to get him his supplies in a timely manner.

It was a miracle that she got everyone strapped into the helicopter for takeoff. As she'd suspected, Jo Beth hated the openness of the chopper and the noise not even earphones totally blocked. out, Marlee didn't blame her. Flying this behemoth after yesterday's smooth ride in the Arrow was like comparing a new Mercedes coupe to a battered postwar Jeep.

At the airpark, she shut down the rotors. Pappy removed his earphones and shouted, "While those guys load your freight, let's go visit Mick."

"Okay, if we don't stay long. I promised Captain Martin speedy service." Marlee jumped down and held her arms up for Jo Beth. Her knees felt rubbery. That was another difference in piloting a helicopter over a light plane.

Pappy sank into the passenger seat of the Caddy and all but petted the dashboard lovingly. "Ain't she a beaut? I forgot Mick said he needed to store her at the airpark so he could make pickups in town. Getting old is hell," the man grumbled in an undertone. Marlee could tell from the comment that Pappy was very aware of the real reason Mick had removed the car from the house. In lucid times the old man held no illusions about his failing health.

In the surgery ward they met Mick in the hall he slowly traversed with the aid of a walker. The determination on his face when he slid his bad leg in front of the good one pierced Marlee's heart. Still, she cracked a joke. That was what Cole used to prefer people do. "Hey, you should demand a motorized skateboard from one of your cute nurses instead of that turtle."

It clearly cost Mick when he tried to hustle to meet them. "I wondered where you all got off to this morning. Don Morrison got our answering machine at Cloud Chasers, so he called Stella. He has another one of Wylie's generator parts. Said it's not his whole order, but it's enough to allow Wylie to run his motor at half capacity if need be. Are you on your way over there?"

"We came for supplies for Captain Martin out at the smoke jumpers' camp. I wonder what Wylie's part weighs? Maybe we could drop his stuff off on our return trip."

"Uh, it's a turbine. Medium-sized, I think."

"I'm almost at capacity with Martin's emergency supply of bottled water. Do you think Wylie needs the turbine before his other order comes in?"

"He will if a storm blows up and knocks out his regular power. No way to second-guess storms this time of year," Mick mused aloud. Resting his whole weight on the walker's handles, he swept the trio with a bright gaze. "Well, by the look of it I'd have to say you're gettin' along fine without me."

Marlee sent him a veiled frown, but he'd turned away. She wanted to say *if you only knew*. Instead, she tapped her watch. "We can't stay, Mick. Martin has a fire burning in the Flathead range."

"Ouch. I hope they get it under control fast. According to this morning's weather news, we've got some wind headed our way from British Columbia."

"Wind? How strong? I called for a weather update before we left home. They didn't say a word about wind. I wouldn't want to get caught in downdrafts in the Huey."

"Who knows really? This time of year, there's no predicting if we'll have sun, rain or early snow. That's why I figure Wylie's gonna want that turbine as quick as you can get it to him."

"Tomorrow," she said, seeing herself putting off the filing for yet another day.

"Any word on when the doctor's going to let you come home?" Pappy asked.

"Yeah, Uncle Mick," Jo Beth broke in. "You and me are gonna get a dog so you can train him while your hip's getting fixed, don't forget."

"A dog?" Pappy hooked his thumbs over his belt. "We talked about that yesterday, didn't we, Mick?"

"Months ago. Then I was too busy to think about training a dog. Now I'll have some free time." He pulled at his pajama trouser leg. "A lot of free time."

"Not so fast," Marlee warned. "If I'm flying freight and you're well enough to chase after a dog, mister…there's invoices and bills of lading that need filing. That office is a disgrace. It could use TLC."

Mick groaned. "The doc wants me walking, sis, not sitting on my butt."

"He said a bad word, Mama." Jo Beth clapped a hand over her mouth.

"Jo Beth, *butt* is part of a person's body. It's not a bad word. Besides, Grandmother Rose isn't here to be offended." Marlee was determined to weed out some of Rose's stodgy rules.

"You said I could call her today. And Dean. When, Mama? When?"

Mick couldn't mask his surprise. "You're letting her phone your mom-in-law?"

"Yes. There were some…developments…last night. You and I need to find time to catch up. Right now, though, I have water and protein snacks to deliver."

"Carry on, by all means." Mick took a hand off the walker and gestured toward the elevator. "I'm glad you have Pappy and Jo Beth along for company today. Some of those smoke jumpers think they're God's gift to women, if you know what I mean."

Marlee rolled her eyes at her brother. "That'll be the day when I can't cool the heels of a few sex-deprived males."

"Right. All the same, call me when you get home."

Doing just that so they could talk about Pappy was high on Marlee's list. They said goodbye and drove back to the airpark. By then the Huey was loaded and ready.

The wind did kick up which made flying the lumbering bird twice as tricky on the trip home after dropping the freight at the jumpers' camp. Marlee had been pleasantly surprised by how nice the camp was. The compound sat about fifty miles from the ranger's station. It consisted of a main log structure and clusters of small, neat cabins. A fenced clearing was home to three small Bell helicopters, probably for spotting and keeping tabs on fires, numerous bulldozers, and a hodgepodge of trucks and jeeps.

Marlee hadn't seen a single smoke jumper other than Captain Martin. And he couldn't have been more polite or less interested in her personally if she'd been made of cardboard.

First order of business once she got home and took messages off the answering machine, was to punch up Rose Stein's number before she lost her nerve. Jo Beth danced around excitedly on her toes. Marlee's stomach did flip-flops waiting for the phone to be picked up at the other end. The "hello" when it came wasn't nearly as crisp as she'd expected.

"Rose, it's Marlee." She dawdled, waiting for the woman she

hadn't seen in weeks to make a snide remark. She heard nothing. Marlee couldn't tell if there was still anyone at the other end. "Rose?" she ventured more tentatively.

"I...yes, I'm here, Marlee. Honestly, I can't bear it if you've called to say something bad's happened to Jo Beth."

"No, no. Nothing of the sort. It's just that she'd like to talk to you. I'm on my cell so you'll understand why I'm limiting Jo Beth to ten minutes. Well, here she is." Marlee quickly pressed the phone against her daughter's ear. It was crazy to have such butterflies over as simple a thing as letting those two talk.

Not wanting to appear to hover or listen in on Jo Beth's side of the conversation, Marlee picked up a stack of filing and hummed while she pulled out drawers and found the proper folders.

In many ways she was sorry her relationship with Cole's mother had come to this. In mulling it over, Marlee realized she probably deserved a share of the blame. When she'd met Cole, his father was alive and Rose was busy with the many unofficial tasks of an admiral's wife. A few months after her and Cole's wedding, Phillip Stein had keeled over from a massive coronary. Rose hadn't yet recovered from that blow when Cole was diagnosed with anaplastic or large cell lymphoma. Maybe Marlee had let herself get so wrapped up in worry, she'd shut Rose out.

Perhaps if her time with her husband hadn't been cut short, partly because of the navy's deployment, Marlee might have seen and warded off problems. No, even taking all things into consideration, it never would've occurred to Marlee that a casual mention to her mother-in-law about Mick's request that they come home to Montana would cause such discord.

Finished with the first pile of invoices, Marlee checked her watch. Less than five minutes had passed. She went to the desk for a second batch. The phone on the desk rang. "Cloud Chasers," she sang out, frankly glad of the interruption.

"Marlee? This is Dean Ames. Me and my dad are home from capturing the Macleans' crazy bull. I sure have a lot to tell Jo Beth."

Marlee heard a deeper voice in the background.

"That's my dad," Dean said. "He says I should ask if this is a convenient time for Jo Beth and me to talk."

The boy tried to sound so grown-up it dragged a chuckle from Marlee. And that felt good, considering how depressed she'd been moments before. "Actually, Dean, Jo Beth is on another phone talking to her grandmother. I promise you're next on her list."

"Goody. Er...Dad wants the phone."

"Two things," the man said so quickly after the boy left, Marlee wondered if he'd been listening in on an extension. "To update you on Gordon's condition," Wylie began, "at noon they moved him to a ward."

"I know, I spoke to a nurse this morning."

"Ah, then you're aware he'll be out in two days. Do you know they're singing your praises around the Maclean household?"

"All the praise should go to Gordon's surgical team. Uh...you said you had two things? What's the second? Or let me guess. You received Don Morrison's message about your turbine."

"Yes. How did you know? Don said he never reached you."

"When he couldn't get me, he called Mick via Stella. I was already tied up with a delivery."

"Ah, so you won't be delivering my turbine today?"

"Not today, no." Marlee picked up a pencil and nervously tapped the eraser on a clear spot on the wood-topped desk. "Excuse me a second." She covered the phone with her hand. "Jo Beth, honey, say goodbye. Your time is up."

The little girl bobbed her head. "I've gotta say bye, Grandmother Rose." Looking unsure, the child extended the phone to Marlee. "She needs to talk to you, Mama."

Marlee started to refuse. "Tell her I'm on another call," she said softly, but urgently. Then curiosity got the best of her. "Wylie...uh.

Oops, sorry, I mean, Ranger Ames. I'll have to call you back. Jo Beth's grandmother is on another line. I won't be a moment. Jo Beth would like to gab with Dean later, too."

"Fine. And call me Wylie," he ordered in a sandpapery growl.

Feeling momentarily frazzled, Marlee hung up the office phone. "Rose," she said, taking the cell in an unsteady hand. "You needed to talk to me?"

"My dear, I wanted to tell you how much the last ten minutes has meant to me."

"Rose…"

"No, don't say anything, please. Let me finish. I've moped around this house feeling like an old fool for making such a stink. So big it seems, I caused doubts as to my sanity. Which my attorney says gave your lawyer ammunition for an injunction barring me from ever seeing or speaking to my granddaughter again. I've started at least fifty letters of apology and have torn up every one. Yet, even without that, you allowed Jo Beth to phone." She broke down, and there was absolutely no mistaking her tears.

"Rose, we were both overwrought at the time. I, ah, don't mean to rush you, but I left a business call on hold." *That was a lie.*

"I'm sorry. And about your brother, too. Jo Beth said he's in the hospital. Now I understand your rush to return to Montana."

Marlee debated telling Rose she hadn't known about Mick's requiring further surgery until she arrived home. She thought better of it, and murmured, "Housework, flying Mick's route and handling the business end of things hasn't left me much free time."

"Goodness, you must've had to hit the ground running, and right after such a draining experience here and a long drive. Jo Beth said you live with someone named Pappy?"

It was a simple query, but Marlee automatically tensed. Then she realized that every time Rose had opened her mouth over the last year it'd been emotionally exhausting. Marlee had let it get to her, but that had to stop.

"Pappy Jack is my grandfather. My father's father. Really I have to go, Rose. I'll do my best to see that Jo Beth phones you every week or so. Or occasionally you can call her."

"Yes, please. Any time at all. I'm always home."

"That's not good. You should get out and do things. I remember you and Phillip entertained, attended the theater and played bridge every weekend. You had groups of active friends."

"Had is the operative word, dear. Things change. That was years ago. I'm afraid anyone Phillip and I knew socially has long since dropped me from their roster."

Marlee felt smacked by a wall of guilt. Without a whimper, Rose had given up the busy life she'd known and enjoyed to devote her days to Cole and Jo Beth.

Words failed Marlee, but it was as if Rose knew the silence didn't bode well. "I didn't mean…oh, dear, do go back to your other caller. Maybe someday…goodness, my eyes are leaking again. Goodbye, Marlee. And thank you from the bottom of my heart. You can't know how lonely I've been." The line went dead. Marlee sat holding the phone for several seconds. Until Jo Beth noticed she wasn't talking, and ran over.

"Mama, you said I could call Dean. If you're flying more stuff to his daddy tomorrow, can we stay there for a while so I can play?"

Because it took some time to make sense of Jo Beth's request, Marlee knew she'd been rattled by the way Rose signed off. What had her mother-in-law been about to say? Did she want to come here for a visit? Gazing out the window, Marlee bit her bottom lip. Oh, she could see it now. Rose-the-tidy, here ordering Mick and Pappy to pick up after themselves.

"Mama, can I stay tomorrow and play with Dean?"

"Jo Beth, I heard you mention the cub to Grandmother. Did she say anything about Dean keeping a bear cub?"

"At first it scared her 'cause she thought Dean and his daddy have wild bears for pets. She was okay once I 'splained they make sick or hurt animals better and put them back into the woods, which is their real home."

"Ah." Marlee smiled. She spared a minute to hug her sweet child. That was something she'd too often missed, being away so much of the time. "Hon, Mama needs a word with Dean's dad before you kids talk. I'm imposing the ten-minute limit again, understood?"

Jo Beth rolled her eyes. "Same as with Grandmother. You keep track, okay? Mama, when will I learn to read better and tell time?"

Marlee dropped a feathery kiss on the girl's nose. "Now that you mention it, I need to find out if Whitepine offers home-school materials."

"Dean's daddy teaches him. Every day he's got lessons in reading, numbers, and I forget, but a bunch of other stuff."

Marlee recalled Mick mentioning that Wylie homeschooled his son. "Uncle Mick and I rode a bus to school when we were kids. It picked us up out at the highway. In the winter the bus was often late due to bad weather. We practically turned blue huddled there by the mailbox." As the Ames number rang through, she smiled at the memories and jotted a note to call the school, and also, Mick.

Wylie picked up on the second ring. "Hi, it's Marlee again. I can deliver your turbine tomorrow morning. Is ten good?"

"Any time. Just roll it out on the runway. All the parts I ordered were listed on the first invoice I signed."

Marlee had his bill in front of her so she knew he'd signed in advance. But Jo Beth would be disappointed if they flew to the ranger's station and she didn't get to see Dean. "Is there a better time? One, uh, when you'll be home?"

"Are you asking for help off-loading the turbine? On the last trip, you made it quite plain you could handle that aspect of your job. My foot's proof of that. It's still black-and-blue."

"Sorry about that! My superiors in the navy noted my temper on a couple of performance evaluations. I didn't mean I'd need help with the delivery. It's…well, my daughter wants to play with your son. If you have prior plans she'll have to understand."

Wylie didn't answer right away. Just as Marlee was about to write him off and prepare an excuse to give Jo Beth, he responded grudgingly. "Yeah, I'm getting worked over at this end, too. Dean has a whole set of castles, knights with horses and armor, and probably a princess in a tower he's been setting up in preparation for your daughter's next visit. I think I can manage to knock off a few minutes, and fix you coffee. It'll give them some extra time to play."

Feeling defensive again, Marlee ground her back teeth together. "There's no need to put yourself out on my account. I'll bring a crossword puzzle book to occupy myself."

"Coffee's no trouble."

"Here, I'm handing my phone to Jo Beth if you'll give yours to Dean." Like hell, making her coffee was no trouble! The man couldn't stand having her invade his space. Was it any woman, or just her? Marlee didn't wait to see if he tried to backpedal any more. She held out the phone. "Ten minutes starts from when Dean says hello," she reminded Jo Beth.

She left them chatting and ran next door to check on Pappy Jack. He was asleep in front of the TV, so she tiptoed out again. Seeing him served to jog her memory. With Wylie already acting resentful, there was no way she wanted to risk bringing Pappy Jack along and having him make some offhand reference to the ranger's absent wife. *That could be dicey.*

Back in the office, she rummaged until she found the number

Mick had listed for Stella Gibson. "Mrs. Gibson? This is Marlee Callen. We haven't met, and I hate to impose on you again so soon. But Mick's still in the hospital and I have a delivery to make tomorrow morning, so I'm calling to see if you're free to stay with my grandfather."

"I'd be delighted," the other woman was quick to say. "Until something opens up in town, believe me I can use every cent of extra income. What time do you need me?"

"Can you come at nine? Unless another order's phoned in, I have just one delivery. I should be home by noon. Speaking of home, Mick thinks that as soon as he's released from the hospital he'll be able to take care of himself and Pappy. I'm worried that he won't be as spry as he thinks."

"I understand stubborn men. I nursed my husband through a long illness. A more intractable man never existed. As long as the nursing home in Whitepine doesn't call to hire me permanently, I'll be glad to pop in to check on the guys when you go on a run."

"There's a nursing home in Whitepine?"

Stella laughed. "Our town's moving into the big time. In the last few years we've got us a big box department store, a super-market, and now a big, lumber and home improvement place is dickering with our city council."

"I've been out of touch. So...have the schools grown? Do you know if there's a home-schooling department?"

"Oh, yes, we've got that now. A lot of ranch moms buy materials and teach their kids at home."

"Thanks, Stella. And thanks for filling in tomorrow. I'll give Pappy breakfast before Jo Beth and I take off." She hung up and saw that the kids were well over their time limit. And they were still yakking away. Marlee reached across the desk and nudged her daughter, then tapped the face of her watch.

Jo Beth sighed, so adultlike. "We gotta say goodbye, Dean.

My mama says so. I'll ask Mama if I can go sit at that watering hole with you. Bye."

"What's this about a watering hole?" Marlee stopped halfway to the file cabinets where she intended to file the next stack of invoices.

"Dean says his dad fixed a fence of branches that we can sit behind so the deer who come to drink water don't know anybody's watching. Dean said maybe we can see a mama doe with two baby deer. They come there almost every noon."

"Honey, I want to be back here by noon. Maybe another time. I know we'll probably be taking them one more order."

"The deer might be gone by then. Dean says when there's frost on the pumpkins, the deer go into the valley to live."

"Frost on the pumpkins signals the start of winter. It's still fall, Jo Beth. There'll be other days, I'm sure, to see deer."

The girl stamped a foot. "I want to see them tomorrow."

"Well, Miss Stein, that kind of behavior isn't going to make it happen. Act nice and I'll at least ask Dean's dad whether visiting the watering hole tomorrow is an option."

The turnaround was immediate. The child psychologist had said to find a reward that worked to alter Jo Beth's tendency toward tantrums. Apparently Dean Ames was one such reward. It was too bad the boy was saddled with such an unsociable father.

THE NEXT MORNING Pappy was alert enough to deliver another lecture about Marlee watching herself around Wylie Ames. "You be careful that man isn't asking you to make all of these deliveries to lure you into his lair."

"He's not trying to lure me, Pappy. In fact Wylie told me to leave his order on the runway. It's the kids who want some time together."

Pappy followed her out to the Arrow, harping all the way. "He could be pretending, Marlee, so you relax your guard and he can get you in his clutches. Otherwise why has he placed so many orders? He never did this with Mick."

"Honestly, Pappy. It's a single order. The parts house is the one to blame for the multiple flights. I think you're watching too much *CSI*. Ah, there's Stella, I presume." Marlee was relieved to see a slender woman with cropped gray hair striding up their lane. How long could they rely on a neighbor? Lord knew, Mick hadn't wanted to discuss the possibility that Pappy needed more specialized care than they could provide. And Mick had a point, this had always been Pappy's home.

The old man turned at once and drew a liver-spotted hand through his hair. "You didn't tell me Stella was dropping by. She's teaching me to play Scrabble. I guess there's no need for you to rush right back, after all."

Marlee stuck around only long enough to introduce herself and Jo Beth to their neighbor. That Pappy Jack had a crush on the woman was so plain, Marlee still wore a big smile five minutes after takeoff.

Don Morrison had delivered the turbine to the airpark as promised. While his men loaded the unit on the Arrow, Marlee took the opportunity to telephone her brother. "Mick, hi. How are you today? I've heard sometimes the third day after surgery is the day surgical patients feel the worst."

"I overdid walking yesterday. Will you try to keep tomorrow open? I think I'll be able to talk the doc into releasing me. Bring the turboprop. There's more room between the seats. They swivel, too. I'll put two together as a cradle for my hip and leg. Oh, bring Pappy and Jo Beth. I found out from a nurse that the nearest animal shelter is between the hospital and the airpark. We can pick out a dog on the way and you'll have the room to load up a good-sized cage as well as me."

"Mick, are you sure about the d-o-g?" She spelled the letters softly, hoping to avoid getting Jo Beth excited.

"Mama, are you and Uncle Mick talking about the dog?"

"So much for thinking she hasn't learned to spell." She chuckled and heard Mick echo her response. "Okay, you guys win. But I'm going on record now. Any dog is totally your responsibility. I only signed on to cook and clean up after people. Not pets."

Mick and Jo Beth were both vocal in their acceptance of Marlee's rule. She put an *X* through the next day on her pocket calendar.

By then the workmen had the turbine loaded and tied down so it wouldn't shift in flight.

A layer of clouds had built over the western mountains. Less than fifteen minutes into the flight Marlee felt the wind begin to buffet the Arrow.

"Mama," Jo Beth said worriedly into her mike. "Quit wiggling the plane. It feels like we're going to fall down."

"We're fine. This is called turbulence, honey." In spite of her confidence, a full storm had moved in by the time the Ames runway came into view. Between her last delivery and now Wylie, or someone had spread gravel over a good two-thirds of the track, for which she was most grateful. At lower elevations it was already raining. She'd been afraid the homemade runway would be nothing but a mud slick.

As Marlee banked and headed down into the wind, she again saw the tall stalwart ranger and his son standing at the edge of what she now knew was the path leading to their house. Man and boy wore yellow rain slickers. Marlee wished she'd brought rain gear. Back home it'd been sunny. The jacket Mick kept in the plane had gone with Gordon Maclean, so it wouldn't keep Marlee from getting soaked today.

When she touched down, she heard the pinging of the gravel striking the underbelly of the Arrow. Rain lashed the windshield.

Busy going through her shutdown process, she didn't realize

Wylie and Dean had left the cover of trees to come out in the storm until Jo Beth's passenger door was yanked open. A yellow slickered arm reached in and draped the girl with a silver tarp of the kind used in mountain survival kits. "Jo Beth, hold this tight around you and run on into the house with Dean," said a deep voice outside the plane.

Removing her headset, Marlee leaned across the seat to thank him as her left hand shoved at her door, held shut by gusty wind.

"Hey, stay put," Wylie called. "I have a hooded jacket for you. You'll swim in it, but I thought it'd cover your legs. Our park weather forecaster said the storm will blow over by noon. I'll unload the turbine later when the rain lightens up."

He slammed the passenger door and in seconds appeared at Marlee's side. As if she were a rag doll, Wylie stuffed her arms into the jacket sleeves, then zipped it up to her chin. Which was good, because the sleeves hung well past her hands. It was when he carefully arranged the hood, which would've impeded her sight, that Marlee was most touched by his thoughtfulness.

He didn't, however, give her a moment to convey her thanks. He pulled her out into the rain, shut her door and gripped her under the arm so tightly her feet almost never hit the gravel. They were deep in the trees, nearly to his house before Wylie let go of her. He glanced over once. Then, as if seeing something in her face that warned she was about to blubber out her gratitude, he sped up and called back, "I have to go cover the motor I tore apart. You know your way into the house. I set up coffee, but you'll need to plug it in."

He disappeared into the dark forest. Her hood fell back and rain slapped her hair as Marlee stumbled to a halt. For every nice thing he did, he did something equally abrupt to cancel it.

"The least he could've done before taking off like a caveman would've been to open the damn door." Determined, she wrapped the long wet sleeves around the rain-slick knob. Eventually, with huffing, puffing and ingenuity, she triumphed. Standing in the mudroom off the kitchen, she shook herself off like a wet pup. Somewhere deeper in the house, the kids laughed and chattered happily.

Okay, so she'd plug in the coffee and wait until the storm outside blew past.

CHAPTER SIX

THE COFFEE HAD FINISHED dripping and Marlee had mugs set out on the counter by the time Wylie showed his face again. He stomped into the mudroom bringing in rain, wind and cold.

Shivering, Marlee moved farther into the kitchen, away from the open arch. "No sign of letup?" *Silly question*. She could see the water streaming onto the floor from his slicker and the way his crow-colored hair lay plastered to his head.

"If anything it's worse." He took off the slicker and draped it over a chair. "After I warm up with that tempting coffee I smell, I'll call the park weather station again." He removed his boots at the door and walked silently past her on sock feet, cocking an ear toward the kid sounds in another part of the house. "Those two are still getting along, I see," he said, gesturing with a mug he snatched off the counter.

Marlee cut her gaze from his rare smile to the steamy mug he extended. "I checked on them once," she said, accepting the handle he thoughtfully turned toward her. "They were so involved in slaying dragons, neither of them noticed me. Dean certainly has a huge set of knights and castles and kings."

"Yeah, but he has few opportunities to enjoy them with other kids."

"Do your friends—or family—not have children? Or don't they visit?"

He crossed to the window and stood looking out at the

dripping trees. His posture was so blatantly male, feet spread, a flat hand in a back pocket. "You think Dean's deprived by my choice of a job?"

"Hardly deprived with that roomful of toys."

"Then your question is really about you angling for an opening to ask what happened to my wife...*his* mother? Is that it?" He turned toward her.

Through misty curls of steam, Marlee studied Wylie's implacable features. "This may come as a shock, but not everyone you meet is panting after the intimate details of your life." She blew on her hot coffee before sipping. "Although it'd serve you right if I was nosy," she said. "Considering how you jumped to conclusions on Thursday and felt free to suppose my husband dumped me."

"I apologized. Look—" he pointed out the window "—I think the rain's slacking off. At least it's no longer hitting the house. Guess there's no need to check those weather reports."

It was obvious to Marlee that he'd trod into uncharted waters and, over his head, wanted to swim his way out. She didn't feel inclined to let him wriggle away. "Then you're aware there's talk circulating as to the whereabouts of your wife? What do you say if someone asks point-blank where she's gone?"

His pewter eyes blazed, then as quickly the fire was banked. Wylie's nonverbal communication shouted his distaste, though he said evenly, "My friends accept she's gone. New people I meet are generally too polite to be so nosy."

"And you encourage the mystery by not clarifying rumors? I think it suits your purpose to let gruesome tales circulate."

A shadow of a smile flirted with his lips. "Really? Gruesome. Why would I?"

Marlee took another sip. "I haven't the foggiest. To maintain privacy? Or to keep well-meaning neighbors from penciling you in as bachelor-of-the-night at dinner parties?"

Relaxing his shoulders, Wylie propped one against the

window frame. He shook his head and saluted her with his cup. "Rangers don't throw a lot of dinner parties. Their wives occasionally arrange barbecues. But you've got their number. Maybe you can explain why married women are so obsessed with pairing up any man who's single, divorced or widowed and over the age of twenty-one."

She smiled, finding his lingering grin infectious. So infectious, that when he grew suddenly sober, she felt prickles march up her spine.

"I tell people the truth. Shirl, that's Dean's mother, took off when he was three weeks old. She left with almost everything she brought to the marriage. And at the time it was obvious that she wasn't interested in being found by me or anyone."

"Heavens, you mean you don't know if she's moldering out in the woods somewhere, or if she was eaten by wild animals?"

"I know," he said grimly. "I received a neat package of divorce papers from a lawyer in Miami a month after she left. Including a document that gave me sole guardianship of Dean. End of story."

He sounded so cold Marlee was afraid he'd seen her flinch. She knew she must be staring, but for the life of her, she couldn't fathom any woman walking off and leaving this rough-edged man with her baby.

It was probably fortunate the kids pounded down the hall and rushed into the kitchen. Their timely entry called a halt to any disparaging comment she might've made.

"It quit raining, Dad. I promised Jo Beth I'd take her to our deer blind." Marlee saw that her daughter was swimming in a fleece jacket Dean must have lent her. "So is it okay if we go to the watering hole? This is about the time the doe always shows up with her fawns."

Plainly anxious to escape, Wylie set aside his mug. "Sure," he said, reaching behind the door for a wool plaid lumberjack shirt. "Are you wearing sturdy shoes?" he asked Jo Beth as he stepped into his boots.

She lifted a foot. Her leather sneakers apparently passed inspection. Wylie and the kids were going under the arch when Dean stopped. "Isn't Jo Beth's mom gonna come with us?"

Wylie's indistinguishable response lacked any semblance of grace. "She probably doesn't want to tramp through the woods."

Irked, Marlee made up her mind to be obstinate. "Oh, but I do. Jo Beth told me about the twin fawns. I'd love to see them." She set her cup beside Wylie's abandoned one. "Thanks for inviting me, Dean."

"Dad, the trees hanging over the trail will be wet. Marlee's gonna need a warmer jacket, don'tcha think?"

Wylie's growl must have been concurrence, because he turned back and yanked open a closet door. An array of shirts and jackets hung on metal hooks lining one wall. He sorted through several and finally tossed Marlee a jacket fashioned from supple leather. It was lined with quilted brown satin. When she put it on and saw how far the sleeves hung off her shoulders and over her hands, she knew it belonged to him.

Because she struggled to reach the bottom of the zipper, Wylie again came to her rescue. Only this time, in the warm confines of the house, without rain beating her in the face, the subtle aroma of masculinity blended with his woodsy aftershave affected her in a way she hadn't expected. She had to hide a smile. The scent stoked desires she wasn't ready to acknowledge.

He took inventory, raising a quizzical eyebrow. She jerked away.

Zipping her jacket seemed to Wylie a simple, nonthreatening gesture. One he'd performed a zillion times for Dean. But Wylie's thoughts stalled there. He hadn't been in hibernation so long he didn't recognize that Marlee was coyly playing up the awareness between them. He'd be damned if he'd go along with her games.

Wylie pulled open the door and waved the others through. Dean and Jo Beth darted by with several inches' clearance. But in such tight quarters there was no way two adults could avoid brushing up against each other.

Wyle held his breath as Marlee swept past like a queen. He'd tried, but she'd done nothing to minimize the contact of their upper bodies. That grated on his nerves. When he slammed the door too hard, the kids came to a halt looking at him curiously. "Doorknob's wet," he said by way of explanation.

"Dean, you lead the others on up the trail. I'll collect a tarp from the toolshed." He veered off after giving his son the directive.

"Why do we need a tarp since it's no longer raining?" Marlee hurried up the path slick with rain-drenched fir needles, and put the question to Dean. She'd hesitated back there, unconsciously watching Wylie take the detour.

"We don't want the seat of our pants to get wet, Marlee."

"Oh, I didn't realize we had to sit on the ground."

"Yep. And now we need to be quiet. We have to walk softly up the trail if we want the deer to come 'round." He'd lowered his voice to a whisper, which had Marlee nodding rather than answering back. *He was the expert.*

With Wylie's longer stride, he soon closed the gap, carrying the tarp he'd collected. In spite of the narrow trail, which was little more than a footpath winding through wet undergrowth that clutched at their bodies from all sides, he managed to pass them and take the lead.

Marlee wished he hadn't. From the back he was too fine to look at. From all angles, as a matter of fact. At least when he was behind her, all she had to deal with was his scent.

All at once he turned and peered at her as she picked her way up the path, bringing up the rear. "You'd have been more comfortable staying at the house by the fireplace. This isn't the most ideal weather for a forest hike."

"I'll be fine." Marlee mustered a smile. It was genuine. She couldn't help it. She admired a take-charge kind of guy. A leader, provided he didn't get too pushy or arrogant. And as long as her abilities were honored and accepted. She hadn't become so jaded working with men that she didn't appreciate it when a man placed himself between women, children and possible danger. Call it an odd quirk for a woman in her male-dominated occupation. But that was a code of ethics she'd been raised with. Pappy Jack and her dad, when he was alive, practiced simple chivalry. They'd also instilled it in Mick.

Wylie shared the same quality. Why else would he strike out first, taking care to shake all excess water off sticky, sagging branches, and prop them aside so they wouldn't slap the kids or her?

They were deep in the woods. Marlee felt terribly isolated even before she noticed how far from the house they'd trekked. Thankfully, from the looks of Dean's excited gestures to Jo Beth, their destination lay right ahead.

Marlee hadn't known what to expect from a deer blind. Certainly something larger than the little spot hollowed out of thick brush. As a kid, when she and Mick played cops and robbers, she'd fashioned hideouts around their house bigger than this one. The tarp Wylie spread out only emphasized how cramped they'd be.

Dean plopped onto his knees and scrambled to the front of the enclosure, then dragged Jo Beth down. Marlee was slower to gingerly wedge in behind her daughter.

Wylie stayed standing. Marlee saw they'd left him little room. Scooting forward as much as she could, she patted the small area of tarp that remained open. He hesitated so long Marlee would've childishly blurted out that she didn't have cooties, except that Dean was making elaborate shushing motions with a finger to his lips.

Then Wylie did sit. At once Marlee saw the error in her earlier thinking. His butt might be narrower than hers, but his shoulders suddenly claimed every spare inch. She found herself sandwiched between Jo Beth in front, the woven, still-wet enclosure on her right, and Wylie's warm imposing bulk on the left.

"Breathe," he ordered very near her ear. That effort earned him an angry scowl from his son.

Marlee did as she was told. But then she was forced to absorb all the masculine details she'd shied from back at the house.

She really tried focusing on what was going on outside the blind, but it was difficult. She was all too aware of the broad chest gently bumping her shoulder as Wylie did what he'd ordered her to do—he breathed. In and out with excruciating regularity. Surely she hadn't been without sex *that* long! Granted, it'd been well over a year. Actually, approaching two. And she was, after all, healthy and in the prime of life.

So was the man right behind her....

At the moment of that discovery, Marlee noticed everyone in the blind had crowded forward but her. A movement beyond the branches caught her eye. A subtle reflection in the pool where the deer came to drink. Suddenly, out of a thicket opposite the blind stepped a dainty creature with a delicate head made more arresting by huge, soft brown eyes. Slender ears whisked back and forth as the doe stretched out her neck and sniffed the air.

The four people in the blind froze automatically. Marlee felt Wylie's strong fingers grip her shoulder—an impersonal touch that didn't seem impersonal at all. Although he was merely trying to alert her as to what came next. Two fawns emerged from hiding, one on either side of the doe. Their ears were too big for their heads and when they spread reed-slender front legs to bend and drink, Marlee worried they'd topple into the pool. She clapped a hand over her mouth to keep from exclaiming her fears. Tears blurred her vision. Happy ones she discreetly brushed away.

Of course, she'd seen photos of baby deer with their softly spotted backs. Viewing them in real life was a special gift. She'd been close to wildlife in some of her military exercises but this experience lent new meaning to the term *communing with nature*. All too soon, though, it was over. The mama deer lifted her dripping muzzle, tensed, then nudged her babies with seeming urgency. As quietly as the three had appeared, they vanished.

"So, Jo Beth, what did you think?" Dean broke the silence gripping the foursome behind the man-made wall.

"They're so pretty." She wiggled around until she could stand and in doing so pushed her mother flat against Wylie.

"Hang on. We're in here like an accordion that needs to unfold." With more agility than Marlee would ever guess a man of his size possessed, Wylie rose. After a battle seemingly waged within him, he extended a hand to her.

Wondering what on earth she'd done to prompt this odd behavior, Marlee accepted his help. Scorching heat streaked from the point of contact between their palms, and caught her by surprise. For an instant, forest noises receded, and Marlee knew from the dark flare in Wylie's pupils that he'd felt the jolt too. Neither released the other's hand for longer than was appropriate, given their circumstances and where they were.

Finally he pulled away first, although he'd plainly experienced...something.

On the return walk down the trail, Wylie hung way back. Marlee swung out around him, but he grabbed her sleeve, causing her to drop behind the kids, who ran pell-mell down the mountain path. Her heart began beating wildly. She was tempted to run, especially since she suspected that his mind, like hers, remained on that brief flurry of sparks.

"Listen, I don't know how to say this other than come right out with it. I'm not in the market for female companionship

Marlee. So save your feminine wiles for someone who's interested."

"Wha…at?" She broke from his grip, and knew her face must've turned bright red, because she felt heat building. What she did was laugh incredulously. "I don't *work* any kind of wiles. And if I were so inclined, I wouldn't waste them on you." Swinging around, she stomped down the path spewing some very colorful swearwords—which petered out before she reached the house.

"Jo Beth!" Marlee stripped off the ranger's jacket inside his mudroom. "We're leaving. *Now*. Tell Dean goodbye." She almost pulled the metal hook out of the wall as she furiously made stabs at hanging up the heavy jacket.

Two frowning faces dived into her line of vision as she wheeled around.

"Aren't you staying for lunch?" Dean asked. "Last night, Dad cooked roast beef for sandwiches. And he made potato bread."

Marlee's mouth watered. She was starved. A hunger probably more pronounced from the taxing hike uphill through the woods, and the mad dash back down. "Maybe next time," she said, preparing for both children to be upset.

Dean took the news with a long face. Jo Beth clouded up as if heading into one of her tantrums. Marlee nipped that fit early, shocking the girl when she yanked up her stiff body and marched out the door, nearly bowling Wylie over. Frankly, Marlee wished she'd knocked him on his butt.

"Dad," an ashen-faced Dean Ames called. "Do something. They're leaving. I want them to stay for lunch." The boy flew at his father and wrapped sturdy arms about Wylie's waist.

He frowned. *Had he misread Marlee because of his own defensiveness?* God, but he found her attractive. A nagging voice said *So, you're blaming her for that?*

Wylie cleared his throat. In spite of her being so skinny and the five-year-old she half-carried, a resisting armful, Marlee was fast making tracks away from the house.

"I'll see what I can do," Wylie told his son, and broke into a jog. Under his breath he revised the statement. "Make that *undo*."

"Marlee, hold up a minute." He thought he was gaining on her. *Yes, she'd stopped.* However, she sent him a mutinous expression, so he didn't move too close.

"Sorry, was there something you forgot to say? Maybe you've thought of a new way to level ludicrous accusations?"

He sucked the inside of his cheek through clenched teeth. "How many ways do you suppose there are to apologize?"

She stared at him. Singed him with a glare.

Wylie bent his head until his chin touched his jacket, and he rubbed the back of his neck hard. "Forgive me. I've lived like a caveman too long."

"Bullshit," she shot back.

"Ma...ma, shame on you!" Sounding horrified, Jo Beth used both hands to shove away from the woman who held her.

Marlee let her wriggle down and saw that Jo Beth had learned to deliver one of Rose Stein's disapproving looks. Which had Marlee shuffling along the path, toward Wylie. "Go play with Dean for a minute, Jo Beth. His dad and I have a few things to iron out."

The girl didn't wait to be told twice. With the speed of the doe they'd watched at the watering hole, she raced back to where Dean sprawled across the tire swing.

"Okay, she's out of hearing. What's with you?" Marlee fumed. "I don't for one minute buy the caveman excuse. Earlier, I was impressed by your seemingly built-in good manners."

"You don't pull punches, do you?"

"Are we arguing?" Marlee hiked up an eyebrow. "Is that's how you get your jollies? If so, deal me out. Better yet, I'll lay my cards on the table. I temporarily fly for Cloud Chasers. A freight service. You place orders. I pick them up and deliver them. You have a son. I have a daughter. They hit it off, both of them being only children. They like to play together. Do I find you attractive? In some ways. In other ways, not only *no,* but *hell, no!* Am I a sex-starved widow dying for a romp between the sheets? Not on your life! Your turn." Palms toward her, she invited him to bring it on.

Wylie let her anger fade a little. He'd rocked back on his boot heels, and crossed his arms over his chest while she fired away. There was not one damned thing wrong with Marlee Stein's aim. Every barb struck true. "I have no excuses to give," he said quietly.

"No she-done-me-wrong song?" she asked sarcastically.

"Okay, there's that."

Marlee found his self-deprecating admission endearing, but she wasn't through being mad. "All the same, don't be taking your beef with her out on me."

Nodding, he loosened one hand from its tucked position and brushed a thumb back and forth across his lips. "Fair enough."

She released her pent-up breath little by little, hunched her shoulders and buried her fingertips in her front jeans pockets. "I never gave it much thought before," she said, frowning slightly. "You and I probably have a lot more in common than either of us wants to admit. No matter how a person loses someone they love, there's lingering pain. People told me time will heal that, but…look at you. You're no poster child for *that* theory."

His gaze lingered on her face briefly, then he shifted his eyes beyond her to the two children who laughed and played on the swing. Both kids were red-faced from exertion. With Dean's shock of red hair and his fair skin, he showed the effects more than Jo Beth, who had brown hair and skin prone to tan rather than burn.

Marlee saw the change in Wylie's eyes the minute they moved

to his son. A gentleness that wasn't there a moment ago. A softening that indicated overwhelming love.

"You must look at Dean and see your wife, which makes losing her harder. I feel the same. At times Jo Beth is the mirror image of her father."

Wylie cleared his throat twice. "I need to stop you right there. By the time she left, there wasn't much love between me and Dean's mom. He was born during a raging ice storm. I never thought a baby…but damn, something changed from the minute I held that squalling, scrappy kid."

"Yeah." Marlee caught her bottom lip with her teeth. The raw emotion in his voice choked her up. Why? Because she had only to recall the moment Jo Beth was placed in her arms to know she shared Wylie's experience. "You know what, Ames, you're not such a bad guy."

That statement shook Wylie out of the mood he'd fallen into, and kindled an easier, freer laugh than he'd allowed before in her presence. "Does this mean, instead of tearing out of here in a huff, you'll stay for a roast beef sandwich?"

"Since you have such a charming way of asking, sure I can do that." Her sudden grin let him know she was teasing.

"I've been told I can blame my tactlessness on the fact that I'm a Taurus."

Told by a woman, no doubt. "Really? I'm relieved to know it's something that simple."

A small smile lingered on his lips. "The kids'll be happy to hear you're staying. You want to tell them to wash up while I go slice the bread?"

"Okay. For the record, you get brownie points for your domestic skills. If you ever end up eating a meal at my house, I guarantee you'll get store-bought bread."

They fell into step alongside each other. "I probably shouldn't admit this, but my bread machine was a wedding gift from one of the other rangers and his wife. Shirl was a waitress, but I learned early on that she had no interest in putting food of any kind on *our* table. I cooked for myself before she came along, and after. A couple of years ago I cleared out the third bedroom and ran across a Crock-Pot and the bread machine, both still boxed. I decided, what the hell, I'd initiate them."

The kids ran up. Wylie kept walking toward the house. Marlee stopped. "Kids," she said, "Jo Beth and I are staying for lunch."

"Yippee!" Dean grabbed the girl's hands and they galloped in circles around Marlee. "Do we have time to go feed Boxer first? I've got a new mountain goat Jo Beth hasn't seen. We ran across him riding back from Macleans' ranch. He broke his leg. My dad splinted it. I helped."

Marlee checked her watch. "Your dad's gone in to prepare lunch. Go ahead but you kids come straight back. And wash afterward," she called, because they'd already skipped off down the path.

It was odd how at home Jo Beth seemed to be here. Glancing around, she was surprised by how calming *she* found it. But any woodsy place would feel relaxing after the hustle and bustle of living in San Diego for the past year.

She opened the back door to Wylie's home and decided she'd better keep those last thoughts to herself. She wouldn't want to make him nervous by giving the impression that she had designs on him or his house. He couldn't have made it more obvious that he was an independent guy who did fine without a woman mucking up his life.

He stood at the kitchen counter, big and imposing. He looked out of place behind a breadboard. Probably because he still wore the lumberjack shirt.

He'd heard her come in, and after slicing the heel of the loaf, glanced up and smiled.

Marlee discovered that she had no defense against the heat that clutched her belly at the sight of his smile.

"Are the kids wringing out the last two minutes of play before they join us?"

"They asked to go feed the bear. And Dean said you guys have a new patient. Jo Beth's never seen a mountain goat except in the zoo. Do you want me to set the table?"

"I've got it covered. Why don't you go see if there's any late tomatoes left on the vines in the garden?"

She almost ran back outside, glad of the opportunity to put aside the feelings he'd incited. She realized it was the little things that she missed about marriage. Like the way light filtered through a stubborn lock of hair falling across Wylie's forehead. The confident way he handled a knife. Trying to blank out those images, Marlee inspected the plants on the other side of the chicken wire. She found three plump red tomatoes, and concentrated on carrying them into the house without bruising them.

She'd dallied long enough that the children met her at the path intersection. "I trust the animals are all right," she said, herding them into the house ahead of her. It was probably cowardly to use them as a buffer, but on the other hand, she thought, *whatever worked.*

"The goat ate grass right off my hand, Mama!"

"Great," Marlee said, awkwardly hugging the excited girl. "I definitely want you to go scrub your hands. You have time. I need to wash and cut these tomatoes."

Jo Beth was still nattering on about her experience with the goat when they all grouped around the table. Unlike the last meal they'd shared, everything seemed more natural this time. When Marlee cut Jo Beth's sandwich in fourths so it would be easier for the girl to pick up, Dean shoved his plate toward her. "Do mine that way, too, please."

She complied.

Wylie picked up the dish of sliced tomatoes. He slid two slices onto each plate. "I don't like 'matoes," Jo Beth announced with a sudden scowl.

"Eat them, young lady," Wylie commanded. "Girls and boys need the good things like vitamin C found in vine-ripe tomatoes." He picked up his sandwich. "Besides," he said, appearing to hunt for the right place to bite into the thick sandwich. "If Dean eats his and you leave yours, he'll be able to run faster."

Marlee was shocked to see Jo Beth pick up her fork and cut off a piece of tomato and pop it in her mouth. She finished her portion well ahead of Dean.

Marlee couldn't help sharing a conspiratorial grin with her host. Wylie was such a good dad, she had to think that with the right woman he'd be a good husband, too.

Whoa! She abruptly set down the second half of her sandwich.

"Something wrong?" Wylie asked after swallowing the bite he'd taken.

Marlee was saved from scrambling for an answer when a two-way radio she hadn't noticed on the counter began to chatter with static.

Wylie rose and wiped his hands on his napkin. Before he reached the unit, a woman's voice broke through the noise. "Station six, this is Trudy Morganthal at Base Camp. Over."

He hit a switch. "Trudy, it's Wylie. What'cha need?"

"We just received a report of a canoeing accident on the lower end of Yaak River. Our chopper did a flyover. Halsey says you're closer if you go in fire road fifteen on horseback than anywhere he could land and hike in." She rattled off additional coordinates of the accident.

The numbers stuck in Marlee's mind. They were talking about a heavily wooded area. She'd been studying longitude and latitude readings to familiarize herself with the area.

"Roger that. I'm on it." Wylie stuffed the paper he'd scribbled on in his shirt pocket. "Any confirmed drowned?" he murmured, again pressing the switch.

"Negative. I gather one girl was banged up on the rocks too badly to hike out."

"Hang on a minute, Trudy." Wylie turned to Marlee. "Have you got time to tag along on this rescue? Depending on how banged up the kid is, I may need you to fly her out to a medical facility."

"A lot of *maybes* there, Wylie." Marlee's gaze moved to the kids. She wasn't sure what he planned to do with Dean and Jo Beth.

"Do you ride?"

"It's been a while. The kids…"

"Dean owns a horse."

"His name is Kaleidoscope, 'cause he's black and white and brown," the boy announced.

Wylie ruffled his hair, then looked at Marlee. "If you ride, Jo Beth can double up with you. I'll tie a first aid kit and an aluminum travois on a pack mule. If the vic can be moved, we can bring her here and fly her out."

"What's my legal responsibility in flying out an injured person on your say-so, Wylie? I hate to ask, but people are sue-happy these days."

"I'd want Trudy to notify Angel Fleet and get them involved. That's if the injured girl requires more help than transporting her to wherever her friends parked."

"I'll need to phone home to let our neighbor Stella Gibson know I'll be returning later than planned. She's staying with Pappy."

He went back to the radio and relayed his plan to the waiting woman. Marlee pulled out her cell and punched in the number to her house.

"All set," she said a moment later. "Kids, finish your lunch quickly. And make a bathroom stop before Dean saddles his horse. Jo Beth, it seems we're about to go on an adventure." She smiled, but truthfully Marlee wasn't at all sure her daughter would be thrilled to ride a horse.

Once they reached the corral where Wylie already had two horses saddled and a mule almost packed, Jo Beth watched Dean saddle his pinto. Her daughter surprised Marlee when she said, "Mama, if Dean gets to ride by himself, why do I have to ride in front of you?"

Wylie answered. "Because, short stuff, Dean's been riding for a few years. When he was your age he sat on my horse in front of me."

"Okay, then," she said, meekly letting him boost her astride the sorrel mare he'd saddled for her mom.

"Those stirrups the right length?" Wylie ran a hand from Marlee's knee down to where her boot slipped into the stirrup, and ordered her to stand a minute.

Apparently not liking what he saw, he moved her foot aside and made an adjustment, a process he repeated on the other side. Marlee's reaction to his impersonal touch had her squirming in the saddle.

If he noticed, her discomfort went without comment. All business now, he swung into his saddle, unlooped the lead rope on the mule, and cantered off.

Marlee hated to think how sore she'd be in the morning. However, focusing on that was infinitely better than fixing her eyes on the muscles moving underneath Wylie's khaki shirt. He wore official ranger garb, and had tied the plaid shirt-jacket behind his saddle. He did the same with slickers for all of them, which told Marlee he was prepared for a shift in the weather or riding after nightfall. Neither prospect overjoyed her. Either would mean taking off from Wylie's runway in less than ideal conditions.

"I wish I'd brought the Huey today," she admitted when he dropped back to check on her at a wide spot in the trail.

"Why? Isn't the Arrow faster?"

"Yes, but I can probably fly a helicopter blindfolded through a hurricane. I think you know—after the remark you made regarding my first landing—that I'm not nearly so confident when it comes to flying a fixed wing aircraft."

He held her gaze briefly. "Ah, so that snippy little *I can fly anything with wings* remark you threw in my face was a bit of female machismo?"

Her chin shot up stubbornly. "I am pretty damned good."

"Mama, you said a bad word." Sitting in front of her, Jo Beth turned to look up.

Wylie's warm chuckle matched the heat in his eyes. "No argument from me."

As Marlee shushed Jo Beth and attempted not to make anything significant of Wylie's sudden teasing, he raked his heels along the belly of his black gelding. The trail again demanded single file travel, and he dashed forward to lead.

Had an opportunity presented itself later in the trek, Marlee decided she'd have put him on the spot with her own teasing. It didn't, and once they reached the river, and met the beleaguered canoeists, things got too hectic.

Tracie Ledbetter, the sixteen-year-old girl who'd reportedly been slammed into a jagged rock by the swift river, had suffered a broken arm, leg and a head injury bad enough that she drifted in and out of consciousness.

Marlee and Wylie conferred briefly. He said, "I'm afraid she's fractured her skull." He administered first aid to the three ambulatory teens, and felt assured they could make it back to their car under their own power. He quickly assembled the travois and settled Tracie. From a clearing, Wylie called ranger base camp while Marlee tucked blankets around the girl.

Thunder rumbled overhead as they started back. Marlee had earlier avoided placing any importance on his astrological sign. Now she took comfort in knowing Wylie Ames was a Taurus. Reliable, practical and steadfast.

CHAPTER SEVEN

WYLIE LED THE GROUP in single file, keeping a tight rein on the mule that hauled the lightweight aluminum and canvas travois— a conveyance patterned after the old type used by Native Americans. Except the new model had three small wheels across the lower back which allowed for a smoother ride. And it broke apart to fit into a backpack.

Tracie Ledbetter had a wicked-looking bloody bruise above her right temple, along with other cuts and scrapes. She'd worn hiker shorts, a tank top and sandals for her canoe trip. All had gotten soaked. Wylie carried an extra pair of sweatpants and sweatshirt in his kit. Marlee and the second girl from the boat, Julie, had carefully stripped Tracie out of her wet clothing. She wore the sweats and was covered by a wool blanket. Still her lips were slightly blue, and she only roused when Wylie passed a whiff of ammonia under her nose.

Jo Beth was first to notice a change in the patient. "Mama, that girl's not dead. She just opened her eyes."

Marlee, who brought up the rear, had tried to keep an eye on Tracie. At times when the path widened, Dean trotted ahead and blocked her view. This being one of those times, she had to look hard to check. Sure enough Tracie's eyelids fluttered, and she tried to lift her head. To avoid further injury, Wylie had strapped her tightly to the travois.

"Wylie, stop!"

He did at once. Marlee quickly dismounted and ran to the girl's side. "Tracie, can you hear me? My name is Marlee Stein. You were canoeing with friends. Your boat capsized. Do you remember?"

Tracie's eyes opened a slit, closed, then widened to reveal gorgeous blue-violet irises. She was quite pretty, other than her chalk-white face, and blond hair matted with blood and debris from the river.

"Wh-where am I?" she said faintly, growing panicky as she discovered she couldn't move her arms. Adding to her fear, four strangers loomed above her. "I hurt," she whimpered. "Why do I hurt all over?" Again she fought the straps.

"I'm a Glacier Park Ranger," Wylie said quietly as he knelt. "You banged yourself up on a river boulder. A boy from your party has contacted your parents. They authorized us to take you to where Marlee can fly you to a hospital in Kalispell. Do you understand, Miss Ledbetter? We're here to help you."

"The others? Julie, David and Brad?"

Marlee softly stroked Tracie's forehead. "Shaken, but they're fine. Well enough to hike back to where David parked. You were thrown from the canoe. They swam to shore, ran downstream and were able to pull you out."

"It's all fuzzy in my head."

"Well, we're not far from the ranger's cabin and my plane. Don't try to move. We'll get you to a doctor as quickly as we can."

"I feel numb," the girl mumbled. "I hurt everywhere. And you're out of focus."

"Lucky you didn't all drown," Wylie said to impress on her the seriousness of the accident. "We're glad to see you alert. It's a good thing David had his cell phone in a waterproof bag. He contacted the main ranger station, who in turn called me."

Jo Beth crept closer to her mother. "I thought you were dead like my daddy," she whispered to the injured girl.

The little girl's solemnity got to Wylie. He swept Jo Beth up into a hug, and patted her back.

Marlee's vision blurred. Cole had been too weak for a long time to even lift his daughter. Wylie swung her easily aloft. And Jo Beth tucked her head under his chin, which told Marlee her daughter felt secure in Wylie's arms.

That reminded Marlee of how much Cole lost because of his illness. Cancer had cheated the whole family.

After Wylie determined that Jo Beth was okay, he set her astride the mare. "Marlee, do you need help mounting?"

He waited beside the horse, and moved to his only after she said, "No thanks."

"Dean, climb aboard Kaleidoscope. The longer we wait here, the longer Tracie's folks will worry."

"I have a cell phone," the girl said feebly. "Should I let them know I'm okay?"

"Your phone took a bath. And we're so deep in trees and granite, I doubt I have service." He pulled out his phone, checked it and put it back. "Once you're loaded on to Marlee's plane, she can have Angel Fleet send your folks a message." Wylie's statement was nearly absorbed by the dense foliage.

Marlee mounted sluggishly and had to urge the mare to catch up.

They reached the plane twenty minutes later. Marlee saw again how Wylie's strength blended with his tenderness as he manhandled the turbine out of the cargo hold, then took extra care not to jar Tracie too much as he gently set her, travois and all, on cushions Marlee removed from the second set of seats and threw on the floor of the Arrow.

They worked well as a team. Wylie used bungee cords to tie the travois poles to the seat posts for better stability. Marlee tucked pillows between the girl and the posts. "That travois makes a great litter," she said as she buckled in Jo Beth. "I'll make sure I get it back from the ambulance crew. I'll return it when your back order comes in."

"Or drop it off any time you fly up north. Hunting season starts next week. Mick often flew hunters out from town."

"Oh, so you need it ASAP?" She shut Jo Beth's door and rechecked to see that the cargo hold was locked before darting a glance at Wylie.

"I don't know that I'll have call to use it again this season. But…uh…it'd give us a chance… Well, you know, it'll give the *kids* a chance to play together again."

He wouldn't look directly at her, and Marlee noticed that he tugged nervously on an earlobe. Could he actually want to see *her* again? She'd have to give that some thought later on. "Okay, we'll see. Listen, I'd better take off. The clouds have set down on the mountain again. I don't want to get caught in a squall if I can avoid it."

"Sure. Dean and I need to unsaddle and dry off the horses…and I have to move this turbine out of the weather. But will you let me know the doc's verdict on Tracie? I need the info to complete my report," he rushed to say. "I could phone the ward, but this is faster. Plus…I'll know you arrived safe and sound."

"Aw, you care." Marlee couldn't resist teasing him as she climbed in the Arrow. She expected a swift denial, or at least figured he'd point out that safe delivery of Tracie Ledbetter was part of his job. He hesitated, then right before closing her door, said what sounded like, "Hell, yes, I care!"

Marlee was shocked. She would've opened the door and demanded a repeat to prove she'd heard him correctly. But he didn't hang around.

She fumbled to start the plane, unable to keep from watching his muscles strain as he shoved the heavy turbine off the runway. Dean, who still held the reins to the horses and mule, tipped his head back to follow her liftoff. Wylie didn't turn.

In two visits he'd gone from gruff and unwelcoming, to grudgingly tolerant, to all but admitting he'd like to see her again.

"Mama, why are you smiling?" Jo Beth spoke into her headset, startling Marlee.

"I always smile after a successful liftoff."

"Oh. Mama, is Tracie for sure not gonna die?"

Jo Beth's pinched face drove Wylie from Marlee's thoughts. Her daughter had such a soft heart. And she'd been traumatized watching her dad's health decline. Marlee worried once again that perhaps she was wrong to involve Jo Beth in Angel Fleet's rescue missions.

Except, it was Wylie who'd involved them today. But had she not wanted to stay for lunch, he would've made a different decision when the call came in. Another pilot among Angel Fleet's volunteers might have been given Wylie's request. Mick said there were a number of rancher-pilots on the list. *She could remove Cloud Chasers' name.*

"Sweetie, does it bother you for Mama to do Angel rescues? We don't have to do it."

"I like us being angels, Mama. Dean says we do 'portant work."

"Yes, but the work will get done with or without us, honey."

Jo Beth rocked in her seat. She peered out the side window, then out front, then stretched so that she could see out her mom's side, too. "How come aren't there ever any other angel planes in the sky?"

The plane hit an air pocket and dropped. Tracie cried out so loudly they heard her through their headsets and above the throb of the engine. As she'd done with Gordon Maclean, Jo Beth wiggled around in her harness, reached back and touched their patient. "It's okay, Tracie," Marlee heard Jo Beth murmur. "Me 'n Mama are angels. We take hurt people to the hospital, and they get well fast."

Having spent an hour reading Angel Fleet's rules and mission statement, Marlee thought Jo Beth's explanation cut to the heart of what they did: offer transportation to those who might well die without the service. Taking part in such a team was rewarding.

The Arrow flew into a wall of angry clouds. She wasn't so familiar with the Arrow's quirks that she felt comfortable trying to get above it. Edging the wheel forward, Marlee dropped lower and listened carefully to the whine of the Lycoming engine. Feeling the thrust of its 200 horsepower reminded her of trailing Wylie today, astraddle his sorrel mare.

Already she'd begun having twinges along the insides of both legs. Unbidden, another vision crowded into her freewheeling mind. Of another sport that would result in the same sort of twinges. A sport Marlee hadn't engaged in for a very long time. Shortly after Cole was diagnosed, they'd attempted to have a normal sex life. Even in those early days of chemo, they managed to be creative. Finally he got so weak it frustrated him too much to fail.

The sadness that always accompanied such memories, descended now. Outside clouds swirled in one direction then another.

Marlee's mind meandered with the wispy white mist until rain began to batter her windshield. The onset of gusty winds demanded extreme concentration to hold the light plane on course.

All well and good. Replaying parts of her life that were lost served no purpose. And imagining herself involved with Wylie Ames—which had less chance of happening than she had of sprouting wings. Unless today indicated a change in his attitude.

All at once the instrument panel indicated that she was within radio range of the airpark. She couldn't be happier, since lightning cracked a foot from her propeller. It broke up her request for landing instructions.

Steadily dropping, Marlee soon flew out from under the worst of the storm. She sighed the minute her wheels touched down. Her voice steady and calm, she radioed for medical transport for Tracie

Again Angel Fleet had prepared the way. An ambulance sat just off the runway.

The ambulance crew could transfer Tracie without her help. She'd collect Wylie's travois, refuel, then she and Jo Beth would head on home.

But, Marlee discovered that Tracie had blacked out again. And this ambulance team wasn't as competent as the one that had transported Gordon Maclean.

"Mama, are we going to get that big car like last time and follow Tracie?"

Glancing up from stowing down Wylie's travois in the plane, Marlee shook her head. "Sweetie, it's way later now than I told Stella we'd be."

Jo Beth's lower lip quivered. "But…we hafta make sure Tracie's okay. You promised Dean's daddy we would. 'Sides, I wanna know if Uncle Mick's doctor said he can come home tomorrow. 'Cause that'll mean we can pick out my dog."

It wasn't always easy following her daughter's train of thought. Although Marlee had told Wylie she'd get the information on Tracie for his report.

"We'll go on one condition, Jo Beth. I'll phone to make sure Stella can stay with Pappy. If she says yes, we'll drive to town. If she has other plans then we need to go home and be with Pappy Jack."

"Why does he get babysitted? He's grown-up."

Marlee shut the cargo door, and paused in the act of digging out her cell phone. "It's not babysitting. Sometimes older people become forgetful, or mix up the past with the present. It's a bit like reverting to childhood."

Marlee left Jo Beth looking puzzled. She dialed the house and was relieved when Pappy answered, sounding chipper. "I'm in Kalispell. Are you and Stella managing well enough for Jo Beth and me to take the time to visit Mick?"

"We're fine, 'cept the blasted woman's whipped my fanny at checkers. You go on and see Mick. I'm gonna try and convince Stella to play strip poker."

"Pappy…you're kidding, I hope?"

He laughed wickedly, but Marlee heard Stella put him in his place. She hung up feeling better, and left instructions in the airpark office to have the Arrow refueled while they were gone.

Her first trip to the hospital, when Mick had checked in, had stirred up a flood of old emotions. The medicinal, antiseptic scents, such a part of the hospital landscape, always clutched at her stomach and left her queasy.

The receptionist recognized Marlee. "Angel Fleet has had you busy, Ms. Stein. Sometimes we go months without seeing their volunteers. Other times, like now, rescue missions come in batches."

"I hope this is the last one. I know Tracie Ledbetter's parents planned to beat us here. The ranger for the region where the boating accident occurred asked if I'd get particulars on her condition. Is she in emergency?"

The receptionist directed Marlee to the emergency room. Her inquiry sent a nurse scurrying toward a set of pulled curtains. An older version of Tracie emerged, red-eyed but with a smile for Marlee. "I'm Allison Ledbetter. We can't thank you enough. The doctor tells us Tracie has a depressed skull fracture, but said because you got her here so fast, she'll only require a single burr hole to relieve pressure from the fluid. While she's under anesthetic, an orthopedic specialist's going to set the bone in her leg." Alison Ledbetter choked up, with a helpless gesture toward Tracie's examining room.

Marlee clasped the woman's hand. "Tracie's been a trouper. I'm glad I could be of service. And I'll update Ranger Ames. We're glad the other kids were able to walk away."

"So are we. Dave, Tracie's boyfriend, has called twenty times to apologize. The four of them hike and boat in that area often. My husband says it's one of those rare things that can happen anytime, even to experienced outdoors men."

"I think someone's trying to get your attention, Mrs. Ledbetter. Maybe they're ready to move Tracie. If I may, I'll phone tomorrow and see how she is."

"Please do. Oh, and my husband is features editor for a weekly newspaper. He's planning to write an article about the marvelous work of Angel Fleet. I'm sure he'll want to interview you."

Marlee flushed. "I'd rather he talked with their office staff. I'm only flying medical missions until my brother's back on his feet. In fact, he's upstairs recovering from hip surgery. Say, if your husband wants an interesting interview, have him hunt up Mick Callen. He's a war hero who came home to take over the family freight-flying business. Mick recognizes the need for medical flights into Montana's wilderness, which is why he volunteers time and equipment to Angel Fleet."

"Mama, you said we're angels, too."

"This is my best helper." Marlee slid an arm around her daughter's shoulders. "I think she'd make a fine nurse. Jo Beth comforts the people I fly out."

"You're all angels in my book." Mrs. Ledbetter gave Marlee an impromptu hug before hurrying to catch up with her husband, who'd been talking to his daughter's doctor.

Marlee and Jo Beth remained where they were until the orderly turned the corner with Tracie's gurney. "We did good, huh, Mama?" Jo Beth murmured, slipping her hand into her mother's.

"You bet," Marlee replied happily, savoring the shared moment. "Hey, let's go surprise Uncle Mick."

Jo Beth skipped to the elevator. "*Can* I be a nurse, Mama? When I told Grandmother Rose that's what I wanted to be, she said it's a 'pressing job, and I shouldn't be that, or go in the navy, either. She said I should get married and be a mom."

Marlee stopped and punched the elevator button—hard—several times in succession. "Jo Beth, sweetheart, you can *be* anything you want to be."

The door slid open. They got in. Marlee watched the door shut, all the while thinking Rose Stein had some nerve. Especially as Marlee would've liked nothing better than to stay home to nurse Cole and be a full-time mom. Rose had been instrumental in convincing her son that Marlee needed to ship out for a second tour of duty.

Water over the dam. They'd all had to make difficult choices.

Emerging on Mick's floor, Marlee saw the nurse, Tammy Skidmore, pushing a cart loaded with medicine cups. She waved.

"If you're here to see Mick," Tammy said, "you'll have to wait a minute. The doctor just removed one set of clamp sutures, and Lou's in there redressing his wound. When they come out, you can see Mick. I warn you, though, he's grumpy as a bear."

"Bears aren't grumpy. My friend Dean helped heal one. His name's Boxer, and he smiles when Dean brings him ants and berries and water."

Tammy grinned. "You think we ought to give your Uncle Mick ants and berries to improve his disposition?"

Jo Beth giggled.

Marlee interrupted. "I thought Mick would be feeling good, Tammy. He said this morning he thought he'd get to come home tomorrow. No?"

"I'll let him explain the terms attached to going home."

Knowing better than to try to pump Tammy, based on her experiences trying to get information out of Cole's nurses, Marlee led Jo Beth to the waiting room. She sat where she could see Mick's door. Jo Beth spotted a plastic bin filled with toys and headed straight toward it.

Marlee's cell phone vibrated. "Hello," she said in a whisper, because she should've shut it off as all the signs tacked around the hospital said.

"It's raining pitchforks and hammer handles. Why in hell didn't you call and let me know you'd landed? I assume you *have* landed."

"Hello to you, too, Wylie. We're at the hospital waiting to see Mick. Listen, can I call you back on the waiting room phone?"

"Uh, sure. Sorry." He rattled off his cell number.

She called immediately, and Wylie asked, "How's Tracie?"

"On her way to surgery. That knock on the head fractured her skull. A buildup of fluid in that section of her brain is why she was unconscious for so long."

"In that case I'm very glad you came along on my call-out today. I know you had reservations."

"I did." Casting a furtive glance at her daughter, Marlee turned aside and lowered her voice. "You heard how Jo Beth worried about Tracie. I started thinking, what if someone dies on my plane? Gordon or Tracie might have."

"It'd be hard on Jo Beth. But what about you?"

"What about me?"

"You sounded plenty shaken when I phoned after Gordy's accident. And today you'd rather have been anywhere else than at that rescue."

"Yes, but I can reason through my anxiety. Jo Beth is five going on six."

"Dean's just a few years older. He takes it in stride."

"You've probably always taken him on your accident calls."

"It probably wouldn't be my choice," he admitted.

The door to Mick's room opened, and Marlee heard her brother's voice mingle with that of another man. "Wylie, I need to go. Mick's doctor is just leaving his room. I'd like to catch him. I thought he was releasing Mick, but now I'm not sure."

"I hope so for his sake. Speaking of release, I'm going to turn

Boxer out in about a week. Dean said he invited Jo Beth to take part. Can you hop on up? Morning's best."

"Jo Beth really would love to see that. At the moment I don't see why we couldn't come. There's always a chance of a delivery interfering, so I'd rather Dean didn't say anything to Jo Beth if they talk between now and then. Wylie, Mick's doctor got away, but I really must go see my brother."

"Tell Mick hello. And I'll impress on Dean the need for discretion. That may not be easy. I'm sure you've noticed what a motormouth he is."

Marlee found herself smiling. "Are you sure he's your son?" Silence.

Marlee thought they'd been cut off until Wylie returned, sounding impatient. "Don't let me keep you." This time the line definitely went dead in her ear. She frowned as she set down the receiver. Just when she thought they'd gotten over a hurdle, he'd turned stony again.

"Jo Beth! Time to go see Uncle Mick." Marlee made sure the girl had heard her, but didn't wait. She charged on ahead into Mick's room.

His eyes were closed and his sun-bleached hair looked spiky against the white pillow. But it was the tight set of his lips and new lines creasing his cheeks that she noticed. "Hey, twin," she called quietly in case he'd fallen asleep—although a moment ago she'd heard his raised voice.

Mick's eyelids opened slightly. When he saw who'd come in, he yanked his arms from behind his head and struggled to raise himself up on his good side. That was when Marlee knew why the lines were carved deep. He tried, but he couldn't mask his reaction to the pain.

She approached the bed, touching his ankle. "Lie back, Mick. Jo Beth and I can only stay a minute. Tammy said the doctor was just here removing surgical clips. Not fun, huh?"

Mick fell back against his pillow. "This surgery was rougher than my last few. I know I said I'd bounce right back, but…" He scrubbed a hand over his face. "How's it going at home with the business, with Pap and everything?"

"Fine. Good. Everything's A-1, Mick. What did the doc say? I'm guessing he's not going to let you come home tomorrow?"

Jo Beth skipped into the room. "Oh, no! Then that means I can't get a dog."

"Hold on. He never said I can't go home. It's…well, Doc claims I need specialized physical therapy. Three days a week. He's arranged for me to go to the veterans' PT unit…in Missoula," he added with a scowl.

Her fingers tightened on his ankle. "For how long?"

"Six weeks. During our busiest season. Pappy said he took three calls today. Hunters, all repeat customers requesting flights north to lodges."

"Your health takes priority, Mick. Six weeks is nothing. Missoula's a hop, skip and a jump. We used to fly there on weekends just because you wanted to see the university football games."

"I won't turn away customers. Do you have any idea how hard I worked to win them back after Pappy forgot he scheduled them for pickup or delivery?"

"We'll work it out, Mick. Isn't that what you said Angel Fleet does when they have a patient who needs a series of treatments? They book the treatments around a volunteer pilot's availability."

"You've never worked with a Vet Hospital. We're talking government bureaucracy."

"How about going to a private sports medicine clinic?"

"Sure, if I want to shell out big bucks," he said, rolling his eyes.

"Mick, we never talked about my partnership in Cloud Chasers. I have some savings, and Cole's insurance is invested in mutual funds. I'd like to hold the principal for Jo Beth's college, but I'll use the interest."

"I can't let you do that!"

"You can," she said stubbornly. "I insist."

Jo Beth leaned her elbows on the bed. "Uncle Mick, when Mama says she 'sists, you better do what she says."

Mick's features relaxed for the first time since Marlee had entered his room. He ruffled his niece's curls. "I should've remembered that about your mother, squirt." Shifting his grin to his sister, he said, "Okay, we'll do it your way if you can work out a flexible therapy schedule and keep up with family, home and business."

"I am woman!" She yodeled off-key and beat her chest, reminiscent of the way she used to when they were kids.

"Yeah, yeah." The mischief in his eyes instantly cascaded into a deeper emotion of the type Mick Callen rarely showed. "Uh…thanks, sis. I had a feeling I knew what I was doing when I twisted your arm to get you to come home. Since that's settled…I can blow this joint any time tomorrow afternoon."

Jo Beth danced away from the bed. "Yippie! Pappy Jack will be 'cited, too!"

Marlee tried to nix the dog plan to no avail. Mick and Jo Beth drowned her out, and went right on discussing what each had in mind for a pet. Giving up, Marlee snatched a phone pad off Mick's nightstand. She jotted down things dogs needed, like a collar, leash, food, bowls and a bed. By the time they hugged Mick goodbye, she'd accepted the reality they'd be dealing with training a dog.

"Mama, when we get home I want to call Dean and Grandmother Rose and tell them I'm getting a dog tomorrow."

The reference to Dean brought to mind his father's earlier abrupt dismissal. "Jo Beth, I suggest waiting until you actually have a dog to spread the news. Anyway, I really need to make some business calls tonight. While I'm tied up, you and Pappy can look over that dog book Uncle Mick said he has. But you shouldn't get your heart set on having a particular kind. Not until the shelter shows us what dogs are available for adoption."

Marlee steeled herself for an argument, if not another tantrum. Jo Beth merely bobbed her head. And that was the end of it. *Maybe the psychologist was right when she said that in time Jo Beth would settle down.*

From the airpark they flew home through thick clouds that threatened rain, but didn't spill a drop. While she'd previously parked the Arrow on the runway, this time she taxied beneath the canopy.

"Why did you park the plane in the garage?" Jo Beth asked as they got out.

"They call these light planes because they're not made out of very sturdy material. I want the wings covered in case we get snow."

"Why does the sky get so icky in Montana?"

"The seasons are more pronounced here than in San Diego. I just realized you've never seen snow, Jo Beth." Marlee, surprised she hadn't thought of it until now, made the remark as they entered the house.

Pappy roused from his chair by the fire. "Snow? Is that what it's doing?"

"No. I was telling Jo Beth it won't be long. In fact, she and I don't have a winter wardrobe. That's something else I need to put on my list." She took a sheet from her pocket.

Stella gathered up her knitting. "I'll go now," she said. Pappy walked her to the door. On his return, he passed her a stack of messages. "Five requests from hunters. Some are bound for the same lodge. That's good."

"Hey, I remember this Chinese checkers set. You taught Mick and me to play when we were Jo Beth's age, Pappy." Marlee traced a finger over the worn board.

"If that's a hint to teach the girl, I reckon now's as good a time as any. You need to go out to the office and get the schedule planner and call those fellows back before they get antsy and go to a competitor. Mick won't let me make appointments. He's probably right to think I might screw things up," he added with regret in his voice.

Marlee flung her arms around the old man's neck. "You took down their phone numbers, Pappy. That's important. Mick's darned answering machine is so scratchy, it's almost impossible to hear anyone." Delighted to find her grandfather lucid today, Marlee took another minute to catch him up on Mick's condition and the plans they'd made for the next day.

"I said he'd need therapy on that fake hip. Danged kid let the problem go too long. His doc wanted to do surgery last year. Well, nothing to be done now except follow doctor's orders. Say, I hear you flew another rescue today."

"How'd you hear that?" Marlee paused at the door, a scarf half over her head.

"One of those calls is from Don Morrison. He located a pump part Wylie Ames ordered. Don talked to Wylie right after you left with the injured girl. She okay?"

"I need to check on her again. You're sure Don spoke to Wylie after I left the ranger station? I called him from the hospital. He never mentioned a delivery."

"Dunno. You've got enough to do without his business. You already know my feelings on the subject of you making so many stops at Ames's station."

"Pappy, Wylie takes his job as ranger seriously. Really, he's a nice man."

"Ha, he offer to sell you a piece of swampland?"

Marlee didn't think that comment of Pappy's even rated a comeback. But as she crossed the breezeway to the office, she wondered why Wylie had neglected to mention Don's call. Perhaps he assumed she'd bring his order if she and Jo Beth could figure out the timing to see him release Boxer. On the other hand, she'd more or less indicated that work came first. So, if he had a job for her, wouldn't he think it'd ensure that she stop by?

Between calls she continued to puzzle. Had she said something to annoy Wylie? Marlee racked her brain. She'd been rushed, and worried about Mick. Wylie hadn't seemed upset when she asked him not to let Dean tell Jo Beth in advance about releasing Boxer.

When she scheduled customers, Marlee left the mornings open. She told herself she did it so as not to disappoint the kids, and refused to dwell on her own desire to see Wylie and straighten out any misunderstandings.

But her heartbeat quickened at the prospect of seeing him again so soon.

CHAPTER EIGHT

A STEADY DOWNPOUR didn't dampen the spirits of the trio slated to fly into Kalispell to spring Mick from the hospital. Marlee rolled out the twin-engine Seneca. It offered a smoother ride in iffy weather, and had more room inside than the Arrow.

She welcomed this trial run in the larger plane. Tomorrow she was scheduled to ferry a group to a former mining camp deep in Scapegoat Canyon. It was now called Hidden Fern Lodge. An investor had converted the old camp into a posh hunters' resort. Five men from Kalispell, a group of doctors and dentists, had hired Cloud Chasers to deliver them, and also fly them home a week later. Paul Tabor, the doctor who'd reserved the plane, assured Marlee the lodge had a honey of a landing strip capable of handling corporate aircraft. That booking put Cloud Chasers in the black.

Excited to show Mick what it had done for their bank account, she landed and drove to the hospital. First, though, she sent Pappy up to Mick's room, and she and Jo Beth dropped in on Tracie Ledbetter.

The girl's head was swathed in bandages, but she greeted them with a smile. Her room was filled with flowers. "Hey, my littlest angel," she said, high-fiving Jo Beth. "You're both awesome. The ranger and his son, too. If you see them, hug them both for me. The neurosurgeon said I'm lucky you acted so fast."

"It's good to see you looking well. I'll pass the word on to

Wylie and Dean. We can't stay long. My brother had surgery and he's going home today. We're here to pick him up."

"And after we get him," Jo Beth announced, "We're getting a dog."

Tracie smiled. "I have a dog and a cat. If all goes well, in a day or two I'll be home with them."

Marlee took Jo Beth's hand. "Good to hear, Tracie. No more canoes," she joked as they waved and left the room.

Mick met them at the elevator. Tammy was pushing his wheel-chair. "There you guys are. Can you tell I'm anxious to get out of here? Pappy said you went to see the Ledbetter girl. Her dad came to talk to me last night. He's writing a feature about Angel Fleet. You and Wylie impressed the right people, which is excel-lent. Angel Fleet depends on contributions to pay an office staff."

She listened, and chatted with Tammy about flying the mercy flights while Mick signed insurance papers in the business office.

Marlee left then and brought the Caddy around. They all got hugs from Tammy, who told Mick, "I'll miss you, big guy. Mind your therapist, okay?"

His sister nudged Mick meaningfully as they drove off.

"Let's just go get the dog. I can't date someone who's seen me at my worst."

"You mean naked?" Pappy said, reaching up to pop Mick lightly on the back of his head.

"Watch the X-rated talk, you two." Marlee raised an eyebrow.

Pappy sank back in his seat.

"That first road on your right is the one we want to go to the animal shelter," Mick said.

Two minutes later, Marlee groused, "No one said it was gravel. I think we should turn around and forget the dog. This bumping around can't be good for Mick."

"I'm fine." Even as he made the claim he clutched his hip as she hit a chuckhole. "It's not much farther."

Pappy said, "We promised the girl a dog, and a dog she'll get."

Once they reached the shelter, Marlee was even more miffed at Pappy. He convinced Mick he'd be okay using his walker to hike the shelter grounds while they shopped for the perfect mutt. But they insisted on inspecting every dog in the place before choosing one. The part yellow Lab, part American White Shepherd they picked had big feet and floppy ears. The attendant's records showed he was ten months old.

"After you pay," Marlee grumbled, "it'll still take a side trip to buy all the accessories on my list."

Actually it required more than one side trip. They stopped at three pet stores before everyone was pleased with their purchases.

The afternoon waned, and the strain of the extra hours in the car showed on Mick.

"Mama, can my dog sit on my lap on the flight home?" Jo Beth seemed oblivious to the fact that she and Pappy were literally crammed into the Caddy's generous backseat, squished between a wire mesh travel cage and the dog—a far larger dog than Marlee had fixed in her mind. She and Mick had discussed a nice terrier. A *small* dog.

"Absolutely not, Jo Beth. First, he's too big for your lap. Second, he goes in his cage because it's safer for him. Can't have him tossed around the cabin if we hit turbulence. Looking at that sky I'd say we'll be lucky if we don't have a downpour before we get off the ground."

"I think you'd better pull over, Marlee," Pappy said urgently. "This dog's gotta pee, and since that's the part of him draped over my lap, I vote we stop *now!*"

Exasperated over yet another delay, Marlee let up on the gas slowly. "It's only a mile to the airpark. Pappy, you and Jo Beth can snap on his leash and take him for a turn around the parking lot while I settle Mick in the plane and stow all the junk we bought. The doggy paraphernalia," she added unnecessarily, slightly annoyed that she'd had to skip buying winter clothes for herself and Jo Beth.

"This late start isn't entirely our fault, Marlee. You're the one who stopped at two bookstores so you could buy the Ames kid a book on white-tailed deer. He's not even family," Pappy muttered. "And you ordered me to stay in the car the last time you and Jo Beth ran into the mall. Or else the dog could've done his business back there."

Accepting blame rather than arguing, Marlee spotted a rest stop ahead. She eased the big car off the highway, jumped out and yanked open the back door. "Give me his leash."

Pappy snapped the new leash onto an equally new collar and passed it to Marlee. "Too bad you got your mother's temper, instead of your dad's and my sunny disposition, girl."

Hearing Mick snort, Marlee might've expounded on what she thought about the subject of the Callen temper, except that the - dog shot out of the car nearly tearing her arm from its socket. The two things in favor of this dog: he'd been neutered and was housebroken. The major drawback—he was big as a moose, she thought as she grunted and pushed, trying to stuff him back into the car after he'd peed a bucketful. He'd done it close enough to the back door that she was forced to straddle the puddle.

Thinking she probably looked as if she'd gone ten rounds with Rocky Balboa, she slid behind the wheel and scraped wind-tossed hair out of her eyes. "May I again remind you all that I have a substantial flight to make in the morning? What'll you do if what'shisname knocks Mick off his feet, or he gets away from Pappy Jack? It goes without saying that dog is too much for Jo Beth to handle."

"What *is* his name?" Mick asked, twisting so he could eye his niece, who'd thrown both arms around the dog's neck. Pappy was half-hidden by the animal's wiggling backside.

"Can we worry about naming him later?" Marlee turned into the parking lot at the airpark and backed the Cadillac into its numbered space. "Those clouds look more ominous by the minute. Let's load up before the skys open and dump all over us. Frankly, I'm not keen on the idea of smelling wet dog all the way home."

The others did their best to comply. Mick attempted twice to get out of the car and ended up falling back each time, smothering a curse.

Marlee handed Jo Beth the keys to the plane. She waved girl, dog and Pappy Jack off before she stopped to help her brother. "Mick, if you're not able to put any weight on your bad hip, how can you climb into the plane?"

"I didn't do a million chin-ups in my military career for no gain," he said grimly. "I'll grab the sides of the door and swing up using the strength in my arms."

Marlee had her doubts. And it hurt to see what it cost Mick to accomplish that feat. He sank into the copilot's seat, but not before plenty of sweat beaded his forehead, and pain dulled his normally sparkling eyes.

Loading the dog proved the most difficult. After several failed attempts, Marlee said, "Pappy, you climb in and station yourself at one side of the door. Jo Beth, you get on the other. You both pull, and don't let go of his collar. I'll lift his back end and shove."

The dog balked.

"Move his kennel. I think he doesn't like seeing it open."

That trick worked, but it'd taken so long, the storm Marlee was expecting broke directly overhead, and struck with a vengeance. She gave a last hefty push on the dog's rump, then slammed and locked the door. Rain smacked the tarmac and bounced up, soaking her from both directions. Hunching, she swore silently over a ruined linen jacket.

Finally aboard, she shook off her frustration until she saw that the dog hadn't been penned. He made his objections clear with a series of sharp barks followed by mournful howls, all rebounding off the thinly insulated cabin walls, threatening to deafen everyone on the plane.

"Cage that animal now!"

"Mama, he sees the cage and probably thinks you're going to take him back to the shelter."

Marlee gnashed her teeth. "He will go back if you don't have him corralled by the time I warm up the engines. I mean it, Jo Beth. You, too, Pappy!"

"Gee, this is fun." Mick said loudly, and smirked.

Marlee dealt him a dirty look and fired up the turbocharged engines.

The dog let out a surprised yelp, dropped to his belly and slunk into the cage. Pappy quickly shut and locked the wire gate.

"Well, whaddya know?" The old man sank into his seat, and strapped himself in. "They don't call this two-twenty piston engine the double dragon for nothing. Hey, there's your dog's name."

Jo Beth wrinkled her nose. "You want to name him Dragon?"

Pappy chortled. "Piston. A piston is the driving force that makes an engine turn over. He's a driving force, wouldn't you say, girl?"

In the absence of any objection, Pappy's suggestion stuck, and the big lummox had a name.

It took an hour to make the forty-minute flight. Marlee landed at their compound in a gully washer. Feeling the wheels hydroplane in six inches of standing water on the slick runway, she corrected the bounce and counted herself fortunate that Mick had fallen asleep. He roused, though, as the whine of the engines wound down.

"Holy catfish, how did we get home so fast?"

"Fast? I'm assuming the pill Nurse Tammy made you take finally kicked in, Rip Van Winkle. Pappy, Jo Beth, stay and keep Piston locked up until I help Mick out. A lot of water has pooled on the ground. I suspect he'll be unsteady even with the aid of a walker."

"Mama, I want to phone Dean and tell him about Piston. May I?"

The mention of Dean reminded Marlee that Wylie still hadn't

contacted her about picking up his order at Morrison's. "Let me settle Uncle Mick first. You can phone Dean while I see what there is to fix for supper."

"And Grandmother Rose? I want to call her, too."

"It hasn't even been two days since she phoned you. But, hon, she's probably not going to be as excited as Dean to hear all about your new dog."

Much to Marlee's surprise, Jo Beth agreed. Not for the first time, she thought that this move home was the right choice.

Mick hadn't wanted to lie down in his bedroom. Yet, two seconds after he sat on the flowered leather couch, Marlee caught him fast asleep. She covered him with a knitted afghan that belonged to Jo Beth. It was one of numerous such projects Rose had knit over the span of her son's illness. Her mother-in-law's ability to concentrate on something that intricate had always astonished Marlee. She often found herself rereading the same paragraph of a novel five or six times, until she just gave up.

Rose had her good points, she reminded herself as she unloaded the plane. Once she'd found a place for everything, Marlee retrieved Dean's number on her cell as promised and passed the phone to Jo Beth.

Hurrying into the kitchen, Marlee assembled ingredients for a green salad. She tried not to cock an ear toward where Jo Beth chatted happily away with Dean. Marlee expected the boy's dad to ask to speak to her. And she didn't hide her disappointment when Jo Beth brought back the phone and said, "Dean had to go feed the animals. He thinks it's cool that I have a dog. Mama, shouldn't you feed Piston?"

"Your chore, my love." Marlee put the salad in the fridge. "I put the sack of dog food and his bowls in the laundry room, along with his dog bed."

"I want his bed in our room, Mama."

"Okay," she said with only a slight hesitation, despite knowing she'd be the one to get up in the night if the dog needed to go out. "The pet store clerk said give him three scoops of dry food in one bowl and fill the other with water. Jo Beth, hon, did Dean happen to mention if his dad's parts order needed delivering tomorrow?"

"Nope." The girl skipped off with the dog at her heels.

Not knowing whether Wylie was angry got to be too much for Marlee. She put pork chops on to grill, looked up his cell number again, and called. The timbre of his voice made her feel a surge of desire every time she heard it.

"It's Marlee," she said, shaking back her hair. "I know Jo Beth just hung up from talking to Dean. I knew he wouldn't say anything about us coming to watch you turn out Boxer, but according to Mick, you have a back order at Don's. I assume you want it?"

There was silence, even though Marlee was sure she hadn't lost Wylie. "I, ah, am picking up some hunters in Kalispell tomorrow. It wouldn't be any trouble to stop at your place after I drop the men at Hidden Fern Lodge. Or…I can bring your order Friday."

The absence of a response dragged on for so long it embarrassed Marlee. Wanting to end the awkwardness, she finally said, "Wylie, if you've made other arrangements, say so. I know Mick will be sorry to lose your business, but you don't have an exclusive contract with Cloud Chasers." She hoped she sounded businesslike. Inside she shriveled and her stomach knotted. But she'd be darned if she'd grovel, particularly when she had no idea what she'd done to invite his prickly silence.

"I haven't made other arrangements."

Just that, no more. An idiot could hear the reticence in his tone. Marlee tended to be direct, and she hated having to tread lightly, or guess whether or not she'd put her foot in her mouth. "If I've crossed some invisible line, please tell me. I'm dealing with a lot here. Learning to handle Mick's planes, his surgery and Pappy's failing health to name a few." All at once something dawned. "Wait. Is this about the offhanded remark you made when you closed the Arrow's door the other day? Uh, where you sorta mumbled that you care…about me? Heavens, Wylie, I'm not going to jump you." She wanted to laugh, but was afraid to—in case he took that the wrong way, too.

"We should probably let this drop. I've been out of touch for too long."

"With what? People? With feelings?" This time Marlee did utter a strangled laugh. "We military types aren't the best at getting in touch with our inner selves, either. Since neither one of us is likely to win any award for social graces, shall we just get back to discussing your order?"

"It's a crankcase housing I ordered six or seven months ago. No big deal."

"You are such a…a…*man!* Just say yes, bring my stupid crankcase tomorrow, or say hold off and bring it Friday. My pork chops are burning."

"Tomorrow, dammit! I want to see you again," he muttered.

Marlee found herself holding a dead phone. She was aware she was also scowling, because Jo Beth and Piston loped into the room, stopped, and Jo Beth asked shyly, "Was that Grandmother Rose?"

"Ah, no, sweetheart. That call had to do with a delivery. Just let me turn these pork chops and I'll dial Grandmother's number. It's awfully quiet in the living room. Would you run and see how Pappy and Uncle Mick are doing?"

"They're okay. They're both making sleep music."

Marlee flipped two pork chops. "And what is sleep music?"

"That's what Daddy used to say when I woke him up to tell him he was making pig noises while he napped. He said, saying somebody makes pig noises isn't nice. It's kinder to say they're making sleep music."

Tucking the spatula under the next pork chop, Marlee felt tears in her eyes. She quickly turned the remaining chops, opened the phone again and hit speed dial for her former mother-in-law. She shouldn't envy the inside jokes Jo Beth or Rose had shared with Cole. But—damn, she'd missed so much. Little things a wife should be in on.

Hearing Rose's faint hello, Marlee reached out and pressed the instrument into Jo Beth's hand. She busied herself setting the table.

Maybe loss got easier over the years. Her most jealously guarded guilty secret was her resentment that she'd had so little time alone with Cole. It had been forever since she'd acted like a normal wife. If she ever fell in love again, Marlee planned to experience every stage of courtship, love and marriage. She wanted the fun of dating, the dawning blush of discovering new love, followed by a mutual exploration of body and soul—uninterrupted.

As if that would ever happen. Ready-made moms didn't get that luxury.

Meeting someone suitable and then finding time to date were big things. Living in the boonies didn't help. Marlee shook off whatever ailed her and forked the pork chops onto a platter. Bringing out the salad, she called, "Jo Beth, time for dinner. Tell Rose goodbye and go wash. I'll wake up the sleepyheads."

Mick shuffled into the kitchen. "The smell of food woke Pappy and me. He's gone down the hall. The kitchen sink is closer. Mind if I scrub up here?"

"Mick, it's your house."

"No, it's Pappy's." He bent over the walker and soaped his hands. "After dinner I need your delivery schedule, so I can pencil in my therapy appointments. The PT might give me exercises to do at home. That'd save making so many trips."

"I don't mind taking you. I'd rather you let a trained therapist oversee your program. I know you, buster. You'll overdo it."

"Nag, nag, nag." He dried his hands and sniffed the platter of meat. "On second thought I'll let you nag as long as you cook. I'd have died on that hospital food if it Tammy hadn't smuggled me in hamburgers and milk shakes."

Marlee had set a straight chair at the end of the breakfast nook. "Tammy seemed nice. And interested in you, Mick. Were you kidding about not dating her?"

"We exchanged phone numbers, but nothing will come of it."

"Isn't it time you got serious about finding someone special?"

"In Whitepine? Most people our age left years ago. Or they're divorced twice over. Anyway, women take more of an investment of time than I have to give."

"I thought you said you have almost all winter off."

"Have you forgotten what Montana winters are like? Besides, that's when I refurbish planes and catch up on my reading."

"I guessed it was you who'd built those ceiling-to-floor bookcases and filled them. You could start a winter bookmobile, Mick. You might meet a nice prospect that way."

"Marriage prospect, you mean?"

Pappy and Jo Beth came in and sat. "Who has a marriage prospect?" Pappy asked right before he stabbed a large pork chop he split with Jo Beth.

"No one." Marlee passed the salad and rolls she'd heated. "Mick's just confirming what I'd already guessed. The marriage pool in Whitepine isn't very big."

Pappy buttered his roll. "Mick's kinda sweet on a little gal at the smoke jumpers' camp."

"Really?" Marlee glanced up from slicing Jo Beth's meat. "You sly dog. Is it serious? Who is she, and when do I get to meet her?"

Mick turned red to the tips of his ears. "Pappy, you've got a big mouth. Hana Egan and I only ever talk about the books we've read. Anyway, smoke jumpers rarely stick around more than a couple of fire seasons before they move on."

Marlee was about to ask more about the smoke jumper, but Piston trotted up to the table and set his muzzle next to Jo Beth's plate. The girl started to share her meat, but Marlee grabbed the dog's collar. She hauled him to the laundry room and shut him inside. He started to howl and so did Jo Beth.

"No dogs at the table, young lady. Dry those tears and eat, or I'll reconsider letting Piston sleep in our room tonight." Marlee tensed, awaiting the kicking and screaming she'd come to expect.

Jo Beth blotted her wet eyes on her shirt, and tore off a piece of her roll. "Mama, I want to show Piston to Dean. He said the dog could come next time we fly up there."

Though surprised by her daughter's swift change in mood, Marlee didn't want to show it. "I'll have to okay that with Dean's dad," she said simply.

Pappy stopped eating and waved his fork at Marlee. "Mark my words. No good's gonna come of you encouraging those kids to get chummy. Joe Duff says..."

Marlee took another bite. It was Mick who cut off their grand-father. "Joe mishandled the early search for Wylie's wife," he said, referring to the former sherriff. "It wasn't Joe's first screwup, either. That's why he got booted out of office. He's bitter. If I were Wylie I'd sue Joe for defamation of character. God knows Joe made such a stink, his deputies dug up half of Wylie's garden. Even then, he's not the one who petitioned to get Joe fired."

"If you're so smart, what became of Mrs. Ames?" Pappy muttered.

Mick's eyes flashed in annoyance, but he clammed up.

What worried Marlee was how Jo Beth seemed to be absorbing everything, while quietly stuffing her mouth. "Wylie's wife, er, ex, I should say, lives in Florida."

"How do you know that?" Pappy demanded. Mick merely gaped.

"I asked him. Shirl, that's her name, sent him divorce papers a month after she took off. More important, he said, she signed over full custody of their son."

Mick clapped Pappy on the back. "Leave it to a woman to wade in where we men respected the guy's right to privacy."

"That's why the rumors got out of hand," Marlee snapped. "Wylie thinks he explained his situation to someone once, a cop, I assume, and it's settled."

"Or you're gullible," Pappy said, serving himself another pork chop.

"I'm not gullible. I'm just not too pansy-assed to be able to confront him."

"Ah, Mama, you said a bad word."

"I did, Jo Beth," Marlee said, after chewing her last forkful of salad. "And I'm not sorry. When you grow up you'll learn that sometimes men are so obtuse no other word fits." She rose and carried her plate to the sink. Glancing back, she saw Mick struggling to stand with his plate in hand, and she rushed to help him. "Honestly, Mick, ask for help why don't you, instead of hurting yourself."

"Because I'm an obtuse male," he said, pausing to kiss his startled sister on the top of her head. "Do you need me for anything else tonight? If not, I said I'd play a game of Chinese checkers with Pappy. Then I'm gonna crash."

Taking into account what they did for a living, added to the fact that Mick's crash had caused his current condition, Marlee considered it a poor choice of words. "I'm flying those hunters to their lodge tomorrow. Be sure to get your appointments on the calendar while I'm gone." She said nothing about her planned side trip to Wylie's. Pappy would fuss and Jo Beth would want to go along. "Stella's coming at seven to fix breakfast, and again at noon to make lunch. I want everyone to mind their manners and make sure nothing goes wrong."

"Same goes for you, sis. The runway at Hidden Fern Lodge is short and you take off over water. Give the Seneca plenty of fuel to clear the trees across the lake. I watched a small corporate jet take a dive because he carried too big a load." Mick shook his head in warning.

THAT NIGHT MARLEE DREAMED of Wylie, and of falling out of the sky. She distinctly saw him standing at the end of his runway, his face tipped up, his eyes anxious. He raised his arms as if to pluck her from a fall. Twice she jerked awake without ever feeling the comfort of his arms closing around her.

A third time she bolted upright, her breathing erratic. Piston, who'd flopped down between the twin beds got up, padded over, resting his soft muzzle on her bed, and whined. As her eyes adjusted to the darkness, Marlee saw that one of his ears stuck up, while the other flopped over an eye. She reached out and rubbed the velvety fur between his ears. "It's okay, boy. Since we're both awake, why don't I take you out?" As if he understood, he crossed to the door and waited for her to pull on a robe and slide into slippers.

The rain had ceased, but the trees still dripped. Great muddy puddles on the gravel pathways, which Marlee recalled Pappy and her father fashioning when she wasn't much older than Jo Beth. Gazing at the heavens, she gripped the front of her robe under her chin. She wondered if her parents, grandmother and Cole were up there watching out for those left behind. A cold wind blew across the porch. She shivered. "Piston. Come, boy."

The dog trotted obediently up, the tags on his collar clinking musically. Marlee knelt and used the towel she'd grabbed from the bathroom to dry his wet feet and body. He lifted first one paw then the other. Someone had trained him. Marlee was moved to hug the big mop of damp fur. "Okay, you won me over. I wanted a small dog, but I feel good placing Jo Beth, Mick and Pappy in your care tomorrow. Uh, today," she corrected, noticing that the eastern sky was shot through with threads of purple and salmon.

She led Piston back to the bedroom. He went straight over to check on Jo Beth. After a sniff or two, he sank down on the carpet next to her bed.

Marlee quietly gathered her clothes, turned off her alarm

clock and slipped into the shower. She came out, kissed Jo Beth and woke her long enough to say goodbye.

Her early-morning dream had faded by the time she taxied down the runway. Morning had always been her favorite time to fly. A pale sun peeked above the rim of snow-tipped mountains as she swooped down forty minutes later at the airpark in Kalispell.

Don Morrison's delivery crew knew her by sight. She left them loading and tying down Wylie's crankcase housing, then headed for the office where she'd arranged to meet the hunters. Their suitcases, duffel bags and rifles were stacked outside the building. Marlee breezed in. "Good morning, everyone. I'm your pilot from Cloud Chasers, Marlee, Mick Callen's sister. We'll be taking the Seneca parked on runway two. Go on and load your gear. I need to check for wind shears in the canyon region."

She'd expected city doctors and dentists to look sleepy at this hour. Surprisingly, all her passengers were alert and jovial.

"I've been flying with Mick for about four years. I do see a strong family resemblance. I noticed his name on the hospital surgery schedule, I hope he's getting along okay."

"Thanks for asking. He came home yesterday. You are...?"

"Sorry, Paul Tabor." He quickly introduced the other men in the group. They shook hands politely, then the men filed out.

The office attendant printed off the latest weather data. "A dramatic change from yesterday." He handed her the paper.

"Winds might still be dicey up in the alpine country." Marlee folded the sheet and tucked it in her pocket. "That's a beauty of a Cessna being refueled on runway one."

"Sure is. Belongs to a movie producer. He has a retreat that sits between the Clearwater and Swan Rivers. He's been up there a month and is headed home to a warmer place for the winter. Must be nice."

She grinned, removed her shades from where she'd tucked them in her hair and dropped them over her eyes. "To each his own. I haven't seen snow in forever, it seems. I'm looking forward to the white stuff. When's the first snowfall predicted?"

"Soon. A week or two at best. Outside of hunters and a few hearty souls who stick winters out, the hills are emptying now."

Marlee acknowledged the attendant with a lazy, nonmilitary salute. She was enjoying flying Mick's route more than she'd imagined she would. Too bad she hadn't wound up her business in San Diego earlier. By Mick's own admission, he rarely filled supply orders from November to March. So, she was lucky to get her flying fix now.

She ran a discerning eye over her passengers to make sure they were all strapped in. Probably because she was a woman, they held their breath from the start of taxiing to when she rose and leveled out. The flight to the lodge was no piece of cake. Crosswinds slammed the Seneca up, then down, then sideways. Several of her passengers reached for barf bags.

Marlee was determined to land without a ripple. And she did. She turned in her seat once she'd shut down the engines. "Sorry, guys. You'll find a larger plastic container by the door. Cloud Chasers doesn't guarantee the weather. There's no bargaining with Mother Nature." She offered a sympathetic downturn of her mouth.

Paul and his friends, Ben and Norm, sent the sicker guys on to the lodge. Marlee tied up the sack and walked it to the lodge Dumpster. "Need a hand?" she asked the three unloading luggage. They were weighed down with all the bags.

"We owe you a steak dinner for that smooth landing. I don't think some of our party could've stood up as well if we'd blown off the runway like last year."

"Not Mick?"

Paul shook his head. "He was tied up, so Ben commissioned a competitor. Never again. See you a week from today? Or will your brother be flying us home?"

"Me. He's got six weeks of physical therapy. You might say

he's getting a jump on winter break." Smiling, they all waved as she fastened the cargo hold.

Recalling Mick's warning, Marlee punched up her speed and immediately went into a sharp climb. She was aware of her audience below. The three men shaded their eyes and made no pretext of doing anything except watching her takeoff. Circling, she swooped back over the lake and executed a lazy loop. *Might as well give them a show.* Leveling out to a sedate flyover of the lodge, Marlee didn't know what had possessed her. She hoped none of the trio ever mentioned her high jinks to her brother.

She anticipated visiting Wylie, yet felt queasy at the prospect. On her other trips, Jo Beth had always been a buffer. Of course, Dean would be there, but… "Dang," she muttered as his runway came into view. She'd left the book on white-tailed deer she'd bought Dean on the counter next to the note she'd written Mick.

Had she been feeling nerves even then? Admittedly she was somewhat giddy. There were no two ways about it, Wylie Ames caused her stomach to flutter. He had from the beginning, although she'd refused to yield to the possibility. *Implausibility* Pappy would say, and for all she knew, Mick, too. Friends or not, Mick was the protective sort of brother.

But maybe nothing would happen today. Marlee almost had herself convinced. Then, as her wheels touched ground, Wylie stepped out from under the trees. He wore black boots, dark blue jeans and an open-throated white shirt with the sleeves carefully rolled up over thick forearms. He reminded her of an oak. Big. Sturdy.

Marlee's breath hitched. Her heart rose in her throat before tumbling to meet a jittery stomach. The die had been cast. They connected, all right.

"Oops!" She'd been so busy ogling Wylie she nearly sent the Seneca barreling through the shed at the end of his runway, which he'd told her housed his all-important generator. If she wiped out his alternate source of electricity, with winter so close, it'd most likely end any relationship before one started. *If one started.*

"No brakes?" he asked, the grooves in his cheeks deepening. He raised both hands, an invitation for Marlee to let him swing her down from the cockpit. She was blinded by the sharp memory of last night's dream. The sense of falling. It was too eerie. But obviously she wasn't dropping from heaven into his arms as had happened in her dream.

She shouldn't be so jittery, but she was. That must've been why she tripped and swan-dived out of the cockpit.

Wylie hadn't expected her grand exit. He grabbed her, but almost dropped her. "Whoa!" Adjusting his hands, he held her slightly below the waist. Her silk blouse pulled loose from her khaki slacks, and the skin beneath his fingers felt as satiny smooth as his summer bedsheets. Damn, he shouldn't think of bedsheets while he was touching Marlee. His mind was clear on that. But Wylie's fingers refused to stay still. Of their own accord they slid up and down.

Too much time elapsed. Too much time without words. Wylie knew it. And he still held her suspended in midair. Swallowing with difficulty, he started to swing her free of the wing in order to set her feet on the ground.

The sensation of being suspended had Marlee slinging her right arm around Wylie's neck for stability. The move anchored her to his wide chest. Supported now, she breathed normally. Or rather she did until she realized she was left gazing straight into his eyes, their faces separated by mere inches. Her lips less than a millimeter from Wylie's.

Neither spoke. Then Wylie said, "Wh…aat's happening?" His fingers stilled. His eyes traveled heatedly over Marlee's features as if memorizing each one.

"Nothing either of us went looking for," she admitted giddily.

"My stomach's doing a tap dance." Her fingers toyed with the lush dark hair curling over Wylie's collar.

Inside she shattered like glass. It'd been so long since she'd felt the texture of a man's hair....

"Is something wrong?" He loosened his grip and her legs began to slide down his body.

Feeling desperation and panic and need all clumped together, Marlee threw a second arm around his neck, locking her hands over her elbows to keep her in place. "Don't talk, please, Wylie. Don't ask questions. Not...yet," she said huskily. "Just...kiss me," she begged, a plea few men in their prime could refuse.

Wylie was in his prime. It had been so long since he'd held or kissed a woman who moved him to be masterful yet tender that he couldn't recall when the last time was.

And he didn't need a second invitation. Oh, he might've liked Marlee's eyes open instead of fluttering closed. But then their lips met and that didn't matter. Nothing mattered. Not the fact that he wasn't breathing, or that his muscles shook so badly he'd had to press her against the only solid item around to keep from falling down and rolling on the ground like a man possessed. His bulwark turned out to be a fork where the plane's wing met the metal skin of its body. The backs of his hands felt the steel.

Lord, she tasted sweet. She tasted hot. She tasted... Wylie's brain shut down right there. Accepting that it'd been a long drought, he slaked his thirst.

CHAPTER NINE

"DAAAD!" A STRIDENT, high-pitched cry was slow to penetrate Wylie's senses.

It might not have cut through at all if Marlee hadn't twisted her head and broken their frenzied kiss. "It—it's Dean," she stammered, pushing weakly on Wylie's chest. *Where was he?* "Wylie, I think he's in trouble. That sounds urgent."

Wylie released her and bolted, bumping her shoulder as he tore off down the runway. Oddly detached, Marlee gazed after him. The echo of his rapid footsteps attested to how quickly he'd managed to disengage himself from one activity and flee toward another. She needed longer to get a grip and lick the taste of Wylie Ames, the man, the bachelor, the potential lover, from her lips.

Using both hands, Marlee massaged the tight muscles of her neck. She slowly followed Wylie along the path that led to his house.

It was dark under the tree canopy. Marlee rubbed at the goose bumps suddenly chilling her arms. Had that been Jo Beth shouting, she'd be the one charging away like an avenging angel. That was the responsible Marlee Stein, just as the man who'd disappeared was the responsible Wylie Ames.

In a flash, Marlee returned to his first question, *"What's happening?"* She could've ended it all if she'd said, *"Nothing."* She could've drawn a hard line. Instead, she'd opened the door to possibility by saying, *"Nothing either of us went looking for."*

The stark truth—she'd done more than open the door. She'd... Blushing, Marlee recalled how bold she'd been. What would Wylie think once the dust settled? What would he think of her?

Where was he? Her steps quickened even as she considered returning to the Seneca to off-load the box containing his crankcase housing. But turning back would be a cowardly act. A roadblock thrown up to avoid facing the interest simmering between them.

Deciding to leave the freight for him to deal with, she straightened her blouse and went in search of Wylie and Dean. One thing her military reviews had always reflected about her—she wasn't a coward. And she faced facts. She'd wanted to kiss Wylie. Had wanted him to kiss her back.

Heaving a dramatic sigh, Marlee kicked fallen leaves and hesitated just beyond the big tree that held Dean's tire swing. Loud noises interrupted her musings. Birds squawking as if terrified. Squirrels chattering up in trees that hung over the path.

Sorting through the sounds, Marlee followed the path. A scream rent the air. Almost human, yet so wild, panic made the hair on the back of her neck stand up. *A mountain cat?*

Moving faster, she swept aside briars grabbing at her clothes. She'd heard a jaguar scream like that one time when her unit joined another to play war games on a jungle island. The jaguar later killed a villager.

But wait—she stopped. A limb swung back and struck her so hard she saw stars. What if the cat had gotten into Dean's animal pens? If Wylie and Dean needed help, her going with no weapon wasn't wise. In the distance, she heard Wylie shout, "Get back! Back!"

Marlee remembered seeing a gun cabinet in an alcove off his living room. It might be locked, but maybe not.

Retreating more rapidly, she burst into his house through the back door. Her heart hammered madly. Blood whooshed in her ears as she found the oak cabinet and clawed at the doors. *Locked!* With shaking hands she felt across the top for the key, and knocked one to the floor. Scrambling on her knees, she found it, rose, opened one door and selected a Winchester 94, a gun she knew was reliable. Comfortable with weapons, she threw the bolt and checked the chamber. Empty, as she would've imagined. Nerves still jangling, she yanked out first one drawer, then the other and was relieved to find boxes of shells neatly lined up. She grabbed a handful of those that fit the rifle and stuffed her pockets full.

Worry urging her to run, she left the house and plunged into the thicket, setting a more direct route. The cacophony of sounds reverberating through the trees hadn't abated. If anything, the ground shook and she heard limbs cracking. But maybe *she* was making the ground shake and her imagination had blown this all out of proportion.

Ducking smaller branches that impeded her progress along the nonexistent path, Marlee grew oblivious to everything except what lay ahead. It sounded as if all hell had broken loose. That kept her forging onward. "Wylie? Wylie?"

Fumbling out several shells, she filled the rifle's magazine. Moving toward a light ahead that had to be the clearing, she tripped over an obstacle in the middle of the path. Had she not flung her body sideways she'd have flattened Dean Ames, who huddled white-faced on his knees, out of sight of whatever was taking place beyond.

"Marlee!" The boy jumped up and flung his arms around her waist, and began to blubber, "Dad might be killed. I don't know what to do."

"Dean, honey! What happened?"

"A cougar. Dad's fight'n him with nothin' but a stick. I went to feed the mountain goat. I filled the bucket from the shed, unlocked his gate. I heard a snarl, turned, and there *he* was. His eyes were awful, and he slobbered and hissed. I kicked the feed bucket, ran and hollered and hollered for Dad." Shuddering sobs racked the boy's body.

"Listen, Dean, you have to let me go. I raided your father's gun cabinet. I've got a rifle. But you need to stay back," she said, prying him loose.

"Please don't shoot him. Please! We don't shoot animals. Dad has a tranquilizer gun."

She didn't realize Dean hadn't obeyed her until she stepped into the chaos near the pens, and all sixty plus pounds of him plowed into her back. The clearing told the story of how long man and cat had battled. Shrubs were flattened, some ripped up by their roots. Twigs and leaves were strewn all over. The resinous odor of pitch permeated the air from where the cat had swiped bark off the spindly pines. The mountain goat, blood running down his leg, huddled in a back corner of a cage now closed up.

Sweat stained Wylie's underarms, and a bloody gash lay exposed where ribbons of his sleeve trailed over the hand wielding a too-short stick.

The cat, a dull gold, lean animal was backed against the mesh wire of Boxer Bear's cage. It was driving the cub insane. The cat, as if sensing added danger from a second human, crouched. Ears flat, his mouth open, big paws swiped at the man attempting to drive him into a freestanding, steel-barred cage that sat adjacent to the bear's pen.

Marlee raised the rifle to her shoulder.

Dean screamed loudly this time, "Don't shoot!"

Wylie turned at the sound of his son's plea. And the cat lunged, shearing open his pant leg to his knee. From his curse, Marlee knew the cat had gotten a piece of Wylie, as well. Those two things combined caused her shot to go wide. Her bullet struck a tree above and to the right of the cougar. The crack, however, had the animal twisting in the air.

With Wylie distracted, the cougar sprang. It was pure luck, and Wylie's agility that saved the day. Shifting aside, his altered route drove the cat barreling into the cage. In spite of his own injuries, Wylie's reflexes remained sharp. He slammed the cage door shut. An automatic lock clicked in place, confining the snarling beast, who roared and banged against the bars.

"Dean, run and get the dart gun. Damn cat is going to tear himself apart trying to get out. I need to tranquilize him so we can move him up into the hills." Limping off quickly, Wylie unlocked a shed Marlee hadn't noticed before. Taking tongs off a hook, he removed a frozen hindquarter of meat, probably elk, from a chest freezer. He hauled it to the cage and shoved it through the bars.

The cat flopped down and attacked the raw, frozen meat with the same ferocity he'd displayed earlier against his human adversary. The forest instantly settled into silence.

Marlee sagged against the closest tree. Bullet casings spilled from her pockets.

"Are you okay?" Wylie asked hoarsely. He bent slowly as if in pain and scooped up the fallen shells.

"I suppose this—" she waved a hand at the trampled ground and the cougar "—is all in a day's work for you?"

"The animals were here before us, Marlee. The forest fires this region suffered last year burned out the cougar's normal hunting habitat. He's not the first cat to come down this low in search of food. He probably smelled the fresh rodents we've started giving the cub in advance of his release."

She straightened and with anger she couldn't explain, emptied the magazine into a still-trembling hand. "I'm not going to apologize for shooting. I thought you were about to be his next meal."

Wylie relieved her of the shells and stored them in his pocket with the others. Kissing her before she could pull away, he eased the gun out of her grasp. Propping it against a tree, he tilted Marlee's jaw. His tattered shirtsleeve fluttered across her breasts as he delivered a better kiss, but one tinged with desperation. The sharp, clean scent of his aftershave was mixed with the pungent odor of sweat, reminding her of his recent fight with the big, hungry cat.

The kiss lasted until Wylie heard Dean thrashing back through the underbrush.

Lifting his head with a great deal of reluctance, he grinned lopsidedly. "Thanks for looking after this old rack of bones, Marlee. We make a good team. Before you showed up, there was every chance the cougar might have won." His gray eyes went mist-soft, and he spared a last minute to brush two fingers over her stubborn jaw, which had only begun to relax.

She pushed petulantly at his good shoulder. "You scared the heck out of me."

The boy exploded from the dense undergrowth. He carried the dart gun and two spare darts.

Marlee cast a guilty glance over her shoulder, but Dean was unaware of anything between the adults. Instead, he fell to his knees a foot from the portable cage and peered in anxiously. "Wow, up close he's pretty. I'm glad you didn't hit him, Marlee. I think somebody did. See, Dad? He's got a scar along one hip."

Wylie nodded. "I think you're right. That's probably why he shied at the sound of the gunshot."

"Shied?" Marlee scoffed. "He dived right at you, Wylie."

Shrugging, he leaned the dart gun against the tree with the rifle. "We'll let him eat his fill before I tranquilize him. Then he won't need to go on the hunt immediately after we drop him. That'll give him time to explore his new home."

Marlee's gaze lit on Wylie's torn shirt. "You ought to let someone clean and dress that wound," she said, agitated. "Or is it wounds?" Her sweeping hand drew his attention to his arm and leg.

"Yeah, a cat's claws aren't the most sterile cutting tools. Dean, will you run back to the house and bring the small first aid kit? It's in my truck."

"Aw, dad, I'm pooped. I just got back from runnin' to the house."

Marlee thought the boy did look drained and flushed from his recent exertion. Understandable, as the whole experience must have been traumatic. "Let me go."

"We'll all go," Wylie said tearing his shirtsleeve off at the elbow so that he could manage a cursory inspection of his bloodied arm. I should change out of these clothes. Besides, I'll need to bring the truck out here to load the cat."

"There's a road out here? Then why did we tear ourselves up on that overgrown path of brush and briars?"

"No real road. Four-wheel-drive takes me almost anywhere in the backcountry I need to go. Until it snows. Then I break out the snowcat."

Leaving the dart gun, he collected the Winchester and gestured again toward the faint path. "Ladies first."

She had to pass him to reach the opening. "Ooh, Wylie, those are deep gashes in your arm. Shouldn't you leave the cat and go let a doctor stitch you up?"

"I have butterfly bandages at the house. Since the cut's on my right arm I won't turn down help applying the strips." He used the rifle barrel to shove aside the same vines that had wrapped around Marlee earlier as he appealed to her Florence Nightingale side.

She bit her lip and glanced back at him. "Living so far from town, I suppose you're used to handling emergencies by yourself."

Wylie lifted Dean over a moss-covered log. "It does make me

stop and consider what constitutes a real emergency. For instance, driving to where there's a doctor wastes a full day, and longer when the weather turns bad."

Marlee didn't comment. But she stopped to wonder if the isolation was why Dean's mother had left Wylie. Had Wylie's wife even gone to town to give birth to Dean?

As if he'd read her mind, Wylie said, "All rangers receive advanced first aid training. I can set a clean bone break, doctor run-of-the-mill punctures, scrapes and cuts. I stock snakebite kits. I delivered Dean. As a rule, rangers' wives on outposts spend their last weeks before giving birth in a town that has a hospital."

"I came early and surprised you, didn't I, Dad?" The boy turned shining blue eyes toward his father. He wiped his shirtsleeve across a runny nose, which drew a gentle reprimand from Wylie. "You did, bucko. Listen, no need to be scaring Marlee into thinking life on our station is too primitive."

"Why?" Dean wrinkled his freckled nose.

Over top of the boy's shock of red hair, Wylie sent Marlee a sexy smile. "Well, I want her to feel welcome to drop in any time. Don't you?"

"Sure. 'Cause we're friends." The boy slid a moist sweaty palm into Marlee's free-swinging hand. "You and Jo Beth can visit us any ol' time."

A small knot of contentment balled in her belly. Not so long ago, this duo had been a fortress unto themselves. Wylie had preferred being a loner. Marlee felt she'd somehow passed an important test.

"Marlee, why didn't Jo Beth come with you today?"

She explained that her plane had been full of paying customers. "Speaking of Jo Beth, I need to call home and see how the family's getting along. Wylie, I didn't off-load your freight. I'll take care of it as soon as we finish cleaning your gashes."

"My arm might be a little stiff, but if we work together the crate won't be too much for either of us. I hate to ask, but...I may need help loading and unloading the cougar."

Marlee gave his request a cursory thought. "I'd like to see where you're going to turn him loose. If everything's okay at home, you've got yourself a sidekick, pardner."

A smile passed between her and Wylie, leaving prickles of a different kind marching up Marlee's spine. That sensation signaled an appetite for something that was way more than friendship. Friends had told her it was time she circulated again. Probably none of them had been talking about a recluse with shadows in his past and tons of baggage of his own.

"While you gather up the alcohol, tape and such, I'll touch base with Mick. Did I tell you he was released from the hospital?"

"Jo Beth told Dean. The news took second billing to the new dog, though."

"I'm not surprised." Grinning, she took out her phone as they entered the house. She watched Wylie return the Winchester and shells to the gun case. Then, with a mother's power of observation, she noticed Dean making a beeline for the couch, where he curled around one of the throw pillows. Was it the winking of the sun's rays through the front window that made him look more flushed now?

Mick answered on the first ring, his "Hello," punctuated by a massive yawn.

"Didn't mean to wake you. How's everyone there doing?"

"We had a bit of excitement. Pappy headed out to pick up the mail. He got lost. Took two hours to locate him."

"Oh, Mick. How'd he get lost? The mailbox is at the end of our lane. I didn't mention it while you were in the hospital, but Pappy got...weird...one night. Thought he was in the war." She closed her eyes, regretting what she had to ask next. "I wonder, uh, I mean have you considered that we may have to put him in a home?"

"This is his home."

"I know that, Mick. I also know where we'd be if it hadn't been for him. I'm thinking of *his* safety."

"It'll be okay, sis. Soon as I can cut out these danged pain pills."

She decided to let it go. "So, where and how did you find him?"

"Near as I can figure he got it into his head to walk on down to see Stella. We think he turned at the Hart ranch by mistake. Don Hart was on his way home from town and saw Pappy sitting beside the road. The two lanes are side by side. He just got discombobulated. Are you at the airpark?"

"No, I stopped to deliver Wylie's backorder. We had a bit of excitement here, too." She glossed over the highlights of Wylie's tussle with the cat. "We're back at the house now. The cougar tore open Wylie's arm. I think it needs sutures, but he asked me to butterfly it closed. After that I was going to help him load the cage into his pickup and drop the cat farther up the mountain. Maybe I should skip that and fly home."

"No rush. Stella's here. She and Jo Beth are making pies. Pappy's glued to his afternoon soaps."

"And you? You're not overdoing it, are you?"

"The dog and I were snoozing. I'm being the model patient. Cross my heart."

"Right… Let me talk to Jo Beth." She heard him shout her daughter's name three times. Finally, a breathless little voice said excitedly, "I can't talk, Mama. Ms. Stella's letting me roll out pie crust dough. Then I get to mix the stuff to put inside. It's cherry."

"And here I thought you'd be clamoring to chat with Dean. He and his dad caught a cougar today. Remember, you saw one of those at the zoo? It's a mountain lion."

"Will he get penned with Boxer? I'll see him next time, right?"

"I'm afraid not. I wish I had a camera to take his picture. He's something! Here, I'll let Dean tell you what he looks like. I need to bandage his dad's arm. The cougar clawed him a little. But he'll be fine. Don't worry."

Marlee crossed to the couch and held the phone out to Dean. "It's Jo Beth. I thought you'd like to tell her about the big cat. Dean, are you feeling all right?" She brushed back the boy's hair.

He sat up and took the phone. "I'm just tired."

No doubt a result of feeling panic for his dad. She pointed toward a mantle clock. "When the big hand reaches the two, tell Jo Beth goodbye and send her merrily off to her pie-baking."

Assured that he understood, she sped down the hall in search of Wylie. And found him in the main bathroom. Without his shirt, he was a sight to behold. All bronzed muscle, and a torso that when covered by his shirt, only hinted at those washboard abs.

To keep from appearing too much the drooling female, Marlee entered the small bathroom with sure steps.

Wylie had been attempting to get a look at his deep scratches in the medicine cabinet mirror, and at the same time wring out the bloody washcloth he'd used to dab off the blood. He couldn't seem to get the right tilt to the mirror, and muttered a curse.

"Take my word for it, Wylie. It's not pretty."

"Hurts like hell," he said through clenched teeth.

"No kidding?" Marlee took the damp washcloth from his hand, and rinsed it thoroughly while holding his arm over the sink so she could squeeze warm water over the gaping cuts. There were three, but the center one was deepest. She poured until the water hitting the basin ran pink instead of bright red.

Then she looked through an array of items in a first aid kit sitting open on his bathroom counter. "You think water hurts, wait until I use this disinfectant. You might want to sit on the rim of the tub," she said.

"Nah, just get it over with fast. Before Dean shows up, in case

I let loose some X-rated words. As a rule he's Johnny-on-the-spot to take care of me. He tell you he wants to be a vet? I tease him about practicing on me. Like a month ago he dug a mean sliver out of my foot. I asked if he was calling it my left hind paw."

She poured clear liquid over his arm. "Ow, ow, damn!" he yelped, his eyes open wide, then watering like mad.

"Sorry." She fanned his skin so it'd dry and she could apply the butterfly strips. "I wish Dean had done the dirty work this time."

"I wonder where he got off to?"

"He lay down on the couch when we came in. Said he's tired. I left him with my cell phone talking a blue streak with Jo Beth."

Wylie spoke absently at the part in Marlee's hair, since she'd bent to press on the first Steri-Strip. "This week I caught him napping several afternoons. Yesterday, he said his bones ached. Is that normal for an eight-year-old kid?"

Marlee raised her head which put her eyes level with Wylie's worried expression. "I'm no nurse, but I recall reading in a book on the stages of childhood that some kids suffer growing pains. According to the book, they hurt." She placed three more pieces of tape and took satisfaction in closing the gaping tear.

"Huh! I should probably get a copy. I've been lucky up to now, I guess. Dean's hardly ever been sick."

"Next time I'm in Kalispell I'll see if I can locate the book. Or tomorrow when I take Mick to physical therapy in Missoula. I'll have hours to kill."

"Missoula? That's quite a trek from where you live. Mick can't get what he needs closer to home?"

"You know doctors. Everyone specializes. I suppose it's the same with physical therapists." She finished the middle row and started on the next deepest mark.

"I don't know doctors, thank goodness. I'm healthy, too. In all ways," he stressed. "No...uh...diseases."

That struck Marlee as an odd comment. Until she lifted her

lashes and met his intense gaze, and suddenly knew exactly what he was saying. She fumbled the next butterfly strip.

"You?" he asked casually. Too casually.

"Uh, yeah. Clean bill of health. The navy was rigorous about checking." She heard her own voice, soft and trembly. Her fingers flew, but her thoughts skittered away to areas forbidden till now. For the last year she'd still considered herself a married woman even though Cole had passed away. Now, here she stood, inches away from a man brimming with sexuality.

"Wylie," she said, withdrawing a step after hastily patching the third gouge on his arm. "Now it's my turn to ask what's happening. I mean, I hope I didn't send the wrong message on the landing strip today. I realize I fell into your arms. But I'm not promiscuous." She kept her eyes averted, and made a point of not touching his skin as she deftly wound gauze around his deltoid muscle. Clear to his elbow and back up again to his shoulder, double padding the section over his cuts.

"I never had that impression," he said gruffly. "This is good, Marlee. Thanks." He flexed his arm a few times, and began collecting tape, scissors and gauze.

She curved a hand cautiously over his bare arm. Then she jerked back. "Don't you want me to bind the wound on your leg? I saw the cat get a piece of you when he ripped your jeans."

"I'll take care of it." A flush crept across Wylie's cheekbones. "Damned cat, ah, nailed me in the groin. On the inside of my thigh."

"Oh. Oh! In that case I'll find Dean and get him off the phone." She backed toward the door, and awkwardly pointed down the hall.

The gray eyes drilled her. "I want to say this, Marlee. You're the first woman I've had any interest in for a lo-o-ong time." He drawled this on an exhaled breath.

"Same here. Just chemistry, you think?"

"More like two worlds colliding. I wore these Sunday jeans to impress you," he said wryly.

She banged her elbow on the door casing and winced, plainly uncomfortable at this turn of the conversation. "I'd better let you fix your leg or I won't have time to help relocate the cat." She hastily explained what had happened to her grandfather.

"If I thought Dean could lift half the weight of that cage I'd say go on and take off. Still, I might be able to manage it alone."

"And pop off my handiwork with those butterfly bandages, Wylie? Not on your life."

"You'll be back Friday, right? I'll probably need them rebandaged by then."

"I want to come. For Jo Beth's sake," she clarified. "She'll be disappointed if she doesn't get to see you and Dean release the cub. I told you, though, it depends on how many flights we schedule. Tomorrow I take Mick for his therapy. All of our paying customers have to be juggled around his appointments."

"I understand. You have a life that doesn't revolve around me." He turned his back on her and unzipped his jeans.

Faced with the rigid lines of his back and the hard truth of their separate lives, she had no ready response, so she left.

Wylie heard her footsteps recede down the hall. What had he expected? That she'd deny it? He slammed the bathroom door closed, then muttered, "Who has time for this?" He swore out loud, because it hurt like hell when he stripped off his jeans and poured disinfectant on that tender spot. A pair of brand-new jeans, ruined. Also, his best white shirt had bit the dust. *For her.* He wadded up the clothes and flung them into a corner of the bathroom.

Hell, he wasn't good at relationships. Never had been. They took too much effort. His ranger buddies told him to think about what his life would be like after Dean passed the high school equivalency tests for home schooled kids and went his own way.

Wylie usually sidestepped commenting. At first he'd hoped Dean would follow in his footsteps and take over this station so he'd never be forced to move to town. But realistically Wylie knew that was nothing more than wishful thinking. Dean hankered to work with animals. The kid had a knack for it.

Glowering darkly at his reflection in the mirror, Wylie shrugged on a khaki work shirt and matching pants. Relocating the cougar was an official act. Technically he was stepping beyond the pale in asking a civilian's help. The tranquilizer might wear off before they reached their destination. He'd seen other cats play possum and once dumped out, turn on their captors. For all the dire warnings he heaped on his own head, Wylie limped from the bathroom without the slightest intention of sending his guest off into the wild blue yonder.

Yes, he was interested in Marlee Stein. Rusty though he might be at knowing how to garner reciprocal interest, Wylie couldn't talk himself out of trying. Maybe he needed a book on *that* subject as well as one on growing boys, or whatever it was Marlee had promised to hunt up. Would she take him seriously or deck him if he requested she also buy him a book on dating for dummies? If there was one…

He emerged from the hall into the living room, thinking she might have simply taken off. She hadn't. She sat on the edge of her chair engrossed in a sadly neglected photo album he kept on the coffee table.

"Ready?" She let the pages drift closed before glancing up. "Well, don't you look official?" Marlee jumped to her feet. "We won't break any laws if I tag along in your truck? I happened to notice it's got the park logo."

"I make the rules out here. Dean…"

"He's zonked, Wylie. Can you carry him out?"

"Sure, if you catch the doors. I can't figure this out, the way he's falling asleep in the middle of the day."

She hurried across the room and flung open the door. "The weather's been on again, off again. Maybe he's catching a cold."

"Maybe." Wylie left Marlee to close up the house, and he carried the gangly boy to the kingcab pickup. She dashed around him and opened the narrower back door, then stood aside and watched him buckle his son in, tenderly covering him with a blanket.

Out of deference to the sleeping child, neither adult talked on the bumpy ride to the clearing. The cat had finished his meat, and again paced and gnawed at the bars of his cage.

Dean stirred when both front doors were thrown open. His eyes glittered. Marlee thought they were *too* bright. She reached over the seat and felt his forehead.

Wylie noticed. "Is he feverish?"

"You feel. If so, I think it's low-grade."

As was typical for most kids, Dean ducked his dad's hand. "I'm okay," he declared crossly. "That ol' cat's sure makin' a fuss. Will you look at Boxer? I've never seen him stand up on his hind legs and roar like that." The boy scrambled from the truck and flew to the animal pens. He tried to console the cub.

"Dean, stay back from the bear. He's agitated, and may bite you. Cougars and bears are natural enemies in the wild. He'll settle down once I put the cat to sleep."

Dean instantly tucked his hands behind his back. Sitting on the ground, he turned sad eyes toward his father. "I know you said it's time to turn Boxer loose. But, I don't want to say goodbye. It's too hard."

Because Wylie had gone to retrieve the dart gun and didn't see his son's distress, Marlee walked over, sat down next to him and let him bury his head in the hollow of her shoulder. She felt a kinship with this boy. "I understand. You love him, Dean. It hurts to let go. But life is a series of hellos and goodbyes."

Wylie lifted the dart gun and took aim at the cougar's hind quarters. The cat howled.

"Did that hurt him?" Dean mumbled against Marlee's blouse.

She sheltered him from actually witnessing the flying dart. Her own heart tripped a little faster at seeing the huge animal sink in stages, fighting the drug. "I'm sure it stings, Dean, but your dad wouldn't do this if it wasn't for the cat's own good. If he hunts in the valley, he might kill a rancher's cow. Then the ranchers would band together and go after the cougar." Marlee raked the hair off the boy's clammy forehead. "Your dad said you want to be a veterinarian some day. Doctors— for humans *and* animals—are often faced with making tough decisions."

"Maybe I won't make a good vet."

"You will. Listen, it's done. I need to help load his cage in the back of your dad's pickup. Are you going to be okay?"

Dean nodded. But he didn't get up. Instead he sat chewing on a thumbnail.

"That's unusual behavior for Dean," Wylie said when Marlee joined him. "Also, I've never seen him cotton to anyone like he has to you. Thanks."

"For…?" Marlee struggled, but managed to heave her part of the cage into the back of the pickup.

Wylie slammed and locked the tailgate, and set the dart gun alongside the cage. A myriad of emotions skittered across his face. He trailed his fingertips over Marlee's upturned face. "Thanks for not shrugging Dean off." Wylie swallowed visibly. "Those women I told you friends shove my way? They show plenty of interest in me. None had more than an offhand *hi* for Dean."

Marlee found herself leaning into his touch. "I'm sorry. He's a neat kid. And he has a big, soft heart. Like his dad," she added solemnly. "Contrary to what folks say."

His eyes dark and serious, Wylie traced her cheek, then the

bridge of her nose with a featherlight stroke. "I wish you could get past the rumors you've heard."

She caught Wylie's thick wrist and smiled. "At first I gave some credence to them. But I wouldn't be here today if I hadn't decided they were just nonsense. It's more that the feelings I'm experiencing are new, and they're really jumbled up."

"Tell me about it." Turning the tables, he captured her hand, brought it to his lips and pressed a quick kiss in her palm. "There's no need to rush this."

"This? You mean relocating the cougar?" Seeing Dean walking toward them, Marlee extracted her hand and had resorted to teasing Wylie.

He caught on. "Jeez, there's every need to rush that." He spun, scooping Dean up. "Come on, big guy, what do you say we go find this kitty a new home?"

"Okay." He rubbed his eyes. "I wish Jo Beth had come today. It'd be more fun."

"If possible I'll see she comes on the next trip. Jo Beth bought you a book on white-tailed deer. I was supposed to bring it today, but I left it lying on our kitchen counter. What other kinds of books do you and your dad like? I'm flying Mick to Missoula tomorrow. I happen to know the college bookstore at the university is a treasure trove of great books."

The three discussed favorite books as they bounced along over a little-used fire road. Marlee discovered that she and Wylie shared a taste for suspense stories.

"My library is woefully slim," he admitted.

She decided she'd add a few current releases for the Ames guys to her list of things to buy in Missoula.

The higher Wylie drove up the mountain, the colder it grew in the cab of the pickup, forcing her thoughts from gifts to the upcoming months. Old Man Winter was near, she was sure, when Wylie finally stopped the vehicle and they all piled out. A brisk north wind rattled the pines and confirmed the airpark clerk's prediction that they'd see snow very soon.

She helped Wylie slide the dead-to-the-world cougar into a thicket that was within view of where he'd parked. They huddled in the truck and waited for the cat to wake up. Marlee went back to brooding over the approaching season. It meant these feelings between her and Wylie would of necessity slow down.

Granted, she'd been relieved when he said there was no need to rush but now, facing the prospect of not seeing him until spring, she realized that wasn't at all what she'd like. The cat stirred. He got up, shook himself, glared in their direction, then slunk into the underbrush, off toward the spot where Wylie had tossed out another frozen hindquarter of elk.

All the way down the mountain, Marlee debated whether or not to tell Wylie how she felt. She didn't, but promised herself she'd do it when she came back on Friday. "Bye. See you soon," she called. Dean had gone straight into the house. Wylie followed Marlee to the plane. He unloaded his freight, and now stood by watching her warm up the engines. On liftoff, he smiled and gave her a thumbs-up. His smile warmed a too-cold heart, and she savored the feeling all the flight home.

CHAPTER TEN

THE NEXT DAY, MARLEE planned to talk to Mick about what seemed to be happening between her and Wylie. But because Stella Gibson had been called for a job interview in Whitepine, Pappy and Jo Beth had to go along on the trip to Missoula. Marlee didn't want to bring up the subject with anyone but Mick.

"I don't wanna leave Piston home alone," Jo Beth wailed, resisting the last-minute decision to load everyone on the plane.

"The dog will be fine, honey. Pappy put together that nice pen under the big fir tree. He has plenty of food and water. And he has room to run."

"But he'll miss us. What if he runs away?"

"He can't get out of the pen. Honey, we're only going to be gone a few hours."

"Okay, I guess I'll go."

"You'll have fun. Did I tell you I got a list of books from Dean that he'd love to have? You can help me find them at the campus bookstore."

"Then can I take them to Dean?"

"Soon, sweetie. Maybe Friday."

Pappy growled from directly behind Marlee, "Mick told us about the cougar. Cat be danged. You took a bigger chance going into the mountains with Ames."

Marlee shot a disgusted look over her shoulder. "Pappy, why is it so hard for you to accept that those rumors about Wylie are lies?"

"You've been back in town a matter of weeks. Those stories about him hark back eight or nine years, and they don't go away."

"Then it's time for someone to stand up and shout the truth."

Headset on, Mick had listened with interest to the words flying back and forth. "Way to go, champ. You come out swinging. I hope Wylie knows he's a lucky man."

His sister glanced at him and discovered Mick had seen through her veneer.

He poked her. "Am I in danger of losing my best pilot to that son of a gun?"

She laughed nervously. "It's way too soon for that kind of talk."

"Ah, but there is...something going on? A mutual something is my guess." He gave an exaggerated wiggle of his straight, dark-blond eyebrows.

Marlee leveled the plane in spite of shifting uncomfortably in her seat. "Yeah, I'd call it mutual. We were both caught off-guard."

Mick winked, and a slow smile curved lips shaped very much like his twin's. "Damn!" Mick pointed at the front windshield. "Are those snowflakes?"

"Snow?" Marlee squinted, staring out. She whooped and called, "Jo Beth, look! Your first-ever snowflakes. Change of plans today. Buying winter jackets, snow boots and gloves just topped our list."

"Stella said the almanac predicted an early winter," Pappy said. Almost with too much satisfaction, he added, "Snow will throw a monkey wrench in any big plans you've got to start a romance with Ames. By spring you'll come to your senses."

Marlee hid a smile. At times there wasn't a thing amiss with her grandfather's deductive powers. "Well, you don't have any problems hearing, Pappy. I barely heard Mick over the engine noise."

"All this fuss over a guy getting on in years. I wasn't lost yesterday. I went hunting mushrooms to cook in butter and pour over a good juicy steak."

Mick flipped a switch and muttered, only for his sister's ears, "And that's the prime reason it'd be a waste of time to research assisted living homes. He'd still go off and do whatever he wanted."

She acknowledged that with a nod.

THE WET SLOPPY FLAKES tapered to a steady rain some miles before they landed in Missoula. Marlee's hopes for a good day to run around town were pretty much shot. Still, she dropped Mick at the physical therapist's clinic, and drove the others off in the rental car from hell. It was a beater with a stick shift. That would teach her not to let her brother arrange for a car again.

She thought she'd have hours to kill. Between far heavier city traffic than she'd experienced since moving back to Montana, and the necessity to keep tabs on two people, both of whom tended to wander, she had to go and collect Mick before she'd found half the things on her list.

One look at the taut lines bracketing Mick's lips dashed the tiniest hope that he'd feel like tagging along while she finished errands. "Bad session?" she asked as he eased into the seat beside her.

"PTs are trained in torture. I lost count of how many times I told her my leg didn't bend to that angle even *before* the doctor gave me a new hip."

"You feel like doing lunch?"

He cracked open one eye. "Would anyone mind if we went straight home? They had a TV on at the therapist's. This rain is probably more like sleet closer to Whitepine."

"Oh, no! Piston's outside, Mama. He's gonna be covered in snow."

"Jo Beth, he'll be fine." Marlee took a side road that led straight to the airport. She heeded the warning in Mick's casual comment. No pilot liked the thought of wings icing up. Actually, Marlee was more concerned about the possibility of sleet than snow.

At the airport she requested an update on the weather. Forecasters said she'd hit snow and sleet between Missoula and Whitepine. Now she was glad Pappy and Jo Beth had joined them. The extra bodies had demanded the twin-engine six-seater.

The white stuff fell thicker and faster the closer they got to home. Mick leaned forward, clearly with difficulty, adjusting warm air vents. "Did the forecast mention a possible whiteout?"

"No. Let's see if I can climb out of it."

At eighteen thousand feet visibility improved. Marlee and Mick both relaxed. Pappy fell asleep, and Jo Beth wasn't aware enough about flying to be concerned.

Mick wiped his side window with his sleeve. "If this hangs around it'll put a crimp in the deliveries you have booked for the rest of the week."

"Deliveries, plural? More than food staples going to Ranger Watters on the north end outpost?"

"Everyone's hunkering down for winter. Yesterday I booked supply orders for three ranches. Oh, and Morrison called to confirm that the last of Wylie's parts came in."

"Wow. I have more hunters to carry, too. When's your next therapy appointment?"

"She felt bad making me fly in three days a week, so she gave me exercises to do at home. Next time she needs to see me is two weeks from now."

Marlee didn't camouflage her surprise. "Is that wise, Mick? Your therapist isn't afraid you'll slack off? That would prolong the healing process."

"She has my records from past surgeries. I guess she saw how hard I worked to get better. I'll do the exercises. You think I like being out of commission?"

Marlee gave him a sympathetic smile as she came down through the clouds into the bowl cradling their home. "Look, there's only a little snow on our airstrip." After landing, she taxied into the hangar. "I think I'll spend an hour or so in the office. I have bills to print, plus it's time to arrange for a fuel delivery. And I need to check addresses to see which deliveries can be grouped together."

"Mama, may I phone Dean?"

"Sure, honey. Ask him to tell his dad that we'll deliver the rest of his generator parts on Friday morning."

"Okay."

Pappy and Jo Beth climbed down and headed off to check on Piston.

Mick crawled out with difficulty. "Wylie will be glad to finally get his generator repaired. Take our snowfall and multiply it fivefold. That'll be what Wylie and Al Watters have to deal with. Dang, I wish I wasn't laid up. You haven't flown in snow in God knows how long."

"Don't worry about it. Sandstorms are as bad."

"Okay, okay. But if I can manage to stand for an hour or two tomorrow, I plan to service all the planes. No telling which ones might be called into service. Snow generally causes crack-ups along the mountain highways. Angel Fleet may be busy."

"I guess I worried for nothing. The two calls I've taken weren't so bad, Mick."

"That reminds me. On the office desk is a thank-you note from Mrs. Ledbetter, and a copy of the editorial her husband wrote. Tracie's home and doing great."

"I'm glad: I intended to call her again. I've been busy."

"Busy fighting cougars and who knows what else with my

pal Wylie? Now that the little one with the big ears is gone and Pappy, too, out with the truth. How involved with Wylie *are* you, Marlee?"

She pulled the bags with their purchases from the plane. "Not too much. Yet. We kissed a few times. Neither of us is exactly ready to jump off a cliff. A month ago I wouldn't have believed I could even be this interested." She stared into the distance, and her voice wavered. "I wish I had more time to spend with him before the snow hits. I hesitate to make broad statements based on so little, but Mick, I...uh...think he's a man I could get *very* serious about. I have butterflies whenever I know I'll see him. And I feel, well, empty flying off and leaving him and Dean behind."

Mick whistled. "I'd say you've got it bad. Wylie's not the most talkative guy I know. And more than once he's said that life on a remote ranger site isn't something most women are anxious to settle for. What about you? It's a far cry from San Diego."

She shortened her steps to match his shuffle. "Life under the bright lights is overrated, Mick. Not that anything of *that* sort's come up between Wylie and me, but I think I could be content living a quiet life in the woods."

They'd almost reached the house and heard Jo Beth's giggles and Piston's barks drifting out. "What about your former mother-in-law? I don't imagine she'd stand up and cheer to think you'd found someone else."

"It's not Rose's business what I do." Marlee set down her bags and wrenched open the back door. "I maintain civil communications for Jo Beth's sake. Anyway, this thing with Wylie is pretty tenuous at the moment. Maybe nothing further will develop."

"I've known Wylie Ames four years, and this is the first I've heard of him taking a second look at any woman. I'll give you odds he's gotta be plenty interested to reach the kissing stage."

Marlee hid a blush. "Shh! You're teasing me because you know I'm not going to beat up on you since you're injured and all."

"I'm not teasing," he called after her, but she'd made a clean exit through the kitchen and down the hall.

In the bedroom, Marlee shook out the new down jackets and hung them in her closet. Boot boxes followed. Eyeing the small space critically, she considered whether this might be the right time to move out to the cottage. The house was a bit crowded with three adults, one child and now an overgrown mongrel.

Then again, Mick was still on pain medication. What if Pappy had another episode some night, and Mick didn't wake up? Those spells worried Marlee. How serious were they?

She decided for the moment she'd stay put. She shoved the book on white-tailed deer into the bag, along with two Hardy Boys books and a couple of Manga comics they'd bought for Dean today, plus a few thrillers for Wylie.

As if thinking about Dean had telegraphed his name to Jo Beth, she dashed in and announced, "Mama, I want to call Dean now. Piston sat when Pappy Jack said *sit*. He threw a ball and Piston ran out, got the ball and brought it back. Dean asked if I was going to train Piston. Pappy said my dog's already trained."

"Isn't that something?" Marlee smiled, pulled her phone from her purse and showed Jo Beth what numbers to punch. "Have Uncle Mick tell you when ten minutes are up, okay? Mama's going to work in the office. I'll be back in time to fix supper."

She cut through the breezeway, and was pleased to note that it'd stopped snowing and the clouds had thinned. If Mick serviced the planes tomorrow, she'd collect the freight orders from Kalispell. Marlee turned on her computer and sent the first of four invoices to print. The door opened. Jo Beth skipped in carrying a coloring book and crayons.

"That was a quick ten minutes. Wasn't Dean home?"

"He didn't feel like talking."

"Huh? That's gotta be a first."

"Can I sit on the tall stool and color at the desk?"

"Sure." Marlee cleared the high-topped desk, idly wondering what was wrong with Wylie's son. "Did you remember to give Dean the message for his dad?"

"Yep. I even told him I'm bringing a surprise. He didn't act like he cared."

"Maybe he and his dad were in the middle of chores. I'm sure he'll be excited Friday when he sees all the books you chose."

All evening and part of the next day, Marlee thought Wylie would phone. she expected him to verify that she intended to go up to see Boxer's release and to drop off the last of his order. He didn't call, and of course she anxiously wondered why.

Wednesday morning, Mick managed to service the planes. It was late in the day when Marlee bundled supply orders, made her two scheduled deliveries and picked up another that hadn't been scheduled. The family had not only eaten supper without her by the time she hauled her tired body home, but all three had retired for the night.

Marlee riffled through the pink message slips on the spindle next to the phone. *No change in her Friday flight plans. Still nothing from Wylie.*

She showered and crawled into bed, suspecting that her romance with Wylie Ames had ended before it had really begun.

THE SKY WAS HORRIBLY overcast Friday. Gray clouds threatened foul weather, as did television forecasters, who warned that snow flurries were likely by late afternoon.

Mick had traded his walker for a cane. He padded along the path from the house to the hanger for his morning exercise. Piston loped ahead, sniffing bushes. Stopping, Mick watched Marlee help Jo Beth into the Huey. "Taking the whirly bird, huh? Aren't you worried snow might weigh down the blades?"

"Not today."

"I'll trust your judgment. I'm a fixed-wing man myself. I bought the chopper because the former owner practically gave it away."

She patted the ugly khaki paint. "That's funny. Pappy said you bought the Huey for me. Because you know I like to fly choppers." Marlee hoisted herself into the bubble. "I left sandwich fixings for lunch and put a copy of my schedule under the cheese magnet on the fridge door." She started the rotor spinning, and saw Mick's mouth move, but the noise blocked his words. They exchanged a thumbs-up. As the Huey rose straight above the house, she saw Mick make his way along the walk.

Jo Beth fidgeted in her seat, arms clasped around the package for Dean.

Marlee smiled, adjusting dials. She looked forward to seeing Wylie and Dean, but she managed to contain her excitement a little better than Jo Beth.

"Honey, we have one drop to make at a fish hatchery before we land at the ranger station. You don't have to hold Dean's gift all that time."

"I want to. I wonder if he's got more hurt animals? Will we get to see them, and stay for lunch?"

"Maybe." Marlee debated telling Jo Beth that Wylie planned to turn out Boxer Bear.

The fishery came into sight, diverting her attention. The owners, Mr. and Mrs. Barnett, offered Marlee and Jo Beth a tour of the various growth tanks they used to raise rainbow trout.

"That was fascinating," Marlee said at the end. "Thanks so much." She glanced at her watch and was surprised at how late it had grown. Wylie had said to be there at ten, and it'd probably be nearer eleven.

"Mama, do you think Dean's ever been to a fish hatchery? If not, maybe he can go with us next time. I'll bet he'd like seeing the little fishes get big, and then bigger."

"Probably. It wouldn't surprise me if he and his dad have visited there. I think this is part of Wylie's territory."

"It's getting awful cold, Mama. I'm glad you bought me a new jacket." She hugged it around her chest. "Do you think it's going to snow again?"

"It's supposed to later today. I hope we're home before it starts."

She turned a calculating eye toward ever-thickening clouds as she set the helicopter down dead center in Wylie's runway. As the churning blades slowed, she paid more attention to what Jo Beth was saying.

"Dean and his daddy must not have heard us land, Mama. They always come out, but I don't see them anywhere."

Marlee hoped that didn't mean they'd gone to release the cub, who'd grown significantly during its stay here, judging by what she'd seen the other day. That, no doubt, was a big reason Wylie needed to reintroduce the bear into the wild without delay.

"I wanna take Dean his books. May I? The whirly things stopped."

After shedding her harness, Marlee unfastened Jo Beth's. "I know you're anxious. Okay, you run on up to the house. I'll haul out the last of Wylie's order. But, if they're not home, honey, I want you to come straight back."

"If they're not home, where are they?"

"I don't know. At the pens, maybe. I'd just rather you didn't go to the pens alone."

"Okay, Mama. I won't. I 'member the cougar you told us about."

Marlee pulled on gloves and lifted the first of three cartons from the Huey. A wind gust almost knocked her off her feet. It cut icily through her jeans, but didn't penetrate her new jacket. If Wylie had grown impatient because she was late, she'd feel bad for causing Jo Beth to miss the excitement of seeing Boxer released.

She was placing the second box atop the first when Jo Beth

came pounding back down the path. Marlee straightened. "They're gone?" She felt a sting of disappointment.

"Dean's daddy said Dean's got flu. He wouldn't let me in the house to give Dean his surprise in person. Mama, what's flu, and why doesn't Dean's daddy want me to get it?"

"Flu bugs are kind of like cold germs, except sometimes you throw up with flu. I'm sorry Dean's sick, but I appreciate that his dad doesn't want to spread his illness."

"Oh. Maybe that's why Dean didn't feel like talking to me on the phone, huh?"

"I suppose. Let me get the last box off the plane, then I'll phone Wylie on my cell and find out what's going on for sure."

Her phone rang just then. She flipped it open. "Hello."

"Marlee, I hated to disappoint Jo Beth. Dammit, I want to see you, too, but Dean's been vomiting all morning. Yesterday he was really listless. His temperature is over a hundred. We haven't been around anyone except you and Jo Beth, but neither of you are sick, huh? Jo Beth said you're fine."

"We are. Wylie, I'm so sorry Dean's sick. Who knows how flu germs travel? Maybe they blew in on the wind. What did you do about you-know-what? The bear," she said in a whisper.

"I had to go out at twilight last night and let Boxer go. I wanted it done in case I have to take Dean into town to see a doctor. That's an all-day ordeal."

"For your sake I hope it's a twenty-four-hour bug. That reminds me. In the bag Jo Beth brought to the house is the book I told you about on the stages kids go through. It has helpful hints about dealing with colds, flu, headaches and so on."

"I'll read it now. Shoot, I've got to hang up. Dean's retching."

"Go then. I set the last of your freight on the path."

"I'll have to order something else. To make sure you come again."

Marlee's stomach, already tense, tightened further. It had

crossed her mind that Dean's illness might be a convenient excuse for Wylie to avoid seeing her. He'd just verified that wasn't the case. "No need to go to those lengths or that expense. I'll find some reason to drop in again before winter totally rules out travel."

"Good. That's really good. Marlee…"

"Why don't I check with you later and see how Dean's doing? See how you're doing? Believe me, I know it's hard to watch when someone you love is sick."

After they hung up, Marlee stood there dumbly, savoring the sound of his voice even though he'd disconnected.

Jo Beth's shout snapped her out of her dreamy trance. "Look, look, it's really snowing!" The girl skipped from the protection of the trees, and Marlee caught her sticking out her tongue in a frenzied effort to catch some of the flakes. Already Jo Beth's dark curls sparkled like crystal.

Marlee loped down the runway, dancing in circles, flinging out her arms. She, too, laughed and turned her face up to the sky. Mother and daughter spent several minutes reveling in the thickly falling white stuff. Then reality descended on Marlee. The fact was, she had one last load of freight to deliver. This storm, which wasn't supposed to hit until much later in the day, wouldn't be so exciting if it intensified enough to clog the Huey's rotors.

"Jo Beth, honey, we have to take off. I've got an order for a lodge that your Uncle Mick said is a bearcat to find on a good day."

The girl stopped trying to scrape together enough snow to make a ball. "That's silly. There are bears and there are cats. They're way diff'rent animals."

"It's an expression. Scoot back into the helicopter." Marlee hurried the child along. She was out of breath and her hair was wet but as she fired up the Huey those were the least of her concerns.

Marlee missed the lodge in the hypnotic swirl of fat flakes. She recognized a landmark she knew to be beyond the lodge.

"Blast it all!" She adjusted dials and began making a wide sweeping turn.

"What's wrong. Are you mad, Mama?"

"At myself, sweetie, not at you. Or maybe I'm mad at this snow."

"I love it! Will there be enough when we get home for me to build a snowman? Pappy Jack said you and Uncle Mick made lots of snowmen when you were my age."

"We did. It takes a good amount. This may be enough. Wet flakes pack into better balls, but please don't wish for more wet snow today. At least not until after I deliver this order to the Abernathys, and land us safely home again."

"Okay." The child pointed a finger at something below. "Is that the lodge? It's big and there's smoke coming out of a chimbley."

Marlee hovered. "That could be Mountain Meadows all right. With the meadow covered up," she muttered, sinking lower. "It is, I'll bet. Good thing you've got sharp eyes, Jo Beth. There's the red barn partway down the slope that Uncle Mick said to look for."

Flying off course had cost her almost an hour, she soon learned.

"These supplies are more welcome than you know," Mr. Abernathy, the lodge owner said. He'd dragged a fair-sized wagon out to where Marlee landed, and began stacking the boxes she unloaded. "This morning, after my wife picked up the weather news on our satellite, she fussed and fretted at me, saying I waited till too late to call in our winter supply order."

"According to my reports, this storm wasn't expected to swing so far south until much later this afternoon."

He grunted as he parked a hundred-pound bag of sugar on top of the groaning wagon. "We've found that weather folks in this neck of the woods frequently screw up. We've been here eight years. Are you new to Montana?"

"I grew up near Whitepine, but I've been gone quite a few

years. Does Mick Callen usually make your deliveries? He and I are twins."

"Twins. Whaddya know. My wife's a twin. And our son has twin boys."

"I've heard the twin gene often skips a generation. Hear that, Jo Beth? When you grow up and get married, maybe you'll have twin babies."

"No way." The little girl vigorously shook her curls, making snow fly. "But you can, Mama. I wish you'd have lots of babies."

"Don't count on that, tiddledywink." Marlee saw the wagon was loaded and then some. "I'll carry this last box to the lodge for you, Mr. Abernathy. Do you by chance get cell phone service up here? I think it'd be a good idea for me to phone my brother and see how far south this storm extends."

Clarence Abernathy adjusted the watch cap he wore. "No cell service. We have a mobile unit that operates off the satellite I mentioned. You're welcome to use it. In fact, my wife, Verna, hoped you'd stay and have a bite to eat with us."

"Can we, Mama? I'm hungry. I thought we were gonna eat with Dean and his daddy. But Dean was sick," she added to Mr. Abernathy.

Marlee mounted the steps to the lodge and stamped snow off her shoes. "Before I say yes or no, I'd like to get hold of Mick."

Abernathy introduced Verna, a short woman with tight gray curls and a jolly smile. "She needs to use our phone," he told his wife.

"I made a pot of beef barley soup and have warm bread to go with it. We'd love for you to join us. Oh, here I am blabbing away. Clarence said you need a phone. It's inside, to the right of the door. If you must leave, I'll fill two mugs with soup. You can return them when you bring our order next spring."

The soup smell permeated the house, and Marlee was

reminded of her first lunch with Wylie. She thought of him now, and hoped Dean was already on the mend.

The phone took a while to dial through the satellite. When she finally heard it ring faintly at the other end, no one picked up at first so she let it keep ringing. Mick and Pappy were probably messing around in the machine shop. She was about to hang up when Mick bellowed, "Cloud Chasers."

"Mick, I'm at Mountain Meadows Lodge. It's snowing heavily. The Abernathys have invited us to stay for lunch. What's your weather like?"

"Pappy and I just got back from Whitepine. It was spitting rain with a little snow mixed in. That's pretty much blown over. Wait, let me look. We're tinkering in the shop."

"I figured. That's why I let the phone ring twenty times."

The line went silent for a moment. Then he said, "Must all be happening up your way. The clouds have actually lifted here. I hafta say, though, I expected you two would eat at Wylie's—and maybe share a few dessert kisses."

"Long story there, Mick," she drawled. "Anyway, Jo Beth claims she's starved, and Verna's soup smells delicious." She smiled at the woman standing by, chatting with Jo Beth. "So, we're going to hang out here for the time being."

"Okay. I'm glad you called. Now I won't worry if you run late. My advice is, after you leave the Abernathys, fly due east. Turn south and fly straight down the middle between the Rockies and the Whitefish Range."

"Thanks, Mick. Cheerio," she said lightly, signing off.

"I'm so glad you can stay." Verna Abernathy beamed as she led Marlee and Jo Beth into the family's quarters. "Our last guests left two weeks ago. It's always lonely until Clarence and I adjust."

The talkative couple wasn't keen on letting them—possibly their last human contact until the spring thaw—get away. After they ate all of the soup in the tureen, Verna insisted on showing them the accommodations at the lodge. "Never know when you'll run into somebody looking for a getaway. We pamper our guests. Nature lovers, bird enthusiasts, honeymooners, they all love it here." Verna handed Marlee a stack of brochures. "Frankly, we rely on word of mouth to sell our service. Mountain Meadows isn't a spot for anyone wanting organized activities. We keep a half-dozen horses for folks who ride. Our meals are all served family style."

"I'm sold," Marlee said, thinking the Abernathys had a lot in common with Finn and Mary Glenroe. "I'll be happy to drop some brochures at the airpark. Verna, I'd love to see more. However, we need to head home. I've stayed longer than I led my brother to believe I would."

"You want to call him again?"

"Thanks, but if he's still out in the shop working on engines, he probably won't hear the phone. But I'm sure he'll understand."

Clarence opened the carved lodge door. "Mick's done his share of lingering here. Tell him hello, and Pappy Jack, too. Pappy told me how to thin the trees on our land so the ones we wanted to keep would have room to spread and yet not blow down in a wind storm. That was quite a few years ago. Hate to see how his age is catching up to him."

"Mick and I hate that, too," Marlee murmured. Her words were snapped away on a gusty wind. The snow had slowed, but the wind blew puffs of white off the roof. Ice crunched under Marlee's and Jo Beth's shoes. The child delighted in kicking through it.

Following Mick's instructions, Marlee flew east, then circled to the south. Majestic white peaks rose on her right and her left. She felt like an insignificant insect winging her way down a snow-blanketed corridor. Then, as Mick had said, the snow mixed with rain. As well, the daylight began to fade. That was when it struck Marlee how much shorter days were here compared to Southern California.

Full darkness soon engulfed her. She'd made her share of night landings. Still, her nerves were shot by the time she set down, and a sigh of relief trickled out as the rotors stopped. Removing her harness, she turned to assist Jo Beth.

Then Marlee shoved open her door and almost hit Mick. "Hey, shouldn't you be in the house resting that hip?"

"Hey, yourself. Pappy and I expected you an hour ago at the latest."

"Sorry. I should've called, but you must know how the Abernathys can talk up a storm."

"Yeah, well, it's the storm you flew through that had me worried. And Wylie's called three times in the space of an hour, Marlee."

"Really?" Undisguised pleasure shivered through her.

"It's Dean." Mick spoke softly, glancing every so often at his niece. "He's got a raging fever." Grasping his sister's arm, Mick pulled her to the back of the Huey, where he could talk more freely. "Wylie phoned his GP. The doctor wants him to get Dean to the hospital ASAP. I can't fly him. It's gotta be you."

"I thought Dean had the flu." Fear and confusion clogged Marlee's throat.

"It may be. But I've never heard Wylie freak out like this. I told him when I expected you to land. He's since tried the main ranger station. Their pilots are off training somewhere. And the smoke jumpers can't fly the Bell 'copters in this sloppy weather."

"Of course I'll fly him, Mick. There's no question. Oh, but Jo Beth's going to want to come along. What if Dean's contagious?"

"I thought of that. Stella's at the house playing checkers with Pappy. Who knows what time you'll get back? I figured Jo Beth will be more comfortable having Stella around to share a long evening."

Marlee bit her lip. She felt as though she was shuffling her daughter off on someone else again. And yet, until they knew what was wrong with Dean, it'd be foolish to expose her needlessly. "Mick, are you able to refuel the Huey? I'll phone Wylie and tell him when to expect me. Plus, I need a few minutes to prepare Jo Beth."

"Sure. But call Wylie first. I left him ten minutes ago, thinking he'd contacted Angel Fleet. If he did that, maybe they've assigned another pilot to transport Dean."

Marlee dug out her cell. Wylie answered at once. "It's Marlee. I just got home. Mick said Dean's worse? Have you arranged with another flyer to get him to Kalispell?"

"No. Thank God you called. I phoned two ranchers I know who own planes. This snow has them grounded. Maybe you can't fly in it, either. He's bad, Marlee. Last time I checked his temperature, it'd gone up to a hundred and six."

"That's really high," she said. "Dress him warmly. I'll bring the Huey. Look for me in forty to fifty minutes." Her hands were shaking when she hung up.

"Jo Beth, honey, I have to fly out again. Dean Ames has gotten sicker."

The girl's chin trembled. "Will you make him better, Mama?"

Marlee read in her eyes that she was really asking if he was going to die. Kneeling, Marlee gathered Jo Beth close. "I'm going to fly him to the hospital where we hope the doctors will make him better. Uncle Mick says Ms. Stella's inside. She'll take care of you while Mama's gone."

"I want to go. You said I was a good angel, too, 'member?"

"And you are, sweetheart. Gordon and Tracie were injured. But we don't know if Dean has something you might catch. Sometimes good angels help by staying home thinking happy thoughts. Besides, you haven't seen Piston all day. I bet he missed you."

Mick limped up. "You're fueled and ready to roll."

"Mama, can I call Grandmother Rose? Me'n her made happy thoughts for Daddy."

Marlee hesitated and fought down an old panic. Would Rose

use this against her? Perhaps. But this wasn't about them. This flight was about helping a sick boy. "That'll be fine, honey. Uncle Mick can get your grandmother on the phone." Marlee hugged her daughter one last time and dropped a kiss on her cold nose.

"Take care," Mick said. "This weather could turn into a bitch. Oops, sorry, Jo Beth."

At lift-off, Marlee felt bombarded by more than just weather. Dean meant everything to Wylie—a man she'd discovered strong feelings for. But she couldn't focus on that now. She let the night and the pelting flakes comfort her.

As opposed to earlier when she'd landed at Wylie's and Jo Beth had noted the empty runway, tonight the sidelights blazed. Wylie appeared through the trees, holding his sick son in his arms. She could see his impatience as he waited out the short time it took for the blades to slow their rotation. The worry in his dark eyes was so intense, Marlee's own emotions choked her and she was barely able to greet Wylie, and help him aboard. "How is he?" she mumbled.

"I think his temp's gone up even more. Can we hurry?"

Fear clawed at her, and her hand shook as she started the helicopter. She'd walked this walk. Had spent more nights praying to an empty sky than she could count. *But that was for Cole,* a little voice insisted. *Dean has complications from the flu. Kids get higher fevers than adults, but they're really resilient.* As the chopper rose, white globs of snow splattered against the Plexiglas bubble. Marlee wished Wylie would say something. Anything. He didn't. He shut her out when he most needed a friend.

CHAPTER ELEVEN

DEAN DIDN'T LOOK well at all. His eyes, when he opened them, were glazed. His face was flushed and his lovely red hair had turned dark from sweat. Reaching behind her, Marlee popped the lid on a cooler stocked with juice and water. She motioned for Wylie to help himself. "Under the seat are pillows and blankets."

He arranged the pillows, then patted his pockets and finally came up with a folded white handkerchief. After opening a bottle of water, he saturated the cloth to wipe his son's hot face.

Keeping one eye on flying and the other on her passengers, Marlee saw Dean start to shiver from the cool cloth. She chewed her lip. Was it normal for a kid with the flu to go from burning to chills at the mere touch of a cold compress? Her heart clattered in fear for Wylie. She was well acquainted with the paralyzed feeling that resulted from not being able to help a loved one in need.

The hour before she spotted the sweeping light from the airpark tower seemed endless. By rote, Marlee went through the motions of approach.

The blades were still spinning when Wylie's hand clamped on her shoulder. Marlee took off her earphones and turned.

"Will you watch Dean while I run into the office and get the number for a cab? Damn, I hate to make him wait in the cold until one shows up. I should've phoned ahead."

As the noise from the rotors abated, Marlee heard Dean

rambling on about the cougar. Then he switched to mumbling about Boxer Bear, after which he flopped around, begging for ice cream. She realized it was the fever talking.

"Mick keeps a car here. It'll take a minute to give the order to refuel the Huey. Then I'll warm up the car and swing around to that gate and pick you two up." She pointed, and Wylie's troubled gaze followed her finger. "You'll see my headlights."

"I hate to put you out more than I already have."

His words hit her like a punch in the gut. "I'd do as much for any friend," she said stiffly. Did he think she was interfering? Dean began to thrash harder, and Wylie released her and said nothing more.

She left the cockpit, making allowance for Wylie's behavior as she jogged to the building. The clerk was on the phone, so she used the time to call home. "Mick, are you guys okay? Wylie never thought to prearrange transportation to the hospital. If you don't need me to rush right home, I'll give him a lift." In the background she heard Jo Beth asking if it was her mom on the phone.

"We're fine, sis. You take care of Wylie and Dean. If you have a sec, Jo Beth would like a word."

"I always have time for her. Hi, honey," she said once Mick had handed off the phone. Marlee tried to hide her worry over Dean, and her impatience.

"Mama, is Dean all better? Grandmother Rose was worried after I said you hadda fly and it's snowing."

"It's not snowing hard. I'm driving Wylie and Dean to the hospital. If it's not too late, I'll phone you and Uncle Mick again after Dean sees a doctor."

"Stella helped me write my name, and I counted to five hundred. I have my jammies on, but maybe I can stay up till you call."

"Clear that with Uncle Mick. Honey, I need to go, okay?" She heard Jo Beth's faint goodbye and hung up quickly when she saw the clerk was free.

"I'll be flying out later. Will you fuel the Huey and pull off a new weather report?" The transaction didn't take long. However, on her way to start the Caddy, she saw Wylie already at the gate. Marlee had barely stopped the car when he climbed into the cavernous backseat with Dean, who clearly hadn't improved.

Aiming for the freeway, Marlee searched for something appropriate to say—although in her experience, there was little anyone could offer in the way of comfort.

"I don't want you to get a speeding ticket, Marlee, but can you go faster?"

"I'm pushing the speed limit, Wylie. And the road is slick. It won't do Dean any good if I slide off the highway."

"Right. I appreciate all you're doing. It's just… I feel so damn helpless."

"I know." Fifteen minutes later, she skidded under the hospital portico. After climbing out with Dean, Wylie leaned back inside. "Do you have a flight tomorrow? Depending on what they say, I hope we'll need a ride home," he muttered. "I have stock to feed and water, and Dean has a few wild animals in sick bay."

"Wylie, go sign him in. We can figure out the particulars later. I'm going to park. I'll come in and wait with you until you hear something definitive."

"You're staying?" She heard surprise mixed with relief in Wylie's voice.

"For a while. This storm's supposed to blow over by ten or so. The Huey's fueled, so I can fly any time up to midnight. That's when the airpark shuts down."

"Sure you want to hang around here? You probably have bad memories of hospitals."

"Wylie, there's a car behind me. Go! I'll meet you inside."

He withdrew fast and shut the door. Marlee couldn't help

thinking Mick had been right when he said this illness of Dean's had Wylie freaked out.

She parked and went in, stamping snow off her boots. "I'm a friend of Ranger Ames," Marlee said firmly when the receptionist asked her relationship to the patient. She hoped that wasn't a stretch, since Wylie just seemed so…distant.

The keeper of hospital information supplied directions to the Pediatric Emergency waiting room. Marlee didn't expect Wylie to be there. But he was, his head buried in his hands. He jumped up the moment she entered the room.

"Wylie, what's up?" Marlee sensed his growing despair.

"The pediatrician Dean's family doctor called is admitting him for observation. He's dehydrated, just as I thought. In addition to IVs, this doctor ordered X-rays and lots of blood tests. When they finish poking Dean full of holes, he'll go to a room. Isolation."

Marlee recognized Wylie's dazed expression. She'd been shuffled aside by enough doctors who had more important things to do than coddle their patient's loved ones. "Did you ask to have a cot put in Dean's room?"

"Will they do that? Two nurses in masks whisked him away and said for me to wait here."

Her heart ached for this loving man who was going through so much. Taking him by an arm, she mustered a bolstering smile. "Come with me. We'll be the squeaky wheel that gets the grease."

"I haven't slept in two nights." Wylie rubbed at deep lines underscoring his weariness.

"It's okay if you let me handle this for you. There are times we all need a shoulder to lean on. Even men are allowed to be scared sometimes."

"That b-boy means everything to m-me." Marlee saw how hard he fought to hold back tears.

"Of course. Wait, I'll tackle finding you a bed," she said,

hoping to lighten his heart. She started with the ward clerk and found the woman to be sympathetic and competent. She made a call and moments later promised Marlee a roll-away was being sent to Dean's room. The clerk called Marlee *Mrs. Ames.* Her "Thank you" froze on her lips. Turning away, she let the title echo in her head and found it pleasing.

Wylie rushed to meet her. "I take it your smile means you had success?"

"Yes." She didn't share what had really left her smiling. Instead, she sobered. "Wylie, can I get you anything before I go? A sandwich, maybe?"

He passed a hand over his haggard face. "By morning I'm going to look like a porcupine, if I don't already."

She let her fingers follow his, and indeed his stubble prickled.

"I could do with shaving cream and a razor. A disposable. I don't know if any store's still open. Dean and I both sweat all over this shirt." He plucked at it.

"I'd offer to raid Mick's closet and bring you a few things tomorrow, but you're taller and broader through the chest. You know, I recall seeing a late-night discount store a few blocks down the street. I'll run and see what they have."

He gave her his shirt size, then picked up her hand. He caressed each knuckle. "Are you sure? You've had a long day, too."

"I want to do this for you, Wylie. You're important to me. So is Dean, and you need to stay with him."

"Yeah. There's his nurse." Wylie's eyes, which had cleared briefly, clouded again. "I don't know if they'll let you come into his room. The doctor's worried he may be contagious."

"With what?"

"He's not sure. He asked about Dean's shots. Mumps was a specific concern."

"Maybe the doctor's thinking mumps encephalitis. I went to

high school with a kid who got that. He was really sick, but went on to captain our football team," she added, hoping to allay some of Wylie's fears.

He hugged her before letting her go. The hug felt right, and left a glow that warmed her even though it was still snowing.

Marlee located the store and parked close to the entry. She had no problem finding what she'd come for. Doing this was a little thing, but handing over the money and watching the clerk bag the all-male items felt...well, good. It'd been so long since she'd included anything other than girlie stuff on her shopping list.

She tried not to act as if it was a big deal—Wylie had too much on his mind to dedicate any time to furthering a relationship—but she was definitely coming out of a long deep freeze.

At the hospital again, Marlee wished she didn't have to leave. Wylie slipped out of Dean's room when she tapped on the door. "How is he?" she whispered. The ward had quieted for the night.

"The doctor has two IVs running. I think they gave him something to make him rest easier. Still, I'd better get back to him." He glanced anxiously over his shoulder at the door he'd pulled almost shut. "Thanks for these. I saw a weatherman on TV talking about the snow." He brushed a hand over her snow-damp hair. "Is it safe for you to fly tonight?"

"I'll be fine." She slid her arms around his waist and rested her head on his chest momentarily before pulling back. "How early tomorrow did they say Dean's reports will come back? I want to call you for his results, but I don't want to be a pest."

"I'll be up." He jotted down the room phone number. "They brought a cot, but I doubt I'll sleep." He warmed her chilly cheeks between cupped palms. "I'm not very good at this, Marlee. Listen, just hearing your voicetomorrow—any old time—will make my day."

Marlee clasped his wrists and scanned his serious face. "Same here. I hate to go, but I have to. I need to be in the air before they shut off the runway lights."

He lowered his lips over hers. Sighs escaped them both. She rose on tiptoes, drawing out every last taste before he reluctantly released her. He didn't return to the room until he saw her turn the corner.

So maybe he *was* thinking about a relationship.

Were they to be allowed a second chance at happiness? His first marriage had ended badly. Hers in death.

Was it wicked of her—of them—to kiss with Dean so sick?

On the runway, snow flew in eerie patterns off her rotors as she awaited clearance from the tower. For half an hour, it seemed to Marlee that hers was the only aircraft in the sky. Then she caught the wink of lights from a commercial jet headed for the main airport. It was as if that signaled some normalcy in what was anything but a normal day.

Mick had waited up. He didn't come out in the snow to meet her, but held the kitchen door open as Marlee dashed across from the hangar.

"About time you landed. What's the word on Dean?"

She stamped snow off her boots. "Is that coffee I smell? I've put nothing in my stomach since lunch." She headed for the fridge. "Dean's doctor ordered tests," she said. "Did Jo Beth go to bed without a fuss?"

"That dog is heaven-sent. She wanted to wait up until you got home, but Stella pointed out that Piston was falling asleep on his feet and was probably afraid to go to bed by himself. Jo Beth trotted off, peaceful as you please."

Marlee assembled a sandwich of leftover roast beef and cheese. "What's my schedule tomorrow? Wylie's hoping he can take Dean home."

"Next thing booked is picking up the hunters."

She took a bite, and accepted the mug he passed her. Sinking down on a chair, she said, "Have you seen a recent weather report? I thought this was supposed to blow over."

"Those weather guys make things up as they go. We won't know the truth until we wake up in the morning." He yawned. "I'm going to hit the hay."

Marlee finished her snack, but dumped the coffee. She didn't want to be too wired to sleep. She turned off the lights and tiptoed into the bedroom. Piston woofed quietly as Marlee sat on her bed. A beam from the lamp's night-light fell softly on Jo Beth. Suddenly compelled to make sure her daughter had no fever, Marlee settled a hand on the girl's forehead.

Jo Beth opened her eyes. "Hi, Mama. Is Dean okay now?"

"Shh, honey, go back to sleep. He's not well yet. Soon, I hope."

"Grandmother Rose said I should make him a get-well card. Pappy Jack helped me cut out pictures of animals to glue on the card. He let me cut up his hunting magazine, 'cause Dean loves wild animals."

"If I fly them home tomorrow, I'll give it to him. I don't want you around him until we find out for sure what's making him sick."

"That's what Grandmother said when I told her I didn't know why I had to stay home. Mama, Grandmother Rose has loose ends."

Marlee puzzled over the sleepy comment. "Oh, you mean she's *at* loose ends?"

"Uh huh! Can she drive up to visit? Then her ends won't be loose anymore."

"Is that what she said?"

"Not 'xactly. She wants to see us, though. Uncle Mick said she's an old bat. People can't be bats, can they? 'Cept for pretend at Halloween?"

Marlee grabbed her nightgown and stood. "Sweetie, I want you to try and go back to sleep. I need to shower, then I'm going to sleep, too."

She made a mental note to ask Mick to watch what he said.

Of course, anything Mick or Pappy knew about Rose Stein came from Marlee. She hadn't had many kind words last year during their custody tussle. Now, with distance, it was easier to view Rose differently. She'd lost her husband and son. After having her granddaughter virtually to herself, Marlee had waltzed in one day and announced she was taking Jo Beth a thousand miles away. Even though Marlee shared Rose's grief over Cole, she'd been away so much, Rose probably saw her as a stranger walking off with the only person she had left. She'd been desperate. The custody hearing had wasted time, energy and money. Marlee's lawyer had said from the outset that in ninety-nine percent of cases, the parent's rights topped a grandparent's claim.

Could the two of them come to terms on discipline and everything to do with raising Jo Beth if Rose came to Montana? It'd be good for Jo Beth if Rose could work out a visit. Cole would want that.

MORNING LIGHT STREAKING in the bedroom window nudged Marlee awake. Or was it a phone ringing that woke her? She leaned up on an elbow as it rang again, then stopped. Either the caller had given up, or someone had picked up the phone.

She stretched lazily, wondering about the time. All at once, Piston shook and ran to the door growling. She almost didn't hear the soft knock. Before she got up the door was shoved open, bopping Piston in the nose. He ran whining to Marlee.

Mick poked a tousled head around the door. "Sorry." He sounded croaky. "Angel Fleet's on the phone asking if you can fly a patient from Kalispell to Seattle. Possible meningitis."

"Seattle?" She crawled out of bed, grabbed her robe and followed Mick into the hall. "How long a flight is it? And what's the weather?"

"Three hundred and some miles. It's raining."

"It'll eat up a whole day flying there and back." A gamut of things ran through Marlee's mind. Not the least of which—she'd told Wylie that she'd be available to fly him home if the doctor released Dean.

"What's wrong? You've flown longer missions."

"Yes, but...Mick, will you see if they can find another pilot? I was out all day yesterday and half the night." She waved a hand toward the still-sleeping Jo Beth.

"Ah, you need to spend more time with the squirt. Okay, I'll ask them."

He left and Marlee returned to her room to pull on jeans and a flannel shirt. She dug around for warm socks and had picked up her boots when she heard the phone ring again.

This time she met Mick limping out of the kitchen. "It was Wylie, wondering why you refused to fly him and Dean to Seattle. I said we didn't know Angel Fleet's patient was Dean."

She felt dizzy and nauseated. "Oh, Mick! I...I...meningitis?" Shocked, she covered her open mouth with a fist. "If it's bacterial, that's really bad." Slowly she uncurled her fingers. "Uh, will you jot down the particulars, please? And call Angel Fleet to let them know I reversed my decision. But...I can't head out without waking Jo Beth. Mick, do you think Stella's free today?"

"Will you calm down?"

"Yes. Yes, I have to, so Wylie won't see what a basket case I am."

"Listen, relax. I flew a girl to Seattle once who had a heart condition every doctor here said was hopeless. There they operated and closed a hole in her heart, and she's fine. At Christmas, I heard from her mom. The kid's a cheerleader."

"Thanks, Mick."

Jo Beth sat up. Piston licked her face and she giggled. The sound, like no other, spurred Marlee toward hope for Dean. Wylie loved him so much he *had* to get well.

"Honey, I hate to go off and leave you again, but Dean's dad called. The doctor wants Dean to see a specialist in Seattle. That's in Washington state. It's a ways from here. I may not be back until really, really late tonight."

"Okay. I just want Dean to get better. Will you give him the card I made? It's on the Chinese checker board."

"I'll help you dress and brush your hair. Uncle Mick's going to call Ms. Stella to see if she can come again. If not, you and Piston will have to be very good for Uncle Mick and Pappy while I'm gone."

"I will." She stripped off her pajama top and held her arms up for the sweatshirt her mom pulled over her head.

"Tiddledywink, I love you to pieces." Marlee blew raspberries on the girl's stomach while stuffing Jo Beth's legs into corduroy pants. They both giggled, then Jo Beth threw her arms around her mother's neck.

"I love you, Mama. And Dean, too. You're worried about him, huh?"

Marlee checked her response. "A little. He and his dad need us to send them happy thoughts today, honey."

"I can do that. Will you bring me something from…what's that place?"

"Seattle. I'll see if I have time to shop. Do you remember the black-and-white whales at Sea World in San Diego? Those were Orcas from Puget Sound, right near Seattle. Maybe I can find a book on whales."

"And when Dean's better he can read it to me."

Mick limped in again. "I'm getting my exercise this morning. Okay, Wylie and Angel Fleet both confirmed they'll have an ambulance waiting at the airpark in forty-five minutes. And I cleared the day with Stella."

"I'd better shove off." She handed Jo Beth her shoes and socks.

"Maybe you ought to toss in an overnight bag. I downloaded weather stats. Ugly storm sitting right off the Pacific. It could break at any time." He opened her closet. "Here. Throw a change of clothes in your old navy flight bag."

"Darn, I wish I could fly the Huey. For this flight, I'd better use the Seneca."

"That's what I figured. Pappy's fueling her as we speak."

"He okay to do that? The last thing I want is to run short of fuel on this flight."

"Pappy has spells. With stuff like this, he's mostly reliable. You'll want to check your fuel gauge in any case. I trust you do that no matter who fuels your plane."

"I do, yes. Okay, I'll throw some essentials in the duffel. Wylie had me buy him a shirt and a razor last night. After another day, his jeans will stand up by themselves."

"I'd offer a pair of mine, but he's taller."

"That's okay. I'll probably have time while the doctor's examining Dean to run out and buy Wylie jeans."

Mick met her a few minutes later, and handed her a cooler. "I put in water, soda, and some PB&J sandwiches."

She brushed a kiss over his cheek. "Mick, are you limping more today?"

"I'm always stiffer in the morning. The sutures are healing. I actually feel pretty good."

"Don't overdo it, okay?" Marlee slung her navy bag over her shoulder, gave Jo Beth last-minute instructions and a big hug and shifted the cooler so she could take the get-well card. On the way to the hangar, she stepped in Pappy's larger, icy footprints.

Her grandfather was coiling the fuel hose. He looped it over its hook, and dusted his hands on his pants as she approached.

"Fill 'er up?"

"To the brim. Girl, ah…" The old man cleared his throat and kicked at frozen tufts of grass. "I know I said some harsh things about Ames. The boy, he's a cute tyke. I want you to know I'll be pulling for him. Old geezers like me, we can't argue if St. Peter trumpets. But young guys like Cole, and kids, well…"

"No talking like that, Pappy. You think Mick didn't need you when he came home all shot up?" Marlee hugged him, and teared up at the raw emotion lurking in his eyes. "I'm counting on you to ride herd on Mick and Jo Beth till I get back."

He tossed off a salute. "Aye, Captain." For a minute she was afraid Pappy had drifted into the past again. Until she heard him laugh. As she taxied out and down the runway, she found herself in a better frame of mind.

Just under forty minutes later, she rolled to a stop across from a red-and-white ambulance. One look at Wylie's vacant eyes and she knew he'd had a rough night.

Dean wasn't thrashing about or sweating profusely this time when they loaded him into the plane. Strapped to the big gurney, he looked small and defenseless. His red-gold eyelashes made dark shadows on sheet-white cheeks. Most of the color had even leached from his freckles.

Fearing Wylie might shatter at the slightest hint of sympathy, Marlee assumed a briskly professional air.

After they were aloft, he asked, "Why did you tell Angel Fleet no when they contacted you?"

"I had no idea they meant Dean, Wylie. I turned them down because you'd said you might need me to fly you home."

"Uh, thanks, then."

"You're welcome." She dropped her sunglasses, fuming a bit at his implied accusation as she climbed out of the rain. "What are you doing about feeding your animals?"

"I phoned Josh Maclean. He'll ride over to my place today. I know his folks can't spare him longer if I have to stay in Seattle." Wylie dropped his chin to his chest and rubbed his temples. "I asked the doctor where in hell Dean could've contracted a bacterial meningitis. Even with all the fancy tests, he said he's not sure it is meningitis."

Marlee didn't want to say that unfortunately in the world of medicine, sometimes that was just how it was. She struggled to keep her opinions positive, though she wasn't without bias. And yet, she believed Cole's doctors had done everything possible for him.

Wylie lifted his head and gazed gloomily out the side window.

She wanted to take his hand and assure him that where they were headed someone had answers. It was obvious that Wylie was hurting. And Marlee hurt for him. But she of all people knew doctors didn't have all the answers.

The trip was long, miserable and silent. Angel Fleet had arranged for her to land at Boeing Field. She taxied to where the tower directed her.

"Come with us in the ambulance?" Those were Wylie's first words in hours.

"You go. I'm going to rent a car. Mick said there were storm warnings off the coast. I may have to hunt up a hotel."

"Me, too. So, you'll follow us, right?"

"I'm resourceful, Wylie. I'll find you."

As it happened, Angel Fleet had reserved her a rental car. Stuck in traffic, Marlee used the time to phone home. "Mick, we've landed. Wylie rode in the ambulance. I picked up a rental. Don't tell Jo Beth, but Dean was too drugged for me to give him her card. I'll see he gets it, or I'll leave it with Wylie."

"Take care, and don't worry about us. We're fine."

The hospital, big and rambling, reminded Marlee of the one in San Diego. She had to muster courage from somewhere deep inside just to go through the doors. But unlike Cole's ward, this place catering to kids had both color and warmth.

She found Wylie pacing, wearing grooves in the waiting room floor. "Hi," she called softly, so as not to bother others sharing the room. She unfolded Jo Beth's card from her purse. "Jo Beth made this for Dean. Will you see he gets it?"

Wylie smiled as he read the card, then tucked it in his back pocket. "He'll like that she thought of him. I'd about decided you'd run into trouble."

"No. Just traffic. Where's Dean?"

"At lab and X-ray again. The other doctor faxed records, but since some tests were inconclusive, the pediatric internist here wants them repeated. God, Dean's always been a high-energy kid. Did you see how listless he was?"

Wylie was going through his own private hell, Marlee knew. Part shock, part bewilderment. She also noticed he hadn't made use of the razor. But still, he looked ruggedly gorgeous.

"Did they say how long he'll be? I passed a cafeteria. You won't do Dean any good if you collapse, Wylie."

"I look like hell, huh?"

"I didn't say that. But you do look like a man in need of sustenance." Taking charge, Marlee left word at the nursing station where they'd be.

Wylie let her lead him off. "I'm not used to anyone giving two hoots about me."

"Get used to it, buster." She linked their hands.

He stopped outside the cafeteria and brought their locked hands to his lips. He kissed her fingers. "I'm not good with words, Marlee."

"I don't need them." With her free hand, she combed back his dark hair.

The lean muscles along his jaw rippled, then relaxed. He might have been struggling to come up with something more to say, but Marlee shoved open the door. The odor of bacon engulfed them.

"Mick sent sandwiches. They're in a cooler out in the rental car. Peanut butter and jelly. His favorite. But it'd probably stick in our throats just now. How does soup sound?"

"I should probably try and eat."

"Find a table. I'll check out the soup and see if they have toast. Is there anything you simply can't choke down?"

He shook his head. Marlee encouraged him with a smile and a small nudge toward the tables. Friends had done the same for her. She felt like an old hand.

She chose vegetable soup and rye toast. She doubted either of them needed more coffee. Then again, it might be a long evening. She filled two paper cups they could take with them and snapped on lids.

He sat near a window in a quiet corner of the room. Marlee slid his portion off the tray. "Eat," she ordered, before removing her own and placing the tray on an empty table.

Wylie picked up his soupspoon. Steam curled around his face and his stomach growled. "Part of me says I need this."

Marlee waited anxiously until she was sure he intended to eat, whether or not he wanted to. She shook out her napkin and dipped her spoon in the thick soup.

They heard a loud crack near the window followed moments later by a rumble that shook the ceiling, silencing the noise in the room. "Man, it's awful out," Marlee said, gesturing with her toast at the rain beginning to batter the plate glass. "Looks like the reports Mick got from the weather bureau were right for a change. If this lightning doesn't let up, I won't be flying anywhere tonight."

"Dean hates storms." Wylie pushed his half-finished bowl aside, and grabbed his toast. "I've got to get back there." He reached for his coffee.

Marlee rose, too.

"Stay and finish eating."

"After you check on Dean, I'll try to find out how long this storm is expected to last." She efficiently bussed the table and returned the tray. Wylie strode out of the cafeteria. She ran to catch up. And was nearly out of breath as she followed him into the waiting room.

A youngish doctor in wire rimmed glasses entered the room from a door opposite. "Mr. Ames, I was just coming to find you. Our lab tech has preliminary test results. The good news is we don't believe your son has meningitis."

"And the bad news?" Wylie asked slowly, his color draining.

Marlee hung back, holding her breath.

"Diagnoses that aren't obvious take time. You don't want us jumping to conclusions," the doctor said. "Dean's resting with the aid of an IV drip. I've ordered close monitoring overnight in ICU. Mere precaution," he added hastily. "I can see you haven't had much rest. Why don't you check into a nearby hotel, and leave a number where you can be reached. Hopefully by morning I'll have more definitive results." He handed Wylie a business card.

When Wylie didn't say anything, Marlee came up behind him so close she knew he must feel her presence. "Can Wylie see Dean before he leaves the hospital?"

The doctor peered around Wylie. "Mrs. Ames?"

"No. A family friend. It's storming. Dean doesn't like thunder."

The doctor—Marlee read his name tag as Dr. Lefowitz—called to a nurse. "Take Mr. Ames to ICU unit three. I assure you, we do everything humanly possible to make our patients and their parents comfortable."

"I'll wait," Marlee murmured. "The thunder's still banging away. Since I need to find a room, too, we might as well book into the same hotel. And I have a car." She sat, prepared to wait as the men disappeared.

Having decided the safest thing would be to spend the night, she went out to the lobby to phone home. "Mick, we're feeling the brunt of that storm you mentioned. How is it there? No snow? Can I talk to Jo Beth?

"Hi, sweetie, it's Mom. The doctors are taking good care of Dean. It's raining hard here, and there's a lot of thunder and lightning, so I can't fly home until tomorrow."

"Did Dean like his card?"

"His dad promised to give it to him when he's awake. Wylie says Dean will love it. Oh, I see Wylie coming now. We've got to find a place to stay, hon. You and Piston sleep tight, okay? I'll call you in the morning."

Jo Beth said goodbye without a fuss, a relief to Marlee. It was hard being away from her.

"Dean's asleep," Wylie announced. "They wouldn't let me leave the card. Sterile room and all. I hate going off and abandoning him." He frowned at the still-swinging door.

"We can sit here all night if you'd rather."

Wylie bit his lower lip. "I'd probably fall off the chair."

"Then let's find the hotel closest to the hospital. The doctor made it sound as if there're several in the area."

They walked out into hammering rain, rolling thunder and lightning that lit up a black sky in jagged forks. Marlee pulled out keys and pointed to where she'd parked. They ran to the compact car between the bursts of light.

Wylie was the first to spot a hotel sign, and jumped out to see if they had a vacancy. Marlee watched the hypnotic swish of the wiper blades until he reappeared waving two key cards. Relieved it was so easy, she parked, grabbed her bag and sped to the door.

"I packed a few things in case I had to stay. I see you're wearing the shirt I bought you."

"Yeah, but I skipped shaving and forgot to bring the razor. The desk clerk said the hotel store's open." He handed Marlee a key card. "Our rooms are next to each other. Fourth floor. Do you want to go up? I'm going to phone the doctor's service and leave the hotel's number, then I'll detour past the store."

"Okay. I don't need anything from the store, so I'll go on up. Goodnight, Wylie. Wake me if there's any news."

As Marlee rode the elevator, she wished she was stuck here with Wylie for a much different reason. Sighing, she entered her room, switched on the light and tossed her bag and purse on the bed. She wanted a shower, but waited, thinking Wylie might stop in when he came up. He'd looked so bleak. He might want to talk. She recalled the nights she would've liked just knowing she wasn't alone.

Ten minutes passed. She heard his door open and shut. *So much for that thought.*

As she turned her shower taps, she heard his go on in the next room. She couldn't help that her imagination ran wild. Her bed was turned down. A big inviting bed…

Waiting for the water to heat, Marlee dumped her duffel on the bed and unwrapped the chocolate from her pillow. Along with the clothes she'd packed, a small ditty bag provided by the navy fell out. Obviously it'd been in there since her last mission. She unzipped the bag and checked its contents. Toothbrush and paste. Utility soap, not milled like the soap in the bathroom here. Bandages. Antibiotic cream. Bug repellant. Lip balm. Sunblock. Condoms? *The navy thought of everything.*

Marlee scooped up the items and tossed them back in the pouch.

In the steamy bathroom, she tore the paper off the better-smelling milled soap, and stepped under the spray, willing the tension out of her body.

CHAPTER TWELVE

MARLEE WAS RINSING her hair when Wylie's shower stopped. She toweled off, smoothed on moisturizer, then turned on a hair dryer hanging on the wall. It drowned out sounds from next door, but didn't impede her errant thoughts.

It felt all too intimate, showering a thin wall away from Wylie. Or not intimate enough. Showering together could be so…erotic. Suddenly hot, Marlee decided to let her hair air-dry. Humming off-key, she dropped her towel in the shower and changed into her nightgown.

In the next room, she flopped onto the bed and dug out a cross-word puzzle book she'd bought before leaving San Diego. She'd completed only two puzzles. Her mind always seemed otherwise occupied. As it was now. She glared at the wall connecting her room to Wylie's. Her next-door neighbor still hadn't settled down. He was clearly restless, and who could blame him? If Jo Beth were hospitalized, she'd be a mess.

She heard the muffled sound of Wylie's TV. Seconds later, he shut off. She knew the minute he sat down on his bed, and sensed when he got up again. Had he eaten his cream-filled chocolate?

Now he paced like one of Dean's caged animals.

For a decent hotel, the insulation between rooms wasn't worth crap.

Marlee set her book aside. She turned on the TV, muted it and surfed through the channels. No wonder Wylie had turned his off. There was nothing worth watching.

It was obvious neither one of them was going to sleep. He was worried sick about Dean, and she was worried about them both.

She got up and stopped short of reaching for the jeans she'd stuffed in her duffel. To heck with getting back in them. She and Wylie were both adults. Her robe covered as much as any dress, she decided as she slipped into it.

Maybe a drink would help them relax. Her room had a minibar. His probably did, too. She stuffed her room key in her pocket, hauled in a deep breath and opened the door intending to peer around to see if the coast was clear to walk out in a robe.

A yelp left her lips, scaring her and the man who blocked the light.

"Whoa, whoa, it's me." Wylie lowered his hand, which had been poised to rap on her door. "Sorry, I didn't know you were going out."

Her heart still raced from the fright. "I was coming to see if you were still up." *Ugh, that was a lie.* She knew darned well he was up.

Rubbing one bare foot nervously on the other, she drew a hand through still-damp hair. "I thought maybe a nightcap would relax us both. Come on in. We'll see what's in the minibar that suits your taste."

"Beer," he said. "A cold one would taste good. But since you were headed to my room, do you mind choosing from my bar? I just remembered, I left my room number with the doctor's answering service."

Other than his boots, Wylie was still fully clothed, leaving Marlee feeling underdressed, and wishing she had put on her jeans.

As she waited beside him while he opened his door, it struck her that they both smelled like hotel soap and shampoo. She found that reassuring.

At least she did until she noticed he'd shaved. Her pulse skyrocketed.

Stepping over the threshold, after the door closed, she felt the need to do something. Marlee crossed to the bar and checked its contents. "Do you prefer light, dark or imported?" She turned and noticed Wylie's eyes trained on her bare legs. When it was obvious she'd seen him staring, he spun away and hastily rubbed a hand up and down the back of his neck.

"I'm not picky," he managed to croak. "I...ah...maybe shouldn't drink. What if the hospital calls and the beer's knocked me on my butt? Anyway, you probably shouldn't be here in what you have on."

"One beer has that effect?" She'd already extracted two pale ales, and had the cap wrenched off one. "Aren't we adult enough to handle a drink and sit around talking? I'll grant you the reason we're here together is far from fun. But why act like a pair of teens caught sneaking into a no-tell motel? There were many times throughout Cole's illness when I would've welcomed a little human contact."

Marlee handed him a beer, uncapped the other and took a bracing swig.

Wylie set his bottle down without ever bringing it to his lips. "The truth of the matter is, Marlee," he hedged, his face dark and brooding, "I couldn't face being alone tonight. I...just needed to hold someone. And...want to be held a while."

His eyes held raw sincerity.

Without hesitation, Marlee set her bottle next to his on the nightstand. He'd been wrong when he said he didn't know the words. He did. She held out her arms and felt the sash on her robe tangle with the big buckle on the belt Wylie pretty much always wore.

He wrapped her tightly in his arms. His warm breath rearranged her air-dried curls.

She sensed the slamming of his heart, and she was almost dizzy when she felt him harden against her. Even if that wasn't what either of them had in mind, it was satisfying to know she could still evoke that response in a warm-blooded man.

His pensive mood gave way the minute his head bent and he buried his lips in her fragrant hair. Those same lips moved, nibbling her ear and then her neck. "Is this wrong?" he moaned.

"Does it feel wrong?" She sounded breathless.

"No." He shook his head. "We were moving in this direction. But I hate that Dean had to get sick to throw us together."

"Damn, Wylie. I can't tell you how my heart has ached for Dean. And you."

Wylie's fervent kiss cut off the remainder of her admission. Time stopped as they stood, exploring each other with seeking hands. Eventually they ended up bumping against the bed.

And her robe and his shirt lay in a trail on the floor.

Tumbling them down on the bed, he hiked up her nightgown, murmuring, "Raise your arms."

Marlee tried, but before he got it high enough, their tongues were tangled in a searing kiss. She blindly reached out a hand to find the switch to turn off the bedside lamp.

"Don't," he said. "I want to see you. I want to see every inch of you."

"Wylie, I'm not...glamorous. I'm no longer twenty-some-thing." She trapped his hands in the silky material of her gown.

"You're beautiful. I thought so the first time you stepped out of your plane onto my runway. God, I fought it, but on some level, I knew I was a goner."

His earnestness reached a place inside her that had long been ignored. It'd been years since she felt beautiful. The slight tremor in his voice made her feel young again. And carefree in spite of why they were here. And it was plain where they were headed. He leaned around her and fumbled in the drawer of the nightstand.

"Damn—there's nothing in here but the Seattle phone book, the chocolate I tossed in here earlier and a Bible."

"Will the mood be lost if I run next door? I found my former navy kit at the bottom of my duffel bag. What you're hunting for—well, I discovered a small box of them still in cellophane wrap. The navy looking out for its men and women."

He fell back, belt buckle gaping, and pants unzipped. Flinging an arm across his eyes, he waved her toward the door.

She drew on her robe and fumbled in the pocket for her key card.

She was back within minutes. Wylie hadn't moved a muscle. When she tossed the small box onto his chest, he jackknifed into a sitting position. Fortunately, it looked as though he was still up for the occasion. His eyes never left her as she let the robe trail off her arms.

The sight of him ripping open a Mylar packet with his teeth prompted her to sink onto the bed next to him and mumble, "I hope you're adept, Wylie. It's been so long for me, I may have forgotten how." Her hands drifted up his chest and down again.

His dark eyes glittered in the soft light. "Keep touching me like that. I'll remember everything I need to know."

Moments later, when he urged her onto her back and settled over her, resting most of his weight on his forearms, she thought there was nothing more mesmerizing than his velvet dark eyes shimmering with desire for her. Every bit of feeling she had for him, Marlee poured into her kisses.

The delicious rhythm he set didn't end until she bit back cries of pleasure against his damp flesh. And Wylie collapsed against her with a sigh that was really a groan of satisfaction.

"Nothing wrong with our memories," he remarked.

Marlee traced his eyebrows, cheekbones and lips. "Like riding a bicycle, I guess. You never forget how."

He spoke in the hollow of her throat. "Some rides are way better than others. This was *the* best."

They lay joined together until Wylie found the strength to roll aside. Even then he took her with him, tucking her tight under his arm. "I hope you have no regrets."

"None." She snuggled into him. "Has anyone ever said you taste delicious?" As she touched her tongue to the hollow of his throat, she immediately felt another surge against her thigh. She slid her hands over the sculpted muscles of his back to where his hips narrowed.

"Delicious? No, you are, Marlee Stein." He nipped at her earlobe and growled, "Do you have some trick up your sleeve to do with—chocolate maybe? We're moving into a danger zone here."

She stilled her exploration, tilting her head. "I ate my chocolate. It satisfied…a different appetite," she said with a smile, sliding her fingers up his ribs.

"Dean loves chocolates. I'll save mine for when he feels like eating again. Woman…you're killing me," he said, grabbing her hands. "Just how many of those packs does the navy allow their sailors?"

He found the box buried in the sheet and dumped out another Mylar packet. He ripped it open, fell back after sheathing himself and lifted her astride his hips.

This time he didn't object when she snapped off the light. He'd already watched ecstasy wash over her features. And, Wylie figured, after a second round of lovemaking, if it *didn't* kill him, falling into an exhausted sleep would be nice.

The frantic necessity to prove…anything…lay behind him. This time he lingered over pleasing her. And she did the same for him.

It was an intense pleasure that culminated in low pillow talk and cuddling. A surprise to them both.

"You've erased every shred of my tension," he said, stroking her arm.

"I'm glad, Wylie. Your pain has been my pain." Marlee wriggled closer so she was fully against his side.

"I never thought I'd want a woman sharing my bed every night. I was wrong," he said, lifting her hand to his lips.

"That's the most wonderful compliment I've had in…maybe forever, Wylie."

He said nothing else for so long, she pressed her ear against his chest to see if his breathing had evened out in sleep. But he moved and finger-combed her almost-dry hair. "My marriage was a sham from start to finish," he said quietly. "It shouldn't surprise you to hear how lonely it can get on a ranger outpost. I met Shirl after one exceptionally long winter. She was a new waitress at a café the rangers frequented. She flirted. I fell for her red hair and her smile. We hit it off. I…ah…found reasons to go to town—a lot. But how can I condemn what got me my son?"

Marlee felt his heart begin to jackhammer under her ear. She ran a soothing hand over him. "You don't have to tell me, Wylie. I know you had a disappointing marriage. So did I, albeit in a different way. That's all past."

"Please hear me out."

She rubbed her cheek against his chest hair. The movement was close enough to a nod that his voice rumbled beneath her ear again.

"I was a throwaway kid. So I'm extra careful with a partner, know what I mean?"

Marlee's breath caught. That admission told her a lot of private things about this man she'd come to love. *Love?* She tested the concept, and nearly missed his next words.

"Shirl showed up on my doorstep one morning after I hadn't been to town in weeks. It was the time of year I clear fire roads. She announced straight out that she was pregnant and claimed the baby was mine. Had a little strip in a plastic bag. You know, from the test kits?"

"I've never used them, but I've got friends who have."

"She said she had no one, and once she couldn't work she'd

be in a bind. I don't have folks. I weighed everything and figured I had one choice. I rounded up a couple of buddies to witness a quickie wedding at the courthouse. We went back to my place a married couple, but pretty much strangers. It didn't take long for me to see that was how she wanted to keep things between us. At arm's length."

Wylie played with her hair, Marlee found the motion soothing and his voice hypnotic. She thought she knew then why his marriage had fallen apart. But she hadn't guessed even half of it.

"I won't go into the gory details. Suffice it to say Shirl had a rough pregnancy. Sick seven out of nine months, and she hated the isolation. Nothing I said or did helped. We planned for her to board in town the last month before the baby came. He arrived unexpectedly in the middle of a stormy night. From the instant Dean slid into my hands and squalled, he was the best thing in my life." Wylie's voice trembled.

Again Marlee murmured nothing of consequence and stroked his cooling flesh. He'd already given her a lot to think about, but apparently he wasn't done.

"Dean was about three weeks old. I came in from repairing a broken corral at noon. Shirl was gone. I still have no idea how she arranged it. She left a note saying what I already knew—she didn't love me. Hated the outpost. She said she was sure I'd be a better dad than she could be a mother."

"Wylie, I'm sorry. You *are* a wonderful dad. Dean knows it. Surely that's not something you doubt."

"Here's the kicker. Dean's not my son."

Marlee gasped. She couldn't help it. Pappy had hinted at it once, but she hadn't given it a second thought.

Wylie urged her to lie back. "I mean, he's not biologically mine. I had no idea until I signed and returned the divorce and custody papers. Shirl's lawyer forwarded a letter she'd written, and asked him to send after everything was finalized."

"Wylie, you aren't worried his biological dad might show up and claim him are you?"

"That's never crossed my mind. According to the letter, the guy was a long-haul trucker. He's the one who dumped Shirl in our town."

Marlee slumped back into Wylie's arms. "So, this trucker probably doesn't know he has a son. He's yours in every way that's important." She hesitated. "Why tell me or anyone the truth, Wylie?"

"Well, the blood work they did in Kalispell said Dean's type A negative. I'm AB positive. If this is a deal where he needs transfusing, I can't give him blood because we don't match."

"Wylie, that's why we have blood banks. Blood's available everywhere. Angel Fleet volunteers even fly organs and blood if necessary."

He untangled his fingers from her hair and rained kisses onto her head. "I should've thought of that. Have I said how glad I am you flew into my life?"

Her smile accompanied a long kiss. Several followed. Comfortable ones that led them into a lazy discussion of the future. Until conversation brought them full circle to an earlier statement of Wylie's—that he'd never expected to want to share his bed with a woman every single night.

"It's odd how I feel like I've known you forever, Wylie."

"Long enough to move in with me? You and Jo Beth? Winter's approaching. It's lonesome there for me, and worse for Dean. He'd be ecstatic."

"Housemates, you mean?" Marlee pulled away, trying to see him, but it was too dark. The drapes didn't leak any light from the street lamps.

"I told you I'm not good with words. I had something more permanent in mind."

"Oh. Shoot! Like, marriage?"

"Don't sound so horrified."

"No, no, I'm not. It's just that we've barely gotten involved."

Now it was Wylie's turn to lever himself up onto an elbow. You thought tonight was what? Just about sex? *Not involved?* realize this is sudden, Marlee. What I feel here—" he found her and and spread her fingers over the area where his heart thudded trong and fast "—is happy when your plane lands. A real pit pens up in my stomach when you leave. When I see you disappear into the clouds I don't get a heck of a lot of work done until can call and hear you're all right."

Her fingers curled into his flesh. "I share those feelings," she dmitted warily. "But there are times you blow hot and cold. You're moody and distant, like the other day…" She broke off bruptly. "Oh no! I remember what I said! We were talking about Dean's motor mouth and I jokingly asked if you were sure he was our son. Wylie, I am *so* sorry. I'm glad you've told me the truth ow. Good relationships start with honesty."

He eased back, taking her with him. "I've no more skeletons. o, do you think a relationship is possible?" He couldn't seem finish he question for the yawn.

His yawn led to hers. She stifled it with a hand, and burrowed nto his side. "It's possible. But, Wylie, I have family to consider. et's sleep on all these massive changes we've discussed. I mean, ere's no rush, right? Getting Dean well and home is our number ne priority."

"I've never told a woman I love her. These feelings I have for ou are the closest to what I feel for Dean, and then some. If that's ot love, I'm not sure what is."

"I know you're sincere." She shackled him with an arm, doing er best to rid herself of the panic she couldn't seem to quell. Love won't slip away overnight, Wylie. True love grows day by ay."

He made no further comment. When he remained silent too ong, Marlee lifted her head cautiously to see why. He snored softly.

She wished she could shut off everything running through her head. She couldn't see the clock over his body, but there was no doubt it was many hours before she fell asleep.

She woke up in a strange bed, feeling achy and disoriented. The room was gray. Flopping on her back, she felt the bed shift. She squinted up through gritty eyes, and saw Wylie propped up on an elbow, staring at her tenderly. He swooped down and kissed her. Thoroughly and gently. It was nice.

He slowly straightened. "I slept on last night's discussion. Nothing's changed. I feel exactly the same. You?"

His smile warmed her. The vague aches—and she now recalled their origin—faded. "I could get used to waking up every day like this. If it includes coffee," she teased, tickling his ribs.

Laughing, Wylie rolled over and swung his legs off the bed. "Give me a minute to shower, shave and dress. Then I'll turn the shower over to you and go downstairs—to see if I can find coffee. Will that give you privacy enough?"

"Considering how we spent the night, Wylie, isn't it a little late for privacy?"

"I wasn't sure how you'd feel in the cold light of day."

"It's not light yet. Hey, any word on Dean? Or is it too early?"

"It's early, but I checked. I didn't want to wake you since you seemed to be sleeping soundly, so I shut myself in the bathroom to phone. He had a good night. He's awake. They said the doctor will be in around eight. I don't know if you want breakfast, but I'd like to go straight to the hospital and see him before the doctor's rounds."

"Coffee will do me fine, Wylie. I'm so relieved to hear Dean's awake." She felt around the floor, found her robe and slipped it on as she got out of bed. "What's the weather like?"

"It's still raining. But I think the thunderstorm's dwindled away."

"Good. I need to get home. I'm scheduled to pick up a group of hunters tomorrow morning."

"I won't know what's in store for me until after I speak with the doctor."

"I understand, Wylie. If you have to spend another night, I can stop by and feed your animals."

"That's too much to think about just yet."

"I've found it pays to plan ahead."

He turned from opening the plastic bag that contained the new shirt he'd bought in the hotel store. "Guess I prefer not to waste time planning for something that might not be necessary." He removed the shirt, shook it and threw the bag, cardboard inserts and pins in the trash.

"We differ there." She watched him collect his still-packaged personal items, including a second disposable razor. Or was it a third? He said he'd left the one she bought in Kalispell, but he'd certainly been clean-shaven last night.

"You look so serious," he said, pausing in the bathroom doorway. "Do you think we *should* agree on everything? Wouldn't that make life dull?"

"I know better than that, Wylie." She paused. "It dawned on me that both times I've fallen in love, it's been with a bang."

He broke into a huge grin. "Love, huh? That's a word you were reluctant to use last night. I'll take it!" Whistling, he disappeared into the bathroom and shut the door.

As he soaped and showered, Wylie forced himself to think about all the things that had brought him to a point of declaring his love for Marlee Stein, when he couldn't recall ever having felt anything close to that before.

He'd told her the truth when he said everything had started the minute she set foot on his runway. She was pretty, yes. But it was more. She was feisty, quick-witted and competent. The mere sight of a mother deer with fawns brought tears to her eyes. At the time, his only thought was how she'd react seeing her own baby for the first time. Not like Shirl who'd shoved Dean away. Marlee wouldn't be like that. She was tender and strong.

She hadn't shied away from cleaning his wounds. Wylie saw how she was with Jo Beth. And Dean gravitated toward her, and trusted her. She was the woman he wanted, he told himself, toweling off before sliding into his clothes. He brushed his teeth, combed his wet hair and left the bathroom.

She sat patiently on the bed waiting for her turn. The TV was turned on low to the weather channel. "All done?" She stood and dropped the remote onto the nightstand. But she wasn't prepared to be swept into his arms—and to be so thoroughly kissed it left her weak and clinging to him for support.

"Hmm, nice," she murmured, licking her lips, gazing at him through slitted eyes. "What was that for?"

"You were on my mind the whole time I was showering."

"I can tell." She wiggled against the hard ridge covered by his zipper. "If you'd said something earlier, I'd have suggested saving time by showering together."

"Don't tempt me," he said, setting her down and playfully swatting her backside as he turned her toward the bath. "Last night we used all of your emergency supplies. Next time, I won't be caught short."

"Excuses, excuses." She tsked, grabbing her bag as she slowly closed herself inside the steamy room that tantalized her with the scent of Wylie's aftershave. She yanked the door back open. "Maybe we shouldn't even mention doing this again. That'll mean Dean…" She bit her upper lip, then said, "I'm probably conjuring up trouble where none exists. You'll probably get to take him home."

"I'm sure you can't help relating this to your own experience.

It must've been awful. One day I hope you're able to tell me everything about Cole."

"Some things are better left alone. That was a whole other life."

"It affects who you are. And who Jo Beth is."

"Wylie, I just thought of something. If you and I...well, that's getting ahead of myself, but how would you react if Jo Beth's paternal grandmother popped in?"

"Your husband's mom?" He shrugged casually. "Is that a possibility?"

"Maybe." She clung to the door with one hand. "Listen, it's nothing we need to discuss right now. Time's ticking away. I'll shower and we can drink our coffee on the way to the hospital."

He nodded absently as she withdrew. Wylie could well imagine that Marlee's husband's mother wouldn't be overjoyed to think Marlee was ready to move on. In fact, when Mick talked about his sister moving to Montana, he'd mentioned a custody issue. That was why Wylie took it for granted that Marlee had been through a divorce. The custody battle, he thought now, must have been with her husband's family.

The elevator came and he rode down with a family of five who eagerly chatted about where to go for breakfast. Except for the youngest child, still in diapers.

He waved them out ahead of him and reflected again that in a year or so, if Marlee consented to marry him, this could be them. But as Marlee had said, thinking of having a baby together was getting ahead of himself.

Although the image persisted while he filled two cups and pressed on lids... The two of them hadn't discussed whether or not Marlee could have—or even wanted—another baby. He assumed, though, that if she couldn't have more, it would've come out while they'd scrambled to find condoms. He shifted the stacked hot cups from one hand to the other and pushed the elevator button. It was a wonder couples ever got married a second time, given the number of topics they needed to talk over and settle.

Maybe he'd lived in the backwoods too long.

On the fourth floor, he awkwardly searched for his key card. The room door was wrenched open, and Marlee stood with duffel in hand. "What took you so long? It's unbelievable how badly in need of caffeine I am." She relieved him of one cup, pulled off the cap and drank. "Ah...I feel almost human."

"Uh, my friends talk about how long they have to wait for their wives to get ready to go anyplace. I didn't want to rush you," he muttered.

"In the military, lollygagging wasn't an option. I emptied my room and yours. We can drop the keys, pay our bills and take off."

"I wonder if they'd give us a discount since we technically only used one room."

"Technically I used their soap, shampoo and towels. Oh, and I devoured the chocolate. Hey, maybe it was an aphrodisiac."

Wylie jerked his head, bringing her attention to the cleaning staff who were rolling a cart of supplies off the service elevator. "I know what we did with *other* items."

"The two beers we didn't drink, you mean?" She jabbed him with an elbow as they boarded the elevator.

Teasing fell by the wayside once they left the hotel and got into the car. The fine mist and rhythmic swish of the wipers brought a sobering reality as to why they were here and what they might find where they were headed.

"It's almost eight," she said, rechecking her watch as she turned into the hospital lot. "Traffic was heavier than I'd expected. I should've compared a Sunday drive in Seattle to one in San Diego, not Kalispell." She stopped at the front doors. "I'll let you out so there's no chance you'll miss Dean's doctor. I'll park and be up in a few minutes."

"I shouldn't always leave you to be the one hiking through the rain."

"Go. I won't melt. If Dean is more alert, he'll be champing at the bit to see you."

Wylie wove his free hand around the back of her neck and tugged her across the console for a quick kiss that left them both wanting more.

However, she pulled back with a crooked smile and made shooing motions with her hands.

Last night had been a fantasy. She needed another minute to get hold of her herself. And she hadn't wanted to confess how jumpy her stomach was all of a sudden—which had nothing to do with the jolt of caffeine. In her experience, visits to the hospital rarely ended happily. That was why, rain or not, she dragged her feet instead of hurrying into the sprawling building.

A couple and an older man sat in the waiting room. There was no sign of Wylie. Marlee debated hanging around here versus hunting him down.

Deciding it was cowardly not to find him, she went up to the reception desk. Once the woman got off the phone, she said, "I'm looking for Mr. Ames. The patient is his son, Dean. I'm the pilot who flew them in yesterday from Montana," she added for legitimacy.

"Ah, Montana." The woman's eyes twinkled. "That explains his mighty fine cowboy walk." She followed up her observation with directions to Dean's room.

"Thanks." Marlee didn't bother to correct the woman. Ranger. Cowboy. The two had a lot in common. And she was guilty of walking behind Wylie Ames and fanning her own face to cool off.

Rounding a corner, she stopped. Wylie stood outside a room with a lot of glass windows, talking with Dr. Lefowitz. She scanned their faces, measuring them for bad news.

The men glanced around when she paused behind Wylie. He

reached back, slid an arm around her waist and drew her forward. "Dr. Lefowitz said the first round of blood tests are still inconclusive. He's ordered more. A tech is drawing blood from Dean right now."

"Ah, so you'll be staying another day?" she asked cautiously.

"We were just discussing that. Apparently they gave Dean a shot of vitamin B-12 last night, and he's got color back. And energy. Dr. Lefowitz says it may be some new viral bug." He paused. "I explained my situation at the station, and with the animals."

"And I have to fly home today. I have a schedule to meet."

"Tell you what," the doctor said, flipping through lab slips glued to the chart he held. "The test results won't all be back until Wednesday. We like to save parents the expense of room and board if at all possible during the fact-finding stage. I know people don't think so, but we're conscious of not draining your insurance. I'll let Dean go home for now, but I'd like you to phone my service tomorrow and Tuesday and update me on how you think he's doing. Is he steadily improving, or going downhill? I'll have a nurse get him ready and bring him to the waiting room."

Wylie bobbed his head. "Sounds great."

"Did you see Dean?" Marlee asked during their short walk to the waiting area.

"He's in good spirits. Me, too," Wylie said, taking her hand easily. "I gave him Jo Beth's card. He's making plans to call her. Would you think a virus could wreak such havoc?"

"I'm no doctor, but I'll keep my fingers crossed that's all it is."

Dean was certainly much improved. He was back to talking nonstop all the way to the airport. It was a welcome sign.

On the flight, Marlee and Wylie exchanged small, secretive smiles. By the time she landed on his runway, rain was mixed with snow and Dean was asleep. Wylie threw his jacket over his son. "I'm going to carry him. Don't want to risk a relapse."

"I'd go in with you, but I've left Jo Beth long enough. See you guys."

She saw from the flash of Wylie's dark eyes that it was clearly as unsatisfactory a parting for him as it was for her. Taxiing off, she raised a hand and saw him mouth, "Call me when you get home."

A warm feeling crept over her. It was very nice having someone worry about her for a change.

CHAPTER THIRTEEN

RAIN SOAKED the wind sock at the end of Mick's runway, and as Marlee landed, a gust of wind turned the colorful marker inside out. She steered the Seneca into the hangar. Her fuel gauge said low. Very low. Marlee grabbed the hose and pulled it across to refuel the plane.

Mick hobbled out in the rain. "Hey, what's taking so long? Plane have a problem?"

She glanced up. "Crutches? What happened, Mick?"

"Don't wanna talk about it."

"You fell, right?" Another light dawned. "Over the dog! I knew it!"

He clammed up.

"Are you okay? No long-term effects, I hope."

"More bruised ego. I take it Dean's better? I left Jo Beth talking on the phone with him. That's why I came out. Wylie said the storm moved in so fast, he wanted to make sure you made it home in one piece."

Marlee restored the hose to the hook on their pump. "Not all the tests are back on Dean. He certainly seems better. I'm picking up our hunters tomorrow. Did you book any other flights?" They headed for the house.

"Two. Both supply orders. Angel Fleet called to tag you for Pete Jenner's wife. She needs transport Tuesday to Missoula. Heart surgery. I declined for you. Your schedule's already tight. Also, Rose Stein phoned. She's driving up. Will be here Wednesday."

"What?" Marlee almost ran into the door that Mick held open with his crutch. "When? How? *Why?*"

The kitchen door slammed behind them. "The cottage is ready. I thought we could put her there. Give you two some space."

So much whirled through Marlee's mind. Mainly, everything that had escalated between Wylie and her. She was still trying to come to terms with how she was going to break the news to Jo Beth and Mick, let alone Pappy—he wouldn't be pleased—and now there was Rose added to the mix.

"I can see you're upset. Rose phoned Jo Beth from Salt Lake City. That was the first we heard about this trip."

Marlee sighed. "It's okay, Mick. She's Jo Beth's only grandparent. It'll be fine. I hope," she mumbled.

Jo Beth heard her mother's voice. "Dean, my mama's home." The girl streaked across the room and gave Marlee a one-armed hug. "Dean's daddy wants to talk. Then can we eat?"

Mick laughed. "Stella left some kind of chicken casserole. Jo Beth helped make it. She's dying to show off her newfound cooking skills. Aren't you, kid?"

Nodding her head, the girl passed the phone to her mom.

"Hi," Marlee said cheerfully. She wasn't sure if she had Dean on the line, or if Wylie would be there.

"Hi, yourself. I miss you already."

The mere sound of his voice swept away her mounting stress. "Same here," she said. Her own voice softened.

From the next room, Pappy yelled at Jo Beth to come finish their board game. She galloped off after a final squeeze of her mom's legs. Marlee automatically sought a quieter spot, turning away from the arch that led to the living room. She propped a shoulder against the fridge. Thinking everyone had left her alone she allowed their talk to turn semi-intimate.

She was startled to hear her brother clear his throat directly behind her. Whirling, she felt the force of the Callen eyes demanding answers. "Uh, Wylie...I barely walked in the house. I'll call you later," she promised, "after the household settles for the night." Switching off the phone, she faced Mick, her stance combative.

He leaned heavily on the crutch saddles, his mouth twisted to one side. "Sounds like things must've got interesting between you and Wylie in Seattle. What gives?"

She caved, and words about how she and Wylie figured out they'd fallen in love tumbled one over the other. She skipped details, but added, "I thought you liked Wylie."

"I do." He released a hand and rubbed the bridge of his nose. "I'm just getting used to having you here. Having you fly for Cloud Chasers. And now...but, hey, you never said anything about leaving us."

"I can't...would never...ask Wylie to give up being a ranger, Mick."

"Yowza! You're seriously in love with the guy?"

"I...yes," she said. "It's that simple, really."

They talked at length, about Wylie, Dean, Pappy, Jo Beth and the business. Finally Mick straightened away from the counter and let out a breath. "I'm happy for you both, Marlee. For all four of you." He shifted again and stared down at the rubber tips of one crutch. "Call it envy. But..." He gave a guttural laugh. "Hell, I don't have any prospects. Anyway, Pappy needs me."

She rose on her toes and planted a kiss on her brother's cheek. "His health is declining, Mick. And you're a good man. But you need to get out more. Meet someone. Know any female pilots? This business will provide a good living for a couple, for a young family, even. Unfortunately, you can't afford to hire a full-time pilot. The way it stands, Jo Beth and me, we're eating your profits."

"Nah, you're eating my navy disability." He brushed her jaw with his knuckles, and suddenly the air was cleared and all was well.

Having leapt one hurdle, Marlee brought up the prospect of joining forces with Wylie, over Stella's chicken casserole and the biscuits Marlee made to go with it.

"You mean Dean would be my brother?" Jo Beth grew excited. A moment later, she said, "But Piston's all mine, isn't he?" She cast a veiled glance at her uncle. "Uncle Mick, when Mama was gone I know you fed Piston."

Surprisingly it was Pappy who chimed in, settling the matter. "That dog's bonded with you, girl. Me 'n Mick, we'll go to the shelter and find us another pet."

Her eyes filled with tears, Marlee scrambled out of her chair and nearly squeezed the life out of her grandfather. "Thank you. For that, and, well, for everything." She sniffled, and he waved her back into her seat with a gnarled hand.

"I raised you to know your own mind, girl. I figure Mick'll still fly in your supplies. And I 'spect you face enough opposition from that woman, Rose."

That claimed Marlee's thoughts when she should've been sleeping. And the next day, too, while flying the Huey over hills dusted with snow on her way to collect the hunters.

Paul Tabor eyed the helicopter with distaste. "Will this hunk of junk get us home?"

"You, your partners and all the venison you bagged."

The men hooted with laughter. "Time to confess," Paul said, his expression sheepish. "Hunting is our excuse to get away without our wives. If we ever do accidentally hit something during our week-long trip, Steve knows this guy who'll pick up the meat and package it for a local food bank."

With a new appreciation for the quintet, Marlee helped them load up.

The snow fell fast and heavily, coating the ground by the time she set down at home. She thought about Rose driving alone in this weather. Had she ever been out of California? If she followed the Interstate, she'd probably made Idaho Falls by now, or a bit farther.

"Mick," she yelled, shaking off snow as she entered the house. "What's the weather like south of us?"

"This storm is moving in that direction, why?"

"Rose," she muttered. "Has she called today?"

"Just did. That woman's a driving fool. She's way ahead of schedule. Plans to stop in Dillon, Montana, tonight."

"Shit." Marlee had turned to the local weather channel. "She'll wake up to ten inches of snow. I doubt she's ever driven in it." Marlee made a snap decision. "Check and see how close to wherever she is I can land, and tell her to wait for me at the nearest airfield. I'm going after her in the Huey."

Mick laughed. "If that doesn't discourage future visits, nothing will."

"Yeah, plus I'll have her captive while I explain about Wylie and me. Rose can't pitch too big a fit, or I'll threaten to toss her out without a parachute." She grinned.

Twenty minutes and three phone calls later, Marlee and Jo Beth were in the air.

"Mama, Dean's sick again."

Marlee turned shocked eyes toward her little passenger. "Sick, how?"

"He threwed up again. And he didn't wanna talk."

Marlee hadn't had time to call Wylie, and now she felt bad. Guilty. She'd phone after she hooked up with Rose. During refueling.

The snowstorm chased her, always staying ten or so miles behind. Marlee worried about the return trip. She'd meet bad weather head-on.

Per Marlee's instructions, Rose waited at a small airport. She looked elegant as usual, but more gaunt than before Marlee had left. She got up the minute the door opened, and nervously fussed with her cashmere coat. Marlee sent Jo Beth scurrying on ahead. She needed a moment to make that call to Wylie.

"Hi," she said, injecting sparkle in her tone as she asked about Dean, then rushed to explain what she'd done all day, and where she was now.

"Dean's fever has climbed again. I've talked to Dr. Lefowitz twice. The tests he's waiting for will be back Wednesday. He's asked to see Dean again then." The pain in his voice stayed with her even after they'd made arrangements for her to pick them up at dawn on Wednesday.

"I didn't want to put you out, Marlee." That constituted Rose Stein's greeting. She'd had her hair cut since Marlee last saw her, and the sleek gray bob was becoming. Slim and straight, she wore a tweed pantsuit under her coat, with ankle boots and gold jewelry.

"Jo Beth and I would rather you arrived intact. The truth is, it's tricky driving in snow, Rose. It's tricky flying in it, too. If all of your bags are here, we need to go." She picked up two of her former mother-in-law's designer cases, leaving the cosmetic bag for Jo Beth to lug.

"Grandmother Rose, I told you about my dog, but I never told you I'm getting a brother."

Marlee groaned, and lengthened her stride. She sensed the shock rippling through Rose Stein, and felt it intensify when Rose got a look at the chipped khaki body of the Huey.

"We're traveling in that…that whirlybird? I thought you were flying *planes*, Marlee."

"We have two light planes. This chopper is our workhorse."

Rose grabbed her daughter-in-law's arm as soon as the luggage had been loaded. "Is it really safe for you in your condition?"

Marlee had already boosted Jo Beth inside. The girl was adept now at buckling her harness and donning earphones. "Safe in what condition?"

"Don't play dumb. Obviously you're pregnant. Jo Beth said…"

"She said she's getting a brother. I met a very nice man, Rose. He has a son who's three years older than Jo Beth. And before you take me to task, let me say Cole and I talked about the inevitability of me falling in love again. He gave his blessing. No, more than that, he urged me not to close myself off as you've done. Rose, you're not yet sixty, and you're very attractive."

The barely lined face softened around the eyes. "That's one reason I decided to make this trip, Marlee. I have started dating someone. Our insurance broker. His wife died three years ago. Emmett Nelson. He lives down the block from me. We met at the deli one day."

Marlee couldn't be sure in the fading light, but she thought Rose blushed. At any rate, the news they'd traded gave them each a lot to mull over. Rose let Marlee boost her into the seat, and surprised them both when she figured out how the harness worked.

Thereafter talk remained sporadic. Marlee constantly needed to adjust her course to avoid being battered by the wind-driven snow. Rose was a white-knuckle flyer, but Marlee gave her credit for not complaining.

"My, this area is wild, but beautiful, like a Christmas card," Rose said sometime later, after they'd set down and all clambered out.

Pappy emerged from the house to help unload luggage. Marlee introduced the crotchety old man to the regal and refined woman. They were cordial. Marlee finally breathed easy.

"Jo Beth and I are staying in the main house," she told Rose. "It seemed best, especially after I learned Mick needed additional surgery. The cottage is warm and dry, but it's nothing fancy," she warned as Pappy unlocked the door.

"Marlee, goodness, I'm not a hothouse flower. And Phillip wasn't always an admiral. We managed just fine in cheap housing early in our marriage."

Marlee turned to her just before they stepped over the threshold. "But Cole said your family had money."

"They did, but Phillip was a proud man. We never took a dime from them. And my parents left their entire estate, except for burial funds, to the Sierra Club."

"I didn't know," Marlee said, stunned. "There's so much family history I never learned from Cole, I guess."

They all stood looking around the small cottage that had the essentials and the few personal touches Marlee had added the day she arrived. Rose commented on how nice the pillows looked with the afghan she'd knit.

"We should be getting over to the house," Pappy said. "Stella figured you'd all be starved, and she thought breakfast would hit the spot, given it's midnight. That woman makes a mean waffle with bacon cooked right in it. If I wasn't on my last legs, I'd marry her."

Jo Beth delighted in escorting her grandmother through the breezeway. The girl jabbered on about Ms. Stella teaching her to cook.

Rose hung back for a word with Marlee. "I never thought I'd say this, but I can see the move has been beneficial for Jo Beth. I was an old fool to think I could take the place of her mother and father. I hope the new man in your life and hers will be as generous about letting me visit as you've been, Marlee." Her eyes brimmed with tears.

The last vestige of Marlee's pent-up anger with Rose melted away. Impulsively, Marlee linked their arms. "Wylie has no family, and his son's mom is out of the picture altogether. Dean is a sweet boy, who I know will love sharing Jo Beth's grandmother."

They entered the warm kitchen filled with the aroma of Stella's good cooking. Marlee introduced Rose to Stella. She'd met Mick long ago at Cole and Marlee's wedding. To the surprise of everyone, the two older women hit it off, and discussed favorite recipes and handcrafts, dragging the late-night breakfast out until Mick's yawning brought attention to the actual hour. Jo Beth had long since fallen asleep.

Marlee had intended to touch base with Wylie again, to check on Dean. She didn't want to risk scaring him by phoning at 2:00 a.m. But after walking Stella home through the snow, and then dropping Rose off at the cabin, the cold air had stimulated her. She took a chance on Wylie's being awake.

Though his voice sounded deep and raspy, he answered on the first ring. "Marlee, I hoped you'd call when you got in. I haven't been able to sleep for worrying about you, and worrying about Dean."

"He's no better, then?"

"The pills they gave me to use in case his fever returned seem to be keeping it in check. Today he begged me to let him turn out the last of his wild animals. He's sure that when he goes back to Seattle Wednesday, it'll be a long time before he comes home again. I didn't know how to respond to that."

"No wonder you're so concerned, Wylie. That's just kid-talk," she reassured him. "What time shall we head out? I know you said at first light, which would mean I'd have to land on your runway in the dark. And if it's still snowing…" She let the suggestion trail.

"You're the pilot, I'll let you call those shots."

They turned then to discussing Rose's reaction to the news of Wylie. From there, he pressed to find out who Marlee would want present at their wedding.

"Wylie, perhaps it's too early to talk about the ceremony."

"Because I haven't even given you a ring, you mean?"

"Not that. You know, I'm probably just exceptionally tired. Let me sleep on this, okay? For sure, I want Mick and Pappy there. Pappy Jack missed my first wedding. Jo Beth, but that goes without saying. Simple is great. I'm not big on frills." She almost didn't get the last out for yawning so wide.

"Here I'm keeping you up. I just want to say I'm fine with anything you want. I want whatever makes you happy, Marlee."

"That's sweet. What I really want is for Dr. Lefowitz to find out what's wrong with Dean, and give him whatever it takes to make him well."

"On that we agree. You'll probably want to spend tomorrow with Jo Beth's grandmother. When I hear your plane Wednesday, I'll bundle Dean up and we'll come out to the runway. And this time I'll be prepared to stay overnight. Does that work for you?"

"I think that can be arranged." She settled down to sleep, still wearing a smile.

SOMETIME TUESDAY afternoon a steady downpour swept in to melt and muddy the snow. It was the soaking kind of rain that kept everyone inside, even the dog.

Mick's hip ached. Pappy complained about his joints. And Marlee learned that Rose had a touch of arthritis in her hands. Tempers had frayed by nightfall.

The next morning no one wanted Marlee to fly off to Seattle.

"I'm sorry, Mick. Wylie set this up through Angel Fleet. I promised them I'd make this trip. I'll be back Thursday, honest. I want you to call that PT in Missoula and ask to be seen on Friday. What if you got something out of whack when you fell the other day?"

"I didn't. It's the rain. This is the same weather I came home to after all those weeks in the military hospital. I'm in a mood, that's all. Go. Tell Wylie good luck."

She went, but soon found Wylie's mood to be no better than Mick's. Dean's temperature remained elevated even with the medicine meant to keep it down.

"I don't like this weather," Wylie said, shaking drops off his hair.

"Me, neither." Gritting her teeth, Marlee took off into the wind and was promptly slammed by a gust that had Wylie blanching and Dean crying out in fear.

As far as the naked eye could see, there was nothing but angry gray clouds and steadily slapping raindrops. "It's as if heaven is weeping." Marlee said out loud what she'd been thinking.

Wylie's brows drew together in a scowl. And remained that way for most of the trip.

Once on the ground, he phoned Dr. Lefowitz while Marlee saw to the plane and picked up the rental car.

"Dean's tests are back," Wylie announced as he and Dean climbed in. Both got in back and Dean lay down on his dad's lap after Wylie buckled them in. That forced Marlee to catch his eye in the rearview mirror.

"And…?" she prompted. "What are the results of the tests?"

"He wouldn't give them to me over the phone. He's meeting me at the hospital."

The bad weather made for heavy traffic and a slow drive.

Again Marlee let Wylie out at the hospital's front entrance. "We'll wait for you in the lobby," he said.

"Don't do that, Wylie. It's not a good idea to keep the doctor waiting. Anyway, this is between you and Dr. Lefowitz." Anxiety had begun to gnaw at her stomach, and whether or not she realized it, Marlee distanced herself as a coping measure.

Wylie recognized the ploy. "Soon as we can work it out, you will have an important role in Dean's life. Hurry upstairs, okay? You may pick up on something the doctor says that I totally miss."

There were no parking spaces open in the first lot. Marlee moved to lot two, and then on to lot three. As she locked the car and fastened her jacket, she saw that ten minutes had passed. She broke into a jog. Her fear was silly, she told herself. A result of this blasted weather. Anyone would feel negative. She owed

Wylie support through good times and bad. Besides, they didn't know for sure the doctor's news wasn't good.

There was a crowd at the bank of elevators. Marlee took the stairs. The route took her past a small conference room on the pediatric floor. When she heard Wylie's voice, she skidded to a stop at the partly open door.

"The tests are quite conclusive, Wylie," Dr. Lefowitz said. "Dean has Burkitt's lymphoma. The cause is related to genetic or chromosomal abnormalities in as little as a single lymphocyte in the body."

Marlee's mind and body went numb the minute she heard the word lymphoma. Cole had lost his life to lymphoblastic lymphoma. A cry she couldn't contain burst from her lips and she found the world going black. She fought against passing out, but in so doing, braced herself on the door. It swung in toward the occupants of the room. Just Wylie and the doctor. One glimpse of Wylie's face, which was drained of all color and vitality, spiked Marlee's heart with fresh fear.

Dr. Lefowitz jumped up, but on identifying their intruder, beckoned Marlee in. She literally fell through the opening and stumbled heavily into the chair. Wylie reached for her hand. She found his clammy and cold. Normally he radiated warmth.

The doctor, apparently not noticing anything odd in their behavior, returned to the chart, presumably Dean's record, and flipped forward three pages. "Burkitt's lymphoma is a very aggressive cancer. Fortunately it is sensitive to chemotherapy. Normally very responsive, in fact."

"That's a lie," Marlee burst out, unable to contain the anger and dread building within her. "It's up and down, up and down, and finally all down."

Wylie whirled toward her. "Marlee? What do you know about this?"

"Cole died of lymphoma. I've heard these predictions over and over and over!"

Dr. Lefowitz gazed at her, then asked calmly, "You lost a son? Did he suffer from Burkitt's?"

"Cole was my husband," Marlee said through tight lips. "Is there really a distinguishable difference? Lymphatic cancer is still lymphatic cancer."

"True. But with each case we learn better combative treatments. And with the resources at our hospital, we've successfully treated three other cases of Burkitt's in the last two years. The children are in remission. We hope it's permanent remission." Lefowitz faced Wylie head-on. "It's your decision whether to use our oncology department. I've taken the liberty of asking Dr. Hal Riley to look at Dean and go over our tests. He has others in his multidisciplinary team, as well. But first he needs you to sign for an ultrasound and an MRI. These are noninvasive procedures. With Dean's flulike onset and the tiredness followed by high fever, we both suspect the main tumor will be in his stomach, or at least in the abdominal area."

Marlee heard Wylie's sharp intake of breath. She cast a furtive glance in his direction, and knew he wrestled with raw feelings. Plus, he practically ground the small bones in her fingers to dust. She gently broke his grip, and he instantly planted his elbows on the desk and buried his face in shaking hands.

The doctor closed the chart, retracted the point of his pen and returned it to the pocket of his lab coat. "I'd like to give you a reasonable amount of time to reach a decision, Mr. Ames. Let me say, however, every minute counts."

"Marlee?" Wylie removed his hands to stare at her through tear-drenched eyes.

Her heart plummeted. No man—or woman, for that matter— should have his or her private hell laid bare before others. The torment in Wylie's eyes, and in his one spoken word, was unbearable for her. She twisted her fingers in her lap. She wanted to scream that this was unfair. Unfair for Dean, certainly. And

Wylie. But her, as well. She'd already lived through four years of excruciating agony watching Cole fight and fight…and to what end?

She knew better than scores of other people what Wylie needed from her right now. *Strength!* Lifting both hands, she stroked beneath his eyes to remove the tears that had been trapped by his long lashes. "I take back what I said earlier. Until you've exhausted every test, every treatment, every medicine, there's hope, Wylie."

"Will you stay?"

Did he mean for an hour, the rest of today, throughout the long months of treatment, or was that simple question asking if he could count on her forever? The truth was she didn't have an answer, not to the last.

"Sign for the ultrasound and MRI. I need to find a restroom. I also have to call home. Then I can run down to the cafeteria and pick up coffee. How about we meet in the waiting room in…say, half an hour?"

Dr. Lefowitz pushed up from his chair. He picked up the two sheets of paper on which Wylie had scribbled his name. "You should probably plan to meet in the Oncology waiting area. Two floors up."

The word pierced her to the core. Oncology—the branch of medicine dedicated to the study and treatment of tumors. Nobody, not even doctors, wanted to use the C word.

Too near losing control to do more than nod, Marlee fled the room. She'd passed a women's lounge on her way from the stairs. It was a good thing she found it again readily, because she couldn't see anything through her tears.

She grabbed two handfuls of tissues from a box in front of a wide mirror. Flinging herself into an overstuffed chair, Marlee sobbed her way through tissue after tissue. A woman came in. Marlee vaguely registered that she was tall, thin and wore a navy-blue suit. Hesitating only briefly, the stranger crept out again without a word.

What could anyone say? Dean was eight. He was precocious and had once brimmed with boundless energy. Planned to be a veterinarian. His beautiful red hair would soon be lost to chemotherapy.

Mopping her eyes, she pulled another handful of tissues from the box, wadded the others and tossed them. A stack of brochures on things to do in Seattle fell on the floor. She tried scraping them together.

Wylie needed her to be stoic. And she needed to phone home, but she dared not let anyone hear the quaver in her voice.

Throwing the last shredded tissue into the trash, Marlee made her way to the washbasin and ran cold water over her face and puffy eyes. She waved her hands rapidly in front of her face, hoping air-drying would minimize the blotchy redness.

As soon as she felt able, she went to the pay phone and punched in her home number. Mick answered.

"Mick…Marlee. It poured rain all the way, but we're he-here, at the hospital."

"What's wrong? Dean's report? Your voice reeks of bad news."

"Oh, Mick, it's beyond bad." She tore out more tissues in the telling.

WYLIE DIDN'T KNOW HOW he got from the conference room to Dean's bedside. The hallway, and everything Dr. Lefowitz said on their way, blurred. In figuring his worst-case scenario, he'd never imagined anything this bad.

Two fairly young doctors poked and prodded Dean. Dr. Lefowitz joined his colleagues. Wylie hovered just inside the door. He felt as if he was unraveling, but men weren't supposed to fall apart.

Dean saw him and smiled. That funny, freckle-faced grin righted

Wylie's cartwheeling world. He stepped up to the bed and ran his hand over his son's spiky red hair. Hair Lefowitz had already explained Dean would lose. Wylie swallowed back his pain.

An owl-eyed, blond man introduced himself. "I'm Hal Riley, Dean's oncologist. We'll leave you two for a minute. I'm going to see about that MRI."

Wylie knew they expected him to break the news to Dean.

"Dad, I don't have the flu, do I?" The gold-tipped lashes lifted, and the eyes, no longer shaded, demanded honesty.

"Son, I've never sugarcoated the truth when it came to the injured animals we found and tried to heal." Wylie leaned both elbows on Dean's bed, and he fought to beat back throat-clogging tears. Dr. Lefowitz had given him some simple terms to use. Wylie employed them all. He hadn't kissed his son since Dean was three or four, although they often hugged. He hugged and kissed him now in spite of the IV tubes.

"It's okay, Dad." Dean patted his father's back. "Limb foam. I think that's what Jo Beth said her daddy had."

Wylie drew away, blinking very fast. "Yes, lymphoma...but Marlee said he had a different kind."

Dean nodded solemnly. "When I get finished with the MRI and that other test, I want to call Jo Beth. Her mom will tell her, and then she'll get all sad. Where is Marlee? I want her and Jo Beth to see if they can find me a book on limb foam." He still didn't get the name right, and Wylie let it go.

A movement at the door distracted the pair. Marlee waited uncertainly, juggling two cups of coffee, her purse and a brochure.

"Did Jo Beth send another card with happy thoughts? I did laugh at her stick dog. Now I don't know if I'll ever get to see Piston." He sounded forlorn.

Marlee moved into the room. She handed a steaming cup to Wylie. Her heart pounded. "Hey, sport. I heard you ask for a book on lymphoma. I think that would be dry reading. But you know what I found in the restroom? This brochure about the Seattle Zoo. It sounds fantastic." She pressed the folded, brightly colored pamphlet into his hand. "You do everything your doctors say, and the first day you feel well enough, I'll fly Jo Beth here, and the four of us, you, Jo Beth, your dad and me, we'll visit this zoo. And Jo Beth can tell us if it's as good as the one in San Diego."

The boy stared at the giraffe, gorilla and hippo gracing the shiny paper. "The zoo, Dad. I've never been. Can we go? I bet it'll be loads of fun."

Wylie clearly had to dig deep to answer. Once he got control, he pretended an inordinate amount of interest in the brochure. "Sounds good, fella. Here come Dr. Riley and a nurse. Want me to keep the zoo pamphlet while you go for the MRI?"

Dean handed it over without a word.

Dr. Riley explained in a soft, almost melodic voice, exactly what Dean could expect to happen in X-Ray. "Your mom and dad can wait in the waiting room."

Dean turned. "Marlee's not my mom…yet."

"First things first," Marlee quickly interjected. "The number one item on your father's list, Dean, is restoring you to good health."

A second nurse came in and the two shifted Dean onto a rolling bed. The rollers squeaked, Marlee noticed, as the trio started down the hall.

Wylie looked as though he'd finally hit bedrock. The coffee cup shook in his hand.

"Drink that, you need the caffeine," Marlee said. She'd found the strength to support Wylie, if only for today. "It'll be a while. We should probably do as Dr. Riley suggested, and wait in the waiting area."

"Right."

She felt him morph into the man who'd fought the cougar, and the one who'd trekked through the woods prepared to rescue Tracie Ledbetter from the river. He squared his shoulders and led the way to the bright, cheery room.

They sat side by side and sipped coffee as the minutes ticked past. He probably read the zoo brochure from cover to cover forty times. Marlee would bet he knew it by heart. She'd long since got up and found a bin to dispose of their empty cups.

After what seemed like hours, Dr. Riley appeared. Since there was no one else in the cavernous room, the doctor took the seat next to Wylie.

Turning over a page on Dean's chart, Riley sketched the boy's abdomen and lower internal organs. "Here's the primary tumor. It's attached to both kidneys. And it's big. I'm surprised he didn't complain sooner, although lymphocytic tumors grow fast." He let the pages flip shut. "We have to treat this aggressively. I want to implant an intravenous Broviac Catheter in Dean's chest. This will be the best method of administering large doses of chemotherapy drugs. It's a surgical procedure done under anesthetic. I propose to install the catheter today. Tomorrow we'll inject the first dose of drugs. Hit it hard and hit it fast."

Not for the first time, Marlee marveled at how doctors talked about the human body, almost as if it were a car. She didn't realize Wylie expected anything from her until she discovered he'd taken her hand and was squeezing it, and his eyes, filled with despair, begged her for wisdom.

She dragged her gaze away, focusing instead on the doctor, even though she wrapped a bracing hand around Wylie's wrist. "I fly Wylie and Dean back and forth from Montana. Is this a daily treatment, weekly, or what?"

"Depending on how Dean responds to treatment, I see no reason he can't go home between doses. My group is beginning a clinical study he'd fit into nicely. It's twice a week at first and is aimed at using less toxic doses of chemotherapy drugs more often. We have reason to believe it will increase the cure rate. I just need you to sign these papers."

Wylie heard *cure rate,* and he sat up straighter. He took the pen and scribbled his name on three forms. *Like one of Pavlov's dogs,* Marlee thought. *Oh, how many times had she and Rose done the same thing?*

Dr. Riley got to his feet. He shook Wylie's hand. "Good, good. We'll dive right in. You'll want to stay with Dean as we prep him for surgery."

The men strode off. Marlee stayed seated. Wylie turned. "Aren't you coming?"

"I…can't, Wylie. I'll…uh…go find us a snack. And maybe talk a nurse out of a couple of pillows. These chairs get hard. It's going to be a long night." Her heart was so heavy she wasn't sure she could stay here. Yet going to a hotel was out of the question.

Wylie's gaze caressed her face. Plainly they both were remembering their last night together in Seattle.

Marlee glanced away first. *They might never spend so intimate a night together again.* The mere thought sent a physical pain through her. Spinning, she all but raced out of the room.

CHAPTER FOURTEEN

THE FIRST MAJOR ORDEAL was over, and they were flying home. Dean dozed fitfully. Wylie had left the hospital armed with a folder full of instructions and information. Dean would be returning for biweekly visits to the Oncology department.

Wylie sat and tried to digest the copious amount of information. Marlee wanted to be sure she was clear on his schedule. "On one of my phone calls home yesterday, I had Mick block out tentative dates on the calendar from now through November for Dean's trips. You know, I hope, that if the weather turns really bad you'll probably have to arrange to stay in Seattle for a while."

"I asked a friend, another ranger, to fill in for me on a moment's notice. My area, even the part bordering the park, is generally quiet all winter. I do have company snowmobiles and other equipment we don't want stolen. And there's our horses to feed and exercise."

"It's good that your bosses are so understanding and willing to give you time off. And I never would've expected your insurance to pay part of Cloud Chasers' charges. You're lucky your rep talked you into adding Dean to your catastrophic plan right after he was born."

"Marlee, are we having this conversation about my insurance because you're avoiding what I asked before we left the hospital?"

She pursed her lips.

He glanced at Dean, who appeared to be dozing, but Wylie

edged forward and spoke quietly. "Am I so terrible for wanting to set our wedding date before Dean's treatments take such a huge toll that we risk not having him there?"

"I don't think you're terrible, Wylie. It's just…you need a fortress. I don't think I can be that." Her voice quavered.

Even though she feigned interest in the plane's controls, Wylie reached out and stroked the side of her face. "I didn't ask you to be my fortress, I asked you to be my wife."

She felt her eyes fill. The dark clouds outside her window shimmered fuzzily. "Stop, Wylie. I need to be able to see your airstrip in order to land."

He pulled back. She rubbed a sleeve over her eyes and made a second pass over the mist-shrouded strip. The wheels touched, and she made the turn into the wind and feathered the props. Wylie's shed was merely an outline off her tail section.

He unbuckled himself and Dean, and shoved open the side door.

Marlee sat hunched in her seat. "Please make sure your door is locked down," she reminded shakily. "Bye, Dean." Marlee wiggled her fingers at the yawning, lethargic boy. "Tomorrow I fly Mick to his therapy appointment in Missoula. Any books you'd like me to pick up?"

"More Hardy Boys mysteries. And music for my portable CD player. Dr. Riley said listening to music will take my mind off hurting."

Marlee had to hold it together for Wylie's son, and so mustered a semblance of a smile. Dean sounded like an old soul; not like a kid of eight. "I'll have Jo Beth give you a jingle when I get home." She revved the opposite engine, telling Wylie it was time to cut short this conversation.

He withdrew and shut the door. Marlee studiously avoided watching him carry Dean across to the trail. But she couldn't have seen anyway for her tears. She cried all the way back to Whitepine.

At home, the family saw her condition and gave her space. Except for later in the evening after supper—Rose followed Marlee out to the office when she'd claimed she had to catch up on billing.

"You look like a train wreck, Marlee. You've got to pull yourself together. For Jo Beth, if no other reason. What's the truth about this boy's prognosis?"

Marlee shuffled a stack of bills, and took satisfaction in ripping into envelopes with a dagger letter opener Mick said he'd picked up in Asia. "They told Wylie eighty-five to ninety percent chance for full recovery." She pinned her former mother-in-law with hard eyes. "He believes them."

"Mick said you've lost your heart to this man and his son."

Marlee burst into tears. The dagger fell from her hand and clattered to the floor.

Rose rushed around the desk and folded Marlee in her arms. "You probably think I have no business lecturing. It hurts me so much to see you suffering again. But, you know what, I wouldn't trade one minute of the precious hours I had with Cole. And whether or not you believe me, I regret that I was allowed more time than you. Just your phone calls lifted his spirits for days. Cole needed us both, Marlee."

"I…can…can't go through the highs and lows again."

"Can you stand by and know that Wylie's suffering alone? You say you love him."

Slowly, Marlee's chest stopped heaving and her shoulders stopped shaking. She rubbed the heels of her hands over her eyes until they were dry, or nearly so. She took the tissue Rose extended and loudly blew her nose. "I—I guess I needed a swift kick. Rose…how can I ever thank you?"

"You already have. For loving my son and providing the means for him to get the best care. And for giving me a gorgeous grandchild. Mostly, you forgave this selfish old lady, and allowed me back in Jo Beth's life."

Marlee picked at the tissue. "Dean and Wylie have barely begun their ordeal. Is it fair for me to leave Jo Beth to fly Dean to Seattle for treatments? I could be gone two or three days a week. And Mick's still rocky. Pappy has spells of dementia where he wanders off." She glanced up, but couldn't see through her watery eyes. "Rose, I can't be all things to everyone I love."

"I'd offer to stay, but I don't want to wear out my welcome or cause problems again."

"You'd stay? For a month, even?" The tissue had practically disintegrated. "As long as I set all the parameters for Jo Beth." Marlee dabbed her nose again.

"My lawyer didn't mince words when he sat me down and gave me hell for trying to replace what I'd lost in Cole with Jo Beth. She's your daughter, not mine."

Marlee's jaw sagged. "Rose, you said *hell*."

"I'm slow at it, but I'm doing my best to change. I need to start over. Jo Beth asked today if I could teach her to knit hats. For Dean. He apparently told her the doctor said he'd lose his hair like Cole did. I have a simple pattern I kept altering for Cole, but if you'd rather teach her…"

"Are you kidding? My mother wasn't domestic. All I know about cooking I learned from watching you. I'll teach Jo Beth to skate and ride horses and fly."

Rose smiled. "I'm no competition there. So, it's set? I'll handle the home front for now, and you take care of Wylie and Dean. I hope I'll get to meet them both soon."

"Wylie thinks we should get married before the chemo makes Dean too weak to attend. But I feel I owe it to Mick to work for Cloud Chasers until he's cleared to fly again."

"I'm sure you can figure it all out. Philip and Cole thought you were one of the most competent women they'd ever met. I used to be a bit jealous. Well, I'll leave you to your mail. I'm going to go see if I can beat Pappy Jack at Chinese checkers. I think he cheats."

"He's competitive. I'd forgotten that. Go get him, Rose."

Feeling better, Marlee dispensed with the mail. She should try to reach Wylie. On the other hand, some messages were better delivered in person.

THE NEXT DAY SHE FLEW Mick to Missoula for his physical therapy. The whole family went. While Mick had his appointment, Rose dragged the rest of them from coffee shop, to bookstore, to specialty stores for cooking oils and herbs.

Snow started to fall by midafternoon. "I know everyone's having fun, but I don't like that sky." Marlee looked in her rearview mirror at Rose and Jo Beth. "I told Mick we'd meet him at the college at four. He wanted to walk over and browse in their bookstore. He hoped to get rid of his crutches today." She excused herself to answer her ringing cell. "Ah, Mick, it's you. So, you saw the sky? We're ten minutes away. Pick you up at the clock tower?"

In short order, the weather progressed from flurries to heavy snowfall. Mick, still on crutches, fussed over an inconclusive weather report given to them at the airport. "If we hadn't left Piston, and Stella hadn't gone to see her son, I'd say let's stay here tonight."

Marlee taxied to the appropriate runway. "Did that controller fall asleep?" she muttered several minutes later. Snow blew sideways, obliterating the tower. At last she was given clearance. Everyone relaxed marginally after liftoff.

Twenty minutes out she wished she'd heeded Mick's suggestion to stay the night. It was as if someone had thrown a sheet over the windshield. Pappy was telling jokes but kept breaking off to ask Marlee for instrument readings. Mick was talking nervously, as well.

"Who's the pilot here?" she complained. The plane lurched, tilted, and Marlee wrenched the controls to pull it out of a spin.

"Our left engine flamed out," Mick shouted, stretching as far as his harness allowed. "Wonder what the hell went wrong. I serviced that engine myself."

"Uncle Mick said a bad word."

Jo Beth's grandmother gripped the girl's arm. "It needed saying," Rose told the startled child.

"We've gotta land at the closest airport." Marlee stared out at a near-blizzard. She stayed calm and controlled; the navy taught its flyers not to panic.

"Great idea. Except there are no airports between here and home. Pappy, you left the hangar lights on, I hope."

"I can't remember." His craggy face was ashen.

"It's okay, Pappy. I've landed there often enough I have the coordinates burned into my brain."

Half an hour later, Marlee feared that the turbulence might make a liar out of her. The crippled plane bucked and jerked in the erratic winds. Mick motioned her to start her descent. She realized they were over the runway, and cut power to the single engine too soon. The wheels touched down, but then went into a slide in the snow. She and Mick both had their hands on the wheel. They overcorrected, fishtailed back and forth, and came to a stop directly beneath the beacon shining at the east end of the hangar.

"You did turn on the lights," Mick said calmly to his grandfather, breaking the tension and causing everyone to smile. But it was a sober group that left the Seneca with the day's purchases.

The message light on the kitchen phone blinked red, and the phone was ringing as the weary travelers filed into the house.

Mick grabbed the receiver. "Wylie? Hey, man, we just had an adventure that rivals yours with the cougar. What? Damn." Mick turned to look at Marlee. "Dean's coughing and he's got a fever." He held out the phone.

She took it gingerly. "Wylie, tell me you don't want to fly Dean somewhere right now. We just landed on a wing and a prayer. We're practically in a whiteout, and we blew an engine in the Seneca."

"Dr. Riley is afraid Dean may be reacting to the chemo." She heard the strain in Wiley's voice. "Or else the tumor fought through the two massive doses they gave him and got larger instead of shrinking. There's no way you can land on my airstrip, so I have to load him on the snowmobile and go to the main ranger station. Any chance you can pick us up there in one of your other planes?"

Marlee conferred with Mick. "We have a second engine, but it'll take time to switch them out." She didn't add that it'd be tricky flying through a storm with an untried engine. The urgency of the situation dictated she try. They agreed on an approximate meeting time.

"Has it occurred to you that this is insanity?" Mick said over the whir of the electric bolt remover twenty minutes later. He wiped sweat from his brow, and started on another bolt.

His sister grunted as she took the weight of the section they dropped out. She'd already argued with Mick about not bending or lifting. She couldn't help glancing repeatedly at her watch, however, underscoring the urgency she felt.

Like early-in-the-season storms tended to do, this one blew over before they could finish and test the engine. The flight would still be treacherous, given that the storm had dumped six inches of snow, and the stars and moon were obliterated by clouds. It didn't help that Pappy handed her a crash kit after the new engine sputtered, missed a few times and sparked before smoothing out.

"She just needed a bit of breaking in, Pappy."

"Enemy out there everywhere, girl."

Mick looped an arm around his grandfather's stooped shoulders. "Pap, you trained Marlee. She's got Callen guts. Let's go see if Rose has the coffee hot."

Marlee had needed that encouragement from Mick. Taxiing out of the hangar, she realized how much her whole family meant to her. It was at that moment Marlee exorcised whatever leftover fear had hung on following Cole's battle. She included Wylie and Dean in with prayers for her family. They were soon going to be part of it, come what may.

Blessedly, the main ranger station had a concrete runway. Someone had cleared it with a snowplow. And they'd flared both sides of the runway. She landed, only to be immediately mobbed by rangers. Five big men. Wylie's friends.

"I hope I'm not going to be tested on all of your names any time soon," she said after they'd introduced themselves and helped Wylie load a bundled-up Dean into the plane.

A barrel-chested man, who'd introduced himself as Swede, boosted Marlee into her seat. "We told Wylie nobody would fly in this weather, let alone a gal. Gotta tell you, miss, we heard them engines, and we all agreed Wylie's found himself a winner."

"Indeed he has." Her gaze locked with Wylie's as she said it. There was no time for any other exchange.

They'd been in the air an hour before Wylie had Dean settled. Not until the boy was dozing could he broach anything personal. "The guys all bet me you'd blow me off." He leaned forward in his seat and clasped his hands between his knees.

"What did you think, Wylie?"

"Even if you had, I'd have borrowed a company pickup. I would've driven Dean to Seattle. I'd have arranged to stay there until his treatments are done. Then I'd be on your doorstep insisting you follow through on a promise you made. That the four of us, you, me, Dean and Jo Beth, will visit the Seattle Zoo together. As a family, I hope."

Her heart twisted. "I'm sorry about the way I left things between us last night."

"Do you have any idea how it tore me apart, watching you fly off, knowing you might tell Angel Fleet I'd have to use another pilot?"

"I won't lie. That's what I wanted to do, Wylie. I thought the worst thing I'd ever experience was watching Cole slowly slip away. Believe it or not, it was his mom who helped me see I wouldn't be able to live with myself if I let you go through this ordeal alone and that each day we're given together is precious. If you haven't changed your mind, I want to be at your side."

Hope lit the murky pupils of his eyes. "Is that a roundabout way of saying yes, you will marry me?"

The plane shuddered in a side gust of wind, forcing her to turn her attention to flying. But once they'd leveled out, she didn't immediately answer him.

"What then? I don't get it." He tangled his fingers in a strand of her hair.

"I do want to marry you," she said. "But I'm torn. Mick's business is growing. It's all he's got. That, and Pappy, who has good days and bad ones. Rose said she'll stay a while and help with the house. I thought great, that solves everything. But if we get married, Jo Beth and I will move in with you, and I can't expect Rose to continue helping Mick. Another thing, this plane we're using to fly Dean back and forth belongs to my brother." She sighed and rested her chin on his hand, rubbing her cheek back and forth against his fingers, just to feel connected to him.

"You think I only want to marry you to guarantee having you in my bed every night? Yes, that would be my preference in a perfect world. But we both have proof that's not how life works. I haven't asked you to let Mick down."

"Then why rush to the altar? If we know we're eventually getting married?"

"Call me old-fashioned. But I want to grab every minute I can with you. The other night at the hotel…the sex sort of happened. I don't want to pay for two rooms in the future if we stay overnight in Seattle."

She couldn't help it; she laughed. "Wylie, there's old-fashioned and then there's *old* old-fashioned."

"Okay, okay! That was a stupid excuse." He'd seen her switch the plane over to autopilot, so he used his forefinger to turn her face toward him. "Here's the bottom line. I want to make a baby with you. I'd like us to be husband and wife when we do."

Marlee couldn't deny that the idea of making babies with Wylie had crossed her mind. It had. She never imagined he'd given it any thought. For years, she'd worked with sailors. Nine out of ten of those men cared a lot more about the act that led to making babies. In fact, most guys she knew… Suddenly, Marlee recalled something Cole's team of doctors had discussed at length, but had then dropped.

"Wylie, this wouldn't be because Dr. Riley suggested Dean might one day need a bone marrow transplant? Or the cord blood of a sibling?"

"That's insulting." He flung himself back and let his hands fall idle in his lap. "You must've forgotten what I told you about Shirl and me."

"Oh, my God, I'm sorry, Wylie." It had slipped her mind that Wylie wasn't Dean's biological dad. Should he need that last-ditch effort, which ultimately hadn't been an option for Cole, it'd be next to impossible to find a familial match of blood or marrow for Dean Ames. Sadness again gripped her.

"Listen, Boeing Field is somewhere beneath three layers of clouds. We have to defer this conversation until after I land."

She sneaked a peek when Wylie made no response. He stared out the side window looking cool and aloof. Her heart lurched with the plane as she descended a thousand feet, then two thousand. Damn, she had a habit of sticking her foot in her mouth. Mick could verify that. Rose, too.

It wasn't snowing in Seattle, but wind and rain slammed them around. Fall was definitely sliding into winter. Landing required her total concentration. Any get-down-on-her-knees type of apology would have to come later. Much later, she thought, as an air pocket sucked up the Seneca, then dropped it into a hole, driving her teeth into the tip of her tongue.

"How's Dean?" she shouted, hearing the boy's cry ring out, but not daring to turn around as she was in the approach for landing.

"He just threw up all over." Wylie sounded more frightened than ever before.

Marlee radioed for an ambulance. She berated herself for not having done so earlier.

The new engine wasn't performing as well as she'd like. Marlee debated between asking for a hangar where she could do maintenance or requesting that a staff mechanic go over it so she could go to the hospital with Wylie and Dean.

Once on the ground, he didn't ask her to go, or even meet there. On one level she knew she deserved the cold shoulder. On another, she felt he should cut her some slack. Forget her past, dammit; she'd risked her life to fly them here.

Too many things happened at the same time to have a heart-to-heart talk with Wylie. A maintenance crew appeared, having heard the rough-running engine. And the ambulance squealed to a stop, spraying the water standing on the tarmac everywhere, drenching Marlee's jeans. Wylie climbed into the back with his son.

And Marlee was left gaping after the flashing lights of the emergency vehicle.

"Ma'am, hangar five's available." A man in blue coveralls, and wearing goggles to keep the rain out of his eyes, held out a clipboard with a service ticket. "Did you want to rent a vehicle so you can follow that ambulance?"

"Yes," she said, reaching for his pen and signing to have someone service the Seneca's engines. "I need to clean the interior before you take her, though. Our patient had a little accident. And can you point me to a place where I can change out of these wet clothes?"

The whole routine, plus the few minutes she'd taken to check in at home, took forty-five minutes. As she suspected, Rose had waited up for her call.

"So, Mick thinks Pappy forgot to take his pills? I set them out, Rose. We need to be sure he's not taking a double dose. I know, I know, you said you'd handle that for now. I don't know how Dean is. Wylie went with him in the ambulance. You get some sleep, Rose. I'll wait until a more decent hour to phone, once I've got the particulars on Dean. I'm fine. Yeah, I'm beat, but you know how many times I flew space-available hops home to spend thirty-six hours with Cole before flying back to my duty station. I can do this."

She hung up and got settled in the car.

She'd expected Wylie to contact her when he got Dean checked in, but her cell didn't ring.

In spite of the early-morning hour, freeway traffic was bumper to bumper. With so much rain in this city, she found it difficult to pump up her own flagging spirits. And yet she knew from experience that Wylie needed her to be calm and hopeful.

Over an hour and a half had passed by the time she arrived and got directions to Dean's new room. She expected a team of doctors to be bustling around the boy. Instead, he slept in a dark, four-bed ward. Wylie sat in a chair next to him. His head touched the wall, and his face had gone slack in sleep.

She wrestled with letting him be or waking him up. She was here. Dean appeared to be well cared for. And she and Wylie had things to settle.

Tiptoeing into the room, she bent over him and kissed him awake with soft kisses.

His eyelids fluttered a few times, then flew open. His head banged against the wall, making a racket. Marlee grimaced and rubbed him with a hand to massage away the pain. "Sorry," she whispered. "Got a minute for a lady in distress, Ranger?" She trailed her fingers through his hair, and offered what she hoped was a winsome smile.

He stumbled upright, and hustled her out the door. It swung silently shut behind them. Wylie traversed the hall so fast they were both out of breath on entering the empty waiting room.

"If we're about to go round one in a verbal boxing match," she said, "I'm getting my licks in first. I love you, Wylie. It's as simple and as complicated as that. Simple, because it happened when we least expected love. Complicated, because we're both hauling around a heavy load of past history. I may say certain things due to that. And you may not like what I say. You may throw up a protective shield that I can't penetrate. I guess I'm trying to tell you that I'm willing to work through those times, and do everything in my power to recognize them and ward them off. Phew, that's a long-winded speech even for me. So, what does Dr. Riley think is the matter with Dean?"

A ghost of a smile lifted one side of Wylie's lips. "Dean has a common cold. A hazard of this climate, he said. They shot Dean full of antibiotics, mostly to ward off secondary infections."

Wylie tugged her over to a couch in one corner of the room, and pulled her down onto his lap. "For the record, you did a damn good job of explaining the conclusions I'd already come to on my own. I have a few other things we need to get out in the open. Dean and I rarely, if ever, put the toilet seats down. Haven't needed to. I toss dirty clothes at the hamper, but say *so what* if I miss. That bad habit I have of closing myself off when I'm annoyed irks Dean and everyone I know. I figure it must be love if I'm willing to work at rectifying all of those shortcomings and any more you point out." He drew her slowly against his chest, and when their eyes met and reached an understanding, their mouths met, too.

When their hearts were hammering, Marlee freed one hand and brushed her fingers across Wylie's lips. "If we continue in this direction, we're liable to spend the night in jail for performing lewd and lascivious acts in a public place."

Wylie let his head fall back and willed his body to relax. He sat a minute, then brought his head forward and grinned wickedly. "I'm having a debate with myself—trying to decide whether it'd be worth starting out married life with a police record."

"Not!" She gave him a playful smack with the flat of her hand.

He captured it and held it tight against his racing heart. "Everything we've said aside, Marlee, you're the first woman I've ever met who's made me want to be a better man. I read every scrap of information Dr. Riley gave me. I know we're facing an uphill climb with Dean. I know it's asking a lot of you to make the trek with us."

"Shh." Marlee pressed a quick, hard kiss on his lips, effectively silencing him. "It's my decision whether or not to make this journey. And I've decided. We've jumped one hurdle. I'm ready for the next one. So, hold on for the ride." She smiled warmly. "Now that I see you're in such a mellow mood, I think we should talk about a wedding. Our wedding," she said, suddenly shyer and far less bold.

Wylie whooped, not caring that he was supposed to be quiet here. They made wedding plans over three cups each of black coffee. They would have a no-frills ceremony in the church in Whitepine where Marlee's parents had exchanged vows.

"If circumstances were different I'd invite all of my buddies from the department and everyone who lives in my territory," Wylie said. "If you think the minister will be flexible enough to let us have the ceremony as soon as we see Dean can handle it, I'll forget the others and just ask Mick to stand up with me."

"If you're willing to make allowances for whatever might come out of Pappy Jack's mouth, I'd like my grandfather to walk me down the aisle."

"Done."

They kissed again, and this time two young nurses walked through the room, caught them and broke them apart with a wolf whistle.

On their heels, a rumpled-looking resident, a junior member of Dr. Riley's team, stuck his head in and announced. "Mr. Ames, Dean's fever is way down. We'd like to keep him until his temperature's normal, probably twenty-four hours. Then we'll administer his next dose of chemo. He'll be back on his regular schedule. Also, he's awake. Do you want to give him the news, or shall I?"

"We will." Wylie stood up, took Marlee's hand and pulled her to her feet. "*We* have news that may be even better medicine, Dr. Montego. We're moving up our wedding so Dean can attend before the going gets too rough."

The young doctor shook Wylie's hand and smiled at Marlee. "Well, we've all heard about the family zoo trip he has planned for when his cancer goes into remission. I assume this is an added step leading to that end."

Marlee slid her arm around Wylie's hips. "You assume right. I've been thinking late April or early May will be the perfect time to tour the zoo. Dean and my daughter would love seeing any spring zoo babies."

"That should be about right," Montego said. "Dr. Hal Riley designed a five-to-six-month regimen. The treatment success rate to date has been over ninety percent."

Marlee's hand grew clammy as she heard the prediction spelled out. But she refused to let the past cloud her thinking. She led the way into the room where Dean lay waiting.

CHAPTER FIFTEEN

NO MATTER HOW SIMPLE they wanted it to be, putting together a wedding took time.

Three and a half weeks later, Marlee chafed impatiently. Now that she'd decided she was going to be part of Wylie's and Dean's lives, come what may, she embraced her own with a new sense of purpose.

"What would I do without you two creative ladies?" she said to Rose and Stella. "Thanks to you, I'm getting excited about the ceremony part of our wedding. Cole and I got married in our uniforms in front of a navy chaplain. I told Wylie I didn't want frills this time, either. Maybe I lied."

Rose took the pins out of her mouth. She and Stella were running a hem in a powder-blue chiffon overskirt on a wedding dress they'd just finished sewing. "That was probably the only time his father and I were so mad at Cole we could have disowned him. Our only child, and he didn't let us splurge on his wedding."

"Oh, Rose, I'm sorry. Other things overshadowed the ceremony. Cole and I were both due to ship out. It's sort of the same now. Wylie and I go from week to week dealing with winter weather, and how it affects getting Dean to Seattle for chemotherapy."

Stella stood up and set a pale blue ring of flowers on Marlee's hair. She gathered a short veil of net across the back and pinned it in place. Jo Beth, who'd bounced into the room with Piston at her heels, stopped and clapped her hands. "Oh, Mama, you're as beautiful as my Barbie bride."

That broke the tension that had followed Rose's statement.

"And you are going to be gorgeous in violet, Jo Beth," Stella exclaimed.

"Do I get a flower crown? Dean said he's wearing one of the hats you took him that Grandmother helped me make. "'Cause it'll be summer before he's got hair.'"

"I wish I'd had a camera when Dean wore the cap you knit with the dog nose and floppy ears. Wylie tried his hardest to talk Dean out of wearing it into the oncology lab. He couldn't believe it when all the kids asked where Dean got the hat, and wanted one like it."

"It's a good thing the boy's maintaining a sense of humor. Doctors say attitude helps heal." Rose set the last pin and got up off her knees. "That's as even as I can make this soft material. Be careful taking the dress off Marlee."

"Since Mick and Pappy are out in the shop fixing an engine, we won't be interrupted, so help me out of it here, why don't you?"

Rose lifted the hem. "Mick said a bird flew into the engine. That's what caused it to break down. I never would've thought anything like that could happen."

Marlee reappeared from under the voluminous skirt. "Ordinarily we fly higher. Poor bird must've been fighting the snow just like we were."

"Speaking of snow…" Stella took the dress and draped it over a satin-clad hanger. "I have my fingers crossed that the next storm will hold off until after Saturday. I can't believe you have to fly Wylie and Dean here that morning and then go on to Seattle so Dean can have another treatment on Monday. It's bad luck for the groom to see the bride on the day of the wedding. And you need a honeymoon," she muttered.

"Oh, Stella, don't mention bad luck. With Dean's ups and

downs, we've had more than our share. We're due for a change. We're saving our celebrating for when Dean finishes his treatments."

"How many does he have left?"

Marlee started to say Dr. Riley might have to adjust Dean's schedule, but Jo Beth piped up from the corner. "Dean said his last treatment will be in May. And that's when we get to be a real family, huh, Mama? To celebrate, we all get to go to the zoo. I can't wait! Uncle Mick gave me a calendar to cross off days."

"Mick shouldn't have done that." Marlee stopped buttoning her robe. *What if the treatments failed? Last week Dr. Riley had mentioned a new experimental drug....*

"What shouldn't Mick have done?" he said from the doorway.

His sister whirled. "You shouldn't encourage Jo Beth to mark off the days until the end of Dean's treatments. He's having escalated bouts of nausea and intermittent fevers. They added something to the mix of medicines. He suffered that scary seizure, and it's only December. There are no guarantees," Marlee said, pacing to the window.

Mick studied his sister's rigid back. "That's why it's so important to keep your eye on the end goal. Marking milestones helped me work harder to stay on track. I sent Dean a calendar to match Jo Beth's. Now they're both shooting for that zoo trip."

Rose sat down to start the hand sewing that remained to be done on Marlee's dress. "Since Mick's healing nicely and expects to be given the go-ahead to fly in January, I'm thinking I'll go home then. I talked to my friend, the neighbor I told you about, Emmett Nelson—we've spoken nightly, to tell you the truth—and I've taken the liberty of inviting him to spend Christmas, with Pappy Jack's approval, of course. Emmett booked a flight to Seattle. I thought you could bring him here, dear." She lifted hooded eyes to Marlee. "Mick and I discussed how once he's flying again, he can take Emmett and me to where I left my car. This way I'll have company on the drive back to San Diego."

Flabbergasted was too mild a word for how Marlee felt. "I see you've all done a lot of planning without me."

"You've been preoccupied. Mr. Nelson isn't as old as Pappy, but he served in Nam. You know how Pappy loves swapping war stories." Mick, who walked unaided by either crutches or cane now, crossed the room and grabbed Marlee around the neck. He knuckled her head, mussing her honey blond hair. "Come on, let down your hair. You don't always have to be in charge of everything."

Marlee tried to bring order to the mess he'd left. "Let down my hair, you goof? I don't have to be in charge. I *know* everything is changing. Only, it's changing so fast."

Pappy shuffled in and sat next to Stella. "Mick said this weekend our girl is really gonna marry that Indian fella."

"Wylie is only part Chinook, Pappy," Mick chided. "He says the best part."

"Well, marriage ain't a done deal until the preacher signs the license. Still time to back out, Marlee."

"No," everyone in the room shouted so loudly the old man flung up his hands in self-defense.

"Pappy, I picked your suit up from the cleaners yesterday. I want you to wear it and do the Callen clan proud when you walk me down the aisle."

"Just so you all know… I had Stella take me to see Dennis Addison yesterday. For a look-see at my will. Changed a few things. The bulk of this property and the main house will go to Mick. I put the cottage in your name, Marlee. It's there if you or Jo Beth ever need a place to land for a while."

Marlee and Mick traded startled glances. Was he slipping into the past again? "Pappy? I don't need the cottage. I would like us all to spend the holiday in this house. I'm counting on you to welcome Wylie to our Callen family."

SATURDAY DAWNED. Whitepine and surrounding areas had been spared the storm that had worried Stella.

With Wylie at her side, and Dean in the seat behind, Marlee asked for the fiftieth time, "Dean, are you sure you feel up to a day, well, a half day of festivity?"

He opened one blue eye. His freckles really stood out now that his gold-tipped eyebrows and lashes were gone. Little was left of his beautiful red hair. "What if those other people who live in Mick's house don't like me? What if they think I'm freaky, Marlee?"

"As if! 'Those other people' are my family, Dean, with the exception of Stella Gibson, who helped decorate the chapel and make my dress and Jo Beth's. And you're going to be a part of that family. Everyone will love you." She paused. "Jo Beth may wear you out, though. I've never seen her as excited as when I left this morning."

Wylie searched the depths of Marlee's eyes. "And you? Are you excited? Or are you thinking you made a bad bargain?"

"Never!" Marlee flashed him a huffy glare. "Ahem…by the way, I told you, no frills. I hope you don't blame me for the froufrou Rose and Stella conjured up. Oh, shoot, not just them. I went overboard. I can't say this in front of Rose, but…this is the wedding of my heart, Wylie."

He touched two fingers to her face, his emotions vivid in his eyes.

They landed at Mick's then, and from that moment on, until they arrived at the church, they were all caught up in last-minute details. Except for Dean. He sat in the wheelchair the oncology doctors insisted he use. He hated wearing the mask, also a must. His eyes, which had been lackluster of late, twinkled as Jo Beth fluttered around, and Piston laid his big head contentedly across the boy's lap.

Marlee dressed at the church. She was surprised by how nervous she felt when the organist Stella had found began to play the wedding march. Her heart pounded as Mick shoved Pappy through the door to take her arm.

"You look the spitting image of your grandmother, girl." Hi
eyes watered. "We were married in this church. As were my so
and your mother." He patted Marlee's arm with a palsied hand
"I'm glad I lived to see this day. Wish I had time to see your twi
happily married to a good woman. I feel time slipping away."

"Don't talk like that. Once I get my life on track, I'll find Mic
a really nice woman. You hang in here, Pappy Jack."

They ambled slowly down the aisle. Marlee's heart leape
sky-high when Wylie turned, and so much love flowed towar
her from his obsidian eyes.

They were an odd assortment grouped around the youn
minister. Jo Beth served as Marlee's maid of honor. Mick stoo
up for Wylie, but he stepped back before the ceremony began an
moved Dean's wheelchair into the lineup.

Rose and Stella helped Pappy to his seat after he remem
bered to mumble, "I give this woman in marriage."

Marlee and Wylie had picked out brushed gold, matchin
bands. She was shocked when he worked two rings over th
knuckle of her third finger. "What's this?" she whispered. "Wai
I've seen this…"

"It's a yellow diamond that belonged to your grandmother,
Wylie told her. "Your grandfather pulled me aside and asked m
to present you with it. I was honored and told him so, eve
though he swore he'd make me suffer if I didn't treat you lik
a queen."

"You're both old softies." She smiled through tears, and the
kissed over top of the rings Wylie raised to chin level. All wa
right with Marlee's world, even though the minister faltere
because he hadn't reached the part where the groom kissed hi
bride.

Mick shrugged, motioning the okay for the minister to spee
up the ceremony. Which he did. Then he presented Wylie an
Marlee as husband and wife to the small group of onlookers.

There were hugs, kisses and buckets more tears.

But all too soon, it seemed, Wylie, his new bride and their son flew off to a less happy but important gathering in Oncology.

Shortly after Dean went in for a routine treatment on Monday, Dr. Riley pulled Wylie and Marlee into the hall. He shook Wylie's hand, saying, "I'll get congratulations out of the way, then I need to talk about something more serious. Dean's complaining of chest pain. I thought maybe the wedding was just hard on him, but Dr. Barker says it's pleuritis. That's fluid or inflammation in the sack around his heart. Could be from his mediport. We need to admit him for tests."

"Wylie." Marlee pulled him aside after the doctor left. "I have two freight deliveries to go out later this week. And I need to take Mick in for what he hopes is his last trip to the physical therapist."

"Okay. I'll phone my friend Bud Russell. He'll check on my campsites and feed Dean's menagerie. I've got to stay here, sweetheart."

Marlee's heart fluttered at the endearment. It was too bad they had such a mix of joy and fear at the very time they should be settling down as a family. "We did talk about this possibility, Wylie. Of course you'll stay. I want Dean feeling good enough by the holidays so that we can all spend Christmas with Pappy and Mick."

Wylie kissed her leisurely. Again he didn't care that they were in the hospital waiting room. "That's what I want, too," he said after they eased apart. "Christmas Eve with the four of us at my place…er…our place," he emphasized. "Hey, it's great that Rose gave me her blessing to adopt Jo Beth."

"I judged her so wrong, Wylie. And Pappy Jack. I worried he'd lose control and punch you, or worse, at the wedding. Instead he gave you Gram's ring."

"That's Stella Gibson's doing, I'll bet. She must've shot three rolls of film of the wedding. I think she took so many pictures of Dean and your grandfather in case..." Wylie stumbled. "In case it's the last photos anyone will get of either of them."

"Wylie, don't. It's a temporary setback for Dean. This past week Mick made me understand that we need to rid ourselves of all negativity. *All*, Wylie. We have to think positively about everything."

"I already owe Mick for bringing you into my life. Any chance you can see your way clear to spending at least tonight with me, Mrs. Ames? Hmm. I wonder if *our room* might be available at the hotel down the street?"

"Since we're thinking that positively, Mr. Ames, I'll call and book it, and meet you in Dean's room."

"You remember which one it is?"

"Are you kidding? How could I ever forget?"

CHRISTMAS WAS LESS than Wylie and Marlee had hoped for. Dean's CT scan didn't show the progress his medical team wanted. They'd upped his drug dose. As a result, Christmas Eve at Wylie's was considerably scaled down from what they'd planned.

As if to add to the melancholy, late that night it started snowing hard. They decided Marlee and Jo Beth should go alone to Mick's the next day for the family Christmas gathering.

The two of them were listless in spite of the good food and lavish gifts Emmett Nelson bought everyone. Marlee let Jo Beth call Dean to say they'd put his and Wylie's presents aside to bring home the following day.

"Dean, me 'n Mama will fix another Christmas dinner for when you get well. We'll go to the zoo and then come home and decorate a tree. Won't that be fun?"

"Jo Beth, if I don't get well I want you and Dad and Mo

Mom—" he stuttered as he called Marlee *Mom* "—to go to the zoo anyway. I'll be there in spirit."

"You'll be there in person," Jo Beth insisted, her eyebrows drawn fiercely down.

"At the hospital…you don't know what it's like, Jo Beth. Some kids who have c-cancer…they don't make it."

"I do so know. My daddy's treatment didn't work. But Mama said your lymphoma's different. Your daddy told Uncle Mick most everyone gets well."

Marlee heard Jo Beth's side of the call. She rushed over to her daughter. "Honey, you're talking so loudly you're interrupting Emmett and Pappy Jack."

Jo Beth stamped a foot in the first display of temper Marlee had witnessed in a long while. "Mama, tell Dean we are so going to the zoo as a fambly!"

Marlee swallowed repeatedly, until her voice revealed none of the turmoil she felt or that she saw in Jo Beth. Then she took the phone to speak to the boy she'd grown to love. The boy who'd become her son by marriage. "Jo Beth is right, Dean."

BETWEEN JANUARY, after Mick flew Rose and Emmett off to pick up Rose's car, and April first, Dean received six blood transfusions. The first experimental treatment ended, and a new course began. Marlee lost track of the packed platelets they administered. The lumbar punctures necessary to draw fluid for pathology racked Dean's thin body with pain. Twice, his white blood cell count dipped so low Marlee and Wylie spent the night on their knees in the hospital chapel. Dean lost weight. So much, Wylie was afraid to hold him in his arms. He and Marlee no longer requested their special room at the hotel, even though they spent nights making love with abandon. Wylie said one night, "I feel that if you and I could just get close enough, maybe the tide will turn."

"Yes," Marlee whispered holding on to him for all she was worth.

BY MID-APRIL as Marlee flew to Seattle she saw signs that the land below was breaking free of winter's grip. Trees that had been bare were feathered with green. Rivers filled, and Mick was kept busy delivering fishermen to the swollen streams.

Dean was scheduled for a battery of tests, so Wylie had spent an entire week in Seattle. Phone calls home, no matter how frequent, weren't satisfying to the newlyweds.

Marlee coaxed as much speed out of the Seneca as possible. Adding up the times she'd flown round-trips, she figured she owed Mick a new engine.

Two hours after landing, she hurried into Dean's room and bent to kiss Wylie. It wasn't until the frantic kiss ended that she sensed the change in the atmosphere. Her heart galloped, and she straightened slowly.

Dean wore a cheeky smile. The kind of smile Marlee hadn't seen since the early days. Afraid to assume too much, she glanced warily at her husband.

His double thumbs-up fueled her fragile hope.

"Today, every test showed marked improvement. Of course, he has two more to go, so Dr. Riley said don't crow from the barn roof yet. And even if the results show what he expects, Dean will require a year of close monitoring. Like once a month."

Whooping, Marlee hugged her son. Was she imagining it, or had his body become more substantial since she'd last seen him?

"Can I call Jo Beth?" Dean asked. "Every time we talk, she tells me how many days are left until our zoo trip. I finally believe I might get to go."

Marlee gladly dialed the number. "Jo Beth has news, too. Ask her about the tests she took at school last week."

In no time, the kids were yakking up a storm.

"So, are we going to have a first and fourth grader to home-school come September?"

"We are." Marlee sat on Wylie's lap and looped her arms

around his neck. Bending close to his ear, she murmured, "And come next Christmas or thereabouts, there'll be a newborn added to our household."

"What?" Wylie almost dumped her.

"Hey, no throwing me on the floor. It's not good for mothers-to-be."

Wylie scooped her up and whirled her around the bed. They heard Dean tell Jo Beth, "Our folks are acting like dorks. Huh? Whaddya 'spect, they're adults. Dad, what are you guys laughing about?"

Wylie couldn't get enough of kissing his wife. "To punish him for his smart remarks, I vote we save the surprise until after the zoo trip."

"Okay." Marlee smiled happily against his lips as Dean, unfazed, went back to his conversation with Jo Beth. "But don't expect them to be as impressed by this as by the new arrivals at the zoo. I'm pretty sure baby orangutans will come out the winner."

DEAN'S IMPROVEMENT continued. In a matter of weeks his color returned, as did his energy. And his team of doctors began to speak of long-term remission.

The whole Oncology staff wiped their eyes the day Dr. Riley said, "It's official! Dean's lymphoma is in full remission. It pleases me even more to say that when Burkitt's lymphoma goes into remission, the prognosis of having it remain dormant is very, very good. Above ninety percent."

Marlee crumpled against Wylie's side and sobbed openly. "She's happy," he felt compelled to announce at large as he stroked her hair.

"I think this calls for some kind of celebration," he said abruptly. "Do you think Mick will fly Jo Beth to Seattle? And Pappy. I'll spring for dinner at the top of the Space Needle. The next day, just the four of us will go to the zoo."

"Uh…we have the Arrow. I left Mick the Seneca. We can switch if he comes. He can fly Pappy home in the smaller plane and leave us the larger one. Oh, but we'll have to fly there anyway. Mick needs to deliver us to your house….uh, *our* house." Her racing thoughts slowed. "Wylie, do you have any idea how good that sounds? Now we can move Jo Beth's and my stuff permanently."

"One thing at a time, Marlee. Let's enjoy tonight."

Wylie phoned Mick, who was delighted to hear the news and able to fly to Seattle.

Dinner that night in the revolving restaurant left everyone giddy. Pappy said, "I've read a lot about this joint. Never thought I'd live long enough to look out over a city this way and not have to tip my wings to see it."

Mick ordered champagne. "Here's to losing a pilot, but gaining a brother-in-law and a nephew. Is something wrong with the bubbly, sis?"

"It's not that." She blushed. "Wylie and I have other news. We weren't going to tell *quite* yet, but…oh heck. By Christmas or shortly thereafter you'll have a new niece or nephew, Mick. Dean and Jo Beth will be big brother and big sister."

Jo Beth and Dean gave each other high fives.

"Holy cow! That tops Pappy's and my news, doesn't it, Jo Beth?"

"Yep, but can I tell? Can I, Uncle Mick?" She bounced in her seat, and the minute he nodded, she blurted out, "Mick, Pappy and me went to the animal shelter yesterday. They got a dog that looks 'xactly like Piston. Pappy named him Wingman."

Dean, not to be outdone, tossed his knit cap in the air. "Look, everyone, I have fuzz growing on my head. Dr. Riley said my hair might not even be red any more. It could grow in dark like Dad's and Jo Beth's. Wouldn't that be cool?"

By tacit agreement they made the evening last. Even Pappy Jack and Mick, who intended to leave the city at first light, stayed up late.

That night had produced so many milestones, it stole some of the spotlight from the children's much-anticipated zoo trip. Still, they had a marvelous time. And all four members of the Ames family reveled in the sunshine.

"Instead of staying here tonight," Dean said, later that afternoon, "can we go home?"

No one objected.

They piled into the plane, the kids exclaiming over wild-animal coloring books Wylie had bought them at the zoo store. In flight, Wylie happened to catch Marlee's wistful expression. Prying one of her hands off the wheel, he brought her fingers to his lips. "A penny for them."

"My thoughts?" She turned to look at him. "There's always a kind of letdown at the end of a long, hectic mission. Do you see how beautiful the sky is? I started thinking how my flying days are over. I arrived at Mick's prepared never to fly again. Then his surgery changed those plans. There's something very liberating about soaring through the heavens. I'll miss it. But I'm heading into an equally satisfying, challenging chapter of my life. Wife. Mother. It's impossible to top that."

Wylie sank back in his seat. He wore a contented smile.

On the approach to Mick's runway, Marlee scanned her childhood home that was home no more. "Either Mick has company, or he bought a new plane. Wow, great lines. Twin turboprop Merlin. I'm guessing a four-seater," she murmured, craning her neck as she angled the Seneca into its descent.

"Six seats." Wylie dangled a key in front of Marlee's eyes. Her wheels touched the ground and the plane did the same little hop as it had on her first landing at Wylie's.

He curled the key back into his hand. "Dammit, woman! Should I have bought landing lessons with the plane?"

"Yours?" She slammed the pedals and the Seneca whined.

He waited until the plane came to a standstill.

The kids released their harnesses and crowded forward. "It's yours," Dean, Jo Beth and Wylie shouted in unison.

Wylie alone managed to close Marlee's open mouth—with a smothering kiss. Eyes aglow, he murmured, "I asked everyone, what does a man who loves a no-frills pilot buy her as a wedding gift? Pappy said, 'A plane, of course.' Since the old man scares the hell out of me, that's what I did. With Mick's help."

Marlee's head spun to encompass all the smiling faces she couldn't see clearly for her tears. "Lord, but I love you all." She got the words out past her sniffles.

He managed to get the last word, though. "Here's the plan. We go tell Mick and Pappy Jack hello and goodbye. Then, little mama bird, we'll load up your new toy and fly our family home."

* * * * *

What does the future hold for Mick Callen?
Will he, too, meet the love of his life?
Find out in ON ANGEL WINGS, coming in December!
Turn the page to read an excerpt from this
warm and moving book.

MICK CALLEN MOVED a step higher on the twelve-foot ladder propped against a battered Huey. It was the one helicopter in a fleet of three aircraft belonging to Cloud Chasers, Mick's company, which delivered freight throughout remote northwest Montana.

He stretched to dab lubricant on the far side of the rotor pitch. The movement caused pain in his hip, a sharp reminder that he'd reached too far for the titanium socket a surgeon had installed a year ago. He adjusted his weight and breathed more easily. Damn, he'd have to remember he couldn't make sudden moves anymore. But setting limits wasn't easy for a man who, at thirty-five, ought to be in the prime of his life. Lately he'd spent too much time contemplating his age and physical limitations.

Frustrated, he raised a greasy hand to swipe a stubborn lock of hair out of his eyes, then caught himself and instead rubbed the grease down his coveralls rather than leave a black streak in his blond hair. Mick shifted again and rested the can on the top rung. From this vantage point, he could see a row of white-capped peaks in the distance. A slice of the Rocky Mountains.

Until this minute, intent on servicing the Huey, Mick hadn't noticed the added nip in the morning air. The sky was a deep, cloudless blue. Pappy Jack would've said it was a perfect day for cavorting through the clouds. *Cloud chasing*. Hence the name of their company.

A pang seared Mick's chest. The pain wasn't related to old

injuries he'd sustained in the military when he'd been shot down flying his last mission in Afghanistan. Nor was it the result of subsequent surgeries. Mick recognized this ache. He'd diagnosed it weeks ago as he tinkered with his plane engines. This pain stuck each time he left the house to work solo.

Beginning mid-May, he'd shopped solo, cooked solo, ate solo, flew solo and walked Wingman, his mutt, solo.

Here it was, practically the end of October. Mick realized he'd frittered away six damned months and he still expected to see his grandfather moving around the property. Pappy Jack Callen, Mick's mentor, had always been the real heart and soul of Cloud Chasers.

At Jack's funeral late last spring, scores of residents from the nearby community of Whitepine had come to pay their respects. More than a few of Pappy's contemporaries claimed Mick—and Jack—were lucky once they learned Pappy had said good-night as usual one night and simply didn't wake up the next morning. The friends said that when they died, that would be the best way.

Except they weren't the ones who'd found Pappy lifeless in his bed. Mick had. And not a day passed that he didn't think of a hundred things he should've said the night before to the man who'd long been the rock for Mick and his twin sister, Marlee. Pappy had been everything to them after they'd lost their parents in a senseless car accident some twenty years back.

Marlee assured Mick over and over in the days following the funeral that Pappy knew they loved him. But his sister, newly married and pregnant, didn't have endless empty hours to fill with nothing but rambling thoughts. *Should'ves, could'ves, would'ves.* Those seemed to be the bane of Mick's existence. He'd never been a big one for vocalizing how he felt. He wasn't the touchy-feely type. A fault he'd have to live with, or change. Damn, the change didn't come easy, either.

Pappy had suffered for several years from arteriosclerotic

heart disease, so Mick knew a heart attack had always been a risk. It could also be said that at eighty-six, their grandfather had lived a full life. Jack Callen proudly boasted a distinguished military career. He'd married the love of his life. Had built this home and business from the ground up. He'd raised a son and shepherded twin grandkids toward becoming fine navy flyers and otherwise all-around productive citizens.

By comparison, Mick felt his own life was going nowhere fast.

His new brother-in-law, Glacier Park forest ranger Wylie Ames, said what Mick needed was to find a good woman. Now, that had crossed Mick's mind a few times over the long boring summer. His sister took every opportunity to nag him to phone Tammy Skidmore, a nurse in Kalispell who'd shown enough interest to hand him her phone number the day he checked out of the hospital.

He scowled as he slopped grease on the underside of the rotor. Huh, maybe he *should* pick up the phone and call Tammy. But something held him back. Mick jokingly told Marlee it'd be hard to date a woman who had repeatedly jammed needles into his bare butt. Although that didn't ring true. Mick had lost all modesty after his accident. With Tammy, at least, if they ever reached the point of doing the deed, he wouldn't have to explain all the puckered skin that ran from hip to ankle where he'd been riddled by shrapnel. Mick probably didn't have a single physical asset Tammy Skidmore hadn't clinically observed, so that was pretty much a non issue.

And if he crossed Tammy off his list of available females he was left with slim pickins'. Available, suitable women didn't grow on trees. A couple of old schoolmates in Whitepine had let it be known at Pappy's funeral that they were back in circulation. One was too straitlaced to suit Mick. The other lacked any scruples.

A little voice in the back of his mind niggled. *What about Hana Egan?*

What about her? Last fall, Pappy had told his twin sister that Mick was "sweet" on the smoke jumper. A fact Mick had tripped over his teeth to deny.

"Mick. Mick!" Hearing his name drifting up from the foot of his ladder jerked Mick out of his daydream. He hastily jammed a lid on the grease bucket and began to make his way backward down the rickety ladder.

Stella Gibson was waiting for him at the bottom. Judging by her worried expression, she'd anxiously followed his slow progress. The matronly widow, who lived in a cabin down the hill, had helped Mick in a variety of capacities since his medical discharge from the navy. She cleaned up the house after he and Pappy made a mess of things, and left enough meals in the refrigerator to keep them from starving.

Those months when Mick had been laid up, when Marlee moved home and flew his route, Stella used to ride herd on Mick, Pappy and sometimes Marlee's daughter, Jo Beth. But Stella never made a secret of the fact that she was looking for a permanent job. It was only after Marlee married Wylie, and Pappy passed away, that Mick got smart and hired Stella to work half-time cleaning house, and the other half keeping order in Cloud Chasers' office. That was a task his sister repeatedly said he was bad at.

Just now, Stella stood with hands on hips, obviously ready to give him a motherly lecture. "When I left yesterday, Mick Callen, you told me Josh Manley would be in today to service the helicopter. Why are you up on that ladder?"

Mick set down the bucket, pulled a red rag out of his back pocket and wiped the excess goop off his fingers. "Yeah, well, Josh's mom phoned. His girlfriend conned Josh into driving her and a coworker into Kalispell today. Apparently they're all invited to an early Halloween party at the home of his girlfriend's boss. I gather it's one of those command performances.

The guy giving the bash has an opening for a corporate pilot. I know Josh really wants that job. He's a good pilot, and I can't use him full-time."

"If he gets the job, who'll spell you, Mick? Between the upswing in freight orders, and the mercy missions with Angel Fleet, it seems to me you need a full-time flying partner."

"With winter coming on, Stella, it's a matter of weeks before I'd have to cut Josh's hours. That's the nature of the freight business in upper Montana."

"We've been running in high gear these six or seven months so I never thought to ask. Will my hours be cut over the winter?"

Wingman bounded up, his tongue hanging out. The part Lab, part shepherd, part some unknown breed, nosed Mick's leg until he bent to rub the dog's furry head. "Actually, Stella, I've been juggling my finances, hoping I can afford to spend the winter bumming around some island with white sandy beaches, ice-cold margaritas and bikini-clad babes. I'd like you to look after the place. You know, see the pipes don't break and my planes don't blow away. Up to now, no one's had time to scan in all the old accounts or shred mountains of paperwork Pappy stored in those damned cardboard boxes. I'll pay you to handle everything."

"I can do that. Are you planning to take the dog?"

Mick let the animal lick his chin. "I wish. But this guy's a cold-weather mutt. I intend to make an end run around Marlee and ask Wylie if I can pay Dean to take care of Wingman until I get back next spring. The kid's been good about letting Jo Beth claim sole possession of Piston. Last time I visited them for the weekend, I let Dean take charge of my dog. It evened the odds in their yours, mine and ours household."

Stella's dark eyes sparkled when she laughed. "You'd do that to your poor sister? Add another creature when she's dealing with Thanksgiving, Christmas and having a baby? Last time we talked, she said Dean had rescued a half-grown grizzly who'd been shot by a neighboring rancher. That boy already has twin wolf cubs and numerous small animals in various stages of healing."

"Was Marlee complaining?"

"No. She sounds bubbly, in fact."

"Yeah, she does." Mick straightened and patted the dog. He gazed blankly at the horizon. "I was just thinking, Stella, it's perfect flying weather. I should shake out the chopper and see if the maintenance I did takes care of the rotor wobble Josh was complaining about. Last week when I flew to Missoula for a follow-up visit with the physical therapist, I picked up some things for the baby. I also bought a few Halloween goodies for Dean and Jo Beth. Maybe I'll take myself up to the ranger station. See if Wylie can use an extra hand with the addition he's madly building on their house."

Stella snapped her fingers. "That's why I came to find you, Mick. I took a phone order from Trudy Morganthal at the rangers' base camp, and the smoke jumpers would also like some supplies delivered no later than this afternoon."

Mick's grease-stained fingers fondled the dog's silky ear. "I delivered Captain Martin's winter supplies weeks ago. He said he wouldn't need anything until spring."

"I gather this is private supplies for the smoke jumpers. None of them are in your billing system, which brings up the next question. Will you fly out such a small order for cash? Jess Hargitay promised to pay on delivery."

"I guess. Jess has been with Martin for a few years. Not all the jumpers return each season." He frowned. "I've never known any of them to request private supplies. In fact, I understood they were all leaving next week, except Captain Martin and his assistant."

"Mr. Hargitay mentioned that a group is planning a farewell climb in Glacier Park. One of the taller peaks, but I don't recall which. They've ordered ready-to-eat meals, long johns and miscellaneous stuff."

"Huh. Long johns for sure. I see there's quite a bit of snow up along the ridge."

"If the report I heard this morning is correct, we're liable to lose this fine weather soon. They predict we'll see snow in the valley by early next week."

Mick laughed. "Stella, you can't trust the news channel weather staff to get it right. If you want the skinny on the weather, you need to phone the service pilots use."

She tipped back her head and scanned the sky that was visible through a row of majestic pine trees left to block north winds from battering the house. "You're right." She looked at him again. "So, then, you want me to phone Trudy and this Jess guy and say you'll take both jobs?"

"Sure. Sounds good. I never turn down an opportunity to earn money. What's today? Thursday? Ask Trudy if tomorrow's soon enough to deliver her order. I'll fly to Kalispell this afternoon and fetch the supplies in the Arrow. At first light tomorrow, I'll transfer the load to the Huey. That'll allow me time to phone Wylie and Marlee, and arrange to spend a couple of nights with them."

"I'll confirm the times with Trudy ASAP. Unless you want my help in carting that big old ladder back to the work shed."

"Thanks for the offer, Stella, but my PT said I'm good as new. Maybe better than, what with all the hardware installed in my hip," Mick said with a wink. He forgot the condition of his hand and raked still-greasy fingers through hair that needed more than a trim, as curls fell over his eyes and skimmed the lower edge of his collar.

"You look kind of shaggy. But unless there's someone out in the great beyond you want to impress, I'd say you can get by for another week without hunting up a barber."

Again, a clear vision of perky Hana Egan popped into Mick's mind. Probably because Stella had mentioned Jess Hargitay. Jess gave the impression that he was hot stuff in the eyes of female smoke jumpers. Mick had seen Jess act possessive of several women who'd rotated in and out of the camp. And he'd definitely put the moves on Hana. Yet for all Mick knew, Hana returned Jess's interest. Probably did. His trips to the camp were few and far between, so it wasn't as if he had any inside news.

"Stella, if Trudy needs her order today, buzz me on the house intercom. I'm going to store the ladder and grease, then go clean up."

They parted, and Mick returned the ladder to the shed. On his trip to the house, he took out his cell phone and punched in his sister's number. Her phone rang three times before she answered, and then she sounded out of breath.

"Hey, sis, did I catch you on the run?"

"Mick?" His twin's voice reflected both surprise and delight. "I had my head in the oven when the phone rang. I stopped to take out two pies before I picked up."

"You're baking pies? What's the occasion?"

"I'll have you know I cook a lot more since I acquired a family of two hungry males. Thankfully, Rose sent me her most favorite recipes," Marlee said, referring to her former mother-in-law, Rose Stein. Marlee's marriage to Wylie Ames was his twin's second marriage. Her first husband died after a prolonged bout with cancer. She'd had some problems with he ex-mom-in-law. But Marlee had met and overcome all challenges like a champ.

"These pies," Marlee continued, "are for an end-of-season potluck the rangers are having on Saturday. I'm so nervous, Mick. Wylie said I shouldn't, but this'll be the first time most of his ranger buddies will have met me and Jo Beth. Bud and Ellen Russell—Bud is Wylie's closest friend—came by to deliver a wedding gift from the whole crew. Outside of them, I won't know a single soul at the gathering," she admitted. "I hope my offerings at the potluck are edible, or the women will feel sorry for Wylie. They're probably all wondering how he met me, anyway."

Mick didn't comment. He was trying to piece together the significance of what his sister had said.

"Mick, are you still there? Is something wrong? Oh, no, don't tell me the report from your physical therapist was bad? I meant to phone, but we had a lot going on, what with trying to get the addition finished so Rose has a place to sleep when she comes here for Christmas. You know she's going to help when the baby's born? And do you remember Emmett Nelson, Rose's neighbor in San Diego? He and she will be traveling together. I think they're an item. Are you listening to me, Mick?"

"Yes. I'm fine according to the PT. It's just that I scheduled a couple of deliveries up your way tomorrow. I figured on spending the weekend with you guys. That was before you mentioned you have plans for Saturday. Maybe I'll swoop in for a minute tomorrow afternoon and drop off the Halloween treats I bought for Dean and Jo Beth."

"You will *not* just pop in and out. I have an order sitting at the Kalispell airpark that you can bring. And you'll stay for the potluck. So, if I don't pass muster with Wylie's coworkers, I can hang out with my brother instead of looking like a wallflower."

"Why wouldn't you pass muster? Anyway, the only important thing is how much Wylie and Dean love you. Hey, come on! You flew choppers in a war for pity's sake. Which of the other rangers' wives can claim that kind of guts?" He shook his head. "Are you okay, sis? I've never known you to be insecure."

"You never saw me when I was pregnant. Feeling frumpy comes with the territory."

"Hmm, that explains it. I haven't been around pregnant women—just the one in that fender bender a couple of weeks back. She went into labor at the side of the highway near Whitefish. Angel Fleet had me fly her and her husband to Kalispell. She was a trouper. Her husband was a basket case, though. I hope Wylie won't be like that."

"He won't. Wylie delivered Dean. I'm planning on the local midwife coming in. But if weather doesn't permit it, I'll be fine with just Wylie and Rose on hand. Out of curiosity, what did the woman have, a boy or a girl?"

"A boy. Cute little dude. The dad acted goofy, tapping on the nursery glass and making goo-goo noises. He gave me a bubble-gum cigar. I tried to picture myself in his shoes, but I'm positive I would've acted way cooler."

"If you don't get on the stick and meet a woman, Mick Callen, you won't ever be in that's dad's shoes—and we'll never know if you'd be cool or not."

"Yeah, yeah! Time to hang up. I've gotta go shower and then fly to Kalispell and collect the orders for delivery tomorrow."

"If you don't have to fly on Monday, stay over for an extra day, why don't you? We'll all like that."

"We'll see. I'll toss in a duffel and see what Wylie thinks about me crashing his company picnic. Where is the picnic? Isn't it already too cold?"

"We're gathering at the picnic grounds at the main ranger station to celebrate the closing of the park on Sunday. If that storm hanging out in Canada blows down, Trudy Moranthal says we can eat in the wildlife lecture room."

"Stella heard about that storm. I'll have to check the reports. Maybe I will stay over. How bad are they predicting it'll be? Nothing like the doozy last June that surprised the heck out of everybody? Never seen such high winds. And the rain and light-ning. That monster tore a swath two hundred and fifty miles wide through Idaho and Montana. Every able-bodied person was called out on rescue after rescue."

"Nothing so major, thank goodness. Wylie said he'd never seen a storm cause as much damage as that one. He called it a *derecho*, a Spanish word the weather forecasters use for a big storm that tears up everything in its path, or something. It's a miracle more summer vacationers weren't hurt or killed. I think this forecast is for a few inches of snow, that's all. The kids have their fingers crossed. Probably because Wylie built them sleds out of scrap lumber."

"All right! If I wasn't planning to stay over before, that would've tipped the scales. It's been years since I did any sledding. Expect me around lunchtime tomorrow. I'll see if your kitchen skills have improved." Mick clicked off before the sputtering began.

As Mick fired up the Huey, the breaking dawn gave no indication that the weather wouldn't be a repeat of the previous day. Streaks of purple, pink and gold edged out the deep gray of a rapidly fading night. And there was little, if any, wind.

The thrill of the promised flight lifted his spirits, even if he'd rather be flying a navy jet than this lumbering chopper. Wingman sat in his makeshift harness, one ear perked up. Mick grinned at the dog and could swear the mutt grinned back. "We're a pair, aren't we?" Mick called. The dog raised his head and barked.

As he lifted off, Mick stopped admiring the breaking day and listened carefully for any sign of wobble in the rotors. He much preferred flying fixed-wing planes like the Arrow or the Seneca. He'd bought the chopper at auction to entice his sister back home to Montana from San Diego. She'd flown helicopters in the navy. But if he'd known she was going to meet Wylie Ames, fall in love and marry the guy within a year of moving back, Mick might have passed on buying the Huey. Except, that it'd come in handy on several occasions during his volunteer missions for Angel Fleet. He was getting so he could land the chopper just about anywhere except in heavily treed terrain. For as fast as Montana was being built up, there was still a lot of wilderness left, thank goodness. And as Marlee claimed, the Huey was a reliable workhorse.

He'd been the air a little under an hour when he spotted the main ranger layout below. Mick had realized yesterday that the supplies he'd picked up for Trudy Morganthal were mostly for the weekend ranger barbecue, or potluck, whatever they were calling it. He had cartons of paper cups, paper plates, napkins. Of course, the rangers would use disposable items that were bio-degradable. Trudy had ordered staples to get them through a winter during which no one traveled easily in this part of Glacier Park except by snowshoes or snowmobile.

He landed near the park's two smaller helicopters. Wingman got antsy waiting for the rotors to stop. Mick saw why. They were being greeted by the house dogs, a German shepherd and a good-size collie. Mick released his dog but attached a leash to his collar.

Trudy hurried down the path that led to the buildings. From her hand motions, Mick deduced that she intended to pen her dogs. He waited to open the door until she'd disappeared again.

"I know, buddy, you're disappointed to lose playmates. But maybe those dogs aren't as friendly as you. Come on. I'll walk you into the woods to do your business. Then you'll have to stay in the chopper while I unload Morganthal's order."

Trudy reappeared about the time Mick returned to the clearing. "Where shall I stack the boxes?" he asked.

"My husband and sons and our other rangers are making sure all the campers have pulled out. They'll be closing this end of the park and chaining up the roads until next season. Would it be a terrible imposition if I asked you carry the paper goods to the canopy we've set up for the potluck? Put everything else on the porch. I don't want you reinjuring your leg. Wylie told us about your surgery. In a way, that was his good fortune. Otherwise he wouldn't have met your sister."

"Wylie's right. Marlee never would've taken over my cargo route if I hadn't been laid up. It's not problem moving your stuff, Trudy. I have a handtruck I can load boxes on."

Trudy talked incessantly as Mick loaded up cartons and

trucked them around. He would've told her he'd see her the next day as he'd been invited to the potluck, but couldn't get a word in edgewise.

"Phew, Wingman," Mick said after he'd buckled himself in his seat. "That woman could talk the ears off a mule. I suppose she gets lonely stuck out here. Her husband and his crew are probably gone a lot, tending the park." He slipped on his earphones, and promptly turned his thoughts to his next delivery. Mick wondered if he'd see Hana Egan this trip. A new kind of excitement rose in him, different from the thrill he got from flying. A month ago when he'd delivered the bulk of the winter supplies to Captain Martin at the smoke jumpers camp, Mick had managed a few words with Hana. She wasn't real talkative, and sometimes he had to cajole information out of her. She'd said she'd be going home to California soon.

As he rose above the stand of timber marking the northernmost park entrance, Mick considered how little he knew about Hana. He knew he was drawn by her red-gold curls that snapped to life when she stood bareheaded in the sun. He liked the freckles dusted across her nose. Mick probably thought too much about kissing her shapely mouth, since odds of that happening weren't high. He'd never seen her wear lipstick. Of all her attributes, Mick found Hana's eyes to be her most arresting feature. Given her coloring, a person might expect her to have blue or green eyes, but hers were…gold. Whiskey gold. He'd only spoken with her two, maybe three times—enough to decide that her eyes reflected her every emotion.

Time passed quickly. The smoke jumpers' camp sat halfway between the ranger station and his sister's house. The place looked pretty deserted. He recognized Leonard Martin's battered Ford diesel truck and the assistant's slightly newer SUV. The Jeep belonged to Jess Hargitay. As a rule, smoke jumpers flew in from various camps during times of fire. But

Jess drove in. The station was the seasonal home to maybe six men and women. And the season was at an end, Mick lamented as he landed.

Heck, maybe he'd find out where Hana lived in California. He'd been thinking of island vacations, but California had plenty of white sandy beaches.

He repeated the process he'd gone through at the ranger station. He let the rotors stop fully before he leashed Wingman and the two of them climbed out.

"Hi, Mick."

Hana Egan's sweet voice had him spinning too fast on his fancy titanium hip. Mick felt a deep pain buckle his newly healed muscles. A blistering swearword escaped before he could check himself. He dropped Wingman's leash when he was forced to grab the upright strut on the landing skid to keep from toppling.

The petite woman was quick on her feet. She scooped up the fleeing dog's leather leash. "I didn't mean to surprise you, Mick. Are you okay?" Those whiskey-gold eyes Mick had so recently been thinking about turned dusky with concern.

"I'm fine," he growled. The last thing he wanted was for Hana to judge him a lesser man than Jess Hargitay, who was swaggering toward them. Smoke jumpers tended to be agile, tough and have a penchant for danger.

"You don't act fine," she said. "Why can't men ever admit to shortcomings?"

He tried to discreetly knead the kink out of the long muscle that ran down his thigh. He hadn't limped in a month, but he limped now as he crossed the space between them and relieved her of Wingman's leash. "I wouldn't touch that comment with rubber gloves, Hana. Suffice it to say, must be a guy thing. But I can't answer for all men." He looped the dog's leash through a cross tube at the rear of the landing skid. "I probably need to ask Jess where he wants me to stack his supplies." Still smarting from her words—and the cramp in his leg—Mick lowered his chin in dismissal and started to walk around her.

"Hold on." She touched his hand, then abruptly pulled back. "I saw you dropping down to land, and I hurried over here to catch you before anyone else butts in. I wanted to tell you goodbye, Mick."

"You're taking off for home today, then?" He halted in his tracks and idly rubbed his hand, still feeling the touch of her surprisingly callused hand. Although, considering the job she did, Mick didn't know why he'd be shocked to find her hand wasn't nearly as soft as it looked.

"As soon as six of us finish climbing Mt. St. Nicholas, we'll split up and go our separate ways."

"You heard there's a front moving in?"

"I'm sure Jess scoped out the weather. We're making the climb for fun. It's been a rough summer with fire after fire. This is our last hurrah as a unit before we scatter for the winter."

"Huh. So you aren't all from the same locale?"

"No." The denial was accompanied by a crisp shake of her red curls.

"I imagine you're anxious to get home. What with family holidays like Thanksgiving and Christmas around the bend."

Mick noticed that a brittleness overtook her formerly friendly demeanor. Had he crossed some kind of line? Granted, in the past they'd never got around to discussing anything so personal.

"I struck out on my own at sixteen, Mick," she said briskly. "I took three part-time jobs so I could graduate from high school. Before that I was shuffled through a lot of different homes. There's none I'd remotely call family."

"So you were, what? In foster care?"

"Care? If you say so." She spat the words with distaste. "I hope that's not pity in your eyes, Mick Callen. I've done fine. This winter I'm enrolling in a couple of courses at UCLA. One day I'll have my degree in ecology." She followed that with a halfhearted laugh. "I'm surprised Jess hasn't regaled you with the fact that I'm UCLA's oldest underclassman. But I think I should qualify as a junior this semester."

Mick felt her underlying anxiety over baring so much of her soul. He usually played things cool, too, when it came to spilling his guts. Now he felt moved to share. "This past spring my grandfather died. Pappy. I'm sure you met him."

"I did. Mick, I'm so sorry to hear of your loss. You probably know he bragged about you something fierce. You obviously miss him terribly."

"Yeah. I rattle around the house." Mick dug deep to keep his voice from breaking. It was one thing to share a private grief, and another to show weakness.

"I heard your sister married Wylie Ames. Gosh, does that mean you're totally alone this holiday season?"

"Marlee and Wylie want me to spend a week with them at Thanksgiving. I probably will if I haven't winged my way to a sandy beach in some warmer clime. Their baby's due right around Christmas, and they'll have a houseful with Jo Beth's grandmother coming to help with the baby. Especially if weather forces the midwife to bunk over."

Mick thought Hana's eyes looked wistful as she said eagerly, "They're having a baby? I can't believe you'd want to miss that."

"I wouldn't have a clue what to do around a newborn. By the time I come back in the spring, the baby will be sitting up and there'll be something substantial to hang on to. They don't live far from here, Hana. Maybe if you're not off fighting a fire, I'll swing by and take you to see the baby, since you sound keen on little kids."

She gazed beyond him into the distance, and an awkwardness fell between them. "Uh...maybe."

"My sister wouldn't mind. Hey, you'll be back here next spring, right?"

She lifted one slender shoulder, and Mick's heart slammed hard up into his throat at the possibility that she might not be coming back to Montana.

Wingman started racing around and bounding to the end of his leash, barking his head off. A long shadow fell across the couple. A muscular, dark-haired man wearing a frank scowl strode up and shouldered Mick aside.

"Hana, what are you two jawing about for so long? Kari said you came to collect our supplies from Mick. Everything else is loaded in my Jeep. Come on, you're holding us up. I want to make camp at the fir tree break in time to pitch tents for the night."

Hana didn't respond to Jess Hargitay's order.

Mick felt tension drawing tight as both Hana and Jess raised their chins. Wanting to intercede, Mick tapped Jess's back. "Cloud Chasers' office manager said you'd pay cash for this load, Hargitay." Mick pulled a wadded-up charge slip from his shirt pocket and pressed it into the other man's hand. "Soon as you cough up the *dinero,* I'll haul these supplies to your Jeep."

There had never been any love lost between the two men glaring at each other now. Always cocky and sure of himself, Jess brushed off Mick's hand. Locking eyes with the pilot, Jess reached out in a too-familiar manner, running his fingers through Hana's short curls. "Hey, babe, I'm kinda short this month. Run over and pass the hat among our other four climbers. I'm supplying the wheels and gas to get to the site, so the least all of you can do is spring for food, canned heat and long johns."

Hana opened her mouth as if to refuse. Instead, she ducked under the thickly muscled arm and murmured a final goodbye to Mick.

The air crackled in her wake. Neither man spoke, but they continued to take each other's measure until tall, bean-pole thin Kari Dombroski loped up to hand over a collection of bills and coins.

Mick shoved the money in a pocket without counting it. He hurriedly pulled the supplies out of the Huey.

As if to keep Mick from meeting up with Hana again, Jess relieved him of most of the load, except for a small quantity he snarled at Kari to take.

Wingman lunged at the end of his leash to bark at Jess, and Mick turned his back on the smoke jumpers and bent to calm his pet. "Nice guy, huh, pooch?" he muttered. "If you could talk, I'd ask you what in hell Hana sees in that jackass."

The dog whined and licked his owner's face as Mick untied him and hoisted him into the chopper. Before Mick had his harness and the dog buckled, the mottled black Jeep kicked up dust farther down the dirt road.

As he lifted off, Mick noted with interest that both he and Jess were headed toward the clouds building over the mountain range.

He tried not to think of petite Hana Egan climbing craggy ridges topped by snow and already shrouded in a thickening gray mist.

To distract himself, he projected his worry onto Saturday's potluck. What if the wind was the first taste of the storm up in Canada? If the party was canceled, Marlee would be devastated. Oh, his sister made noises about not wanting to attend, but Mick had seen right through her. She wanted the day to be perfect. And Mick wanted that for her, too. She and Wylie deserved to kick back a bit after nursing Dean, Wylie's son, through Burkitt's lymphoma. Between worry over Dean, and Pappy's funeral not long on the heels of Dean's remarkable remission, the whole family could use some fun.

* * * * *

Set in darkness beyond the ordinary world.
Passionate tales of life and death.
With characters' lives ruled by laws the everyday world can't
begin to imagine.

Introducing NOCTURNE, *a spine-tingling new line from*
Silhouette Books.

The thrills and chills begin with UNFORGIVEN
by Lindsay McKenna

Plucked from the depths of hell, former military sharpshooter Reno Manchahi was hired by the government to kill a thief, but he had a mission of his own. Descended from a family of shape-shifters, Reno vowed to get the revenge he'd thirsted for all these years. But his mission went awry when his target turned out to be a powerful seductress, Magdalena Calen Hernandez, who risked everything to battle a potent evil. Suddenly, Reno had to transform himself into a true hero and fight the enemy that threatened them all. He had to become a Warrior for the Light....

Turn the page for a sneak preview of UNFORGIVEN
by Lindsay McKenna.
On sale September 26, wherever books are sold.

Chapter 1

One shot...one kill.

The sixteen-pound sledgehammer came down with such
fierce power that the granite boulder shattered instantly. A spray
of glittering mica exploded into the air and sparkled momentarily around the man who wielded the tool as if it were a weapon.
Sweat ran in rivulets down Reno Manchahi's drawn, intense
face. Naked from the waist up, the hot July sun beating down on
his back, he hefted the sledgehammer skyward once more.
Muscles in his thick forearms leaped and biceps bulged. Even
his breath was focused on the boulder. In his mind's eye, he
pictured Army General Robert Hampton's fleshy, arrogant fifty-
year-old features on the rock's surface. Air exploded from
between his lips as he brought the avenging hammer down. The
boulder pulverized beneath his funneled hatred.

One shot...one kill...

Nostrils flaring, he inhaled the dank, humid heat and drew it
deep into his massive lungs. Revenge allowed Reno to endure

his imprisonment at a U.S. Navy brig near San Diego, California. Drops of sweat were flung in all directions as the crack o
his sledgehammer claimed a third stone victim. Mouth tau
Reno moved to the next boulder.

The other prisoners in the stone yard gave him a wide bert
They always did. They instinctively felt his simmering hatre
the palpable revenge in his cinnamon-colored eyes, was mor
than skin-deep.

And they whispered he was different.

Reno enjoyed being a loner for good reason. He came from
a medicine family of shape-shifters. But even this secret pow
had not protected him—or his family. His wife, Ilona, and hi
three-year-old daughter, Sarah, were dead. Murdered by Arm
General Hampton in their former home on USMC base in Cam
Pendleton, California. Bitterness thrummed through Reno as h
savagely pushed the toe of his scarred leather boot against sever
smaller pieces of gray granite that were in his way.

The sun beat down upon Manchahi's naked shoulders, grow
dark red over time, shouting his half-Apache heritage. With h
straight black hair grazing his thick shoulders, copper skin an
broad face with high cheekbones, everyone knew he was India
When he'd first arrived at the brig, some of the prisoners taunte
him and called him Geronimo. Something strange happened t
Reno during his fight with the name-calling prisoners. Leanin
down after he'd won the scuffle, he'd snarled into each of the
bloodied faces that if they were going to call him anything, the
would call him *gan,* which was the Apache word for *devil.*

His attackers had been shocked by the wounds on their face
the deep claw marks. Reno recalled doubling his fist as they
attacked him en masse. In that split second, he'd gone into a
altered state of consciousness. In times of danger, he transform
into a jaguar. A deep, growling sound had emitted from his thro
as he defended himself in the three-against-one fracas. It a
happened so fast that he thought he had imagined it. He'd se

his hands morph into a forearm and paw, claws extended. The slashes left on the three men's faces after the fight told him he'd begun to shape-shift. A fist made bruises and swelling; not four perfect, deep claw marks. Stunned and anxious, he hid the knowledge of what else he was from these prisoners. Reno's only defense was to make all the prisoners so damned scared of him and remain a loner.

Alone. Yeah, he was alone, all right. The steel hammer swept downward with hellish ferocity. As the granite groaned in protest, Reno shut his eyes for just a moment. Sweat dripped off his nose and square chin.

Straightening, he wiped his furrowed, wet brow and looked into the pale blue sky. What got his attention was the startling cry of a red-tailed hawk as it flew over the brig yard. Squinting, he watched the bird. Reno could make out the rust-colored tail on the hawk. As a kid growing up on the Apache reservation in Arizona, Reno knew that all animals that appeared before him were messengers.

Brother, what message do you bring me? Reno knew one had to ask in order to receive. Allowing the sledgehammer to drop to his side, he concentrated on the hawk who wheeled in tightening circles above him.

Freedom! the hawk cried in return.

Reno shook his head, his black hair moving against his broad, thickset shoulders. *Freedom? No way, Brother. No way.* Figuring that he was making up the hawk's shrill message, Reno turned away. Back to his rocks. Back to picturing Hampton's smug face.

Freedom!

* * * * *

*Look for UNFORGIVEN by Lindsay McKenna,
the spine-tingling launch title from Silhouette Nocturne™.
Available September 26, wherever books are sold.*

Introducing...

n o c t u r n e

a spine-tingling new line from Silhouette Books.

These paranormal romances will seduce you with dark, passionate tales that stretch the boundaries of conflict, desire, and life and death, weaving a tapestry of sensual thrills and chills!

Don't miss the first book...

UNFORGIVEN

by *USA TODAY* bestselling author

LINDSAY McKENNA

Launching October 2006, wherever books are sold.

✓ *Silhouette*®

SPECIAL EDITION™

Experience the "magic" of falling in love at Halloween with a new *Holiday Hearts* story!

UNDER HIS SPELL

by *KRISTIN HARDY*

October 2006

Bad-boy ski racer J. J. Cooper can get any woman he wants—except Lainie Trask. Lainie's grown up with him and vows that nothing he says or does will change her mind. But J.J.'s got his eye on Lainie, and when he moves into her neighborhood and into her life, she finds herself falling under his spell....

HOLIDAY HEARTS

If you enjoyed what you just read,
then we've got an offer you can't resist!

Take 2 bestselling love stories FREE!

Plus get a FREE surprise gift!

SAVE UP TO $30! SIGN UP TODAY!

INSIDE *Romance*

The complete guide to your favorite
Harlequin®, Silhouette® and Love Inspired® books.

✓ Newsletter ABSOLUTELY FREE! No purchase necessary.

✓ Valuable coupons for future purchases of Harlequin,
  Silhouette and Love Inspired books in every issue!

✓ Special excerpts & previews in each issue. Learn about all
  the hottest titles before they arrive in stores.

✓ No hassle—mailed directly to your door!

✓ Comes complete with a handy shopping checklist
  so you won't miss out on any titles.

- -

SIGN ME UP TO RECEIVE INSIDE ROMANCE
ABSOLUTELY FREE
(Please print clearly)

_____
Name

_____
Address

_____
City/Town   State/Province   Zip/Postal Code

Please mail this form to:
(098 KKM EJL9)   In the U.S.A.: Inside Romance, P.O. Box 9057, Buffalo, NY 14269-9057
In Canada: Inside Romance, P.O. Box 622, Fort Erie, ON L2A 5X3
OR visit http://www.eHarlequin.com/insideromance

IRNBPA06R   ® and ™ are trademarks owned and used by the trademark owner and/or its licensee.